CRYSTAL STORM

CRYSTAL STORM

BOOK **5** IN THE
FALLING KINGDOMS
SERIES

MORGAN RHODES

RAZORBILL

An Imprint of Penguin Random House

RAZORBILL

An Imprint of Penguin Random House
Penguin.com

ISBN: 978-1-59514-822-3

Printed in the United States of America

10 9 8 7 6 5 4 3 2

KRAESHIAN
EMPIRE

JEWEL
OF THE
EMPIRE

THE
SILVER
SEA

THE

AMARANTH

SEA

KRAESHIAN EMPIRE

VENEAS

THE NORTHERN SEA

Mytica

THE IRON COAST

LIMEROS

THE GRANITE COAST

Ravencrest

THE REACHES

The Temple
of Valoria

Limerian
Palace

Scalia

THE IMPERIAL ROAD

THE TINGUE SEA

BLACK HARBOR

PAELSIA

Basilia

Basilius's
Compound

FORBIDDEN MOUNTAINS

TRADER'S
HARBOR

THE WILDLANDS

KING'S
HARBOR

The Temple
of Cleiona

AURANOS

Auranian Palace/
City of Gold

Hawk's
Brow

Elder's
Pitch

THE RADIANT COAST

ISLE
OF
LUKAS

TERREA

CAST OF CHARACTERS

Limeros

Magnus Lukas Damora	Prince
Lucia Eva Damora	Princess and sorceress
Gaius Damora	The king of Mytica
Felix Gaebras	Former assassin
Gareth Cirello	Grand Kingsliege
Kurtis Cirello	Lord Gareth's son
Milo Iagaris	Palace guard
Enzo	Palace guard
Selia Damora	Gaius's mother

Paelsia

Jonas Agallon	Rebel leader
Dariah Gallo	Witch

Auranos

Cleiona (Cleo) Aurora Bellos	Princess of Auranos
Nicolo (Nic) Cassian	Cleo's best friend
Nerissa Florens	Cleo's attendant
Taran Ranus	Rebel

Kraeshia

Ashur Cortas	Prince
Amara Cortas	Princess

Carlos   Captain of the guard

The Sanctuary

Timotheus   Elder Watcher
Olivia   Watcher
Kyan   Fire Kindred
Mia   Watcher

PROLOGUE

SEVENTEEN YEARS AGO

After he read the message, Gaius crushed the parchment in his fist and fell to his knees. His mind was jumbled with thoughts and memories. So many choices. So many losses.

So many regrets.

He wasn't sure how long it was before the echoing sound of footsteps drew him from his painful reverie. The small hand of his two-year-old son, Magnus, pressed against his arm. His wife, Althea, stood at the far end of the room, blocking the light from the window in his chambers.

"Papa?"

Gaius glanced, blurry-eyed, at Magnus. Instead of replying, he pulled the boy's small body against him and tried to take comfort in his son's embrace.

"What was in that message that's upset you?" Althea asked crisply, staring down her nose at him.

His throat constricted, as if fighting to speak the truth of it. He finally pulled back from his son to glance up at her.

"She's dead," he said, his words as dry and brittle as fallen leaves.

"Who's dead?"

He didn't want to answer questions. He didn't want to talk to his wife today, especially not about this.

"Papa?" Magnus said again, confused, and Gaius looked into his son's bright eyes. "Why you so sad, Papa?"

He placed his hands on the toddler's cheeks. "It's all right," he assured the boy. "All is well, my son."

Althea's jaw had tightened, and there was no kindness in her eyes. "Pull yourself together, Gaius, lest a servant happen to see you like this."

And what if they did? he thought. Althea was always so concerned about outward appearances and the opinions of others, no matter who they might be. His appreciation for her attention to detail and royal decorum often outweighed his overall apathy for the woman, but today it only made him hate her.

"Take Magnus," he said, rising to his feet and fixing the stoniest of looks upon his wife. "And send for my mother. I need to see her immediately."

She frowned. "But, Gaius—"

"*Now,*" he snapped at her.

With an impatient sigh, Althea took Magnus by his tiny hand and led him out of the room.

Gaius began pacing his chamber, from the heavy oak door that had the Limerian credo of *Strength, Faith, Wisdom* carved deeply into its surface, to the windows overlooking the Silver Sea. He finally stopped, silently staring down at the cold waters that crashed into the icy cliffs far below the palace window.

It wasn't very long before the door creaked open behind him and he turned to face his mother. The pained expression he wore drew her brows together. Fine lines fanned out around her dark gray eyes.

"My darling," Selia Damora said. "What has happened?"

He held the crumpled letter out to her. She closed the distance between them to take it from him and quickly scanned the short message.

"I see," she said grimly.

"Burn it."

"Very well." Using her fire magic, she set the letter aflame. He watched as the parchment fell in soft black ashes to the floor.

"How can I help?" she asked, her voice calm and soothing.

"You offered me something once . . . something powerful . . ." he said, clutching a handful of his shirt over his heart. "You said it could remove this cursed weakness from me once and for all. To help me forget . . . *her*."

Her solemn eyes met his. "She died bearing a daughter to another man—a man she chose long after you parted ways. I'm surprised you can't put all this far behind you."

"Yet I can't." He wouldn't beg. He wouldn't shame himself that way before the strongest and most powerful woman he'd ever known. "Will you help me or won't you? It's a simple question, Mother."

Selia's lips thinned. "No, it's not simple at all. All magic comes with a price, especially magic as dark as this."

"I don't care. Whatever the price, I'll pay it. I want to be strong in the face of any challenge that lies before me. I want to be as strong as you've always believed I could be."

His mother was silent for a moment. She turned her gaze toward the windows. "You're absolutely certain about this?" she asked.

"Yes." The word came out like the hiss of a snake.

She nodded, then left the room to fetch him what he asked— no, *begged*—for. When she returned, she held the same vial of potion she'd offered him years ago—potion, she said, that would make him strong in both body and mind. It would take away his weaknesses. It would sharpen his focus and help him attain everything he'd ever wanted.

Most importantly, this potion would also help him put his love for Elena Corso firmly where it belonged: in the past.

Gaius took the container that Selia held out to him and stared at the blue glass vial. For such a small object, it felt incredibly weighty in his hand.

"You need to be sure," Selia told him gravely. "The effects of this potion will stay with you until the day of your death. Once you drink it, you will never feel the same as you do now—you will be irrevocably changed."

"Yes." He nodded, his jaw tight. "Changed for the better."

He uncorked the vial, raised it to his lips, and, before he allowed himself any chance for doubt, drank the thick, warm liquid in one swallow.

"The pain will last only a moment," Selia said.

His frown deepened. "Pain?"

And then there it was—a sudden burning as if he'd swallowed molten lava. The dark magic coursed through him, burning everything weak and pathetic away. He heard himself scream from the sheer anguish of it as the glass vial fell from his grip and shattered on the stone floor.

Gaius Damora tried to embrace each moment of agony as his lingering weaknesses burned away, his memories of Elena faded to mere embers, and the desire for ultimate power rose within him like a phoenix from the flames.

CHAPTER 1

JONAS

KRAESHIA

Far across the sea in Mytica, there was a golden princess Jonas wanted to save.

And a god of fire he needed to destroy.

However, an obstacle now stood in Jonas's path on the Kraeshian docks, eating into time he didn't have to waste.

"I thought you said his sister killed him," Jonas said to Nic under his breath.

"She did." Nic's voice came out as barely more than a rasp as he raked both his hands through his messy, bright red hair. "I saw it with my own eyes."

"Then how is this possible?"

"I . . . I don't know."

Prince Ashur Cortas drew to a stop only a few paces away. He eyed both Jonas and Nic through narrowed, silvery-blue eyes that stood out against his dark tan complexion like the glinting edge of a blade at dusk.

The only sounds to be heard for a few long moments were the

squawk of a nearby seabird as it plunged downward to catch a fish and the gentle, steady splash of the water against the waiting Limerian ship with its black and red sails.

"Nicolo," the raven-haired prince said with a nod. "I know you must be very confused to see me again."

"I . . . I . . . what . . . ?" was Nic's only reply. The scattering of freckles over his nose and cheeks contrasted boldly with his blanched complexion. He drew in a shaky breath. "This is impossible."

Ashur raised a dark brow at the boy, hesitating only briefly before he spoke. "In my twenty-one years of life I've come to realize that very little in this world is impossible."

"I watched you *die*." The last word sounded as if it had been dragged painfully from Nic's throat. "What was that? Just another lie? Another scheme? Another plan that you didn't feel the need to tell me about?"

Jonas was surprised that Nic dared to speak to a member of royalty with such insolence. Not that Jonas himself had much respect for royals, but Nic had spent enough time in the Auranian palace, side by side with its princess, to know it wasn't wise to be this openly rude.

"It was no lie. What happened at the temple was not a scheme." Ashur swept his gaze over the Limerian ship, which was ready for imminent departure from the Jewel of the Empire's crowded, busy docks. "I'll explain more once we're at sea."

Jonas's brows went up at the prince's commanding and confident tone. "Once *we're* at sea," he repeated.

"Yes. I'm coming with you."

"If that's what you're planning to do," Jonas said, crossing his arms, "then you'll explain more *now*."

Ashur eyed him. "Who are you?"

Jonas eyed him back. "I'm the one who decides who gets on this ship—and who doesn't."

"Do you know who I am?" Ashur asked.

"Well aware. You're the brother of Amara Cortas, who just recently seems to have made herself the bloodthirsty empress of most of the damn world. And according to Nic, you're supposed to be dead."

A familiar form appeared behind Ashur, catching Jonas's eye.

Taran Ranus had left the docks only a few moments ago, so that he might quickly prepare for an unplanned journey to Mytica. But he was already back. As the rebel drew closer, he swiftly pulled out a sword from the sheath at his waist.

"Well, well," Taran said as he raised the tip of the sword to Ashur's throat. "Prince Ashur. What a pleasant surprise to see that you've strolled into our midst this morning, just as my friends are working to topple your family's reign."

"The general chaos around the Jewel did give that much away," Ashur said, his tone and demeanor surprisingly serene.

"Why have you come back? Why not stay abroad, chasing after meaningless treasure as everyone says you're fond of doing?"

Chasing after treasure? Jonas shared an anxious look with Nic. It seemed that very few were aware that the prince had been presumed dead.

"The circumstances of my return are none of your business."

"Are you in Kraeshia because of . . ." Nic began, then hesitated. "Of . . . what happened to your family? You must know, don't you?"

"Yes, I know." Ashur's expression darkened. "But that's not why I'm here."

Taran smirked. "As the true heir to the throne, perhaps you'll make an excellent tool for negotiations with your grandmother now that your sister's married the enemy and sailed away."

Ashur scoffed. "If that's what you think, then you know nothing about her desire for power—or my sister's. It's easy to see that your rebels are vastly outnumbered. This current uprising will be as effective as the chirp of a baby bird in the shadow of a hungry wildcat. What you really need to do is get on this ship and leave while you still have the chance."

Taran's smirk disappeared. His brown eyes flashed with outrage. "You don't get to tell me what to do."

Jonas felt uneasy about Ashur's attitude. He seemed to be taking the recent news of most of his family's massacre in stride. He couldn't tell if Ashur grieved their loss or celebrated it. Or did he feel nothing at all?

"Lower your weapon, Taran," Jonas growled, then hissed out a breath. "Why are you back so soon anyway? Didn't you have belongings to gather?"

Taran didn't budge. He kept the sharp tip of his sword pressed to Ashur's throat, his biceps flexing. "The roads are blocked. Granny Cortas has decided that all rebels are to be slain on sight. Since we blew up the city dungeon yesterday, there's nowhere to put any prisoners."

"All the more reason for us to go now," Nic urged.

"I agree with Nicolo," Ashur said.

The angry squawk of a bird caught Jonas's attention. He shielded his eyes from the sun and looked up at the golden hawk swooping above the ship.

Olivia was getting impatient. That made two of them.

He willed himself to remain calm. He couldn't afford to make any rash decisions.

Just then, an image of Lysandra slid into his mind, along with the sound of her laughter. *No rash decisions? Since when?* she would have said.

Since you died and I couldn't save you.

Pushing his grief away, Jonas forced himself to focus on the prince.

"If you want any chance to board this ship," he said, "then explain how you've managed to rise from the dead only to walk right up to a group of rebels like you've only been out for a tankard of ale."

"Rise from the dead?" Taran repeated, his furious expression giving way to confusion.

Ignoring Taran, Jonas searched for any sign of intimidation in the prince's demeanor. A signal that he feared for his life, that he was desperate to escape his homeland. But only serenity filled his pale eyes.

It was unsettling, really.

"Have you ever heard of the legend of the phoenix?" Ashur asked smoothly.

"Of course," Nic replied. "It's a mythical bird that rose from the ashes of the flames that originally killed it. It's the symbol for Kraeshia, to show the empire's strength and ability to defy death itself."

Ashur nodded. "Yes."

Jonas raised his eyebrows. "Really?" he said.

Nic shrugged. "I took a class with Cleo on foreign myths once. I paid more attention than she did." He flicked a wary look at Ashur. "What about this legend?"

"There is also a legend of a mortal fated to one day do the same—return from death to unite the world. Grandmother always believed that my sister would be this phoenix. When Amara was a baby, she died for a brief moment but came back to life, thanks to a resurrection potion our mother gave her. When I recently learned of this, I had the same potion created for me. I'm not sure

I truly believed it would work, but it did. And as I rose at dawn in the temple where I'd died the night before at my sister's hand, I realized the truth."

"What truth?" Jonas demanded after Ashur fell silent.

Ashur met his gaze. "That *I* am the phoenix. And it's my destiny to save this world from its current fate, beginning with stopping my sister from her dark need to blindly follow in my father's footsteps."

The prince fell silent again as his audience of three stared at him. Taran was the first to laugh.

"Royals always think so damn highly of themselves," he sneered. "Legends of heroes who defy certain death are as old as legends about the Watchers themselves." Taran glanced at Jonas. "I'm going to cut off his head. If he gets up after that, consider me a believer."

Jonas didn't think Taran was being serious, but he didn't want to take any chances.

"Lower your weapon," Jonas growled. "I'm not going to tell you again."

Taran cocked his head. "I don't take orders from you."

"Do you want passage on this ship? Then yes, you *do* take orders from me."

But still Taran didn't budge, and his gaze grew only more challenging.

"You giving Jonas a problem, Ranus?" Felix's voice boomed out, just before he came to stand at Jonas's side.

Jonas was grateful that Felix Gaebras—with all his height and muscles—was on his side. A former member of the Clan of the Cobra, a group of assassins who worked for King Gaius, Felix's ability to cast a deadly and intimidating shadow was no accident.

But Taran was just as deadly and just as intimidating.

"You want to know about my problems?" Taran finally lowered

his blade to his side, then nodded at the resurrected royal. "This is Prince Ashur Cortas."

Felix peered skeptically at the prince with his good eye. After spending the last week imprisoned and being mercilessly tortured for poisoning the Kraeshian royal family—a crime Amara had blamed on him—it was his *only* eye; the other was covered by a black eye patch. "Aren't you supposed to be dead?"

"He is." Nic had stayed very quiet, never taking his attention off of the prince, wearing an expression that was equal parts stunned and confused.

"I'm not." Ashur spoke patiently to Nic.

"It could be a trick." Nic's brow furrowed in concentration as he studied the prince carefully. "Perhaps you're a witch who possesses enough air magic to change your appearance."

Ashur raised a dark eyebrow, as if amused. "Hardly."

"Witches are female," Taran reasoned.

"Not always," Ashur replied. "There have been a few notable exceptions over the centuries."

"Are you trying to help your case or not?" Jonas asked sharply.

"He's Amara's brother," Felix growled. "Let's just go ahead and kill him and be done with it."

"Yes," Taran seconded. "On that, we agree."

Ashur sighed, and for the first time, there was an edge of impatience in the sound. Despite any threats, he kept his attention firmly on Nic. "I understand your hesitation in believing me, Nicolo. It reminds me of your hesitation that night in the City of Gold, when you left the tavern . . . The Beast, I believe it was called. You were drunk, lost, and you looked at me in that alleyway as if I might kill you with the two blades I carried. But I didn't, did I? Do you remember what I did instead?"

Nic's pale face flushed in an instant, and he cleared his throat.

"It's him," he said quickly. "I don't know how, but . . . it's him. Let's go."

Jonas studied Nic's face, unsure whether to believe such a promise, even from someone he'd very recently begun to trust. His gut told him Nic wasn't lying.

And if Ashur wanted to bring a halt to his sister's evil machinations, believing himself to be this legendary phoenix who'd risen from death, true or not, then he could possibly be an asset to their group.

He wondered what Lys would have to say about *this* situation.

No, he already knew. She very likely would have put an arrow through the prince the moment he'd appeared.

The glint of Taran's sword again caught his attention. "If you don't lower that weapon, I'm going to have Felix chop off your arm."

Taran laughed, an unpleasant crack of a sound that cut through the cool morning air. "I'd like to see him try."

"Would you?" Felix asked. "My eyesight's not as good as it was, but I think—actually, I *know*—I could do it real fast. It might not even hurt." He chuckled darkly as he drew his sword. "No, what am I thinking? It's going to hurt very badly. I'm no ally to any Cortas, but if Jonas wants the prince to keep breathing, he's going to keep breathing. Got it?"

The two young men glared at each other for several tense moments. Finally Taran sheathed his weapon.

"Fine," he said through clenched teeth. The tight smile on his face didn't match the cold fury in his eyes.

Without a word, he shoved past Felix and boarded the ship.

"Thanks," Jonas said to Felix under his breath.

Felix watched Taran's departure with a grim look. "You know he's going to be a problem, right?

"I do."

"Great." Felix glanced at the Limerian ship. "By the way, have I mentioned that I get really seasick, especially with the thought of Amara's undead brother on board? So if our new friend Taran tries to cut my throat while I'm vomiting off the side of the ship, you're the one I blame."

"Understood." Jonas eyed Nic and Ashur warily. "Very well, whatever fate awaits us on the other side, let's set sail for Mytica. All of us."

"Thought you didn't believe in fate?" Nic muttered as they made their way up the gangplank.

"I don't," Jonas said.

But, to be honest, only a small part of him believed that anymore.

CHAPTER 2

MAGNUS

LIMEROS

The sun rose in the east while Magnus waited at the bottom of the steep cliff for his father to die. He watched tensely as the pool of blood around the king's head grew, becoming a large crimson stain on the surface of the frozen lake.

Magnus tried to summon something inside of him other than hatred for Gaius Damora. But he could not.

His father had been a sadistic tyrant his entire life. He'd given away his kingdom to an enemy as if it were nothing more than a meaningless bauble. He had secretly ordered the murder of his own wife, Magnus's mother, because she stood in the way of the power he craved. And, just before he fell from the cliff, the king had come within mere moments of ending the life of his son and heir.

Magnus jumped when Cleo's hand brushed against his.

"We can't stay here," she said quietly. "It won't be long until we're discovered."

"I know." Magnus glanced at the four Limerian guards who stood nearby, awaiting orders. He wished he knew exactly what to tell them.

"If we hurry, we can make it to the docks of Ravencrest by sunset. We'll be in Auranos within a week. There we can find help from rebels who won't sit back and let Amara take everything away from us."

"Does that make me a rebel now too?" he asked, almost able to find the humor in such a statement.

"I think you've been a rebel longer than you'd care to admit. But yes. We can be rebels together."

Something stirred deep inside of him at her words, a kind of warmth that he'd repressed for far too long.

The king—with help from Magnus—had destroyed Cleo's entire life, yet she still stood by his side. Fearless. Brave.

Hopeful.

He kept thinking that this was only a fevered dream, that this perfect version of the princess might fade as the sun rose higher in the sky. But as the day grew light, she still stood by his side. She wasn't a dream.

Magnus raised his gaze to hers. Yesterday had been a blur of desperation and fear. It had been the absolute worst day of his life, which had been turned utterly inside out the moment he'd finally found her in the woods, alive and fighting with all her strength to survive.

He'd confessed his love for her in a pathetic heap of messy words, and she hadn't turned away from him, disgusted. This beautiful golden princess who had lost so much . . . she'd said she loved him too.

It still didn't seem possible.

"Magnus?" Cleo gently prompted when he didn't respond

immediately. "What do you say? Shall we make our way to Ravencrest?"

He was about to answer, when the king drew in a hoarse, rattling breath.

"Magnusssss . . ."

His gaze shot to his father's face. The king's eyes were open now, and he raised his arm a few inches, as if reaching for his son.

Impossible. Magnus forced himself not to stagger back from the man in shock.

"You should be dead by now," Magnus managed, his throat painfully tight.

The king made a strange, coughing sound then, and if Magnus didn't know better, he'd swear it sounded like a laugh.

"Not . . . that simple . . . I'm afraid," the king sputtered.

Magnus could see Cleo's eyes blazing with hatred as she looked down at the man. "Why did you say my mother's name?"

The king glanced up at her, his gaze narrowed. He licked his dry lips but didn't reply.

Magnus looked at Cleo with surprise. The king had spoken the name Elena in what had seemed like his dying gasps. Had he really meant Queen Elena Bellos?

"Answer me," she demanded. "Why did you speak her name when you looked at me? You said you were sorry. Sorry for what? What did you do to her that you would need to be sorry for?"

"Oh . . . dear princess . . . if only you knew." The king's words were less like dying gasps this time and more like the sluggish statement of someone who had just awoken from a deep slumber.

The guards had drawn closer to them at the sound of the king's voice.

Enzo gasped as King Gaius pressed his hands against the blood-spattered snow and raised his head from the icy ground.

"What dark magic is this?" The guard's wide eyes glanced over to Magnus, and he immediately bowed his head. "Apologies, your highness."

"None required. It's an excellent question." Uneasily, Magnus drew his sword and held it as steadily as he could to the king's chest. "You should be broken beyond repair, like a bird that flew into a window. What dark magic *is* this, Father? And is it strong enough to save you from a sharp steel point?"

The king glanced at him with a thin-lipped smirk. "You'd so easily wish to finish a man who's grasping at the smallest edge of life?"

"If that man is you, then yes," Magnus hissed.

His father was helpless, weak, bruised, and bloody. It would be the easiest kill Magnus had ever made. And well deserved. So very well deserved.

One jab, one small gesture, could end this. Why, then, did his sword arm feel trapped in stone, unable to move?

"The earth Kindred . . ." Cleo whispered, touching the pocket of her cloak where she'd put the crystal orb. "It's healed him. Is that what this is?"

"I don't know," Magnus admitted.

"I don't think the Kindred's magic has anything to do with this." The king now sat upright, his legs stretched out before him. He looked down at his hands, scraped and bleeding from holding on to the edge of the cliff. Gaius took out a pair of black gloves from inside his torn cloak. He slid them on, grimacing from the effort. "As I fell, I felt the darklands reaching for me, ready to claim another demon for their ranks. When I hit the ground, I felt my bones shatter. You're right: I should be dead."

"And yet, you're sitting and speaking," Cleo said, her words clipped.

"I am." He peered up at her. "It must be taking quite a lot of restraint from you right now, princess, not to beg my son to end my life."

Her eyes narrowed. "If I didn't think your guards would kill him a moment later, I would."

Magnus looked toward the silent guards now flanking them. Each one had their sword in hand, their expressions tense.

"Point well made." The king took a deep, steady breath. "Guards, hear me. You will obey all commands of Magnus Damora from this moment forward. He will not be held responsible for anything that has, or will, happen to me."

The guards glanced at each other with strained and uncertain expressions before Enzo nodded. "Very well, your highness," he said.

"What deception is this?" Cleo spat out. "Do you think we'll believe anything you say?"

The king smiled. "*We.* How very sweet it is that you two have traversed this dangerous maze together and come out on the other side holding hands. How long have you two been working together against me? I'd no idea I had been so blind."

Magnus ignored the king's attempt to throw him off course. "If this isn't Kindred magic, what is it?"

With total disregard for the sword Magnus held, the king slowly and shakily pushed himself up to his feet. "Melenia told me that I was destined for immortality, that I would be a god." He let out a small, bitter laugh. "For a time, I actually believed her."

"Answer my damn question," Magnus snarled again. He jabbed the blade forward, leaving a shallow scratch on the king's throat.

Gaius flinched, his expression darkening in an instant. "There's only one person responsible for the magic that helped me survive today. Your grandmother."

Magnus didn't believe him. "What common witch could possess magic as strong as this?"

"There was never anything common about Selia Damora."

"You expect us to believe anything you say?" Cleo snapped.

The king looked at the girl without a lick of kindness in his eyes. "No. I wouldn't expect a child to understand the complexities of life and death."

"Wouldn't you?" Her fists were clenched at her sides. "If I had a sword in my grasp right now, I'd end you myself."

The king laughed. "You could certainly try."

"You look like you're already dead." Magnus realized the truth of his words as he spoke them, his father's pale appearance no healthier than a corpse—his skin slack and bearing a grayish tinge, his bruises mottled browns and purples, his blood so dark it appeared black. "Perhaps Grandmother's healing magic wasn't as strong as you'd like to believe."

"This isn't healing magic." His brow glistened with perspiration despite the frigid morning air. "This has only prolonged the inevitable."

Magnus frowned. "Explain."

"When what little magic remaining within me fades, I will die."

His father's bluntly delivered statement only filled him with more confusion.

"He's lying," Cleo said through clenched teeth. "Don't let him manipulate you. If this isn't earth magic, then it's blood magic that keeps his black heart beating."

Magnus glanced at the guards, taking in their troubled gazes and furrowed brows before returning his attention to his father. "If this is true, how long do you have?"

"I don't know." He inhaled, and Magnus heard the hard edge of pain in his breath once again. "Hopefully long enough to fix some of the mistakes I've made. The most recent ones, anyway."

Magnus turned his face away, disgusted. "Unfortunately, we don't have enough time to go over a list as endless as that."

"You're right." Gaius gazed at Magnus, past the sword. "Perhaps I can fix only one, then. In order to defeat Amara and reclaim Mytica, we will need to unlock the full power of the Kindred."

"For this, we need Lucia's blood and the blood of an immortal."

"Yes."

"I have no idea where to find her."

Disappointment crossed the king's pale expression. "I must go to see my mother immediately. She'll use her magic to find Lucia. I would trust no other witch with this task."

"Go to her? How?" Magnus frowned. "Grandmother has been dead for more than twelve years."

"No, she's very much alive."

He stared at the king in shock. Magnus's memories of his grandmother were sparse, foggy glimpses of his childhood and a woman with black hair and a cool gaze. A woman who had passed away shortly after his grandfather's death.

"He's trying to confuse you." Cleo took Magnus's hand in her own, drawing him away from his father and out of earshot from both him and the guards. "We need to go to Auranos. There's help there. Help we can trust, without question or doubt. Those loyal to my father's name will not hold the king's crimes against you, I promise."

He shook his head. "This is not a war that a few rebels can win. Amara's become too powerful, she's gained too much with barely any effort. We need to find Lucia."

"And if we're successful in finding her? What then? She hates us."

"She's confused," Magnus said, an image of his younger sister appearing in his mind. "Grieving. She feels betrayed and lied to. If she knew that her home was in trouble, she would help us."

"Are you sure about that?"

If Magnus were honest with himself, he'd have to admit he wasn't sure about anything anymore.

"You must go to Auranos without me," he spat out the words, as distasteful as they were necessary. "I can't leave yet. I need to see this through to the end."

She nodded. "That sounds like a good plan."

His heart twisted into a vicious knot. "I'm glad you agree."

"You are, are you?" Cleo's cerulean eyes flashed with cold fire, and Magnus almost started at her harsh words. "You think that after all of this . . . ?" She threw her hands up in the air in lieu of finishing her sentence. "You are completely *impossible*, do you know that? I'm not leaving here without you, you idiot—"

His brows shot up. "Idiot?"

"—and that's the end of this discussion. Got it?"

He stared at her, once again stunned by this girl and everything she said. "Cleo—"

"No, no more arguments," she cut him off harshly. "Now, if you'll excuse me for a moment, I need to clear my head. Away from *him*." She tossed the last word at the king and, with a glare, marched away, her arms crossed tightly over her chest.

"I see such passion between you now," the king said as he drew closer to his son, his lips twisting with distaste. "How terribly sweet."

"Shut your mouth," Magnus growled.

The king kept his gaze on the princess as she paced angrily nearby. Then he turned toward the guards. "I need to speak to my son in private. Give us space."

All four guards immediately did as requested and moved away from Magnus and his father.

"Privacy?" Magnus scoffed. "I don't think anything you have to say to me anymore warrants that."

"No? Not even if it's about your golden princess?"

Magnus's hand was on the hilt of his sword in an instant, fury rising within him. "If you dare threaten her life again—"

"A warning, not a threat." His father regarded his outrage with only weary patience. "The girl is cursed."

Magnus was sure he hadn't heard him correctly. "Cursed?"

"Many years ago, her father was involved with a powerful witch—a witch who didn't take the news of his marriage to Elena Corso well, so she cursed Elena and any future offspring that they would die in childbirth. Elena nearly died giving her firstborn life."

"But she didn't."

"No, she died with her second."

Of course Magnus had heard about the former queen of Auranos's tragic fate and had seen the portraits of Cleo's beautiful mother in the hallways of the golden palace. But this couldn't possibly be true.

"It's said she suffered greatly before she finally passed." The king's voice had become not much more than a rasp. "But she was strong enough to see her newborn daughter's face—and to name her after a wretched, hedonistic goddess—before death finally claimed her. And now this witch's curse has surely been passed to that daughter."

Magnus regarded his father with utter disbelief. "You're lying."

The king sent a fierce frown at Magnus. "Why would I lie?"

"Why would you lie?" he repeated, a dry laugh rising in his throat. "Oh, I don't know. Perhaps because you wish to manipulate me at every turn for your own amusement?"

"If that's what you think . . ." The king flicked his wrist toward Cleo, who was speaking with Enzo now and sending impatient looks toward Magnus and his father. The hem of the scarlet gown she wore peeked out from beneath the dark green fabric of the cloak she'd stolen the night before from a Kraeshian guard. "Get her pregnant and you'll witness her die in anguish, lying in a deep pool of her own blood as she brings your spawn into this world."

Magnus had all but stopped breathing. What his father claimed couldn't possibly be true.

But if it was . . .

Cleo began to close the distance between them, her hood down, her long blond hair fanned over her shoulders.

"Witches casts curses," Gaius said to Magnus quietly. "Witches are also known to break curses. All the more reason for you to come with me to see your grandmother."

"You tried to kill me and the princess."

"Yes, I did. So the decision of how you'll proceed lies with you now."

Cleo reached Magnus's side with Enzo behind her, and she frowned as she looked between father and son. "What is it? Not more plans for me to hide myself away in Auranos, I hope."

The horrific image of Cleo lying dead on bloody sheets was now locked in Magnus's mind, her eyes glazed and lifeless while nearby a baby with cerulean eyes cried endlessly for its mother.

"No, princess," Magnus managed. "You made your thoughts on that quite clear, even if I strongly disagree. I wish to be reacquainted with my grandmother after all these years. She will use her magic to help us find Lucia, who will help us reclaim Mytica. Agreed?"

Cleo didn't answer for a moment, her brow furrowed in thought. "Yes, I suppose it makes a sickening kind of sense to seek help from another Damora." She blinked. "Magnus, you've become very pale. Are you all right?"

"Fine," he said tightly. "We leave now."

"Amara will wonder where I've disappeared to without word," the king said. "That could cause problems."

Magnus sighed. "Very well. Go and make your excuses for leaving your bride's side. However, if you try to cross me, Father, I assure you that your death will come far sooner than you anticipate."

CHAPTER 3

AMARA

LIMEROS

Empress Amara Cortas sat upon a carved, gilded chair in the villa's smaller than adequate main hall. It was a temporary throne, but it did nicely to prop her up so she could easily look down upon the two very different men who kneeled before her.

Carlos was the captain of the Kraeshian guard, a man with bronzed skin and black hair, his shoulders impossibly broad. He had more than enough muscles to fully fill out his dark green Kraeshian uniform, its golden clasps, which attached the black cape, glittering in the candlelight.

Lord Kurtis Cirillo was younger, thinner, more sallow in appearance, with dark hair and olive green eyes. While Amara would prefer a larger castle to spend her current days, this villa was the finest home for miles around, and it belonged to Kurtis's father, Lord Gareth.

"Rise," she commanded, and they obeyed.

Both men waited for her response to the updated news of yesterday's siege and capture of the Limerian palace.

As Amara composed her thoughts, she winced from the large and rather painful lump on the back of her head she'd acquired last night. The sack of icicles that she held to the injury had started to melt.

"Of the dozen casualties," she finally said, "was there anyone of importance?" For this, she turned to Kurtis, who would know nobles from lessers much better than her guard.

"No, your grace," Kurtis replied quickly. "Mostly Limerian soldiers and guards, a few servants. Only those who attempted to stand against you."

"Good." Twelve wasn't an unacceptable number to perish considering how many people had allegedly been at the palace to witness Princess Cleiona's speech at the time of the siege. From Carlos's report, three thousand citizens from nearby villages had made the journey to hear that hateful girl spread more of her lies.

She scanned the red and black banners lining the stone walls bearing the Cirillo family crest: three snakes entwined. For a kingdom of ice and snow that supported very little wildlife that Amara had noticed, Limerians did seem to value images of serpents.

"Your grace . . ." Kurtis's reedy voice chirped.

"Yes, Lord Kurtis?"

The young man's face was pained, his mouth set in a grimace that had become familiar to her in her short time in Mytica. She wondered whether this was a permanent look for the kingsliege or whether it was due to the unfortunate injury he sustained just before she met him. There were fresh bandages on the bloody stump at his wrist where his right hand used to be. "I hesitate to broach a subject that Carlos believes we mustn't bother you with."

"Oh?" She glanced with surprise at her guard, who looked at Kurtis with naked hatred in his steely gaze. "What is it?"

"I've heard concerning talk amongst your soldiers about your reign—"

"My lord," Carlos bit out, "if there is a problem with the men I command, I will come to the empress myself. This matter does not need the opinion of a Limerian."

Kurtis scoffed, as if insulted by Carlos's bluntness. "Does the empress not deserve to know that her own soldiers speak of abandoning their posts rather than be ruled by"—he hesitated, but only for a moment—"a *woman*?"

Amara willed herself to be calm as she handed the melting ice to a nearby maid. "Carlos, is this true?"

The guard looked ready to spit molten glass. "It is, your grace."

"Yet you don't feel this is a concern?"

"Talk is talk. None have taken any action as yet to leave this mission to return to Kraeshia. And if they do, they will be severely punished."

She studied the man's face, a man who had been loyal to her father not so very long ago. "How do you feel about having me as the first female ruler of Kraeshia? Will you continue to take my orders without wishing to abandon your post?"

He straightened those massive shoulders. "I am loyal to Kraeshia, your grace, therefore I am loyal to whoever is on the throne. I assure you, I have control over my men."

"Yes, but the question is, do I?" It was the reason she hadn't celebrated her victory of becoming empress quite yet. Her control felt delicate, like ice newly formed over a lake. There was no way to know for certain if it would shatter the moment it was met with pressure.

All the more reason why she needed the magic released from her water Kindred. The small aquamarine orb hidden in the pocket of one of her gowns in the wardrobe was useless to her now. She had to figure out how to unleash the powerful magic inside.

"Your grace," Kurtis said, and she couldn't help but notice that his expression had lightened some since delivering the news Carlos had wanted concealed from her. "I have also heard them speak of Prince Ashur's eventual return from his travels."

"Oh? And what of it?" Pain flared from her head wound, radiating in waves. She would like to lie down for the day, to rest and heal, but an empress couldn't afford to indulge in even the slightest bit of weakness.

"As your older brother, they feel that he will reign as emperor. They believe that your position is a temporary one only. And they feel, once news of your family's deaths reach him wherever he currently is, that he will return without hesitation."

Amara took a deep breath and counted, slowly, to ten in her head.

Then she counted to twenty before pushing a small smile on her face.

"Is this also true?" she asked Carlos as sweetly as she could.

The guard's face seemingly had turned to stone. "It is, your grace."

"Truthfully, I hope they're right," she said. "Ashur certainly is the first in line to the throne before me, so of course I will relinquish my title the moment he appears. We can mourn our lost family together."

"Your grace," Carlos said, bowing deeply, his brows drawn together. "Your grief is shared by us all. Your father, your brothers, they were all great men."

"Indeed they were."

But even great men could be felled by poison.

Amara had been trying very hard not to feel like a venomous scorpion who lured unsuspecting victims into her lair. She knew she wasn't the villain in the story of her life. She was the heroine. A queen. An empress.

But without the respect of the soldiers she needed to expand her kingdom, she had nothing. Carlos might not believe a few dissenting whispers were important, but soon they could become the voice of a full rebellion.

For now, despite her title, she had to tread carefully until she had the magic she required to hold on to her newfound power.

One day very soon, Amara Cortas would not answer to any man, not ever again. They would answer to her.

And if they were counting on her brother's return to chase the girl from the throne she had taken with strength and sacrifice, then they would be sorely disappointed.

After all, one of those sacrifices had been Ashur himself.

"I am grateful that you chose to tell me this," she addressed Kurtis again. "And if my brother does arrive, please know that I will welcome him with open arms." When Kurtis bowed, she shifted her disappointed gaze to the guard who would keep the talk of treason a secret from her. "Carlos, what is the status on the search for Princess Cleiona?"

"A dozen men, including the king, are still out searching for her, your grace."

Less than a year ago, before she was taken in by the conquering royal family and married to Magnus, Cleo had been a spoiled princess who had lived a pampered Auranian life. Amara knew what a demanding and difficult girl she *really* was, despite the sunny and golden demeanor she might have presented socially.

Last night, Amara had made the mistake of underestimating Cleo and offering her her friendship. She'd quickly come to regret it.

The princess's drive for survival nearly equaled her own.

"Make it two dozen guards," she instructed Carlos. "She couldn't have gotten far."

Carlos bowed. "At your command, your highness."

"Actually, I'm sure the princess has frozen and is now three feet under the fallen snow." King Gaius's voice stole Amara's attention from her guard. She looked up to see that the man had entered the hall and was slowly moving toward her, flanked by two of his guards.

Kurtis and Carlos immediately bowed before the king.

Amara swept her gaze over Gaius and her eyes widened with shock. His face was bruised, all banged up with cuts and scratches. There was a sickly grayish pallor to his complexion. His neck was smeared with blood, which was caked in the creases of his hands and underneath his fingernails.

"Carlos, fetch a medic immediately!" she commanded as she rose from her throne to meet the king halfway across the large room.

"No," Gaius said, raising his hand. "That won't be necessary."

Only last night when he'd left to search for the princess, he'd been a handsome man with dark hair and deep, if often cruel, dark brown eyes, tall and strong, but now he looked as if he had crawled up out of his own grave.

Amara gave Carlos a nod to do what she asked anyway, and the guard immediately left the hall. "What happened to you?" she asked, injecting concern rather than simply shock into her tone.

The king rubbed his shoulder, his face a mask of pain. "I took a rather nasty fall while searching for the princess." His expression tightened. "But I'm fine."

A lie if ever she'd heard one.

Gaius swept his gaze over the kingsliege, lingering on his injury. "Good goddess, boy. What happened to you?"

Kurtis glanced at his bandaged stump, his face reddening and his cheek twitching. "When I attempted to escort your son's wife out of the palace yesterday, he attempted to stop me."

"He cut off your hand."

"He did," Kurtis admitted. "And I feel it's a crime that deserves punishment. After all, I only acted on your command."

"I must sit." Gaius gestured for one of his red-uniformed guards to bring him a chair, and he all but collapsed into it. Amara watched him with growing alarm. This was not a man who normally showed any kind of weakness at all. This was the result of a fall, he said?

If he was close to death for whatever reason, she needed him to tell her how to unlock the Kindred's magic before it was too late.

"Yes," Gaius continued, his voice barely more audible than a gasp. "Magnus has certainly made some questionable decisions recently."

Amara tried again. "Gaius, I insist you see a medic."

"And I insist that I'm fine. On to other, more interesting topics, I've brought you a gift." He gesturing at one of his guards. "Enzo, bring in the girl."

The guard left the hall and returned a few moments later with a pretty young woman with short, dark hair.

"This," the king swept his gaze over the girl, "is Nerissa Florens."

Amara raised a brow, managing to find a trace of humor in the unexpected introduction. "I've never received a girl as a gift before."

"You need an attendant. Nerissa tended to Princess Cleiona and, I've heard, is greatly skilled at her job."

Instead of feelings of peevishness provoked by being presented with a nobody, Amara found her interest piqued. "I assume this means you're loyal to the princess."

"On the contrary, your highness," Nerissa replied, her voice strong. "I am loyal only to my king."

Amara narrowed her gaze at the girl and took her in, top to bottom. Short hair wasn't a common style, not in Kraeshia or

Mytica. It spoke of someone who didn't have time for vanity. Yet Nerissa was quite attractive. She had a graceful nose, widely set eyes, and a flush to her tanned cheeks. She stood proudly, far more proudly than any servant Amara had witnessed before.

Amara finally nodded. "Very well, Nerissa, I do find myself in need of a skilled attendant. However, if you say you're loyal only to the king, I will need to ask him to transfer that loyalty to me now. Gaius?"

"Yes, of course," the king replied without hesitation. "Nerissa, Amara is your only concern now. Watch over her and attend to her every need."

Nerissa bowed her head. "Yes, your highness."

Amara continued to assess the girl. She couldn't be much older than her own nineteen years. "You don't seem afraid of me."

"Should I be, your highness?"

"The palace where you earned your living was taken by a foreign army, its prince and princess deposed. And here you stand before the conqueror. Yes, I think you should show some fear."

"I learned a long time ago, your grace, that no matter what I might be feeling on the inside, I should show only strength on the outside. Apologies if that philosophy is not acceptable to you."

Amara studied the girl a few moments longer, thinking that they had this much in common. "It's fine, Nerissa. I look forward to learning more about your time with the princess."

"Yes, your grace."

"Good," the king said. "Now that that's taken care of, Lord Kurtis . . ."

"Yes, your majesty?" Kurtis straightened his back like a soldier coming to attention.

"While I'm gone, I'd like you to make the arrangements to

relocate the empress to the Limerian palace. Your father's villa may become a bit cramped, and of course it lacks the level of accommodation that my wife deserves. When I return, I will expect to find you there."

Kurtis bowed. "I will do exactly as you say, your majesty."

Amara watched the king with growing confusion. "Where are you going?"

Gaius grunted as he pushed himself out of the chair, struggling to his feet like a man twice his age. "I need to lead the search for my son."

"On the contrary," she said. "What you need is bed rest and time to heal from your fall."

"Again," he said tightly, "I find myself in disagreement with my new wife."

She kept the smile on her face.

"May I speak to you? Privately?" Amara asked as sweetly as possible.

"Of course," he said, nodding to a nearby guard, who quickly swung the door open and ushered everyone out. As the room cleared, Amara closed her eyes and took several deep breaths in an attempt to force herself to handle this conversation delicately.

"If you insist on going on this quest," she said, "I think you should leave the air Kindred with me for safekeeping."

Perhaps *delicately* was slightly beyond her particular skills.

But Gaius was unfazed. "I don't think so," he replied simply.

Amara's gut tightened. "Why not?"

He raised a dark eyebrow. "Oh, please. I admit I may not be completely myself at the moment, but I'm no fool."

So it would seem. "You don't trust me."

"No, not at all, actually."

Amara reined in her frustration. The king had no idea that she also possessed a piece of the Kindred and she had no intention of telling him. "I will earn your trust."

"And I will earn yours. Someday."

She closed the small distance between them and took his hands in hers, noticing his grimace of pain as she did so. "We can begin today. Share with me the secret of unlocking its magic. The answer is here, I know that. Here in Mytica."

"That much I haven't tried to hide."

She had been thinking nonstop about this during their journey here across the Silver Sea. So much time to think, to worry, to plan. "I can only assume that your daughter is an integral part of this, just as she was integral to finding the crystals in the first place."

His expression closed up. "Is that what you think?"

"Yes." She would not fear this man and his reputation for violence when crossed. She was the only one to be feared in this room, in this kingdom, and one day in this entire world. "Perhaps it's Lucia, not Magnus, that you seek on this ill-timed journey."

"My daughter eloped with her tutor and could be anywhere."

"I'm right, aren't I?" A smile spread across her features. "Lucia is the key to everything. Her prophecy expands far broader than I already thought. Don't look so grim, Gaius. I told you that you could trust me, and you can. I'll prove it. We will find her together."

"I do want to find her, but I assure you, she is not the missing piece of this puzzle you seek."

She wouldn't receive a confirmation from him about this. Not today, perhaps not ever. She forced herself to smile sweetly and nod. "Very well. I will be patient then and focus on moving to the palace while you're gone."

Gaius studied her closely, looking into her eyes so intensely that Amara couldn't be sure if he was trying to memorize her face or read her thoughts. She held her breath as she waited for him to speak.

"I'll return as soon as I can." He drew her closer and kissed her cheek. She forced herself not to recoil from the oddly unmistakable scent of death upon him.

He held her gaze for a moment longer, then turned and left the room without another word.

She took a seat upon her throne, waiting until Carlos returned with the medic. Amara dismissed the woman and summoned Carlos before her.

The guard kneeled at her feet, his attention on the floor. "Your grace, I see now that I should have told you what Lord Kurtis did. I assure you that all is well, and I don't believe there is any reason for you to worry."

"Rise." When he did as she commanded, she didn't bother to smile. Smiles were exhausting when not genuine. "You will tell me everything from now on, no matter how seemingly unimportant. If such a transgression happens again . . ." The words *I will have you flayed* were ready on her lips, but she chose not to speak them aloud. ". . . I will be very angry."

"Yes, your grace." He blinked. "Was that all?"

"No." With annoyance, she rubbed the lump on the back of her head, wondering how long it would take before it healed. "The king will be leaving soon to search for his son. I want you to send two or three of our best men after him."

"To assist?"

"No." This earned a genuine smile. "To catch my new husband in a lie."

CHAPTER 4

LUCIA

THE SANCTUARY

As Lucia slowly drew closer to the crystal city she'd only ever seen in her dreams, she recalled some advice her mother had given her once. It had been before a banquet. Lucia was no more than ten years old and wishing desperately that she could stay in her chambers and read instead. She always tried her best to avoid social gatherings, certain that no one liked her, that they thought the daughter of King Gaius was an awkward and uninteresting girl who wasn't worth their important time.

"It's when we feel the most uncertain," her mother had told her, *"that we must appear at our most confident. To show weakness is to allow others to prey upon it. Now brush your hair, lift your chin, and pretend you are the most powerful person in the room."*

Lucia now realized, with an unexpected thud of sympathy in her heart, that this was precisely what Queen Althea Damora had had to do every day of her life.

She hadn't realized it at the time, but this was truly excellent advice.

With a lift of her chin, a straightening of her shoulders, and the thought that she was both powerful and confident beyond all imaginings, Lucia quickened her pace across the lush green landscape of the Sanctuary toward the city, where she would find Timotheus and ask for his help.

If he said no and cast her away, the mortal world would surely perish.

The city became more impressive the closer she got to it. She didn't know what the citizens of the Sanctuary called this place or if it even had a name; she called it the crystal city because, from afar, in the meadow where she walked, the metropolis appeared to rise up from the emerald-green grass, shimmering like an unexpected treasure against a cloudless blue sky. It wasn't a treasure in the way people said the Auranian palace, which was set with threads of real gold, was. Rather, this city was white and sparkling, ethereal from end to end, made up of spires and towers of varying heights. The image of it before her was like an intricate illustration ripped right from the binding of a confiscated storybook.

She fought to maintain her composure even though she wanted simply to stand there in awe at the sight of it.

Lucia would allow herself only one thought now: *Find Timotheus.*

The immortal had warned her about Kyan. It was a warning that Lucia had foolishly ignored. Kyan had so convinced her of his own struggles—struggles that, she'd thought at the time, had paralleled her own. She'd been so full of vengeance and hatred when she finally met Timotheus that not even the most glaring truths could have penetrated the steel wall she'd built around herself, let alone have made their way to her heart or mind.

No, she hadn't been ready to hear the truth back then.

If only she could be more certain that she was ready to hear it now.

She reached the end of the meadow and stood before the threshold that led into the crystal city. For a moment, Lucia just stood there, eyes closed and breathing.

"Timotheus despises you," she muttered. Then, after one more breath, she took a step and entered the city. "And, if necessary, you are going to fall on your knees and beg for his help."

The thought of begging didn't exactly sit well with her. As the daughter of King Gaius, Lucia had never needed to beg for anything, not once in any of her seventeen years alive. The very thought of doing it now put a rancid taste in her mouth.

But she would swallow what little pride she had left and do it. There was no other choice.

The shining archway that led into the city itself dwarfed her, and as she walked through it, she saw her wide-eyed gaze reflected in its surface. The arch was etched with symbols—squiggles and lines that she didn't recognize, but she felt something from them. A cool, shivering sensation moved through her from head to foot, momentarily stopping her in her tracks. Then she moved closer to the surface of the archway, tentatively pressing her hand against one of these markings.

There it was again—she felt the power of this gate through her fingertips. She pulled her hand back, remembering the crystal monolith in the Forbidden Mountains, only that had been a warm sensation. She knew she could have absorbed that magic to help Kyan draw Timotheus out of the Sanctuary to his doom.

This magic was the opposite—cold instead of warm. If she'd left her hand upon its surface, could it have stolen her magic the way Alexius had taught her to steal Melenia's?

The thought sent a shiver of fear though her, but she ignored it and pressed on, passing under the archway to fully enter the crystal city.

At first glance, it was difficult to take in the view of the city. It was so bright, Lucia put her hand on her forehead to shade her eyes. From a distance, it had appeared to be made of diamonds. Closer up, she saw a city of white buildings and glass structures that reached up to the sky. The pathways were pebbled with small iridescent stones, and she followed one such pathway deeper into the city.

She'd yet to see a single living creature in this place, be it bird or person. There was an eeriness here, she realized. A quiet that challenged even the strict rules of the sternest librarian in the Limerian palace library.

The only sound she could hear was the beating of her own heart.

"Where is everyone?" Her whisper sounded more like a shout, nearly making her jump.

Lucia squeezed her hands together and reminded herself again of her mother's advice: pretend to be confident.

And so she continued deeper into this place. All the buildings looked almost identical, polished and gleaming, but Lucia couldn't tell what each one was.

Still, the city felt strangely familiar to her.

The ice maze, she thought. Yes, this city reminded her of a large version of the ice maze on the Limerian palace grounds that a friend of her father's had gifted to her for her tenth birthday.

And, she realized with a sinking feeling, she was already lost within it.

"Who are you, mortal? And how did you get here?"

Lucia started at the voice, like a crack of lightning waking her from a deep sleep. In the span of one heartbeat, she spun around and summoned her magic without a single thought.

Immediately, a bolt of fire lit up her right fist. She tried not to feel dismayed that she'd unconsciously chosen to defend herself with Kyan's element.

The trigger of her defensive instincts stood before her: a young woman in a long white robe, regarding Lucia with a stunned expression. Her hair was as red as the fire blazing up from Lucia's hand.

An immortal, beautiful and eternally young.

As soon as the immortal moved her gaze to the fire, her eyes widened with shock. "I know who you are."

Taking a shaky step backward, Lucia doused the flames. "Do you? Then who am I?"

As the fire gave way to smoke, the girl appeared to compose herself, blinking rapidly. "The sorceress reborn."

"Perhaps I'm just a witch."

"A mortal witch could never enter the sacred city. No mortal has ever entered this city."

The last thing she wanted was to scare anyone, especially this immortal who could help her find Timotheus in this labyrinthine city. In recent weeks, violence and intimidation—not to mention her newly acquired magical ability to extract the truth from mortal tongues—had been the primary tools she'd used to survive, and it seemed she still had a ways to go in terms of breaking that habit.

"Then there's no reason for me to deny who I am," Lucia replied slowly, carefully.

A smile spread across the girl's face, chasing away Lucia's fear. "Melenia told us that you would walk among us again."

The name made Lucia's back stiffen. "Did she?"

She nodded. "She promises that we will all be able to leave here soon and be free to come and go as we please, finally, after all these centuries."

Melenia seemed to have made a lot of promises to a lot of different people.

Before Lucia killed her, that was.

She took a deep breath, forcing away memories of the evil immortal so she could focus entirely on the present moment.

"What is your name?" she asked.

"Mia."

Though this girl had so far appeared to be nothing other than sweet and friendly, Lucia would not allow herself to forget that Mia was an ageless immortal, a Watcher, not born of man and woman but created from elemental magic.

"My name is Lucia." She straightened her shoulders, lifted her chin, and tried to feel powerful. "And I'm here because I need to see Timotheus. Do you know where he is?"

"Yes, of course." Mia nodded, but the mention of Timotheus had dulled her gaze, and a distasteful look appeared on her beautiful face. "I'm on my way now to the city square, where he's called for a gathering. He's agreed to emerge from his current life of solitude and give us a few moments of his time"—she said this with an edge of disdain that Lucia couldn't miss even if she were deaf—"to answer our questions."

The confirmation that he was here, that the immortal hadn't suddenly disappeared just when she needed him most, drew a deep sigh of relief from her lungs.

"I want to be there to hear what he says," Lucia said. Perhaps he would warn the others about her, if he hadn't already, as well as the threat of the fire Kindred.

She knew the immortal had visions of the future and could receive prophesies, a gift—or a *curse*, Timotheus had said—that he'd inherited from Eva, the original sorceress. He could even enter Lucia's dreams, just as Alexius had, and in those dreams he could read her mind. It was possible he knew every move she ever made, had followed every step she'd ever taken.

The thought made her cringe with shame and embarrassment.

"I don't want Timotheus to see me yet," she said to Mia. "And I don't want to alarm any of your friends with my sudden presence in your world. Will you help me?"

Mia nodded. "Of course I will. However, to remain unseen, I'll need to lend you my robes."

Lucia looked down at herself. The dark red cloak she'd been traveling in was torn and singed from her battle with Kyan, and it made her stand out in this city of brightness like a splash of blood on newly fallen snow. "Yes, that would help."

Mia slipped the beautiful white robe made from a finely woven, shimmering material off her shoulders. Beneath, she wore an equally exquisite silver gown, intricately beaded with small crystals, that bared her arms and hugged her body.

Lucia looked at her with surprise. "You dress far fancier under your robes than anyone I've seen attend even most elaborate banquet."

"Do I?" Mia smiled at this, her eyes shining with pleasure. "I've witnessed mortal gatherings in hawk form but have never been close enough to truly experience such grand events."

"Perhaps I'll take you to one someday in gratitude for helping me today," Lucia said as she quickly slipped the robes over her clothing.

"That would be wonderful." Mia hesitated, as if uncertain what to do next, then slipped her arm through Lucia's. "Come with me."

If only Mia knew what Lucia was responsible for, she doubted the immortal would be so welcoming to her. Everywhere she'd gone with Kyan, Lucia had left destruction and death in her wake. She'd run away from her family, hating them for keeping important truths from her all her life—about her prophecy, her magic, and that she'd been stolen from her birth family. She had no friends, no allies, and no possessions apart from the clothing on her back—clothing meant more for a peasant than a princess.

No, that wasn't entirely true. She had one other possession, a very important one: her ring. She glanced down at her right index finger, upon which she wore a gold filigree band set with a large purple stone.

If not for this ring, she would be dead.

All the more reason for her to be here and to have the chance to speak with Timotheus face to face.

Mia led her deeper into the city. Lucia followed, pulling the hood of the white robes up over her long dark hair. They walked alone for a long while through the crystal city's maze until, finally, she began to see others. Many wore robes like the one Mia had given her, and they were all moving in the same direction. Disguised as one of them, no one gave her a second glance. She was able to continue to observe these immortals and their shining city without interruption.

Every being here was so beautiful, each more so than the last. Even the most attractive mortals couldn't compete with these creatures. Their skin, all shades from palest alabaster to deepest ebony, radiated with light that seemed to glow from within. Their eyes were like shining jewels of every color, their hair like the finest strands of the most precious metals.

How strange it must be to live in a world, she thought, *where everyone and everything is perfect.*

Alexius had been beautiful like this—she'd seen it in her dreams. When he'd exiled himself, he'd become mortal, and that glow had faded. He'd become more three-dimensional, his angles more crooked. He'd become more real.

She saw now that she'd liked that—the transformation of immortal Alexius into real Alexius—more than she'd realized at the time. To be in love with someone perfect beyond compare would have become rather tiresome after a while.

Lucia gritted her teeth as oceans of unbidden memories rose up within her. A wave of grief and rage washed over her as she was confronted by the same memories she'd spent the last few weeks trying to forget.

Alexius had ultimately given his life to save hers.

But from the moment she'd met him in the first dream he'd pulled her into, he'd been deceiving and using her at Melenia's magical command, attempting to learn her secrets and manipulate her into awakening the Kindred.

No, she thought, and with that one firm word she forced away the memories. She swore she wouldn't think about him. Not now, not ever again. Not if she could help it.

They reached an expansive clearing in the center of the city. The ground there was laid with reflective tiles. It reminded Lucia of the mirror in her palace chamber where she watched as her attendants readied her to a state of beauty that would please her mother. From beneath her hood, she watched as two hundred immortals converged in the clearing.

"This is like the public square back home," she said under her breath.

"We meet here for gatherings, and Melenia used to speak to us from the tower regularly to brighten our days . . . until she disappeared . . ."

Lucia bit her tongue. Not even the confused and fearful tone in Mia's voice would make her regret ending the immortal elder's life.

She looked up at the smooth crystal cylinder set in the center of the clearing. The structure reached so high up that she couldn't see the top. "What is this?"

"The elders make their home in this tower. Timotheus hasn't

left it since Alexius exiled himself to the mortal world. Many believe he's been in mourning."

Now Lucia's teeth sank into her tongue so deeply she nearly drew blood.

"How many elders live here?" she asked. She realized that learning about this new place was helping to ease her mind and keep her from spiraling back into thoughts of the past.

"There were six originally."

"And now?"

"This is one of the questions we have for Timotheus." Mia's expression turned grave. "And he must have answers today."

"Or what? What happens if Timotheus doesn't come out today with the right answers? What if this crowd he's gathered is not pleased?"

Mia glanced around at the others surrounding the base of the crystal tower, taking up only a fraction of the space available in the square. "Many feel that the time of elders has passed. At their command, we've searched for the Kindred, and to many it has been nothing but a fool's errand, meant to distract us from the truth."

"What truth?"

Mia shook her head, her expression tightening. "The fact that you're here gives me hope that they're wrong."

Lucia was about to ask more questions, to get to Mia's hidden meaning, but before she could, there came a rustle in the crowd and a rise of angry shouting voices.

She looked up from the depths of her cowl. Her breath caught in her chest as the smooth surface of the crystal tower flickered and filled with light. Then the clear image of Timotheus appeared on this bright surface, his face the height of three men.

Her mouth fell open at the sight of this unexpected magical projection.

The image of Timotheus raised his hands, his expression grim as the crowd of Watchers, including Mia, began to chant a handful of words that Lucia couldn't understand, in a language she'd never heard before today. The sound of it made the chill she'd felt at the gates return to her, and she wrapped her arms tightly around herself and tried not to shiver.

Timotheus waited until the chanting ended and a hush fell over the group.

"You asked to see me," Timotheus said, his voice loud and his tone confident. "Here I am. I know you have questions. That you have worries. I hope to ease your minds."

The crowd had fallen silent after the chanting, so silent that the city felt as still and empty as it had when she'd first entered it.

"You wish to know more about the current whereabouts of missing elders and immortals. You wish to know why I have rendered the gateway to the mortal world unusable so that you're unable to leave our home even in hawk form. You wish to know why I haven't emerged from this tower in recent days."

Lucia watched Mia's face and the faces of the other immortals, their gazes transfixed on the gigantic shining image of Timotheus as if he were an omnipotent god who'd rendered them all into silent, immobile marble statues.

She'd never thought to ask Alexius how an elder's magic differed from other immortals. But now she saw that elders like Timotheus had complete command over others of their kind. The audience was under his spell—everyone was completely still as he spoke.

Yet he had no control over the defiance that still shone in their eyes.

Timotheus's image didn't flicker like a candle. It remained solid and bright. And Lucia was reminded again that he resembled

Alexius so much that the two, if mortal, could have been mistaken as brothers by blood.

"Danaus and Stephanos. Melenia. Phaedra, Alexius, and Olivia. All missing from our already dwindling numbers. You fear that I have masterminded every one of these recent disappearances, but you're wrong. You believe we should be searching for our missing people in the mortal world, yet I won't let you leave.

"What I'm doing," Timotheus continued, "what I have done . . . is because a great danger has risen in the mortal world, a danger that affects everything we've worked so hard and so long to protect. With so few of us left, I've done only what I must to protect you all. And I only ask for your trust for a little while longer, before all will be revealed."

His words didn't help tame the fierce looks in the eyes of the immortals. Lucia wasn't surprised by that. She'd heard hundreds of speeches by her father over the years. He was a true master at public speaking even when presented with an audience who despised him.

King Gaius knew when to lie, when to give false hope, and when to make promises of gold when, more often than not, such promises ultimately meant nothing.

Still, such speeches given at key times were more than enough to prevent riots. More than enough to keep Limerians in check and rebel numbers low.

People clung to the possibility of hope.

Timotheus did not speak of hope. He told the truth but gave no details, making him sound like more of a liar trying to conceal his misdeeds than the King of Blood ever had.

And, it seemed, he wasn't finished yet.

"You've all seen for yourselves that our world is dying. The leaves are turning brown and dry, more and more every day.

Despite the prophesies of Eva's magic returning to us, you've begun to believe this is a sign of the end. But you're wrong. The sorceress has been reborn. And right now, this very moment, she stands among you."

A gasp caught in Lucia's throat as the large projected eyes of Timotheus seemed to look directly at her.

And the eyes of the immortals who hadn't moved or spoken since Timotheus's speech began collectively widening with shock.

A bolt of panic shot through Lucia, and all of a sudden it was as if no amount of pristine white garments could stop her from feeling completely naked.

"Before the burden of visions was passed on to me," Timotheus said to the crowd, "it was Eva who bore the weight of them and foretold that a girl born in the mortal world would become as powerful as an immortal sorceress. I can now confirm that Lucia Eva Damora is the sorceress we've been waiting a millennium for. Lucia, show yourself."

Silence continued to reign in the mirrored square, a haunting kind of quiet that seemed to consume Lucia, pressing in on every side. A cold trickle of perspiration slid down her spine.

Heart thundering in her chest, she again held tightly to the advice her mother had given her—advice she'd resented for too many years to count.

Pretend to be confident even when you are not.

Pretend to be brave even when you're so frightened that all you want to do is run away.

Be convincing in this act, and no one will know the difference.

With that thought, Lucia raised her chin and pulled back the hood of the borrowed robes. Every pair of eyes was on her immediately, followed by a collective gasp as the immortals were released from whatever magic Timotheus had used to render them so still and silent.

Then, one by one, their glowing, beautiful faces filled with awe. Each immortal, including Mia, surprised Lucia by sinking to their knees before her.

CHAPTER 5

CLEO

LIMEROS

Cleo, Magnus, and the remaining two guards carefully journeyed from the surface of the frozen lake to the top of the cliffs. There, Cleo grimaced as she glanced over the side at the sharp drop the king had taken to the bottom—a drop she would have taken as well had Magnus not pulled her back.

Cleo turned to Magnus, ready to speak her concerns about the king's plans aloud, but something stopped her cold. Magnus was bleeding.

Immediately, she tore off a long piece of fabric from the hem of her crimson gown—which, thanks to the misadventures of the last day, was already ripped in several places—and took hold of his injured arm.

Magnus turned to her, surprised. "What?"

"You're injured."

He looked down at the sleeve of his black cloak that had been sliced through to the skin, and his expression relaxed. "It's just a scratch."

Cleo glanced at the guards in their red uniforms, which perfectly matched the color of her gown. They stood a dozen paces away, speaking quietly with each other. She could only guess at the subject—witch's potions, elemental magic, or dead kings come back to life.

Cleo would rather focus on something tangible at the moment. "Hold still," she said, ignoring Magnus's protest. "Actually, let me get a closer look at the wound. I want to make sure it's not too severe."

Grudgingly, Magnus pulled up the edge of his cloak and rolled up the sleeve of his tunic. Cleo cringed at the sight of the bleeding sword wound but was composed again in an instant as she started to bind it with the strip of silk.

He watched her with interest. "You're much more skilled at this than I would have thought. Have you treated injuries before?"

"Once" was all she was willing to say, preferring to concentrate on her task.

"*Once*," he repeated. "Whose wound did you bind?"

Cleo neatly tucked the ends of the fabric into the binding before she met his gaze. "No one important."

"Let me take a wild guess, then. Jonas? It seems he's the one most likely to be injured at any given time."

She cleared her throat. "I think there are topics more pressing than the rebel to discuss right now."

"So it *was* Jonas." He let out a hiss of a sigh. "Very well, a subject for another time."

"Or never," she said.

"Or never," he agreed.

The king had left them with instructions. Speaking only to Magnus—to Cleo he gave only sneering looks over his shoulder—he said he would meet them that evening at a village inn a half day's journey east. The king claimed that this village was on the path that lead to his mother.

To Cleo, everything the king said amounted only to lies on top of lies.

"Are you sure I can't convince you to go to Auranos?" Magnus asked, admiring the tight binding she wove around his arm. "It would be safer there for you."

"Oh, yes, that's exactly what I want right now. To be safe and sound and entirely out of the way. Perhaps you can send these guards with me to make sure I do exactly as I'm told."

He raised a brow and turned his attention to her face instead of her handiwork. "I know you're upset."

She couldn't help but let out a hollow laugh at the understatement. "That man"—she jabbed her index finger in the direction the king and his guards had gone to return to Amara's villa—"is going to be the death of both of us. Actually, he nearly just was!"

"I know."

"Oh, you do? That's wonderful. Wonderful, really." She began pacing back and forth in short, worried steps. "He's lying to us— you have to know that."

"I think I know my father. Better than anyone else, certainly."

"And what? You're counting on him having a conscience? That he's suddenly decided to change his ways? That, magically, he's suddenly chosen to be the solution to all our problems?"

"No. I said I *know* him, which means I don't trust him. People don't change, not as quickly as that. Not without having previously proved that they are capable of change. He's been hard and cruel and driven all my life . . ." He frowned and went silent again, his gaze scanning the frozen lake far below them.

"What's wrong?" Cleo said as gently as she could so as not to discourage him from talking. The way he frowned . . . he must have been remembering something.

"I have these memories . . . they're very foggy and distant. I can't even be sure they're memories instead of dreams. I was young, barely old enough to walk on my own. I remember having a father who was not nearly as cold as my mother. One who told me stories before I went to sleep."

"Stories of demons and war and torture?"

"No. Actually . . ." He frowned deeply once again. "I recall one about a . . . dragon, but a friendly one."

She stared at him blankly. "A *friendly* dragon."

He shrugged. "Perhaps it was only a dream. Many things from my past seem like dreams to me now . . ." He trailed off, his expression turning stern. "I don't want you involved in this. How can I convince you to go to Auranos?"

"You can't, and this is the last we'll speak of it. I'm in this with you, Magnus. No matter what happens."

"Why?"

Cleo looked up at him, her heart full. "You know why," she said softly.

His expression grew pained. "Such cryptic language has always confused me. Perhaps you still don't trust me enough to speak plainly."

"I thought that we'd successfully put concerns like that aside."

"Perhaps in part. But are you trying to convince me that you didn't think I wasn't going to obey my father's command and end your life at the side of that cliff? Because there's no way you can. I saw the look in your eyes—the fear, the disappointment. You believed I'd kill you just to get into his good graces again."

The guards weren't close enough to overhear, but it still felt like a discussion meant for a much more private moment.

Still, he'd asked for her to speak plainly. "I admit, you were very convincing."

"I was trying to be convincing, given that both of our lives were in jeopardy. But didn't you hear me? I called you *Cleiona*—I'd hoped you would take that as a sign not to doubt me." He shook his head. "Then again, why wouldn't you? I've given you little reason to trust me."

He started to turn away from her, but then she took his hands in hers. "Wrong. You've given me countless reasons to trust you."

Magnus stared at the ground, his forehead furrowed in a deep frown, before his gaze flicked up to meet hers. "You're determined to come with me to see my grandmother."

Cleo nodded. "She could be the answer to everything."

His jaw tightened. "I can only hope you're right."

So this witch would find Lucia, and then they would go to her, and beg for her help to rid Mytica of Amara. She had to admit, she didn't like the idea of relying on the assistance of the young sorceress. "Do you honestly think that your sister will help us?" she asked. "The last time we saw her . . ." She shuddered at the memory of Lucia and Kyan arriving unannounced at the Limerian palace. Kyan had nearly burned Magnus to death with his fire magic.

Lucia had stopped him, but then turned her back on her brother when he'd asked her to stay.

"I hope she will help," Magnus replied tightly. "This darkness that has emerged along with Lucia's magic . . . it's not really her. The sister I know is kind and sweet. She does well in her studies— far better than I ever did—and devours every book she sees. And I know she cares about Mytica and its people. When she learns about all that Amara has been up to, she will use her *elementia* to put a stop to it."

"Well," Cleo said, trying very hard to ignore the trickle of poison that had leaked into her chest at the sound of such brotherly praise, "she sounds absolutely perfect, doesn't she?"

"Of course she isn't perfect. None of us are." The edge of his mouth quirked up. "But Lucia Damora is extremely close."

"How unfortunate, then, that she's currently under Kyan's influence."

"Yes." The edge of amusement that had been in his gaze faded away and was replaced by steel. "He possesses the fire Kindred. You have earth. Amara has water. My father has had air for quite some time."

All of a sudden, Cleo's mind emptied of all other concerns. "How long has he had it? Or should I ask, why didn't I know about this before today?"

Magnus blinked. "I'm sure I mentioned it before."

"No, you certainly didn't."

"Hmm. I know someone was present when I received this news. Nic, perhaps."

She couldn't believe her own ears. "*Nic* knows that the king has the air Kindred, and neither you nor he told me?"

"Jonas also knows."

She gasped. "This is unacceptable!"

"Apologies, princess, but it's only been less than a day since we agreed to share more than loathing and distrust."

Memories of the cottage in the woods returned to her vividly: a night of fear and survival leading to a very unexpected encounter.

Cleo bit her bottom lip, her previous outrage all but forgotten. "My head's still spinning from everything that's happened."

"Mine too."

She glanced at the guards to see that one of them paced back and forth, as if in an agitated state.

"Let's make our way to the meeting place," she said firmly. She opened the front of her cloak to look at the crimson gown beneath. "I hope I can find new clothes in the village. This is the only thing I have to my name, and it's torn."

Magnus's gaze traveled slowly down the length of her. "Yes. I remember tearing it."

Cleo's cheeks heated. "It should be burned."

"No, this gown will never be destroyed. It will be displayed in great prominence for all eternity." His lips curved into a smile. "But I agree, you are in need of better traveling garb. The color is rather . . . eye-catching."

She felt his warmth as he slid his hand down her arm, his gaze fixed upon the gown Nerissa had found in the palace for her to wear for her speech.

The closer Magnus got to her, the more her heart sped up. "Perhaps we can discuss this later, at the inn, in our . . . room?" she said softly.

Then, without warning, Magnus let go of her. She felt a sudden waft of cold air as he took a step away from her. "Actually, I'm going to make sure that you're given separate quarters."

She frowned. "Separate?"

"You and I will not be sharing a room for the foreseeable future."

She stared at him blankly for a long moment, his words making no sense. "I don't understand. Why not? After last night, I thought . . ."

"You thought wrong." His face had gone very pale. "I won't put your life at risk."

Still, he spoke in riddles she couldn't easily solve. "Why would my life be at risk if we were to share a room?" She watched as his expression turned tortured and he raked a hand through his hair. "Magnus, talk to me. What is it?"

"You don't know?"

"Clearly I don't. So tell me!"

Reluctantly, he did as she asked. "A witch's curse is the reason your mother died in childbirth. And that curse is why you, too, will die if you become pregnant."

All she could do is stare at him in absolute shock. "Your father told you this."

He nodded once, his jaw tight.

"And you believed such a ridiculous tale, just like that?"

"Don't make it sound so foolish. I'm not a fool—I know there's a possibility he could be lying to me. But I still refuse to take such a chance."

"What chance?" She frowned, feeling stupid that she didn't follow.

He took her by her shoulders tightly, gazing intensely into her eyes. "The chance of losing you."

Her confusion washed away, replaced by a swelling warmth in her heart. "Oh."

"My grandmother is a witch. If there is truly a curse on you, she will break it."

It seemed impossible that she'd never heard of something so serious before, but her father had always been secretive, especially when it came to magic. He'd never told Cleo that he'd had a witch put a protective spell upon the entrance of the Auranian palace, one only Lucia was powerful enough to break.

Perhaps this was similar.

Her thoughts went to her mother, and her heart broke to think of the woman she never knew, destined to die giving her life.

"If this is true," she said after a moment, still refusing to fully believe such a far-fetched possibility, "I've heard of other methods to prevent a pregnancy."

"I won't risk your life until this curse is broken. And I don't give a damn if my father is lying to me. I won't take the chance that he's right. Do you hear me?" Magnus's voice had grown darker and quieter, sending a shiver down her spine.

She nodded. "I hear you."

Could it be true? She hated to think it might even be a possibility. Why wouldn't her father have mentioned such a horrible thing?

Now she needed answers every bit as much as Magnus did. All the more reason to see his witch grandmother.

Cleo noticed that the agitated guard who'd been pacing had suddenly drawn closer to them.

"Your highness . . ." the guard said.

Cleo tore her gaze from Magnus's to look at the guard, shocked to see that he had withdrawn his sword and was now pointing it at them.

Magnus pushed Cleo roughly behind him. "What is this?" he hissed.

The guard shook his head, his expression strained and a bit frantic. "I find that I cannot abide by the king's orders. The empress and her army are in control of Mytica now. Limerians have no say over their futures anymore. To continue to align myself with those who wish to deceive and oppose the empress would be committing treason. Therefore, I must turn you over to the empress."

Cleo stared at him with shock. "You disgusting coward!"

He cast a withering look at her. "I am a Limerian. You are an enemy, no matter whom you've married. You," he said, the word twisting with distaste, "are the reason everything we've cherished in Limeros for generations has been destroyed."

"My, you give me much more power than I actually have." She straightened her shoulders and narrowed her gaze. "Lower your weapon immediately and perhaps I won't demand your execution."

"I don't take orders from any Auranian."

"Do you take orders from me?" Magnus asked, his tone edged in acid.

"I would," the guard replied. "If you still had any power here."

Hands fisted, Magnus stepped forward, but the guard responded by raising the blade to the prince's throat. A gasp of fear caught in Cleo's throat.

"Do you even know my name, your highness?" the guard sneered. "The empress does. She knows everyone's name."

"Amara Cortas clearly has an amazing ability to retain useless facts." Magnus glowered at him. "So, what? You mean to march us up to her? Expect her to accept this generous gift with open arms and an appointment for you to captain of the guard? Don't be a fool."

"I'm no fool. Not anymore. Now come with me. Resist, and you will die."

The guard then grunted as the tip of a sword appeared through his chest. He lost his balance and dropped to the ground in a heap.

Standing behind him was the other guard, wiping his comrade's blood from his sword with a handkerchief. He glared down at the fallen guard with disgust.

"Pathetic weakling. I had to listen to his blabberings, his plans. I disagreed with each and every one. Please excuse his disloyalty, your highness."

While so relieved her legs nearly gave out from beneath her, Cleo exchanged a concerned glance with Magnus.

"What is your name?" Magnus asked the dark-haired guard.

"Milo Iagaris, your highness."

"You have my deepest gratitude for intervening. I take it we can depend on *your* loyalty?"

Milo nodded. "To the very end."

Cleo let out the breath she hadn't even realized she'd been holding. "Thank you, Milo," she said, casting a hateful look down at the dead guard lying by her feet. "Now, let's leave this traitor far behind us."

Cleo used her green cloak to shield the shocking red of her dress and the brightness of her hair during the journey to the village.

After hours of travel via several modes of transport, including walking, wagon, and horseback, she, Magnus, and Milo arrived at their destination, exhausted. As luck would have it, the innkeeper's wife was a seamstress from whom Cleo was able to acquire some simple new garments. Then, true to his word, Magnus escorted Cleo to her separate, private room.

Too exhausted to discuss the matter of the curse any further than they already had, Cleo shut and locked the door, collapsed onto the hard bed, and fell asleep immediately.

The morning sunlight woke her rudely, and as soon as her eyes were open she shielded them to block out the glare. Moments later, the seamstress knocked and brought in a basin of warm water to wash up with. Cleo was grateful for the chance to finally clean off the dirt that had accumulated on her skin during her travels. After she washed, she slipped into her new plain cotton dress and spent the next several minutes working hard to pick the tangles out of her hair with a silver comb left next to the basin.

As she finished up, she eyed her reflection, halfway expecting to see someone completely different. It felt as if so much had changed in a matter of mere days. But there in the mirror was simply the same Cleo she always saw. Golden hair, blue-green eyes that had lost only a bit of the weariness that started creeping into them only a year ago, and freshly seventeen years old.

She turned from the mirror with a sigh and reached for the chair over which she'd slung the cloak she'd stolen from a Kraeshian guard during her escape from Amara's borrowed villa. She inspected it in the bright light, looking for tears, but was pleased to find it intact.

As of today, her only possessions were a borrowed gown, a stolen cloak, and an obsidian orb.

And, of course, her memories.

Before she had a chance to consider everything that she'd lost over the last year, she was interrupted by a very loud grumble in the pit of her stomach.

When was the last time she'd eaten? She honestly couldn't remember.

Cleo left her room and peered down the hallway, briefly wondering which room belonged to Magnus. She drew the hood of her cloak close to her face, just in case someone was about at this early hour who might recognize her, then descended the creaky wooden staircase down to the inn to search for breakfast.

The first person she came upon in the empty dining room was tall, with broad shoulders and dark hair. He wore a black cloak and, with his back to her, gazed out of the front windows toward the village center.

Magnus.

She quickly drew toward him and placed her hand on his arm.

Instead of Magnus, King Gaius turned to face her. Cleo yanked her hand back as if it had been scorched. She took an immediate step back from him, then managed to tamp down her initial shock and rein in her composure.

"Good morning, princess," he said. His face was as pale as yesterday, still bruised and cut, with dark circles beneath his eyes.

Speak, she commanded herself. *Say something, so he doesn't think you're terrified of him.*

He raised a dark eyebrow. "Has the wildcat lost her tongue?"

Damn, but he looked so much like Magnus in the shadows of the inn. The very thought made her stomach roil with disgust.

"Not nearly," she said evenly as she drew her cloak tighter around her shoulders. "But she'd advise you to keep your distance if you want to keep yours."

"An empty threat," he said drily. "How predictable."

"If you'll excuse me, I'm going to go back to my room."

"You certainly could." He moved to take a seat at the nearest table, which was soon to be occupied by hungry patrons, and sat down heavily, groaning as if the movement caused him pain. "Or perhaps this is a good time for us to talk."

"There's no time that's good for that."

The king leaned back in his chair and regarded her silently for a moment. "It was Emilia who was blessed with her mother's particular beauty. But you . . . you certainly inherited her fire."

Hearing this snake mention her mother again turned her stomach. "You never did answer my question from before. How do you know my mother? Why was it her name on your lips in your dying moments?"

His lips thinned in a grimace. "It was a mistake, speaking her name."

"You're still avoiding the question."

"I believe this may be the longest conversation you and I have ever had, princess."

"Tell me the truth," she snapped. "Or is that even possible for you?"

"Ah, curiosity. It is a dangerous beast that will lead you down dark alleyways to an uncertain fate." He scanned her face, his expression pinched. "Elena and I were friends once."

Cleo laughed at that, surprising herself at the sharp sound of it. "Friends?"

"You don't believe me?"

"I don't believe you have *any* friends, let alone that my mother was one of them."

"It was a different time, back before I was a king or she was a queen. Sometimes it feels like a million years ago."

"I don't believe you were friends with my mother."

"It doesn't matter if you believe me or not. It was over and done with a very long time ago."

Cleo turned away from him, disgusted that he could even attempt to make such a claim. Her mother would never have chosen to spend time with someone as vile as Gaius Damora.

"Now I get to ask a question, princess," he said, standing up and putting himself in between Cleo and the staircase.

She turned slowly to give him the haughtiest look possible. "What?"

"What do you want with my son?" he said, enunciating each word.

She stared at him. "Excuse me?"

"You heard me. Are you planning to continue to use Magnus for your own gain? If so, then bravo to you. You've done an exceedingly fine job turning him against me. His many weaknesses have long been a disappointment to me, but this—" He shook his head. "Do you have any true idea what he's given up for you?"

"You don't know anything about it."

Gaius scoffed. "I know that not that long ago my son aspired to be a leader, willing to do what it took to one day meet his great potential. I'm not blind. I saw how quickly his head was turned by your beauty. But beauty is fleeting, and power is forever. This sacrifice, the choices he's made lately surrounding the subject of *you* . . . I don't understand his reasoning. Not really."

"Then perhaps you *are* blind."

"He doesn't see everything that's at stake. He only sees what's happening in the moment, before his eyes. But you do, don't you? You know how you want your life to be ten, twenty, fifty years from now. You've never given up on your desire to reclaim your throne. I admit that I underestimated your drive, which was a grave mistake."

"Why wouldn't I want to reclaim what's rightfully mine?"

"Be careful, princess," he said.

"This isn't the first time you've told me to do just that. This time, I can't tell if you mean it as a warning or a threat."

"It's a warning."

"Just like the warning about the curse that my mother passed to me?"

"Yes. Just like that. You don't believe it?" He leaned closer. "Look in my eyes and tell me if I'm lying about something as important as this. Your mother was cursed by a hateful witch and she died giving birth to you because of that curse."

Cleo took a moment to study the king who spoke lies so easily. If he were anyone else, anyone at all, she would be concerned for his health. Even during their short, unpleasant conversation, his face had grown paler, his voice drier and raspier. His broad shoulders were now hunched over.

She celebrated his decline and would equally celebrate his death. If he expected anything else from her, he would be sorely disappointed.

But his eyes—clear, steady, cruel—held no deception that she could see.

"You can see the truth," he said, his voice hoarse. "Elena could too, all too often, when it came to me. She knew me better than anyone else."

"You don't deserve to speak her name."

"That's quite an accusation, princess, especially considering it was *you* who murdered her."

Cleo's eyes began to sting as the weight of the guilt she'd always carried with her—that her life came at the price of her mother's death—rose up in her chest and crushed her. "If what you say is true, the curse is what killed her."

"It certainly helped. But it was you who stole Elena's life. Your sister didn't succeed, but *you* did."

Each word felt like a blow. "Enough of this. I won't stand here for another moment and let you insult me, intimidate me, and lie to me. Listen to me very clearly: If you so much as attempt to harm me or Magnus again, I promise I will kill you myself."

With that, Cleo turned away and started toward the stairs, not caring if she had to wait another eternity for breakfast. She refused to be in the King of Blood's poisonous presence for another moment.

"And you listen to *me*, princess." Gaius's voice followed her like a rancid odor. "This love you think you feel for my son? The day will come when you will have to choose between Magnus and power. And I know, without a doubt, that you will choose power."

CHAPTER 6

JONAS

THE SILVER SEA

On the third day at sea, Jonas stood with Nic at the bow of the King of Blood's ship, its black and red sails catching the wind that would return them to Mytica in four more days. Olivia, in hawk form, kept a watch upon him from above as she did for most of the day, her large golden wings stretched out as she soared.

He wished he could turn into a hawk so he could be that much quicker in his return. Life aboard a ship was not for him; the constant rocking motion beneath his feet was disorienting and made his stomach churn. Although, he had to admit, he was doing better than some. Felix hung over the railing to their right, his face an ugly shade of green.

"He wasn't kidding about his seasickness," Nic said.

"No, he certainly wasn't," Jonas replied.

"I feel bad for him."

"He'll survive."

"Fearsome assassin, you said? Didn't he hunt bounties for King Gaius?"

"That's right. Former fearsome assassin for King Gaius. Currently fighting the good fight as he embarks on a long and arduous path to redemption. And also currently heaving his breakfast into the sea as an offering to any fish who may give assistance."

"I can hear you, you know," Felix managed as he clung to the railing at the edge of the ship.

Jonas tried to repress a grin, the first one he'd felt on his face in ages. "Yes, we know."

"This isn't funny," Felix growled.

"I'm not laughing. Not out loud, anyway."

Felix said something unintelligible but unmistakably unpleasant under his breath, then groaned. "Can someone please kill me and put me out of this misery?"

"I volunteer," said Taran as he descended from the crow's nest. He'd insisted on climbing up there, displacing a crew member, to keep a lookout for any Kraeshian vessels.

"Shut up," Felix snarled. Then his face tensed, and he threw himself against the railing to be sick again.

Jonas grimaced. "Anything I can do to help?"

"Just . . . leave me . . . to die."

"Fair enough." He turned away from his sick friend to regard Taran as he picked up the sword he'd left at the bottom of the pole. "What are you up to now, might I ask?"

"I'm going to sharpen my sword."

"It seems like you've been sharpening that blade since we set sail."

Taran glanced at him. "And . . . ?"

"Must be the sharpest blade ever, ready to kill those who deserve it," Nic said, sharing a knowing look with Taran. "Well done."

Jonas sighed and took Nic by his bicep, directing him out of Taran's earshot. "We need to talk."

Nic slipped away from Jonas's grip. "About what?"

"Your hate of Magnus is consuming you, and it's becoming a problem."

Nic scowled. "Really? How odd that you'd say that, since I haven't mentioned that bucket of scum in days. Besides, since when did you become *his majesty's* personal bodyguard?"

The thought was ludicrous. "I'm not. But the prince sent me to Kraeshia to kill his father. We're in an alliance with him."

"You might be in an alliance with that monster, but I'm not." Nic's cheeks flushed as he jabbed a finger in Taran's direction. "Magnus killed his brother. Your so-called alliance has nothing to do with either me or him."

Jonas had heard about the murder of Theon Ranus over the last few days and how the former Auranian guard had been involved with Cleo before Magnus had stabbed him through the back.

Yet another reason for Cleo to despise Magnus, he thought. He'd had no clue about any of this, but that Cleo had lost someone she cared about . . . just like Jonas had lost Lys . . . it only made him feel closer to her.

Taran had every right to seek vengeance on the prince, but it was nothing but a distraction from the larger problem of Amara and the king, of three magical crystal orbs imprisoning elemental gods, and of Jonas's own need for vengeance against the fire Kindred for killing Lysandra.

"Fine," Jonas said, absently scratching his chest. "You and Taran can do what you want when it comes to the prince. But I want no part of it."

"Agreed."

Jonas scanned the deck, seeing Taran and Felix and a few crew members, but one person was notably missing. "Where's that other prince we need to worry about?"

Nic didn't reply for a moment. "Likely in his quarters, being silent and meditating, or whatever it is prophesied phoenixes do to spend their time while at sea."

With each day that passed, Jonas felt more and more sure that allowing Ashur passage aboard this ship had been a mistake. At best, he was simply the misguided brother of the power-mad empress who'd used and manipulated Felix nearly to death; at worst, he was completely insane and would get them all killed.

Jonas had never been much of an optimist.

"Do you believe the legend is true?" Jonas asked.

"I don't know," Nic said, exhaustion and sadness in his tone. "All I know for sure is that I watched him die, and now here he is, alive and aboard the very same ship we are."

"Have you ever heard that legend before? Of somebody who's returned from death to be the savior of the world?"

Nic shrugged. "When I was a kid, I remember reading a story that was very similar. But there are thousands of legends that aren't true."

"The Watchers are a legend that's true," Jonas pointed out.

"Yes, and it's possible that this phoenix tale could be the same." He noticed Jonas still scratching his chest. "Do you have a rash?"

Jonas grimaced. "No. I guess this long journey to Mytica is making me itchy with impatience." He paused. "Listen, you know Prince Ashur better than any of us. Right?"

"Well, I've known him *longer*," Nic allowed.

"I need to know more about his plans. If he sees you as a friend, he'll trust you. You need to uncover the truth about why he's not simply marching up to his evil sister and taking his rightful place as emperor."

"I can tell you why. Because Amara would try to kill him again. Besides . . . I don't think he wants to be interrupted when he's meditating."

Just the word *meditating* raised Jonas's hackles. That was what Chief Basilius claimed to be doing when he believed himself to be a prophesied sorcerer who would save the world.

He'd been certain the chief's belief had to do with Princess Lucia's prophecy, but perhaps this phoenix legend had further reach into Paelsia.

"Talk to Ashur," Jonas said. "Seek his guidance. Rekindle your friendship."

"You mean you want me to spy on him for you."

"Yes, exactly."

Nic let out a long, shaky sigh.

Jonas frowned. "Unless there's some reason why you'd rather keep avoiding him. Is there something I need to know?"

"No, no," Nic said, perhaps a bit too quickly, Jonas thought. "I'll go now, see what he's up to. You can depend on me, Jonas. Whatever I have to do to ensure Cleo's safety, I'll do it."

Jonas nodded. "Glad to hear it."

He watched as Nic nodded and left, his steps tentative at first but growing more purposeful as he disappeared around a corner.

"Something's up with those two," said Felix, sidling up behind Jonas. "I don't know what it is, but I'll figure it out."

The sour scent of seasickness hit Jonas like a slap, and instinctively he covered his nose with his sleeve and glared at his friend.

"You stink," he said.

Felix shrugged. "Sorry."

"Do you mean you'll figure out what's going on between Nic and Ashur?"

"Yeah."

"Friendships can be confusing—especially when they involve royals."

"Wouldn't know. Never been friendly with a royal before."

"What about Amara?" Jonas regretted his question the moment it left his lips. A stony look crept over Felix's face, obliterating anything soft or lighthearted. "Apologies. Forget that I mentioned her."

"Wish I could forget *her*." A muscle in Felix's right cheek twitched. He stroked his eye patch as his good eye glazed over with deep thoughtfulness.

It was that same unsettling, blank look again, one Jonas had seen several times on his friend's face. It was the look Felix got just before he killed someone.

Olivia had healed Felix's superficial wounds, but some injuries went deeper than skin and bone.

The young man Jonas had found in that dark dungeon was not the Felix he remembered. When he was rescued, there was relief in his gaze, but there was also a deep anguish there. And that anguish remained to this day.

"If you're worried I still have a soft spot for her," Felix finally said, "don't be. I'll be happy to tear her apart with my bare hands if I get the chance."

Jonas put his hand on Felix's shoulder. "You'll get your vengeance."

Felix laughed humorlessly. "Yeah, that's the plan. If I can get her, then get this fire bastard too, well . . . that's all I could hope for in what remains of this pathetic life of mine."

"Kyan is dangerous." Jonas hadn't figured out how exactly to deal with the fire god yet. In fact, he had yet to fully come to terms with the idea of a Kindred transfigured into flesh and blood.

"Yeah? So am I." Felix cracked his knuckles. "All I need is a few moments with him. If he looks like a man, walks and talks like a man, he might have a heart like a man that I can rip right out of his chest."

"You'll be killed before you have the chance to lay a finger on him."

"Then I'll be happy to meet up with Lys in the everafter much sooner than I thought."

Jonas surprised himself by letting out a snort at that, which earned him a sharp, searing look from Felix. "She'd be surprised to know how much you cared about her."

"I didn't just care about Lys. I *loved* her."

"Sure you did." What happened to Lysandra was still an open wound to him. Even her name spoken by someone else made him flinch. "You barely knew her."

"I know how I felt. You don't believe me?"

Jonas knew it would be best not to lose his composure by engaging in an argument about Lys, but he feared he was too close to the edge to control himself. "If you really loved her, perhaps you should have been there to help protect her."

Felix narrowed his eye, making his glare even more menacing. "You don't want to start this with me right now."

"Perhaps I do. After all, you suddenly claim that you were in love with her." Jonas stared at him for a long, silent moment, his forehead growing hot. "But I'm the one who had to stand there and watch her die."

"Yeah, you *watched* her die. If she'd been with me instead of you I know she'd still be alive." Felix took one threatening step closer, and then Jonas saw his gaze go blank like the skilled assassin he was.

Jonas wasn't afraid, though. This conversation had quickly made outrage flare up within him. "True love, huh? Were you thinking about Lys while bedding Amara? Or was it only after you heard she was dead?"

He saw Felix's fist only after it had already connected with his nose. He heard a crunching sound, felt a wash of pain, and then a rush of hot blood trickling down his face.

"You know what the worst thing is? It's that Lys didn't love me, she loved *you*," Felix snarled, "and you let her die, you useless shit."

The splitting pain of his broken nose—of Felix's accusations, of the memory of Lys's final horrific moments—hit Jonas like a cannonball to his gut. Rather than drop to his knees in the face of this pain, he clenched his fists and threw a glare of sheer hatred at his accuser for making everything more painful than it already was.

All of a sudden, without Jonas making a single move, Felix gasped. His smug look vanished, and then—as if an invisible giant had scooped him up off the ship's wooden deck and tossed him like a rag doll—he flew backward twenty paces. Felix had to grab onto the railing to keep from falling off the side of the ship and into the sea.

"What the hell—?" Taran's voice called out from behind Jonas. "What just happened?"

Jonas couldn't find the words to reply. He could only look down at his tightly clenched fists. In the fading light of dusk, he realized with stunned disbelief that they were glowing.

He turned to Taran with wide eyes. Taran, his sword held loosely at his side, stared at Felix, slack-jawed.

He hadn't noticed Jonas's glowing fists.

Felix gingerly pushed himself up from the deck, his attention fixed on Jonas, a thousand unspoken questions harbored within his confused expression.

Without uttering another word, Jonas turned and hurriedly made his way to his cabin, stumbling over his own feet to get there.

He swung the door open and went immediately to the tarnished mirror in the corner, by the small porthole.

His hands, though no longer glowing, trembled violently.

Jonas's chest burned and roiled, felt as if there was a swarm of maggots trying to bore directly into his heart. He grabbed his shirt and tore it open, not bothering to unbutton it first, to expose the creatures that tormented him.

But they weren't there.

Instead, there was a mark. A mark that hadn't been there until now. A black swirl, the size of a man's fist, in the center of his chest.

The mark of a Watcher.

The sharp sound of a gasp wrenched his attention away from his reflection and to the open door. There stood Olivia, now in mortal form and wrapped in a dark gray robe.

"What is happening to me, Olivia?" he managed to blurt out.

Olivia's emerald-green eyes were wide and glossy as her gaze moved from his bare chest up to his face.

"Oh, Jonas," she whispered. "Timotheus was right."

"What is this mark on me?"

She drew in a shaky breath, then closed her eyes with forced calmness. She raised her chin slightly and looked him directly in the eyes. "I'm sorry."

He was about to say "For what?" when the image of Olivia blurred and darkened at the edges.

Jonas didn't remember falling, but he felt the rough floor against his face for a brief moment before unconsciousness claimed him.

CHAPTER 7

LUCIA

THE SANCTUARY

Before Timotheus's large and shining image vanished from the tower, he asked Mia to accompany Lucia inside. While all other immortals kneeled before her, their heads bowed, she nervously followed the Watcher to the base of the elder's residence. A door in the surface of the tower, invisible to her until she was only an arm's reach away, opened before her.

The tower itself was fifty paces in circumference and bare of any furnishings on the ground floor. Bare of anything except smooth white walls and a mirrored floor that matched the ground outside. She followed Mia into a room so small that she knew she could nearly touch each wall if she stretched her arms out to either side of her. Lucia eyed the opaque crystal doors uneasily as they slid shut.

"Can you speak now?" Lucia ventured. "Or are you still under Timotheus's spell?"

"I can speak," Mia said, her voice hushed. "And in the short time we have together, I must urge you to be careful."

Lucia searched the immortal's face, frowning at her troubled tone. "What do you mean?"

"We needed the prophecy to be true, to be proven, and you've finally arrived. Yet I now worry that what happened to Melenia, whatever Timotheus did to her, the same could happen to you. Be careful with him. No matter what he might tell us, we no longer trust him."

Lucia grappled to find the words to speak, to ease Mia's mind that Timotheus didn't harm Melenia, that the elder had chosen her own fate by being greedy, malicious, and bloodthirsty, but the crystal doors slid open before she could say anything at all.

They were no longer on the ground floor. Lucia stepped past the doors into another white room, this one easily the size of all her palace chambers combined. From the floor-to-ceiling windows at the far end of the room, Lucia could see the entire city—the mirrored square, the intricate maze of crystal buildings, and the rolling green hills beyond the gates.

Lucia turned only to see the barest glimpse of the girl before the doors shut behind her. She rushed back to them, pressing her hands against the smooth surface and trying to pry the doors open again.

"How did you get here, Lucia?"

Timotheus's voice made her freeze in place before she slowly turned to face him. Across the room—and no longer a flat, two-dimensional projected image—stood the last immortal elder.

She wasn't sure if she should feel relieved to be in his presence or awed by the magic she'd witnessed today. "I'm sure you're surprised to see me here, but—"

Timotheus raised a glowing hand and, flicking his wrist to his right, sent her flying sideways with great speed. She hit the nearest wall, hard. Though her feet were now firmly on the floor, she found that she was stuck there, an invisible force pressing her up against it.

Timotheus then raised his hand again, his eyes narrowed to slits, and her feet left the ground. Her throat constricted, and suddenly she couldn't breathe.

"I don't know what dark magic you used to travel here," Timotheus growled, "but did you honestly think you could just stroll into my city and murder me? That I wouldn't try to defend myself? You're more of a fool than I already thought you were."

"N-no!" Lucia struggled against the invisible choke hold he'd trapped her in. "That's ... not ... why ..." She tried to get the words out, to explain herself, but she didn't have the breath to speak.

His expression held no kindness at all. "You already made your plans for me very clear in your dreams. Still you know nothing, child. You would rather believe a monster's rant than your own eyes and ears. And now you've put me in quite a predicament. My fellow immortals believe you to be the salvation for which they've waited a thousand years. Little do they know you're nothing but a disappointment."

With the shreds of strength she still possessed, Lucia summoned her own magic. Clenching her fists, she conjured fire, the blazes jumping high from both of her hands as she glared at the man who'd just thrown her around like a rag doll. Remembering Alexius's most important lessons, she placed all her focus on absorbing rather than resisting Timotheus's magic. With a mighty heave, she inhaled the air magic that held her to the wall, and as the grip on her throat began to loosen, she found that stealing this immortal's magic was nearly as easy as smelling a fragrant rose from the Auranian palace courtyard.

Moments later, her feet were back on the ground.

She watched him warily, her fists blazing. "You assume the worst of me, and I can't say that I blame you for that. But did you ever see me kill you in your visions?"

"I will douse your pathetic flames," he said, ignoring her question. A small tornado of air now swirled around his hands.

"And I will steal your air and use it to smother you, right before I set you on fire."

The barest edge of worry slid through his gaze. The realization that this immortal feared her fueled Lucia's confidence, and her fire magic burned brighter.

"Kyan has taught you much," he said.

"Yes. More than you realize even now. And here I thought you knew everything."

"I'm flattered you would think so."

"Don't be." Lucia focused on reining in her darkness, then doused her flames. "I didn't come here to kill you."

He cocked his head, the only sign of his surprise. "Then why have you come, sorceress? How is it *possible* that you've come? And where is your good friend?"

Again, Lucia's eyes began to sting, and she was horrified to realize that she was about to start crying. She forced herself to hold back her tears, knowing that the success of this meeting depended on her staying strong.

"Kyan is dead," she said, holding tight to her resolve. "I saw who he really was—*what* he really was—and I realized I was wrong. All this time, I was wrong about him. I was wrong to help him. I didn't know he wanted to destroy the world."

Timotheus's expression hadn't changed at all. "Perhaps not, but you knew he wanted to kill me. And you agreed to help him."

"I'm not here to kill you, I swear it. You were right to warn me." She slid her hand over the cool purple stone on her ring. "If it wasn't for this ring, I'd be dead. It shattered the monstrous form of fire he'd taken on, and then next thing I knew . . . I—I was here."

Lucia went on in a steady rush of words that left no space for a response, telling Timotheus everything she could about her time with Kyan. She told him of their journey into the Forbidden Mountains in east Paelsia, where they'd found the crystal monolith hidden beneath a sheath of black rock. The monolith was full of power—power Kyan wanted to use to draw Timotheus from the Sanctuary. In Kyan's imagining, Lucia was to drain his magic, as she'd done with Melenia, making him vulnerable and easy to kill. Then Kyan and his elemental siblings would be free of their crystal orbs forever, with no elder immortal alive to return them to their prisons.

Lucia told Timotheus that she had felt sorry for Kyan, who had been used for his magic for all his existence. Who yearned to have his family by his side and the chance to truly experience life.

"But that's not all he wanted," she said, her voice no more than a whisper now as she reached the end of her story. "He saw weakness in all mortals, weakness that disgusted him. He wanted to burn it all away, to reduce everything and everyone to ashes, so the world could begin again as part of his quest for perfection. The other Kindred surely want the same thing."

Finally, she looked at Timotheus, expecting to see a mask of shock on his face. But all that she saw in his eyes was weariness and understanding.

"I see," he said.

Feeling bolstered by his gentle response, Lucia went on. "I assume the blast of magic that killed him triggered something in the monolith and that it was the monolith that opened a gateway that led me here. When I realized where I was, I knew I had to find you. You're the only one who can help me."

"Help you with what, Lucia?"

She felt the shameful spilling of hot tears down her cheeks.

"Help me make amends for all I've done," she croaked, surrendering to her sobs. "I'm sorry . . . I'm so, so sorry. I was wrong. And I . . . I nearly did help Kyan destroy everything. There would have been no world left, thanks to my stupidity. No safe place for my child to grow up."

Timotheus was quiet, regarding Lucia with curiosity. "Your *child*?"

Lucia sniffed, her surprise at his reaction working to calm her sobs. "My child. Mine and Alexius's."

Timotheus blinked. "You're pregnant?"

Lucia wiped her eyes with the sleeve of the borrowed robe. "You didn't know? You're the one who hinted that this was the cause of my fading magic. You told me in our last dream together that Eva's power faded when she was pregnant with a half-mortal child. You must have foreseen this!"

Timotheus blinked once and then sat down heavily on the pure white chair by his side. "I foresaw nothing like this."

"It must be why I can be here. Right? I'm mortal, but the baby . . . my baby must be half-immortal." She shook her head. "Which I don't really understand, since Alexius became mortal when he exiled himself."

"Exiles still have magic within them in your world, even though it begins to fade the moment they leave here. That, combined with your magic . . . it is possible. But I don't understand why I didn't see it before today." His gaze snapped to hers as he scrambled to his feet. "I used my magic on you. I could have hurt you—hurt the child. Are you all right? Do you need to sit down?"

Lucia shook her head. "I'm fine, really." She slid her hand over her flat belly. "It's very early still. I've been sick several mornings, but that's all."

Timotheus gave the smallest of smiles. "You were right to come to me."

Finally, she relaxed the last bit of tension she was holding in her muscles. "I'm glad you agree."

His rare smile fell quickly away. "Kyan is not dead."

She stared at him. "What?"

Timotheus held out his hand. A moment later, a flame sprang up on his palm. "Fire is eternal. It cannot live or die; it can only be contained. Kyan *is* fire magic. And if fire magic still exists, then so does he."

Lucia pressed her hand against her open mouth, her just-calmed heart back to pounding once again. "What do we do? How do we stop him?"

"Contain, not stop. He must be imprisoned again."

"How?"

He didn't answer her. Instead, he turned and moved toward the large windows. Lucia quickly followed him.

Just then, a horrible thought occurred to her. "Kyan believed you're the only one who can imprison him again. But you don't know how, do you? Eva may have, but you don't."

She watched his shoulders grow tense beside her as he remained silent, keeping his gaze fixed on the Sanctuary beyond the city walls.

"All this time . . ." she murmured, trying to contain the shaking frustration growing within her at not having all the answers she needed readily available to her. "All this time, I thought your vague hints and enigmatic riddles were meant to annoy me, to toy with me while you waited for the exact right moment to strike. But now I see why you couldn't tell me anything real. You really don't have all the answers."

"Far fewer than I'd like to have," he gritted out.

"We're in great trouble, aren't we?"

He glanced at her next to him. "Yes, we are. Like you believed of me, I believed that you might be the one who knew how to stop this magic that threatens to destroy us all. That Eva's vast knowledge had somehow made its way into your stubborn mortal mind."

Timotheus had a great talent for making nearly everything he said sound like an insult. Lucia chose to ignore this one. "It didn't. At least, not yet."

He nodded. "I know your ring is powerful. Eva used it when dealing with the Kindred, and she was never corrupted by them."

"Corrupted . . . like Cleiona and Valoria. I have my own vision and I saw it—I think I saw what happened. They touched the orbs and . . . the magic"—she shook her head, trying to understand—"it . . ."

"Possessed them," Timotheus finished for her, nodding. "Changed them, and cast them away from our world forevermore. After the great battle a thousand years ago, the Kindred were lost between worlds. And lost they remained all these centuries—until you entered the time line. Melenia too was corrupted, but in a different way. For all her claims of power and intelligence, when she touched the amber orb, the being who now calls himself Kyan was able to communicate with her. He manipulated her into doing his bidding."

She could barely believe his words, but after getting to know the fire god, they made a sickening kind of sense. "She claimed she loved him, that she'd waited for him for all these centuries. But when they were reunited, he cast her away like she was nothing to him."

"I'm not at all surprised. Fire can't love; it can only consume." He considered her for a silent moment. "Because of your ring, Kyan will be in a weakened state. You must find his amber orb before he regains his strength."

"I never saw the orb in the first place."

"Still, I would guess he would keep something so important like that with him. That orb is one of his few weaknesses, and to allow it into anyone else's hands would be to open the opportunity for imprisonment. Therefore, you must find it. The first place to search would be the site of your battle."

She nodded stiffly. "Are you certain about all this?"

"There are no certainties in situations like this, I'm afraid," he admitted.

"So I'm learning. Especially about Melenia." She refused to feel any sympathy for the heartbroken immortal, but she now understood her on a deeper level. She hadn't become a goddess like Cleiona and Valoria. Her corruption had resulted in an addiction to Kyan, making her into a tool for him to use and manipulate and, when he no longer needed her, to cast away like rubbish.

Alexius hadn't cast Lucia away, but she knew very well what it felt like to be used and manipulated.

"Melenia was smart and resourceful before her corruption, long before she turned against Eva," Timotheus said. "She was one of the few left who knew the secret I must keep about this world. The secret that keeps me trapped here."

"What secret?"

"The leaves," he said. He drew one from the folds of his cloak, a single brown leaf, crumpled and dead. She took it from him, and it disintegrated with the slightest bit of pressure in her grasp.

She shrugged. "Dead leaves. It happens."

"Not here. It's a sign, a small one, that the magic is fading. Even with the Kindred found and scattered across Mytica, it's too late to stop it."

"Stop what?"

"This world . . . what's left of it . . ." He paused, and when Lucia was certain he wasn't going to continue, she followed his gaze out toward the greenery beyond the city arches, hills, and valleys that seemed to go on forever.

"What's left of it?" she repeated, not understanding. "I'm not sure what you mean."

"My fellow immortals panic at the sight of a dying leaf, all the while ignorant that it could be much, much worse." He turned to her with a grim expression, and she met his gaze. "You need to know what could happen to your world. Look again at my beautiful Sanctuary."

Lucia blinked, then turned once again to survey the pristine view. Only now, beyond the city, the greenery she'd admired didn't stretch as far as before. A mile, perhaps two, beyond the city gates, the land turned to scorched and blackened earth. And, like a jagged cliffside, it then dropped away entirely. The blue sky had turned to a sheet of solid darkness, no stars to be seen.

The Sanctuary consisted of the city and perhaps a mile of greenery before all beyond it was destroyed.

"What happened?" she choked out.

"An immortal named Damen was created at the same time as Eva, but with the power to kill. He acted only out of a fiery need to destroy, just as the fire Kindred does. The only difference is that Kyan has no real choice over what he is and what he wants. Damen had a choice, and he chose to hurt us. To try to end us. And finally, so many years after his attack, there isn't enough magic left here to sustain the little that remains of this dying world. Without the Kindred to replenish the life of this realm, the Sanctuary has wasted away to this mere shard, with only a fraction of my kind still in existence. I use my magic to conceal the truth from the others and to try to hold what remains of this world together for as long as I can."

No one should have such a horrible burden all alone, she thought, sickened by the very idea of what he'd shared with her. "The Kindred. If the crystals are returned here, will that help you?"

He cocked his head. "It won't fix what is gone, but it would save what's left."

Lucia nodded, feeling the resolve building within her. "Then that's what I need to do. I need to find and imprison Kyan, wherever he is now, locate the other Kindred orbs, and bring them back here. Then my world and the Sanctuary will be saved."

Of course she knew it wouldn't be nearly as easy as it sounded.

Timotheus didn't smile at this suggestion, but a sliver of hope flickered in his eyes.

"Are you going to say something?" she prompted when he fell as silent and still as his fellow immortals during his speech. "Or are you going to direct me to the nearest gateway so I can get back to the mortal world?"

"You must have heard me say earlier that I've disabled all gateways."

She waited. "So . . . *enable* one again."

"Without more elders, that will take time."

"My magic could help you."

"No. It must be mine. You must hold on to yours for when you next face Kyan." He nodded, as if to himself. "You will stay here in the tower. Rest. Eat. Regain your strength. As soon as I can, I promise I will help return you to your world so you can attempt to do what is necessary to save us all—if that's truly what you want."

It was. Lucia had never wanted anything more.

CHAPTER 8

MAGNUS

LIMEROS

"Tell me, Father," Magnus said, holding tight to the reins of his horse with his gloved hands. "Have you hidden my grandmother in a block of ice? Is that where she's been all these years?"

The king didn't reply to this, not that Magnus expected him to. He'd stayed silent for the half day they'd been traveling so far. They'd acquired five horses from the innkeeper before they'd left that morning, and they rode single file, with the king and Milo at the front, Magnus in the middle, and Enzo and Cleo bringing up the rear.

He preferred to ride in front of the princess. Without her constantly in view, he could think without distraction. So far, Magnus could tell they traveled east, but he had no clue as to their final destination.

He wondered if the four men trailing behind them knew?

When the king demanded a rest near a river, Enzo and Milo got to work building a small fire. Magnus slid off his horse and approached his father. He was disturbed that the man looked even worse than when they began—his face as pale as the snow they stood on, so pale he could see the blue and purple veins beneath his skin.

"Amara has soldiers following us," he said.

"I know," the king replied.

"Plan to do anything about that? I can't imagine your new wife would be pleased to know you lied to her about the reason for this journey."

"I'm sure my new wife would be surprised if I hadn't." The king nodded to Enzo and Milo. "Take care of them."

The guards nodded, mounting their horses, and galloped off without delay.

Magnus knew perfectly well what "take care of them" meant, and he didn't object.

"How much farther will we be traveling?" he asked.

"We're headed to the Reaches," the king replied.

Magnus's eyes widened. "The Reaches? So it seems my block-of-ice theory isn't that far off after all."

The Reaches was a stretch of land close to the Granite Coast, consisting mostly of frozen moors and icy valleys. It was the coldest place in all of Limeros. The ice there never melted, not even when those in the west experienced the brief temperate season that they considered summer. There was only one village located in the Reaches, and Magnus assumed that that frozen little town must be where Selia Damora had been kept hidden all this time.

The king didn't divulge more information. He turned his back to Magnus and went to the river to fill his waterskin. Magnus walked over to Cleo, who had her fur-lined cloak pulled tightly around her face.

"How do you stand this temperature for so long?" she asked him.

He barely noticed how cold it was. "It must be my frozen heart."

"Here I thought that had melted just a little around the edges."

"Oh, no." Magnus couldn't help but smirk. "All Limerians have frozen hearts. We melt into puddles in places like Auranos, with its relentless heat."

"You're making me miss Auranos. I love the warmth there. And the trees, the flowers . . . flowers everywhere. And the palace courtyard . . ." Her voice trailed off, and Magnus could see the wistfulness in her eyes. She took a seat on a fallen log, pulling her gloves off to warm her hands at the fire. Magnus sat down beside her, keeping his father in view.

"There are courtyards in Limeros," he said.

She shook her head. "Not the same. Not nearly the same."

"True. Are you thirsty?" He offered Cleo his waterskin.

She eyed it warily. "Does that contain water or wine?"

"Sadly, only water."

"That's too bad. I could use some wine today to help warm me up."

"I couldn't agree more."

His gloved fingers brushed against hers as Cleo took the waterskin from him. She took a long sip and handed it back. "Enzo and Milo have gone to kill the men who are following us, haven't they?"

"They have. Does that bother you?"

"I think you may have suddenly confused me with the girl I was more than a year ago, one who would have shuddered to learn of such violence."

He raised his brow. "And now?"

"No more shuddering. Just shivering."

He had the urge to put his arm around her to help keep her warm, but kept his focus instead on the fire before them.

"Don't worry, soon we'll be back on our horses, headed for the even more frigid Reaches." He picked up a stick and poked the small fire with it.

"How soon until we get there?"

"A day. Two at the most, as long as my father doesn't drop off of his horse."

"I wouldn't mind witnessing that."

He smiled at that visual. "Me neither."

"What do you know of your grandmother? I know you haven't seen her for many years, but do you remember anything that could be useful?"

He tried to think back to his childhood, which wasn't a time he enjoyed dwelling on. "I was no more than five or six when I presumed she'd died . . . It was just after my grandfather had been buried. I can't even remember anyone telling me that directly, but when people suddenly disappeared, I'd discovered that it usually meant they were dead. I remember a woman with black hair and a white streak right here . . ." He stroked a lock of Cleo's hair that fell over her forehead, wishing he weren't wearing leather gloves so he could actually touch her. "And I recall that she always wore a silver pendant of snakes twisting together."

"Charming."

"I actually liked it."

"You would." She flashed a smile, but it quickly disappeared. "Do you think your father has the air Kindred on him right now?"

The king was crouched by the river, his head lowered as if he didn't have the strength to hold it upright. Magnus watched this frail version of the man he'd been afraid of all his life.

"Probably not. He likely hid it somewhere before he left." He cocked his head, reconsidering her question. "Then again, he would fear someone might find it, so it's very likely on his person."

"So you're saying you have no idea."

"That's exactly what I'm saying." He snorted softly. "You have your Kindred, though."

She held out her hand to show him the obsidian orb. "It saved our lives," she said, gazing down at the black crystal. "We know it works—we've witnessed it cause two quakes. But I need more. We need more."

"We'll get more," he assured her. "My father wouldn't come all this way if he didn't think my grandmother could be helpful. And I wouldn't have come all this way if I didn't think she might be a help in breaking the hateful curse on you."

Her expression shadowed at the reminder. "We'll see. Clearly, it's possible to unleash the magic if Lucia is involved. She helped Kyan harness the fire Kindred's power."

The thought of it caused him near-physical pain. "Perhaps. But we don't know that for sure."

"I can't think of another reason why he'd be capable of magic like that."

"If so, then she could do the same for us," he said.

"I fear you're hopelessly optimistic when it comes to your sister."

Magnus swallowed hard. "I fear you're right, but that doesn't mean I'm wrong."

It wasn't long before Enzo and Milo returned, nodding to the king that the deed was done.

Slowly, and with help from Milo, King Gaius got back on his horse, and they continued on.

It turned out to be three days of travel, which included frequent stops so the king could rest, taking them through small snow-covered villages and ice-encrusted cities. Amara didn't have soldiers patrolling this far east yet, so they didn't have to try to avoid being seen by those who might send word to the empress that King Gaius now traveled with both Magnus and Cleo at his side.

Just as Magnus was ready to demand more answers from his father—answers he was sure he wouldn't receive—they came upon a village in the Reaches called Scalia. It looked no different from the others they'd passed through, yet Magnus felt that something had changed. His father now rode with his shoulders straight rather than slumped.

They followed the king as he took them along a row of stone cottages, each identical to the next. Smoke rose from each chimney, so thick in the frigid air that it resembled puffs of cotton.

The king slipped off his horse, then looked to Magnus. "Come with me."

"It seems we've arrived," Magnus said to Cleo.

"At long last," she replied. Despite her dry tone, he could see the hope in her eyes.

They followed the king as he approached the door of the second cottage on the left. He paused for a moment, straightening his spine. Magnus was shocked to see such hesitation in his father. Finally, Gaius took a deep breath in, raised his fist, and pounded three times on the door's surface.

It took several long moments before the door creaked open inward and a woman looked out at them. Her eyes widened immediately.

"Gaius," she said, her voice barely audible.

It was her—Magnus's grandmother. She looked different—older, of course. Her black hair had turned a dark gray, but the white streak in the front still remained.

"Mother," Gaius replied, his tone void of emotion.

Her gaze swept past the king to Magnus and Cleo. "This is quite a surprise."

"I'm sure it is," the king said.

Selia's gaze moved back to the king. "Gaius, my darling, what has happened to you?" Before he could reply, she opened the door wider. "Come in, please. All of you."

The king gestured for Milo and Enzo to remain outside and stand guard, but then he, Magnus, and Cleo entered the small cottage.

"Please sit." Selia indicated some modest seating around a small wooden table. "And tell me why you look so desperately unwell."

The king sat stiffly upon one of the chairs. "First, in case you don't recognize him, this is your grandson."

"Magnus," she said, nodding. "Of course, I'd know you anywhere. You've barely changed." Her eyebrows drew together as she patted his cheek, her gaze lingering on his scar.

"Trust me, I've changed a lot," he said. "This is Princess Cleiona Bellos of Auranos, my . . . wife." For the first time since their forced marriage, he tasted no bitterness or resentment in the word.

"Cleiona Bellos." The woman's assessing gaze slowly tracked toward the princess. "Elena and Corvin's youngest daughter."

"Yes," the king hissed.

Selia raised a brow. "You didn't take the Damora name upon your marriage to my grandson?"

"No. I chose instead to continue to honor my family name," Cleo replied, "since I'm the last Bellos."

"I suppose that's understandable." Selia's attention returned to the king. "Now, tell me how you came to be in such dire shape, my son. I assume this is the reason for this long-awaited visit?"

Magnus heard no accusation in her tone, only concern.

"One of the reasons, yes," the king admitted. And then he

briefly told the woman about his fall from the cliff, without giving specific details about *why* he fell.

Selia all but collapsed into a chair when he finished. "Then there's very little time. I feared this would happen one day, and I could only pray to the goddess that you'd come to find me if it did."

"You know what to do?" the king asked.

"I believe so. I only hope it can be done in time."

"Why are you here?" Magnus finally put his thoughts into words. "Why did you disappear all those years ago only to . . . live here, in Scalia, of all the undesirable places in Limeros?"

She eyed him quizzically. "Your father didn't tell you?"

"No. But to be truthful, my father doesn't tell me very much. I thought you were dead." He gritted his teeth, angry all over again that this secret had been kept from him for thirteen years. "Clearly, you're not."

"No, I'm not," she agreed. "What I am is in exile."

Magnus shot a look at the king. "For what reason?"

"It was her own choice," the king replied weakly. "There were those on the royal council who demanded her execution—those who believe to this day that her execution was carried out privately. Instead, your grandmother came to live here. And here she has stayed all these years without anyone in this village—or at the palace—being any the wiser for it."

"Why would anyone demand your execution?" Magnus asked, sharing a look of confusion with Cleo.

"Because," Selia began slowly, "I confessed to poisoning my husband."

Magnus shook his head, confused. "But I saw Father poison him."

"Did you?" She regarded him with interest. "Then you saw the poison that I supplied to him. Gaius couldn't take the blame and the throne, so I made everything easier so that he could rule—much better than Davidus ever could." She said it so simply, as if they were discussing the weather. "It hasn't been so horrible, really. This town is sometimes unbearably cold, but it's pleasant enough most days. I have friends here, which helps to pass the time since my son's last brief visit. What was it, Gaius . . . five years ago?"

"Six," Gaius replied.

"Sabina visited me twice since then."

"You were her mentor. I'm not surprised."

Cleo remained silent, but Magnus knew she was filing information away in that beautiful blond head of hers.

"There's no more time for talk." Selia stood up from her chair. "We must leave immediately for the city of Basilia."

"What?" Magnus shot a look at his father. "That's in west Paelsia."

The king too looked surprised by this. "It's a long journey. And we've only just arrived here."

"Yes, and now we must leave. I have a friend in that city who can supply the magic I need to help you before it's too late."

"What I need more than that, Mother, is your magic to help us find Lucia. She's gone missing just when I need her the most."

"So the prophecy was true," Selia whispered. "And you didn't tell me until now? I could have helped her as I did Sabina."

"I chose to use tutors who didn't know of the prophecy."

She said nothing for a moment, then nodded sharply. "You were right to be careful with her. However, finding her current location will be a challenge. After all these years in hiding my magic has faded to a point that it's useless to me. The answer for this too lies in Basilia. We will go there and get what we need for the next steps in our plan." She took the king's hands in hers, smiling. "At long last, everything is coming together. But I need you well."

"I never knew you were a witch," Magnus said, choosing to remain mostly silent until now, watching and listening.

Selia glanced at him. "I told very few this secret."

"And you feel that you can restore your *elementia*?"

She nodded. "I haven't had a need to do so for years, but to find my granddaughter, to acquire the magic necessary to heal my son . . . it will be worth it."

"My father recently told me about a curse . . ." He glanced at Cleo, whose expression was bleak.

Selia's eyes widened. "Yes, of course. The tragic curse on Elena Bellos. I'm so sorry, Cleiona, for your loss."

Cleo nodded. "I am too. I wish I could have known my mother."

"Of course you do. Even though my magic is weak, I can still sense this powerful curse all around you when I concentrate. I won't say that it will be easy, but I promise to do everything in my power to break it when my magic is strengthened."

The tight knot in Magnus's chest finally loosened just a little. "Good."

He saw relief in Cleo's eyes as she nodded. "Thank you," She said.

"What is this magic in Basilia that could help me?" Gaius asked as Selia grabbed a canvas bag and started shoving some of her belongings into it.

"Magic that once belonged to the immortals themselves," she told him. "An object of great power that very few know exists."

"And what object is that?" Magnus asked.

"It's called the bloodstone. We will find it together, and when we do I am certain it will fully restore your father to his former greatness."

"That sounds like a valuable treasure," the king said. "One you've never mentioned to me before today."

"I didn't tell you everything I know, Gaius."

"No. I'm quite sure you didn't."

Their voices became distant echoes as Magnus considered the existence of this bloodstone . . . another rock imbued with great power and magic that could allegedly heal even someone who already looked as if they had been dead and buried.

Forget his father, Magnus thought. That was magic he wanted for himself.

CHAPTER 9

AMARA

LIMEROS

Since childhood, Amara had enjoyed taking long walks in the tropical splendor of the Jewel of the Empire, relishing in its vibrant colors and warm weather, often with Ashur by her side. The kiss of sunlight gave her renewed hope when her father had been particularly cruel or her brothers Dastan and Elan ignored her very existence. In Kraeshia, no one had to wear heavy fur-lined cloaks or huddle close to fires to keep from freezing.

Yes, she missed her home desperately and longed to return there when she finally had what she'd come here for. Then she would say farewell to this frozen and unforgiving kingdom once and for all.

She turned from the main hall's large windowpane, framed with ice crystals, which looked out at the villa's snow-covered grounds, to regard Kurtis. He'd entered the hall to bring the daily news, and he currently knelt before her, his arms full of papers.

"Rise and speak, Lord Kurtis," she commanded as she moved toward her small throne.

"Preparations are under way for you to move to the Limerian palace tomorrow, your grace," he said.

"Excellent." Gaius had suggested the move three days earlier, before his departure, and she'd rather not stay at the villa any longer than absolutely necessary.

She strived for patience as Kurtis struggled, one-handed, to sort through his armful of papers.

"Have my men reported anything on my husband's current whereabouts?" she asked.

He scanned a few more pieces of parchment before replying. "No, your grace. Not yet."

"Really? Nothing at all?"

"No." He gave her a thin smile. "But I'm sure he'd be pleased to know that his wife is so eager to have him return to her side."

"Yes, of course." Amara regarded him for a moment in silence, still trying to decide whether or not she'd come to value his presence over the last few days. According to Gaius—and Kurtis himself—this young man had been a worthy grand kingsliege, one who'd held command of Limeros for months before Magnus arrived and tore his power away.

Amara's gaze drifted to the stump of Kurtis's right arm. Despite the dressing of fresh white bandages, a blotch of blood had begun to seep through.

"What other news is there?" she asked, taking a sip from her goblet of cider that Nerissa had provided earlier.

"My father, Lord Gareth, has sent a message."

"Read it to me."

He unrolled the parchment, dropping several others pieces of paper to the floor. "*Great Empress, first, my deepest congratulations on your marriage to King Gaius, a true and dear friend of mine. He sent word to me about the current situation in Mytica, and I wish for you to know that I understand the situation and embrace this chance to serve my glorious new empress in any capacity you may require."*

Yes, Amara thought wryly, *I'm quite sure he does, given that the alternative is death or imprisonment.*

"For now," Kurtis continued, *"unless you command my services elsewhere, I will remain at the Auranian palace in the City of Gold. Please know that I shall welcome any and all Kraeshians as friends and allies."*

"Very good." Amara gifted Kurtis with a small smile when he finished. "Your father sounds a great deal like you. Very amenable to unexpected changes."

Kurtis returned her modest grin with a simpering one of his own, telling her that he took this wry observation as a compliment. "We both have a knack for recognizing greatness in a leader."

"That's very wise of you," she said through teeth made to ache by Kurtis's cloying comment.

In her periphery, she saw Nerissa enter the room with a tray of food and wine. The girl quietly placed it on a table. When Kurtis immediately gestured to her to leave, Amara turned toward the door.

"Stay," Amara commanded her. "I want to speak with you."

Nerissa bowed. "Yes, empress."

"Lord Kurtis, is that all the news for the day you have to share with me?"

Kurtis's back stiffened. "I have many more papers to read to you."

"Yes, but do they contain anything important?" She raised an eyebrow and waited. "Vital? Any news of my soldiers on the brink of a revolt against their new ruler? Or news of Prince Ashur's imminent arrival?"

"No, your grace."

"Then you may leave us."

"Yes, your grace." Without another word, Kurtis bowed his head and left the room. In the few days she'd known the kingsliege, she'd realized one important thing: He took commands very well.

Nerissa waited by the door.

Amara stood up from her throne and smoothed her skirts as she approached the girl. "Bring the wine and come with me."

Nerissa did as instructed, and Amara led her to her living chambers, a series of rooms that were more comfortable and much less formal. "Please, sit," she said.

Nerissa hesitated for only a short moment before taking the seat next to Amara, who had chosen an overstuffed velvet armchair positioned in front of the vanity mirror.

Cleo had known a great deal about the Kindred. There was a chance her attendant might have overheard something important that might help Amara, especially in terms of Lucia's importance in the matter. Amara planned to coax out whatever Nerissa might know.

"We haven't had a chance to speak privately since you were assigned to me," Amara said. "There is much about you that makes me curious, Nerissa Florens."

"That you would be curious about someone like me is an honor," Nerissa replied politely.

"*Florens* . . . That's an unusual surname for a Mytican. Yes?"

"Quite unusual, yes. But my family isn't from Mytica. Not originally. My mother brought me here when I was a little girl."

"And what of your father?"

"Killed in a battle when the city of my birth was invaded."

A small gasp escaped Amara's lips. "You speak so bluntly and without emotion. It's as if you're a Kraeshian like me."

The corner of Nerissa's mouth twitched, almost a smile. "My origins aren't any more Kraeshian than they are Mytican, although your father did try his best to change that. My family was from the Gavenos Islands."

"Ah, yes." That made perfect sense. *Florens* did sound very much like the surnames common in the Gavenos Islands, a cluster of small kingdoms that Amara's father had easily conquered when she was just a child. "I'm surprised you've chosen to reveal this to me."

"Not at all, your majesty. I have no ill feelings about something your father did more than fifteen years ago." Nerissa sighed. "According to my mother, our home was a horrible place before it became part of the Kraeshian Empire. The war gave us a reason to leave."

"But your father . . ."

"He was a brute. He beat my mother regularly. He did the same to me when I was a mere toddler—though thankfully I don't have any memories of that. No, it was a blessing, not a curse, for us to be forced to start a new life in Mytica."

"Your mother must be a very brave woman to take on such a challenge all by herself."

"She was." Nerissa smiled softly, her light brown eyes distant in memory. "She taught me everything I know. Alas, she passed away four years ago."

"My condolences for your loss," Amara said, sincerely. "I am curious to know what specifically such a formidable woman chose to teach you."

Nerissa raised a brow. "Shall I be honest, empress?"

"Always," Amara said, and she had to force herself not to lean toward her new companion too eagerly.

"The most important thing she taught me was how to get anything I want."

"What a valuable skill."

"Yes, it's certainly proven to be."

"And how did she suggest you do that?" Amara asked with curiosity.

"By giving men what *they* want first," Nerissa said with a smile. "After we fled the islands, my mother became a courtesan. A very successful one." At Amara's look of shock, she shrugged. "During my childhood, a normal day for her consisted of activities that would make most people blush."

Amara had to laugh. "Well. That is rather unexpected—but, frankly, admirable. I would have liked to know your mother, I think."

She also would have liked to have known her own mother, the one who gave her life for Amara's. Strong, brave women were meant to be celebrated and remembered, not discarded and forgotten.

Amara noticed this sort of strength in Nerissa. After all, she must have done something right to get this far unharmed. "I must ask, assuming that you were at the palace during the siege, how is it that you came to be here at the villa? Did the king bring you here immediately?"

"No, his guard Enzo did," Nerissa said matter-of-factly. "He was concerned for my well-being."

"Beyond that of any other attendant at the palace?"

"Oh, yes." Nerissa gave her a wicked smile. "After the occupation, Enzo brought me here to work elsewhere in the villa. When the king noticed this, he chose me to attend to you. Making Enzo believe that we are much closer than we really are has benefitted me greatly, wouldn't you say?"

"Indeed, I would say that." Amara's smile began to spread. "We have more in common than I'd have ever thought."

"Do we?"

Amara nodded. "I'd like you to use this very special skill you have to get to know my soldiers, to find out what they say about me. Specifically, if they have any intention of defying a command from an empress rather than an emperor."

Nerissa pursed her lips briefly before speaking. "Yes, Kraeshian men are not as open to such a change, are they?

"I suppose I'll find out if they are or not in time, but I'd much rather have prior knowledge of any uprising."

"I will certainly do what I can."

"Thank you." Amara studied Nerissa, waiting for any reluctance, any flinch at what she'd asked for, but there was none. "I see why men like you, Nerissa. You're very beautiful."

"Thank you, your grace." Nerissa raised her gaze to meet Amara's. "Shall I pour you some wine?"

"Yes, please pour us both a cup." Amara watched her do as she asked, while imagining the girl doing the same for Cleo and Magnus. "How many attendants did Cleo have?"

"In Auranos, several Limerian girls were assigned to her, but they weren't to her liking. After I arrived, she needed no one else."

"I'm sure. Tell me, is she in love with Prince Magnus? I would have thought no, given that he was her enemy not so long ago, but now I'm not so sure, given the direction of her recent speech."

Nerissa handed Amara a goblet of wine and sat back down in her chair, sipping at her own glass. "Love? I'm not so sure. Attraction, surely. For all her innocent looks, I know the princess is an excellent manipulator." She looked away. "I shouldn't say such things."

Amara touched her hand. "No, please. You must speak freely with me. Nothing you say will be held against you. All right?"

Nerissa nodded. "Yes, your grace."

"Tell me, did the princess ever mention to you what she knew of the whereabouts of Lucia Damora? Have they been in contact at all since her elopement?"

Nerissa frowned. "All I know is that Princess Lucia ran off with her tutor, and it was quite the scandal. No one, to my knowledge, has seen her since—unless you believe the rumors."

Amara lifted her gaze from her wine to the lovely girl's face. "What rumors are those?"

"That the king has concealed the truth all these years—that his daughter is a witch. And there have been tales in recent days of a witch who's been traveling across Mytica, killing anyone who stands in her way and burning down entire villages."

Amara had also heard these rumors. "Do you think it's Lucia?"

The girl shrugged. "More likely these are tall tales of villagers looking for ways to explain an errant spark from a fire lighting up their town. But, of course, I don't know for sure."

This girl had no useful information today, but Amara had enjoyed their talk. She reached forward and squeezed Nerissa's hand. "Thank you for speaking with me. You have certainly proven your worth to me today, and I promise I won't forget that."

In one fluid motion that was as graceful as it was bold, Nerissa entwined her fingers with Amara's. "I'm happy to help in any way you need me to, empress."

Amara looked down at their joined hands with shock but didn't pull away. The warmth from Nerissa's skin sank into her own, and she realized how cold she'd been all morning.

"That is very good to know." Amara paused, considering the lovely young woman before her with growing interest. "The days to come will be challenging, and it's good to know I now have someone I can trust."

"Yes, you do."

Finally, and a bit reluctantly, Amara slid her hand away from Nerissa's and placed it lightly on her goblet. "You may leave me now."

Nerissa bowed her head. Amara watched her stand up gracefully and move slowly to the door. She paused and glanced over her shoulder. "I will be nearby if you need me. Whenever you need me."

Without another word, the girl left the room.

Amara sat there for some time, considering the conversations she'd had with the intriguing Nerissa, as she finished the wine in her goblet.

Alone in her quarters for the first time all day, Amara stood and went to her wardrobe. She slipped her hand into the folds of her emerald-green gown and pulled from it the greatest treasure she'd ever possessed. Cradling it in both hands, she stared deeply into the aquamarine orb.

The water Kindred.

"An exact match for Cleo's eyes," she said, realizing this about the crystal's brilliant blue hue for the first time. "How annoying."

She watched the black, shadowy strand of pure water magic swirl within the orb.

"Does Lucia know how to release you?" she whispered to her prize. "Or are you nothing more than a rock, as disappointingly useless as you are tantalizing?"

Something warm brushed against her shoulders. She gripped the cool crystal and scanned the room, her brows drawing together.

"What was that?" she said aloud.

There it was again: a warm breeze sweeping by to caress her, this time from the opposite direction.

"*Empress . . .*"

Her heart rate quickened.

With haste, she returned the orb to its hiding place. She circled the room, searching for the source of the eerie voice and the hot breeze that made the hair on her neck stand on end.

She heard a deep rumble from the fireplace in the corner of the room. Amara whirled around and gasped. The fire that the servants had lit at dawn had dwindled to embers. Now, it was once again blazing, more gloriously than she'd ever seen it before. Amara's trembling gaze then drifted above the fireplace. Dancing atop the wick of each and every candle on the mantelpiece was a flame—the candles had somehow ignited themselves.

Amara sucked in one desperate gasp of air and then forgot how to breathe entirely. The vision she had on the ship that brought her here reappeared in her mind, vivid and clear and haunting. Ashur, the brother she'd killed, returning from beyond death to avenge her.

"Ashur . . . ?" she ventured cautiously.

"I am not Ashur."

Amara went as still as a corpse at the sound of the deep male voice that echoed through her mysteriously fire-licked room. It was a voice that came with no body—the one thing Amara could be sure of was that there was no one else in the room with her.

"Who are you?" she managed.

"You possess the water Kindred."

Amara's spine froze as if pierced with a dagger of ice. Now she was sure of it: The voice, not the least bit muffled, the way it would be were someone speaking from outside her heavy steel-and-wood door, was coming from inside the room.

Pushing past the thrum of her pounding heart, Amara managed to say, "I don't know what you're talking about."

"Don't insult me with lies."

She wanted to cry out for help, but from what? No. First she needed to know what she was dealing with. "Tell me who you are and what you want," she said, puffing out her chest. "I am in command here, and I refuse to be intimidated by a bodiless voice."

"Oh, my little empress," the voice taunted. *"Trust me, there is far more to me than a mere voice."*

Without warning, the flames flared up, and Amara slammed herself against the wall. The fire blazed so brightly that she had to shield her eyes against its blinding white light.

"Come and see for yourself."

Thankful for her layers of skirts, which helped hide the quivering of her knees, Amara moved closer to the flames. With more caution than she'd ever applied to any task before, she peered into them. Seeing nothing but all-consuming flames, she moved closer, until she could feel the heat threatening to singe her skin. Then . . . there it was. She swore she could see something—someone—looking back at her.

A shriek escaped her throat as she scrambled back from the fire. She reached for the chair behind her to keep from toppling over.

"I am Kyan," the face in the flames told her. *"I am the god of fire, released from my amber prison. And I can help you find what you seek."*

Amara's whole body trembled. She was certain this had to be an illusion, a dream. She tentatively reached toward the flames, feeling the palpable heat, and tried to speak with the boldness she needed to shield her fear.

"You . . ." she began, her voice hoarse. "You are the fire Kindred."

"I am."

Amara felt like her entire world had shifted. "You can speak," she managed to say.

"I assure you, I can do much more than that. Tell me, little empress, what is it that you want?"

It took her another moment to gather herself together and try to take hold of the situation. "I want to find Lucia Damora," she told the face in the flames.

"*Because you believe she can release the magic in the crystal you currently possess. And with that magic you will be more powerful than you already are.*"

"Yes." Her breath caught in her throat. "Is that magic—the magic of the water Kindred—is it like you? Conscious, knowing, thinking . . . ?"

"*Yes. Does that frighten you?*" There was the distinct sound of amusement in the deep voice.

She straightened her shoulders. "I'm not afraid. I possess the water Kindred, which means that the magic within it—"

"*Belongs to you,*" Kyan finished.

She waited, barely breathing now, until he spoke again.

"*I can help you, little empress, attain everything you've ever desired. But first, you must help me.*"

"How?"

"*The very sorceress you named destroyed my physical form believing she could destroy me as well. But fire cannot be destroyed. However, I can only remain in this world as a mere whisper of my true form. With your help I will be fully restored to my previous strength, and then I will give you more than you've ever dreamed possible.*"

He paused, as if to let what he'd said sink in.

What he spoke of was straight out of Kraeshian legend, a magical creature beyond this world who promises to grant one's wishes.

A heady mix of fear and curiosity consumed her. The thought that she'd been in possession of a crystal orb that had an entity like this within it all this time boggled her mind. Elemental magic . . . but with its own consciousness. *Incredible,* she thought.

Still, there were doubts rising within her. "You make great promises, but you show me nothing tangible."

The fire blazed higher, and she jumped back. "*There are others*

I can go to, others who would agree to whatever I ask for without hesitation. Yet I chose you because I can clearly see that you are greater than all of them combined. You have taken your power with strength and intelligence beyond that of any man who's ever existed. You are better, stronger, smarter than your enemies and more deserving of greatness than the sorceress."

Amara's cheeks flushed. His words felt like a healing balm for her bruised hope for the future. "Tell me more. Tell me how to release the magical being within the water Kindred to help me solidify my reign as empress."

He didn't speak again for a moment, and she searched the flames for his face. It flickered in and out of view as the fire burned. It seemed that the fire god could appear and reappear at will. *"Blood and magic. That is what you need—what we both need. The blood of the sorceress and the magic of a powerful witch. When the pieces are in place, I will be restored to my former glory, and you, little empress, will become infinitely powerful."*

A shiver of pleasure coursed down her spine as she stared into the flames. "What do I need to do?"

"The correct question is: Where do you need to go?"

She drew in a breath and nodded. "Where?"

The flames shifted, the shades of reds and oranges, whites and blues growing brighter and more vibrant as they did.

"Paelsia."

CHAPTER 10

LUCIA

THE SANCTUARY

Lucia learned that the tower where Timotheus resided was called the Crystal Palace. At one time it had housed all six original elders. Now he was the only one left.

"It must be lonely," Lucia mused, half to herself. "Being here all by yourself with the burden of all of these secrets."

"It is," he replied, but when Lucia looked up to meet his gaze, he had already glanced away.

"I want to see Melenia's chambers."

"Why?"

"Because . . ." She thought about how to rationalize the need to see where her enemy, the woman who had plotted her death since before Lucia had even been born, had spent her existence. "I just need to see it."

She thought he'd argue, but instead he nodded. "Very well. Follow me."

Timotheus led her to a long corridor with doors that opened on their own as they approached and shut softly behind them as they continued down the hall. Lucia traced the white walls with her fingertips. She could feel Timotheus's eyes on her as they walked.

"You have questions, many questions," he said.

"A lifetime of them," she agreed.

"I can't tell you everything, Lucia. While it's true that you've reached out a hand in friendship today—"

"You still don't trust me," she cut him off. "I know."

"It's not that. Not entirely, anyway. So many secrets have died with the other elders, and now that I'm the only one remaining, these secrets are one of the few weapons I have left to protect myself."

"I understand," she told him. "I really do."

He frowned at her. "How is it you've managed to mature so much in so little time?"

She almost laughed. "Don't sound so confused by that."

"The new life growing within you must have made all the difference in helping to change the childish, spoiled behavior and previous tantrums I'm more accustomed to with you."

"Timotheus, such compliments. They will go to my head."

He let out a soft snort of amusement as they approached a set of gleaming golden doors. Timotheus pushed them open to reveal Melenia's chambers.

Lucia gaped at the sight of the expansive room, the same size as the one in which she'd met with Timotheus. But that room was stark and barren of any personal touches. This one was just the opposite.

It felt like walking into the chambers of a queen in the finest palace. There was a regal seating area in the center of the room with soft white velvet lounges. Overhead a crystal chandelier sparkled, catching the light streaming in from the floor-to-ceiling windows lining the room. Lucia looked down as she walked, taking in the intricate floor made of silver and inlaid jewels.

There were flowers in every color imaginable, as fresh as if they were picked that day. They peeked out from a dozen large vases placed upon glass tables throughout the room.

Lucia walked past all of this grandeur to the far wall. It was overlaid with a checkerboard pattern of silver and glass. Etched into the silver tiles were the elemental symbols—a simple spiral for air, a triangle for fire, a circle within a circle for earth, and two parallel wavy lines for water.

"A shrine," Timotheus explained. "Many immortals have one in their homes so they can pray to the elements."

"I've heard that some old witches do the same," Lucia mused, brushing her fingertips over the symbol for fire.

"Not exactly the same," he said. "But similar."

"Melenia prayed here to Kyan, wanting him to return to her."

"I'm sure she did."

"And he was able to speak to her, in her mind, telling her lies. Making her promises that they'd be together when he was released if she helped him." Timotheus didn't reply to this. He didn't have to. "I hate that I feel even a little bit sorry for her now that I know how Kyan manipulated her. It was so much easier just to hate her."

"Don't feel sorry for Melenia. She could have fought harder against him."

"How do you know that? Perhaps she tried and failed."

"Perhaps," he acknowledged.

Lucia touched the other elemental symbols. "Have the other three Kindred ever been released?"

"Not to my knowledge. Not in a physical form, anyway."

Had Alexius known any of this? she wondered. He must have come there to meet with Melenia. This was where the beautiful elder had told him what to do. He'd been corrupted with her words and magic right here in this very place. Yet Alexius had fought in the end.

Lucia wanted to believe that he had fought from the very beginning.

"You told me Alexius was your friend," she said.

"Like family to me."

"I haven't said this before, but I'm so sorry for your loss."

"And I'm sorry for yours."

She swallowed the lump forming in her throat, trying to focus on something else. She placed a hand on her stomach. "I've been thinking about what to name the baby, and I'm struggling to find something that fits. I want to choose something strong, something worthy. A name my son or daughter will come to appreciate as they grow older."

"You have plenty of time to decide."

"Yes, I suppose I do." Lucia absentmindedly picked up a small golden chest sitting on the nearest glass table. It was about the size of the jewelry box Lucia had found in Princess Cleo's Auranian palace bedchamber. She lifted the lid to see a shining golden dagger lying within. She picked it up and studied the blade.

"Is this what Melenia used to carve the obedience spell into him?" she asked, breathless.

In one smooth motion, Timotheus plucked the dagger from her hand, put it back in the box, and closed the lid.

"It is," he said, looking down at the box with a furrowed brow. "If I destroy it, I worry that would release the dark magic trapped within. I should put it somewhere else, somewhere no one will ever be able to find it again. The worlds will be safer that way." He paused. "Are you finished looking around? I assure you, there's nothing to find here except unpleasant memories and regrets. I would know better than most."

Lucia exhaled shakily and nodded. "I'm finished."

"Then I will have Mia show you around the city. After my unexpected announcement, my fellow immortals will want to see you again before you must return to your home."

As if by magic—and Lucia had no reason to believe it was because of anything else—Mia was waiting for her at the base of the tower. She already knew what Timotheus had suggested. Mia appeared nervous. Despite however many centuries or millennia old she might be, she seemed younger than Lucia herself. Lucia gave her a warm smile.

Mia smiled back and, taking Lucia's arm in hers, accompanied her outside.

While the pressure of finding Kyan when she returned to Mytica weighed heavily on her mind, Lucia was curious to learn more about this city and its occupants—including what immortals did to pass their time.

She took in the sights around her as they walked. A couple dozen Watchers were crouched on the ground. They worked diligently, creating an expansive piece of art directly on the mirrored city square by placing tiny colored crystal fragments in intricate patterns.

"This piece represents air, and they've finally finished it," Mia said, taking Lucia to the top of a nearby building so they could see the artwork from above. "Isn't it lovely?"

"Very," Lucia agreed. The design was of detailed spirals in many different shades of blue and white, and it reminded Lucia of a beautiful mosaic she'd seen on the wall of the Auranian palace library. Only this was ten times that size and had to have taken the artists months to produce.

The artists stepped back from their work, smiling at each other and wiping the sweat off their brows.

Then, to Lucia's surprise, they each took a golden-handled broom and began to sweep away the crystal shards, destroying their impressive work.

"What are they doing?" she exclaimed.

Mia just looked at her with a frown. "Clearing the space so they can begin again, of course."

"Such a waste of a beautiful piece of artwork!"

"No, no. This is how it's meant to be. It shows that everything that exists must one day change—but what is destroyed can be created again with patience and dedication."

As Lucia pondered this, still disturbed that an incredible piece of beauty couldn't be made to last, Mia took her to the group of immortals. Their eyes filled with hope at the sight of her, and they asked if she would like the honor of beginning the next mosaic. Lucia chose a handful of red crystals, as fine as sand, from a long golden tray. She sprinkled some in the center of the area, eyeing Mia to see if she'd done this correctly.

Mia smiled and clapped her hands. "Excellent. I'm sure you've now inspired them to make an incredible dedication to the fire Kindred."

Lucia's stomach sank at the thought that she'd unconsciously chosen red rather than any other color.

Well, of course I did, she thought. *It has nothing to do with Kyan. It's the color of Limeros.*

"You must be hungry," Mia said, leading Lucia to an outdoor courtyard where fruit hung heavily from the trees. Lucia looked around, realizing just how very hungry she was. She reached up to pluck a dark red apple from its branch. Mia did as well, taking a big bite out of the piece of fruit and prompting Lucia to do the same.

When she sank her teeth into the crisp skin, the taste of the apple made her eyes widen with shock. She'd never experienced anything so sweet, so pure, so delicious.

"This is the best thing I've ever tasted!" she said aloud, nearly giddy.

She devoured it quickly, having to force herself not to eat the core and seeds as well. As she boldly reached for another, she felt a sharp and unexpected twinge in her belly. She placed her hand over it and looked down, frowning.

"What was that?" she murmured.

"Are you all right?" Mia asked, concerned.

The twinge was only momentary, and Lucia shook it off. "I'm fine. Likely my stomach was just expressing gratitude for some food after so long."

Lucia decided to take strength from this food, from the immortals who looked at her with hope rather than fear, and from the friendship of Timotheus and Mia, as she waited impatiently to return home.

It was impossible to judge the passing of days in a place where it was always light, but Lucia enjoyed two deep sleeps while she was in the Crystal City.

Then Timotheus had Mia bring her back to the tower. Lucia gripped her new friend's hands. "Thank you for helping me."

"No." Mia shook her head, meeting Lucia's gaze with such sincerity it nearly stole her breath. "Thank you for coming here. Thank you for being someone we can believe in. One day I know we will meet again."

"I hope you're right." Lucia reluctantly released Mia and followed Timotheus into the crystal tower.

This time, the doors he guided her to slid open into a dark, cavernous place.

"We're underground," Lucia guessed.

"We are."

She was about to ask another question when she saw something fifteen paces away, an object that glowed with violet light. As they drew closer to it, Lucia realized what it was.

"A monolith," she gasped. "Like the one in the mountains."

Timotheus nodded, his features shadowed by the uneven light. "There is one of these in each of the seven worlds—yours and mine being only two of them."

"Seven?" Lucia's gaze shot to his. "You're saying that there are five more worlds beyond ours?"

"Your mathematical abilities are truly impressive." He raised a brow. "Yes, seven worlds, Lucia. My kind was created to watch over these worlds before Damen destroyed everything we held dear. Now we only watch over your world." His expression darkened at the mention of the truly evil immortal. "These monoliths were created to allow travel between the worlds. Damen drained that magic so he could easily walk between worlds at his whim. This destruction is what made the mountains void of life, and it's the cause of your kingdom turning to ice and Paelsia turning to stone."

Lucia stared at him as he delivered this gigantic piece of the mysterious puzzle of Mytica in a single breath. "Why, then, is Auranos still beautiful?"

"Because of the goddess they worshipped—that some still worship. The goddess who was once an elder like myself."

"Cleiona."

He nodded. "She managed to protect the kingdom she'd claimed while Valoria failed to do the same. Sometimes it seems as if it was only yesterday that I last saw them both. We've all lost so much, never again to be found . . ." Timotheus grimaced as he spoke of the goddesses. Then he blinked hard, as if to clear his mind. "You've been here long enough, Lucia. You must go now and attempt to stop Kyan."

Lucia almost laughed at his consistently harsh tone. "I think I'll miss your candor. And I'm not going to attempt to stop him, I *will* stop him."

"I hope for all of our sakes that you're right."

She looked up at the glowing monolith. "How do I use this to help send me back?"

"Press your hands to its surface, and the gateway magic will do the rest." When she hesitated, he raised a brow. "Don't tell me that you're doubting my word."

"If I thought you were lying to me, you'd already be dead." A small smile crept onto her face as his eyes widened. "Two of us can be blunt, Timotheus."

"Indeed."

"Farewell," she said, ready to leave. Ready to return to her home, find her family, and ensure Kyan would never harm another soul.

Timotheus's surprised expression faded, replaced by something she could only describe as sadness. "Farewell, Lucia."

She pressed the palms of her hands against the cool, glowing crystal monolith. The light emanating from it quickly brightened to a pure white glow. Lucia forced her hands to keep pushing while she squeezed her eyes shut.

The very next moment, Lucia found herself on the ground with the wind knocked out of her and her feet swept beneath her. Gasping for breath and more than a little confused, she quickly pushed herself up from the dry, brittle earth and spun around in search of Timotheus.

But she was no longer in the Sanctuary. One brief glance at her surroundings told her that she had returned to the place in the mountains where she'd battled Kyan. Though it was day, she still recognized the place, and the air was every bit as cold as it was when she was there last. Cold—and rippling with an unsettling sensation that she instinctively knew to be an atmosphere of impending death.

Damen, an immortal, had caused this by leeching the magic from the monolith. His touch may have been all that was necessary to cover it in stone, hiding its magic for all these years until Kyan burned that stone away. There was nothing here—no birds, no mammals, not even a single insect crawled upon this land. There were no trees or shrubs of any kind here, save for a small oasis where they'd found the monolith.

For a moment, she felt such dread in her heart that it seemed certain that Kyan had been there the whole time, waiting for her to return. She froze, looking around, her fists clenched and ready to fight.

But there was nothing there. No one. Only Lucia.

And it was well past time she left.

As she walked across the scorched ground littered with crumbled rocks, she discovered with a flash of happiness the purse she'd thought was lost. It still contained more than enough coin to pay for an inn for several nights.

Continuing on, she came upon the gaping hole in the ground where Kyan had exploded. At the bottom of the deep depression in the rock, something sparkled even in the meager light this deep in the mountains.

Nothing ever sparkled here.

She moved toward it tentatively, leaning forward to pick up a smooth rock: the source of the strange glinting. Lucia brushed a thick layer of ash from its surface. She staggered backward, clasping a hand over her mouth when she saw what was underneath.

An amber orb.

Kyan's prison was no larger than the apple she'd eaten in the Sanctuary.

"Oh," she gasped, turning her head in every direction to once again make sure she was truly alone.

She held the thing up, squinting as she tried to catch it in what little daylight was able to emerge from behind a curtain of clouds above the mountains. The amber orb was transparent straight through: no cracks, no abnormalities, no imperfections.

Once, she might have thought such a treasure was beautiful. Not now. Not this treasure. But it was a sign that she had the lead, and for that she was grateful.

If she possessed this crystal, she had the means to stop Kyan before he put his plans of world destruction into play.

After allowing herself a small grin at this victory, she made her way out of the mountains and started upon a several hours' journey west for a small village she knew, where she and Kyan had made their plans to trek into the mountains. There she'd learn if anyone had seen or heard about Kyan since they'd been there last.

She would redeem herself for her past mistakes, and aligning with the fire Kindred had, by far, been her biggest mistake of all.

Near dusk, Lucia finally entered the familiar inn and warily glanced around the busy tavern, half expecting to see Kyan slurping from a bowl of soup.

Exhausted from her travels, she took a seat at the very same table the two of them had shared the morning after she realized she was pregnant.

"I remember you," spoke a female voice. "Welcome back."

Lucia looked up at the barmaid approaching her table. "And I remember you. Sera, yes?"

This barmaid had seen Lucia and Kyan together. She'd been the one who told them that the answers they were looking for could be found in the mountains—and she'd been right.

"Yes, that's my name," Sera said with a smile. "Where's your handsome friend?"

"We were separated during our travels. Has he been back since we left here?"

"Afraid not."

"Are you certain?"

"Believe me, I'd remember if he had." The girl winked. "Care for a drink?"

"Yes," she said, all of a sudden realizing how desperately thirsty she was. "I'll have . . . peach juice."

"We only have grape juice."

"That's fine."

"Anything else? Something to eat, perhaps?"

Lucia felt a twinge in her belly at the suggestion. "Yes, that would be wonderful."

Sera glanced over at a full table of loud men, who Lucia now realized were all dressed in identical green uniforms. "Apologies if I'm a bit slow to serve you tonight," she said. "I'm the only one here, and I need to make sure our other guests are well taken care of. It's probably a good idea that we keep them drunk and happy, don't you think?"

"I suppose." Lucia eyed the men with curiosity. "Who are they?"

Sera turned to her, surprised. "It's only been a few days since you were last here. Surely you must know about the Kraeshians."

Lucia snapped her gaze to Sera's. "Kraeshians?"

Sera nodded. "We're now under a Kraeshian occupation, with thousands sent here to enforce their laws upon all of Mytica, including this little forgettable village. These men arrived here yesterday."

"Sent by Emperor Cortas?" Lucia's chest grew more constricted every moment, until she was having trouble breathing.

Sera raised her brows. "These soldiers told me that the emperor and two of his sons were killed by a rebel who's been captured and punished for the crime. Only his daughter, Amara, survived. She's the empress now of Kraeshia . . . and Mytica. At least, until her brother Ashur returns from his travels, they say."

Lucia's heart nearly stopped. She gripped the side of the table so tightly that she was sure she would break it in two.

She fought to control the emotions storming within her. The worst thing she could do now would be to blow her cover by losing control of her magic and causing damage she'd have to pay for later.

"And where is the king?" Lucia managed.

"I don't know."

Lucia remembered boldly revealing her magic in front of the Kraeshian princess, but Amara had acted so very calm about it. Encouraging, even. Lucia had determined she'd deal with any ramifications of confirming the rumors about her magic the next time she saw the girl, but she hadn't seen her again.

And now Amara was empress.

Something was terribly wrong, and she needed to know what had happened to her family.

"Sera," Lucia said, pushing past the fog of shock in her quest for answers, "have you heard anything about the prince? Prince Magnus?"

"I'm afraid news is scarce here, but with all this fresh blood in town"—Sera smiled over at the table of Kraeshian soldiers—"we're getting some information. Apparently, the prince tried to steal the throne from his father while the king was away in Kraeshia. I heard he was put to death for treason, along with his new wife."

For several long moments, all Lucia could do was stare. "No," she finally uttered, her voice cracking as she did.

Sera frowned. "What?"

"He can't be," she gasped. "He can't be dead." Lucia lurched to her feet, her chair screeching against the floor as she did. "I need to find him—my father. Find my brother. This isn't right, none of it. And nobody knows the real danger that's waiting. No one knows how much trouble everyone's in."

As she muttered frantically, the table of soldiers began to look up, one by one. Soon she'd gained their full attention, and a few of them got up from their table to come to her side.

"Is everything all right over here, miss?" one of the soldiers asked. He was the largest man in the group, with gray-blue eyes and dark brown hair.

"Everything's fine," Sera answered quickly, nodding and smiling tightly as she did. "Don't mind her, she's just very weary after a long journey."

The soldier ignored her, focusing only on Lucia. "You didn't come here with plans to give the empress any difficulties, did you?"

The *empress*. The thought of Amara having both Kraeshia and Mytica under her little thumb made Lucia sick to her stomach.

"Difficulties?" she said through clenched teeth. "I hope not. But that depends on how quickly you and your empress decide to leave Mytica and never look back."

The guard laughed and glanced at his compatriots. "I'm sure you alone are going to make us leave, yes?"

Gently, as if wary of startling a beast, Sera touched Lucia's arm. "Please sit down," she whispered in her ear. "I'll get your meal. These soldiers have been very kind to us so far, and they've promised that Empress Amara will make sure that the future will be bright for Paelsians. The empress appreciates our wine, and she has a plan to start exporting it overseas. Soon we will all become as wealthy as Auranians!"

"Promises," Lucia said tightly. "Silly promises, nothing but words. You know what else is made up of words? Lies."

"Little girl," the soldier told her, "do what your friend suggests and sit back down. We're under orders to detain anyone with rebel tendencies. I don't think you want that, do you?"

A dark chuckle came from the back of Lucia's throat. "*Little girl*," she repeated, sneering. "You have no idea who you're dealing with."

The soldier laughed too, leaning down to get right in her face. "I know exactly who I'm dealing with. A mere child who's clearly had too much wine. I'm going to give you one more warning. Sit down, and we won't have a problem."

Lucia squeezed her right fist, ready to summon fire. She would burn these insolent men to ashes and wouldn't bother to warn them.

This kingdom belonged to the Damoras. Not to Amara Cortas.

Sera wrung her hands. "Please, do as he says. Sit down and cause no more trouble."

"You think this is trouble? I haven't even *begun* to cause—"

And in one quick, violent burst, a sharp plume of pain exploded from Lucia's core. She cried out, believing at first she'd been gored through her middle, and her deep wails burned her throat as she clutched at her stomach and dropped to the floor.

"What's wrong?" Sera gasped.

"My—oh, no. *No!*" Lucia screamed, the sudden agony now far too much for her to bear . . .

And then the world fell to darkness all around her.

When Lucia woke, she was in a dark room, lying on a firm cot. Sitting in the chair next to her was Sera, holding a cool cloth against her forehead.

Lucia tried to sit up, but failed. Her body was weak, her muscles as sore as if she'd just attempted to trek across three kingdoms in a single day.

Sera eyed her with worry. "I thought you were going to die."

Lucia stared at her, the horrible knowledge she'd gained in the tavern coming back to her in sharp, jagged pieces. "I'm still alive. I think."

"Oh, you're alive all right. And you're damn lucky, too. When the Kraeshians arrived yesterday, there was a man—a Paelsian who patronized the tavern almost nightly—who stood up to the occupying soldiers. Guess what they did to reward his bravery? They drowned him in a bucket of water. The rest of us aren't so foolish."

Lucia stared at her, horrified. "This is wrong. Those soldiers— Amara—they shouldn't be here. They *can't* be here. I need to stop them."

"I think you have more important things to think about. Like finding that friend of yours?"

She eyed the girl warily. "How do you know finding him is so important to me?"

Sera sighed, then took the damp cloth away. She placed it on the side of a basin, then reached for a glass of water, which she brought to Lucia's lips. Momentarily forgetting her suspicions about Sera's preoccupation with Kyan, Lucia drank eagerly, grateful to be able to gulp down the cool liquid, which tasted like life itself to her parched throat.

"I understand why you might be angry with him," Sera said. "Men are stupid and selfish. They're not the ones who need to be responsible. They can have their fun with whomever, then wander off to the next girl who looks at them twice."

"Trust me," Lucia said with a weak scoff, "it wasn't like that with Kyan."

Sera took the empty water glass away and put a fresh cloth back on Lucia's forehead. "So you just magically found yourself with child, did you?"

Lucia stared at her, mouth open in shock. "How do you—?"

"How do I know?" Sera laughed nervously. "I helped you into bed. I removed your robes so you wouldn't overheat. The condition you're in would have been obvious to a blind man."

Lucia stared at her a moment longer, as Sera reached down to press her right hand to her belly. She looked down at Sera's hand, and as she took in the silhouette of her body covered in the canvas bed sheet, her eyes widened.

The last time she'd examined her stomach, it had been flat, and her gradually fading magic and morning nausea had been the only signs of her pregnancy.

But something had changed in the time between finding Kyan's crystal and entering the tavern. Because what Lucia stared at now, with horror in her eyes, was that very same stomach, but it was no longer flat like it was when she'd left the Sanctuary.

Instead, what she looked upon now was a great swell at her middle, an impossibly large belly. And it belonged to her.

CHAPTER 11

JONAS

THE SILVER SEA

Slowly, light returned to his world, and Jonas opened his eyes. Olivia stared down at him, her eyes warm and welling with relief.

"I'm glad to see you've finally returned to us," she said.

He groaned and stretched his arms. "How long was I out?"

"Four days."

His eyes shot wide open, and he sat up with a jerk. "Four days?"

She grimaced. "You weren't unconscious the entire time, if that helps. There were times when you woke, delirious and flailing about."

"No, that actually doesn't help at all." Jonas jumped up from the cot and stumbled to the mirror. The strange spiral, much more intricate and detailed in its design than the simple symbol for air magic, was still there. He'd hoped it had just been a bad dream.

"I have the mark of a Watcher," he said.

"So, you know what it is."

"Phaedra had one." The Watcher who'd sacrificed her immortal life to save his had proven who and what she was by showing Jonas her mark. Hers had been different, though. It had been the same shape, but it had been a mark of gold that swirled and moved upon her skin as if to prove its magical origins. "And I know you have one too."

"I do." Olivia opened her cloak just a little to show him the edge of the golden mark upon her dark skin. He'd only seen flashes of it when she'd changed into her hawk form.

Jonas turned from the mirror to look into her emerald eyes. "I'm not going to beg you, Olivia. I'm simply going to ask you to please tell me more about this, about the prophecy there is about me. I've tried to deny its reality, but now I need to know. What's happening to me? Am I . . ." He grappled to put his thoughts into words. "Am I turning into one of you?"

The thought was so ludicrous that he wanted to retrieve his words after he'd spoken them. But what else was he supposed to think?

Olivia twisted her hands, and for a moment, he thought she might try to escape, to turn into her hawk form and fly away to avoid his questions. Instead, she sighed and came to sit on the edge of his cot while he stood tensely by the porthole.

"Not exactly," she said. "But you are a rare mortal indeed, Jonas Agallon. One touched by our magic at two very vulnerable times in your life—both when you were moments from death. With me, when I healed your shoulder, and with Phaedra, after you'd been stabbed by the Limerian soldier. You don't know how rare that is."

Those were two moments in his life he'd prefer to forget. "Perhaps not. So tell me."

"I was there when Phaedra gave her life for yours—as a hawk, I watched from the top of another tent."

His took a sharp breath in. "You did?"

She nodded grimly. "I watched with horror as Xanthus ended her life, watched her turn back to the magic we're all created from. And I watched as some of that magic entered you, only moments past the point when you would have died without her intervention."

"I . . . I didn't feel anything."

"No, you wouldn't have. You shouldn't have. And it wouldn't have made any difference at all if not for the fire Kindred's own magic rising up nearby. It worked to strengthen Phaedra's magic within you. But that wouldn't have been enough for *this* to happen." Olivia nodded at his mark, which he now scratched absently. "I used earth magic to heal your shoulder when you were, again, on the brink of death, and I watched as you absorbed it like a sponge absorbing water. That magic has remained within you, joining with Phaedra's, just as Timotheus foresaw."

Jonas tried to understand, tried to deny this, tried to stop his heart from beating like the wings of a trapped bird within his chest. But then it suddenly occurred to him that he shouldn't want to deny such incredible news.

"I have *elementia* within me," he said, his voice raspy. "That means I can use it to fight Kyan and to cast Amara away from the shores of Mytica." The more he considered this possibility, the more excited he became. "I need to go above and tell the others. They must be so confused about what happened—what I did to Felix. But this is amazing, Olivia. This will make all the difference in the world."

He was a witch! A male witch! He had denied the existence of *elementia* and those who wielded it all his life, yet now he had this very magic at his fingertips.

Olivia caught his arm as he made for the door. "It's not that easy, Jonas. Timotheus didn't foresee you as a practitioner of magic, only as a vessel for it."

"A vessel? Impossible. You witnessed what I did. I threw Felix across the deck with . . . air magic, yes?"

"That's true. But that was an anomaly. It was merely a sign that this magic within you has matured, and that expenditure of energy alone rendered you unconscious for four days."

He shook his head. Frustration stirred within him, eating away at his excitement. "I don't understand."

Olivia loosened her grip on his arm. "I know, and I apologize for your confusion. Timotheus keeps his knowledge very close, since he doesn't trust many immortals, not even me. He hasn't even shared the extent of your prophecy with me for fear that I'd tell you and you'd try to avoid it." Her jaw clenched. "I've already said too much."

He groaned. "You say just enough to drive me mad with curiosity and dread."

"You can't tell anyone about this."

"Can't I?" He pointed at the door. "Everyone on deck saw me do that. What am I supposed to do? Deny it?"

"Yes, actually." She raised her chin. "I have explained to them that it was my doing. That I saw Felix from above hit you, and the reason I am here is to protect you. Of course they believed me."

He stared at her. "They believe that you intervened with your own magic."

"Yes."

"And I'm not to say anything about this."

"No. Not a word." Her expression turned earnest. "It's too dangerous. There are those who would target you, knowing that you're a mortal filled with immortal magic."

"Immortal magic that I can't access." He stared down at his fist, remembering how it had glowed above deck.

"You don't believe me, so you must see for yourself." She

gestured to the door. "Go ahead and try to break open this door with the air magic you so easily channeled the other day with Felix."

It sounded like a challenge. Jonas looked past Olivia and furrowed his brow with concentration as he raised his hand toward the door. He focused on the attempt to summon this magic within him so hard that his hand began to tremble, his arm began to shake . . . but nothing happened.

"It means nothing," he grunted. "I simply need to practice."

"Perhaps," Olivia allowed gently. "I only know what little I've been told."

Disappointed, Jonas let his arm to drop to his side. "Of course, we wouldn't want anything to be too easy for me. Being a witch, harnessing *elementia* at will . . . wouldn't want that, would we?"

"Actually, it would have been incredibly useful to you."

He glared at her. "You're not helping."

"Apologies." Olivia grimaced. "The others are concerned about you. They'll be pleased to know that you've finally woken up."

Jonas went to the porthole and looked out at the expanse of sea. "How much farther to Paelsia?"

"We're nearly there."

"I slept almost the whole way." He let out a shaky breath as he tried to come to terms with everything he'd learned. Denial would waste time they didn't have. "What have I missed?"

"Not that much, actually. Taran continues to sharpen his blade in anticipation of killing Prince Magnus, Felix still suffers from his sickness of the sea, Ashur remains in his quarters much of the time, meditating, and Nic lurks around, and when the prince emerges, he watches him in a rather curious manner."

"I did ask Nic to keep an eye on our resident prince. Best not to trust a Kraeshian, not even one who claims not to be our enemy."

Jonas blew out a breath as he tightened the ties on his shirt. "All right, nearly to Paelsia. Good."

"Good?" she repeated.

He nodded firmly. "If there's a prophecy that requires me to be a full vessel of *elementia*, I want to know what it is as soon as possible. And that's not going to happen while we're stuck at sea, is it?"

"No," she allowed. "It's not. But truly, Jonas, I know nothing more than that. I'm so sorry."

He nodded with a single jerk of his head. "Whatever it is, I can handle it. I'm sure I've handled much worse in the past."

To this, Olivia had no reply at all.

Jonas tried very hard not to let that trouble him.

CHAPTER 12

MAGNUS

PAELSIA

Since the journey to Basilia would take at least three days from the Reaches on horseback, there was no time to waste with constant stops for a dying king and an old woman. Selia arranged for an enclosed carriage to carry her and her son.

When Magnus suggested that Cleo ride with them inside instead of on horseback, so she wouldn't have to face the bracing cold, he was rewarded with a piercing look.

That would be a "no."

Gaius directed them on a path that would take them each night through a town with an inn, where they rested, ate, and slept in separate locked rooms.

Seven long nights had gone by without falling asleep with Cleo in his arms, but each night he dreamed of her and the cottage in the woods. In waking hours, he chose not to share this with her. He didn't want her to get a swelled head about her effect on him, so he kept his near-constant want to touch and kiss her to himself.

In the last village they rested, Enzo and Milo's task was to fetch the group clothes befitting innocuous travelers passing through Paelsia. They succeeded in finding cotton frocks for Selia and Cleo and plain leather trousers and canvas tunics for themselves, Magnus, and Gaius.

Magnus looked at his cream-colored tunic with distaste. "Didn't they have black?"

"No, your highness," Enzo said.

"Dark gray?"

"No. Only this color and a robin's egg blue. I didn't feel that you would favor the blue." Enzo cleared his throat. "I can go back to the shop."

He sighed. "No, it's fine. I will make do with this."

At least his cloak and trousers were black.

He emerged, ready to begin the last leg of their journey to the west coast city, to see that Cleo, looking like a beautiful peasant girl in her simple dress, was smiling at him from next to her horse.

"You look like a Paelsian," she commented.

"No need for insults, princess," he growled back, but fought his grin as they mounted their horses and started moving.

A small eternity later, which was actually no more than half a day, they finally—and thankfully—arrived at their destination.

Magnus had heard many stories about Basilia, the closest thing Paelsia had to a capital city. The city served ships visiting Trader's Harbor and stir-crazy crew members eager to disembark their vessels in search of food, drink, and women.

The stories rang true.

At first glance—and smell—Basilia was vastly overpopulated and stunk of both human waste and corruption. Dozens of ships were docked in the harbor, their crews flooding the shores and mingling in the streets, taverns, inns, markets, and brothels of the seaside city. And it seemed every bit as hot as Auranos at the height of summer.

"Disgusting."

Magnus glanced over to see that King Gaius had opened the carriage's window to peer out at the city center with distaste. His eyes were bloodshot, and the dark circles beneath them looked like fresh bruises against the sickly paleness of his complexion.

"I despise this place," he said.

"Really?" Magnus replied, guiding his horse alongside the carriage. "I find it rather charming."

"No, you don't."

"I do. I like this . . . local color."

"You're not nearly as good of a liar as you might believe."

"I suppose I can only aspire to be as accomplished at deceit as you have been."

The king glared at him, then shifted his gaze to Cleo, who was riding in front of Magnus and behind the guards. "Princess, if I recall correctly, it was a market not so far from this very city where you found yourself with Lord Aron Lagaris and the wine seller's son he killed, yes?"

Magnus immediately grew tense as he looked to the princess for her response. She didn't reply for several seconds, but he could see her shoulders were tense through the thin material of her dress.

"That was a long time ago," she said finally.

"Imagine how differently things might have turned out had you not been lusting after wine that day," the king continued. "Nothing would be as it is now, would it?"

"No," she said, glancing over her shoulder to meet his gaze. "For instance, you would not have fallen to your near-death after forfeiting your kingdom to a woman. And I wouldn't be watching your failure with the greatest joy in my heart."

Magnus fought a smile as he eyed his father, waiting for his rebuttal.

The only reply was the shuttering of the window, blocking the view of his father's face.

The carriage rolled to a stop at a place called the Hawk and Spear Inn that, though it stank slightly of sweat and a mysterious kind of musk, Magnus deemed the most acceptable establishment in town. King Gaius, assisted out of the carriage and into the inn by Milo and Enzo, and trailed by Selia, quickly bribed the innkeeper to evict all of his guests so that the royal party could have ultimate privacy.

As the former guests filed out in a parade of grumbles, Magnus watched Cleo look around at the Paelsian inn's meeting hall with displeasure. It was a low-ceilinged, large room that had many worn wooden chairs and chipped tables at which guests could eat and lounge with their companions.

"Not up to your high standards?" Magnus asked.

"It's fine," she replied

"It's not an Auranian inn with feather beds, imported linens, and golden chamber pots. But it seems acceptably clean and comfortable to me."

Cleo turned from a table into which someone had roughly carved a set of initials. The glimmer of a smile touched her lips. "Yes, to a Limerian, I suppose it would."

"Indeed." The princess's lips were far too distracting, so Magnus turned and joined his father and grandmother, who stood by the large windows looking out at the stables where their horses were being tended to.

"So now what to do we do?" Magnus asked his grandmother.

"I've asked the innkeeper's wife to go to the tavern down the road and deliver a message to my old friend to come here," Selia said.

"You can't go there yourself?"

"She might not recognize me. Also, this is not a conversation to have where there are curious ears likely to overhear. The magic I seek must be protected at any cost." She put a hand on Gaius's arm. There was a sheen of perspiration on the king's forehead, and he leaned against the wall as if it was the only thing keeping him vertical.

"And until then what shall we do?" Gaius asked in a voice that had weakened substantially since their arrival.

"You will rest," Selia told him.

"There's no time for rest," he said grimly. "Perhaps I will inquire if there's a carpenter nearby who can create a coffin in which to transport me back to Limeros."

"Come now, Father," Magnus said, allowing himself a wry smile. "I'm happy to do that for you. You should do as Grandmother says and rest."

The king glared at him but didn't speak again.

"I'll take you to your room." Selia put her arm around her son, leading him through the hall, toward the stairs, and up to the rooms on the second floor.

"Excellent idea," Cleo said with a yawn. "I'm going upstairs to my room as well. Please alert me if and when your grandmother's friend arrives."

Magnus watched her leave, then nodded at Enzo to follow her. He'd asked the guard to take extra care in watching over the princess and keeping her safe. Enzo was one of the few he trusted with the task.

"What shall I do?" Milo asked Magnus.

Magnus scanned the hall, which also contained a small bookcase full of ratty-looking books, nothing like the vast selection he'd come to value in the Auranian palace library.

"Patrol the neighborhood," Magnus said, plucking a random book off the shelf. "Be sure that no one has yet realized that the former king of Mytica is temporarily residing here."

Milo left the inn, and Magnus tried to focus on reading a tome about the history of wine production in Paelsia, which mentioned nothing about the earth magic that was surely responsible for the drink, or the laws preventing export to anywhere but Auranos.

After thirty pages of the dreck, the innkeeper's wife, a small woman who seemed to have a constant, nervous smile fixed to her face, returned with another woman who was older, with lines around her eyes and mouth, utterly ordinary in appearance, and wearing a drab, unfashionable gown. This must be the woman Selia asked for, Magnus thought.

As the innkeeper's wife disappeared into the kitchen, the older woman glanced around the seemingly vacant inn until her gaze fell on Magnus.

"So you're the answer to all our current problems, are you?" he asked.

"Depends what your problems are, young man," she replied curtly. "I would like to know why you called me here?"

"It wasn't him, it was me," Selia said, descending the wooden staircase at the far end of the hall that led to the private rooms on the second floor. "And it's because I'm in search of an old friend. Do you recognize me after all these years?"

For an utterly silent and excruciatingly long moment, the woman stared at Selia with a strange mixture of fire and ice in her eyes. Just as Magnus began to fear they'd made a grave error in trusting his grandmother, the woman's cheeks stretched into a big smile, cheerful wrinkles fanning out from the corners of her eyes.

"Selia Damora," she cooed in the candlelight, her tone much

gentler than when she'd first entered the inn. "My sweet goddess above, how I have missed you!"

The two women rushed to each other and embraced.

"Shall I summon the others?" Magnus asked. The sooner his grandmother got what she needed from this woman, the sooner they could leave this place.

"No, this doesn't require a group discussion," Selia said without tearing her gaze away from her friend. "I have missed you as well, Dariah."

"Where have you been all this time? I lost count of how many years had passed so long ago."

"All that matters is that I'm here now. Frankly, I'm a little surprised you're still in Basilia after all this time."

"I could never give up the profits of my tavern—each year is better than the last. So many sailors with coin to spend and thirst to quench."

"Many thirsts, I'm sure."

Dariah winked. "Exactly." She turned toward Magnus. "And who is this young man?"

"This is my grandson, Magnus. Magnus, this is my friend Dariah Gallo."

"A pleasure." Magnus forced the best smile he could onto his face, but he knew it would look more like a grimace.

"Oh, my. Your grandson has grown so very tall and handsome."

Selia smiled. "Yes, grandsons sometimes do that by the time they reach eighteen."

Dariah swept her wrinkled gaze over the length of him. "If I were younger . . ."

"If you were younger, you would have to fight his pretty young wife for his attentions."

Dariah laughed. "And perhaps I'd win."

Magnus suddenly longed to return to the book about Paelsian wine.

Selia joined her friend in her laughter, then once again adopted a serious but good-natured tone. "I haven't only come to Basilia for a reconnection between old friends. I need information on how to acquire the bloodstone."

Dariah raised her eyebrows. "Goodness, Selia, you waste no time."

"I have no time to waste. My power has faded over the years, and my son is dying."

In the stretch of silence that followed, Magnus stayed quiet. This stone, if it was real, sounded like something that could aid him in increasing his power, like the Kindred.

Selia drew Dariah over toward the bookshelf. She motioned for her to sit down on a wooden bench next to her, then took the other witch's hands in hers. "There is no choice. I need it."

"You know I don't have it."

"No. But you know who does."

Dariah shook her head. "I can't do this."

"I'm asking you to contact him—I know you can find him. He needs to arrive as quickly as possible."

A thousand questions prodded at Magnus, but he stayed silent, listening.

Power like this potentially delivered right into his very hands. It sounded much simpler than the complicated process of finding the Kindred.

The witch's expression darkened. "He'll never let you have it, not even for a moment."

Selia's grip on her friend's hands tightened. "Let me handle him when he gets here."

"I don't know . . ."

Selia's eyes narrowed. "I know it's been a very long time, but I feel I must mention the favor you owe me. A favor you promised to repay in full."

Dariah looked down at the floor.

Magnus watched, barely breathing. The witch slowly looked up again, her face pale. She nodded with a small jerk of her head. "It will take time to draw him here."

"He has three days. Will that be a problem?"

The witch's jaw tensed as she rose to her feet. "No."

"Thank you." Selia stood and kissed Dariah on both of her cheeks. "I knew you would help me."

The smile of their greeting was now nothing more than a memory. "I will alert you the moment he arrives."

Dariah didn't linger—with a last look at Selia and Magnus, she left the inn.

"Well," Magnus said after all had gone silent again. "That must have been quite the favor you did for your friend."

"It was." Selia glanced at Magnus, a small smile on her lips. "I shall now check on your father. His health is my only concern right now. Soon, when my magic is restored and he is well again, we can face the other obstacles that stand in our way."

"I will strive for patience," Magnus said, knowing he would surely fail at this.

By now, night had fallen, and Magnus retired to his small private room. It had a full-size bed rather than the unacceptable cots in the communal sleeping area down the hall. The window gave him a second-floor view of the street outside, lit with lanterns and, even after nightfall, busy with citizens and visitors to the city.

There was a soft knock at his door. "Enter," Magnus said, knowing it could only be one of the four people with whom he'd traveled to Paelsia.

The door opened slowly, and as the visitor revealed herself, Magnus's heart began to thud hard against his chest. Cleo peered in at him.

He stood up and met her in the doorway. "My grandmother's friend was here."

"Already?" Her brows raised. "And?"

"And . . ." He shook his head. "It seems that we are forced to wait here for three days."

"She can get the bloodstone, though?"

"Yes," Magnus replied. "I've only just been reunited with my grandmother, but she strikes me as the sort of woman who can get pretty much anything she wants."

"And this is all so that this magical stone will save your father's life." Cleo said this without emotion, but a hardness had formed behind her aquamarine eyes.

"He doesn't deserve to live," Magnus said, agreeing with what was left unspoken. "But this must be a necessary measure on the way to our ultimate goal."

"Finding Lucia."

"Yes. And breaking your curse."

She nodded. "I suppose there's no other way."

He watched her carefully. "Was it only information you came to my room seeking, or is there something else you require this evening?"

Cleo raised her chin so she could look him directly in his eyes. "Actually, I need your help."

"With what?"

"All the riding we've been doing. It's done horrific things to my hair."

Magnus raised a brow. "And . . . you came here needing my help to chop it all off so it's no longer a problem?"

"As if you'd allow that." She grinned. "You're obsessed with my hair."

"I'd hardly call it an obsession." He twisted a lock of the warm golden silk around his finger. "More like an often painful distraction."

"I apologize for your suffering. But you will not be cutting my hair, tonight or ever. The innkeeper's wife was kind enough to give me this." She presented him with a silver-handled hairbrush.

He took it from her, looking at it quizzically. "You want me to . . . ?"

Cleo nodded. "Brush my hair."

Just the thought of it was ludicrous. "Now that I'm forced to dress as a common Paelsian, you mistake me for your servant?"

She shot him a determined look. "It's not as if I can ask Milo or Enzo . . . or, for goddess's sake, your father or grandmother to help me."

"What about the innkeeper's wife?"

"Fine." Cleo snatched the brush back from him with a scowl. "I'll go ask her."

"No, no." He let out a sigh, half-amused now. "I'll help."

Without hesitation, she returned the brush to him. "I'm glad to hear it."

He stepped aside to make way for her. She walked in, sat on the end of his cot, and looked at him expectantly. "Close the door," she said.

"Not a good idea." Magnus left the door ajar and slowly came to sit behind her. Awkwardly and with great trepidation, as if about to skin and clean an animal for the first time, he held the delicate brush up to her hair. "I've never done this before."

"There's a first time for everything."

What a ridiculous sight it must have been: Magnus Damora,

son of the King of Blood, brushing a young woman's hair at her request.

And yet . . .

Whenever Magnus took on a task, he preferred to do so thoroughly, to the fullest extent of his abilities. He applied himself in the same way now as he took up a lock of Cleo's long, silky hair in his grip and slid the brush down the length of it. The warmth of her hair slid through his fingers, making a pleasant shiver course down his spine.

"You're right," he told her, his voice low. "Horribly tangled. Irreparably so, I think."

He was only teasing her—her hair was perfect, just as it always was—but then he came to the first knot.

She winced. "Ouch."

"Apologies." He froze in place, but then frowned. "However, you *did* ask me to do this."

"Yes, of course I know that!" She sighed. "Please continue. I'm used to being tortured by my attendants, and they're used to ignoring my wails of pain. You can't possibly hurt me any more than they have. Only Nerissa has the skill to do this without pain."

"Yes, I've heard how very skilled Nerissa is," Magnus said, unable to keep from grinning. Now, having a more complete picture of Cleo's hair-brushing history, he tackled the task at hand with more determination. "So much hair, so many opportunities for tangles. Why do women bother?"

"Perhaps I should braid it like a Paelsian chieftain?"

"Yes, I imagine that would be a look befitting an Auranian princess, even one forced to wear an ugly cotton dress," he said drily, not letting on how amused he was by the image. "Every girl in Mytica would want to copy it." As gently as possible, he worked the brush through another section of hair that currently resembled a pale yellow bird's nest. "You should know, I mean to claim the bloodstone for myself."

"I assumed so," she replied.

That surprised him. "You did?"

She nodded, and the hair slipped out of his hands, covering the tantalizingly bare nape of her neck. "I saw it in your eyes when Selia first mentioned it. It was the same look I saw in your father's eyes."

"And what look is that?"

"It doesn't matter."

Magnus put the brush down. Gently, he guided Cleo by the shoulders until she was mostly facing him, then took her chin gently in his hand. "Yes, it does. What look did my father and I share?"

She met his gaze with hers, her expression now wary. "A look of icy greed, like this stone is something you would kill for."

"I see."

She searched his face, as if seeking answers there. "In that moment, you looked so cold and so much like your father—I . . . didn't like it."

All his life, he'd been told how much he was like his father—in both looks and temperament. Eventually he'd learned to stop fighting those comparisons, though they never ceased to unsettle him.

"I must admit, lately I find I *do* need to be like my father. There are certain situations that practically require me to be as cold and ruthless as possible. If I were to have shed tears over every life I've taken over the last year, I'd have dried to a husk long ago. So, yes. I suppose I am quite like my father in many ways."

"No." Cleo shook her head. "That's impossible."

"Why do you say that?"

"Honestly?" She drew closer to him, cupping his face in her hands. "Because I've never wanted to do this to your father."

She brushed her lips softly against his. A small, tortured groan came from the back of his throat as he forced himself to make fists with his hands at his sides to stop himself from taking hold of her immediately.

"Princess . . ."

"*Cleiona . . .*" she corrected him, her lips still far too dangerously close to his. "Although, I must admit that I no longer fully appreciate having been given the full name of an immortal who stole and murdered for her power."

"True leaders often must be ruthless enough to steal and murder. If they don't, someone else will."

"A charming philosophy, all too true, I'm afraid. But perhaps we can think of something else for you to call me when we're alone together."

He raised a brow. "I'll consider it."

"Good." She bit her bottom lip, drawing his attention back to her mouth. "Now close the door. And lock it."

"That is a very, very dangerous suggestion."

"Or leave it open. Perhaps I don't care." Cleo kissed him again, parting her lips this time. He found his composure and restraint slipping away with breakneck speed as her tongue slid against his.

"I truly don't wish to tell you no," he whispered against her lips.

"Then don't."

Magnus groaned again as her hands slipped down his chest and beneath his tunic to slide over his abdomen and chest with no barrier between them. He gripped her waist and pressed her down upon the bed, covering her completely with his body. She was so small, yet so strong, so passionate.

How could this callous world create a creature so beautiful? If her beauty wasn't a gift from the goddess, it surely had to be a gift from her mother . . .

Suddenly, Magnus jerked upward, covering his mouth with the back of his hand.

"What?" Cleo gasped, her cheeks flushed.

He pushed up to his feet and gathered his cloak. "I need a drink. I'm going to investigate the tavern up the road."

Cleo lay on his bed, watching him, her hair a half-mussed arrangement of golden curls cascading over her shoulders all the way to her waist.

Utterly, *painfully*, tempting.

"I understand," she said quietly.

He was about to leave without another word, but he turned back to face her.

"Before I leave, know this. When the day comes that this curse is broken, I promise you that the door to whatever room we're in will be locked, and I'll allow nothing or no one to interrupt us."

With that, he turned away and left her there, staring back at him.

Yes, he desperately needed a drink.

"Wine," Magnus grunted at the barkeep as he entered the shabby but lively tavern known as the Purple Vine. He slid several coins across the bar. "Make sure you refill my glass whenever you see it empty," he said. "And no conversation."

The barkeep smirked, then greedily swept the coins off the counter and into a ratty old purse. "Very well."

The barkeep did as Magnus requested and paid much attention to the level of liquid in his cup. As Magnus drank gulp after gulp of the sweet Paelsian wine, the night began to look much brighter.

The last time he'd tasted wine, he'd returned to the Limerian palace to find his wife making a speech. She was soon interrupted by enemies who barely let him escape with his life. After that experience, he'd considered completely swearing off the drink.

Cleo's visit to his room tonight had certainly made him revoke that vow.

"Our entertainment might put you in a better mood, friend," the barkeep said, despite Magnus's request for silence. Magnus was about to reproach him when the barkeep made a nodding gesture toward the middle of the tavern. "I promise you that the Goddess of Serpents is rather a spectacular sight to behold."

Goddess of Serpents? Magnus rolled his eyes and pointed at his glass. "More."

Someone on the other side of the huge tavern hushed the boisterous crowd as the barkeep poured more wine into Magnus's cup.

"All will worship at the feet of our resident beauty!" the man across the room called out. "Bow before her incredible power. And welcome the Goddess of Serpents!"

The crowd responded with great hoots and hollers as a young, dark-haired woman, scarcely clothed, with a large white snake draped around her neck, appeared on a small stage. Next to the stage was a trio of musicians who began to play an exotic tune that sounded more savage than intoxicating to Magnus. As the music began its first crescendo, the young woman began to writhe about in what might be considered by some to be a dance, but to Magnus it looked more like the solicitations of a courtesan.

He drained his glass, uncertain how many times he'd done so since arriving. It didn't matter. Not now, when things seemed so much better to him than they had earlier, when desire for Cleo had nearly blinded him to its dangers.

Perhaps they *should* share a room, he thought now as a he watched this strange woman twist her way across the stage. Perhaps seeking an elixir to prevent pregnancy would be sufficient protection.

Or perhaps he should focus on the fact that his kingdom had been stolen, his father was near death with his grandmother wishing to save him with a magic rock, his sister was aligned with a man focused on burning his way through Mytica, and Cleo had a deadly curse upon her. The fact that he was slowly going mad with desire for his wife truly was the least of his concerns.

Suddenly, something caught his eye: a flash of red hair. Now that shade of hair was possibly a rarer sight than Cleo's in Paelsia. He couldn't help but be reminded of Nicolo Cassian, the only person he'd ever met with hair that unfortunate color.

Magnus chuckled into his wine at the thought. No, Nic likely was still safely—or not so safely, Magnus really didn't care either way—over in Kraeshia, the idiot having volunteered to join Jonas on his failed mission to kill the king.

He turned his attention again to the Goddess of Serpents. Just as he thought he was starting to understand the rhythm of her movements, she paused, waving at the musicians to stop playing.

"Is it you?" she asked, the room now silent. She was clearly addressing someone specific, but Magnus couldn't see him from his seat at the bar. All he could see was the growing excitement on the dancer's painted face as her expression grew more certain. "Jonas!" she called now with more confidence. "Jonas, is that really you? My darling, I thought you were dead!"

Jonas?

Another odd coincidence—must be.

The snake dancer stepped down from the stage and into the tavern crowd, from which she pulled a young, dark-haired man.

Magnus froze. He craned his neck, trying to see around the heads of other patrons. The dancer threw her arms around the young man, twirling around in her visitor's embrace until he faced in Magnus's direction.

Shocked and open-mouthed, Magnus stared at the sight before him.

It was Jonas Agallon. Here, in the very same tavern as Magnus.

"What are the odds?" spoke a familiar voice next to him, articulating his very thoughts.

A wave of displeasure washed over Magnus even before he turned to discover what he already knew: that red-headed Nicolo Cassian now stood directly beside him. "You."

Nic poked him in the shoulder, letting out a bark of a laugh as a splash of ale spilled over the edge of his large tankard. "It seems as though fate is finally kicking you in the arse, don't you think, your highness? And I'm more than happy to bear witness to it."

"Your visit to Kraeshia did nothing to diminish your charm, I see," Magnus said, dismayed that he drunkenly slurred his words every bit as much as Nic did.

Nic smiled, but his unfocused eyes held no humor at all. "Prince Magnus Damora, I'd like you to meet a good friend of mine."

Annoyed at the use of his name in a public venue, Magnus turned, expecting to see some lowly rebel or another. But instead he was met with a face he saw only in his nightmares.

"Theon Ranus," he managed. The pleasant, tingling warmth of the wine he'd consumed disappeared in an instant, leaving him utterly, devastatingly cold as he faced this apparition.

"You're mistaken," said the young man, a dead ringer for the first person Magnus ever killed. With cold eyes filled with nothing but single-minded hatred, he pulled out a knife and held it to Magnus's throat. "I'm his brother, you son of a bitch."

CHAPTER 13

CLEO

PAELSIA

"Where are you going, princess?"

The words halted her at the main door of the Hawk and Spear Inn. Cleo looked over her shoulder to see Enzo standing in the shadows behind her.

"I'm going to the tavern at the end of the road," she said. "Not that it's any of your concern."

"It's late."

"And . . . ?"

Enzo straightened his shoulders. "I think it's best that you stay here, where it's safe, princess."

"I appreciate your opinion, but I disagree. Magnus is there, and I'm surprised and rather dismayed that you didn't go with him. What if he's recognized?"

"The prince made it very clear to me that my sole duty is to ensure your safety, princess."

She blinked rapidly, as if trying to wink away her surprise at this interesting revelation. "Really. Well, that makes things much simpler. You will come with me to fetch the prince and ensure that neither of us are put in harm's way."

She allowed him no time to argue as she turned and exited the inn, leaving the door open behind her for Enzo to follow and pulling up the hood of her cloak to cover her hair and shield her face.

Enzo trailed close behind her without further argument as she eyed the people on the street, the carriages moving past, the sound of horse hooves clopping against the gravel road. She followed the sound of drunken laughter and music toward the tavern that surely had to be Magnus's destination. Above the large wooden doors was a bronze sculpture of a bunch of grapes on a vine.

She read the sign. "The Purple Vine. How appropriate a name for a tavern in Paelsia. And how deeply uninspired."

The prince was so drawn to the taste of wine that he didn't care what would happen if anyone recognized his royal face. He loved to drink so much that he was willing to risk getting killed in the midst of a stormy brew of Paelsians. And what a truly stupid way to die that would be, she thought.

"I've heard of this place," Enzo said, looking up at the entrance. "Nerissa once worked here as a barmaid."

She raised a brow at him. "Really?"

He nodded. "She said it was an interesting experience."

"I had no idea she'd lived in Paelsia."

"She's lived everywhere, it seems. So unlike me, who has never ventured beyond Limeros until now. How boring she must find me."

"I assure you she finds you anything but boring." To hear Enzo speak of her friend made Cleo's heart ache. She had no doubt Nerissa could look after herself, better than any other girl—and possibly boy—she'd ever known, but . . . Cleo couldn't help but worry for her safety. She hated the thought that she might be in danger while being forced to work close to Amara.

Cleo took a deep breath as she and Enzo pushed through the front doors. Inside the tavern were at least two hundred smelly, dirty patrons.

She scanned the faces, searching for Magnus in the crowd.

This tavern was unlike anything she'd experienced during her two previous visits to Paelsia. Her knowledge of the area was limited to poor markets, decrepit villages, and wide expanses of wasteland.

And the locked sheds of angry, vengeful rebels, she reminded herself.

This place, despite its rather rough and shabby interior, looked like it could exist in Hawk's Brow, the largest city in Auranos. Lighting the large room were dozens upon dozens of candles and lanterns set up along the bar and tables. Hanging on the high ceiling above were several large wooden wheels, each one set with candles on the spokes. The floors were nothing more than hard-packed earth; the tables and chairs were made of roughly chiseled wood.

To Cleo's left was a small stage upon which a young woman with black hair and golden streaks painted upon her tanned skin writhed around rather explicitly. Around her neck was a large white boa constrictor, the likes of which Cleo had only ever seen in illustrated books.

"Enzo, please, just help me look for Magnus. Start with the areas with the most wine."

"Yes, your highness."

Cleo drew the hood of her cloak closer to cover her hair and tried to ignore the leering glances of many of the brutish-looking men who passed her. When she felt someone cup her buttocks from behind, she spun around to punch the offender, but her swinging fist connected only with air.

Furious, she tried to spot whoever had touched her in the

crowd, but she froze in place when she heard a familiar name shouted out.

"Jonas!" It was the painted snake-woman, pausing her performance to run to a young man in the audience. "Jonas, is that really you?"

Cleo, eyes wide, looked toward the stage.

Jonas had returned from Kraeshia. And of all the places in Mytica he could have turned up, he was here!

How could this be?

She turned to look at Enzo, but another face caught her attention instead. A young man strode through the crowd, moving in opposition to the sea of faces turned toward the stage

Bronze hair, tanned skin, tall, and leanly muscled . . .

All she could do was stare, certain that her eyes deceived her.

"Theon," she whispered, the name catching in her throat.

The memory slammed into her then of a moment when everything seemed clear—she loved him, and nothing else mattered. Not his station, not the disapproval of her father, not the stern look that Theon had given her before he kissed her, tinged with fear at the thought that he'd lost her forever.

And then the sound of hoof beats when Magnus and his soldiers arrived.

The pride in her heart as Theon faced Magnus's men and won.

And the horror as she watched the life leave Theon's eyes forever as Magnus stabbed him in the back.

"If your guard had backed off when I told him to, this wouldn't have happened," the son of the King of Blood had said.

"He's not just a guard," she'd whispered in reply. *"Not to me."*

Often, it felt as if it had happened a thousand years ago. Other times, it was as if he'd died only yesterday.

Yet here he was.

"Princess?" Enzo asked, frowning at her look of absolute shock.

Cleo didn't answer him. Her legs were numb as she began to move without thinking, wending her way through the crowd toward him.

Hot tears splashed her cheeks, and she viciously wiped them away.

The crowd thinned this far from the stage, which allowed her to keep her murdered bodyguard in sight. Tight in his grip flashed the glint of a sharp blade.

And then she saw Magnus.

This apparition of the young man she'd loved and lost approached Magnus, who stood at the bar, eyeing Theon with as much disbelief as Cleo did. Then, so quickly she almost didn't see it, Theon grabbed Magnus, hard, and pressed the blade to his throat.

She screamed inwardly, her entire body turned to coldest ice in an instant. She looked now to Magnus, his expression resolute, his jaw tight, his dark eyes void of emotion.

"Cleo?" Someone was blocking her path—a boy with freckles and red hair. "Oh, Cleo! You're here! You're alive!"

"Nic?" She spared him a moment's glance before grabbing his shoulder and digging her fingers in. Behind him, she watched as blood trickled down Magnus's throat from where this ghost from the past dug his dagger into his flesh. "What's going on? Why is this happening?"

Suddenly, a third person approached the silent altercation between Magnus and Theon, which had so far gone unnoticed by the rest of the patrons, whose gazes were still directed toward the stage. It was a young, dark-haired man, broad-chested and heavily muscled, wearing a black eye patch.

He held a chunk of wood in his grip, and with it he hit the ghost of Theon, hard, on the back of his head. The dagger clattered to the floor, and the victim's body slumped, unconscious, next to it.

"Magnus!" Cleo called out.

Finally, Magnus tore his gaze from the young man on the floor to meet Cleo's.

His eyes narrowed. "You shouldn't be here."

She gaped at him. *That* was what he chose to say to her right now?

The brute nodded down at the body. "He's not going to be happy with me when he wakes up."

Cleo rushed to Magnus's side, quickly assuring herself that the wound on his throat was shallow. She spun to face the young man with the eye patch. "Who are you?" she demanded.

He bowed. "Felix Gaebras, lovely young lady. At your service. And who are you?"

"This," Magnus said, gingerly touching his neck, "is Princess Cleiona."

Felix's eyes widened. "Ah, so *this* is the Golden Princess. It all makes sense now."

"And who"—she pointed at the floor with a shaky finger—"is this?"

"That," Felix replied, "is Taran Ranus, Theon's twin brother."

Cleo felt herself go cold. *"His twin brother?"*

Magnus's jaw was tense. "It was so kind of Nic to introduce us tonight, don't you think?"

From next to her, Nic looked down at the unconscious young man, then met her shocked gaze. "I think we all need to talk," he said.

"Clearly!"

"I agree," Magnus said stiffly. "I know a place that is much more private than this. Find Jonas, and come with me, all of you."

Felix leaned down, picked up his unconscious associate, and threw him over his shoulder. "Where are Jonas and the others?

Did the dancer tie him up with her snake and drag him away? I'll go find him."

Cleo didn't wait—she needed fresh air. She needed to breathe normally and bring her heart rate down to a regular pace.

Twin brother, she thought, stunned. *Theon's twin brother.*

Yet Theon had never, not once, mentioned to her that he had a twin brother.

Nic was at her side, swaying slightly with each step he took as Enzo escorted her outside. She glanced over her shoulder to ensure herself that Magnus was close behind.

"You're drunk," she said, turning to Nic and finding herself exceptionally angry with him and with everyone present.

"Extremely. And also extremely happy that you're here." He gave her a big sloppy kiss on the cheek, reminding her of the slobbering puppy her father brought back to her and Emilia after a long stretch of travels. As her heart rate returned to normal, she allowed herself to give in to her overwhelming sense of relief that Nic had returned from Kraeshia alive and well—and that he was here with her again.

Felix exited the tavern, still bearing the weight of Taran Ranus.

Behind him walked Jonas, who scanned the area before his gaze landed on Cleo.

She watched as a smile spread across his handsome face.

"I *knew* you were alive." Jonas quickened his steps to reach her. He grasped her around her waist, and lifted her off the ground, spinning her around in the air. "It's so good to see you."

Any other day, she would be smiling just as wide as the rebel. "Explain to me what is going on."

"Yes," Magnus said, his dark eyes fixated on Jonas. "An explanation for your arrival in this city coinciding with our own would be greatly appreciated."

"I'm shocked to say, it's almost good to see you too, your highness." Jonas gave the prince the edge of a smile.

It wasn't returned.

"Our friend here's getting a bit heavy," Felix commented.

Magnus eyed the unconscious body he carried with a sour look. "Follow me."

Another girl joined their entourage, and Cleo recognized her instantly—she had accompanied Jonas and Lysandra when they were last at the Limerian palace.

Cleo remembered her name: Olivia. But a proper greeting could wait.

She hooked her arm through Nic's as the group followed Magnus back to the inn. "Why are you so drunk tonight?"

"Oh . . . so many reasons. I've recently come to believe you were dead, for one. Therefore, I was going to drown myself in ale to stifle my grief."

"I'm very much alive."

"And I'm very much happy to see that."

She allowed him a smile. "And there are other reasons for your thirst?"

"None that have chosen to join us tonight, but I hesitate to mention that just yet. You've had quite enough of a shock already. I'm sure he'll catch up eventually. He does that."

"You're making no sense."

"No, I'm sure I'm not."

Her meager smile fell away when she glanced at Felix and his burden. "Did Theon"—it hurt to say his name, even after all this time— "ever say a single word to you about having a twin brother?"

Nic shook his head. "Not a word. When I saw Taran at the docks in Kraeshia, I nearly keeled over with shock. Taran doesn't talk about it, but I assume they were estranged. Still, he took the news of his brother's death hard."

"Yes, I saw that." She exhaled shakily. "How did he learn it was Magnus who killed Theon?"

Nic shrugged. "I told him, of course."

Her stomach sank at the exact moment her anger began to rise. "Of course you did."

"I should have stayed by your side." He took her hand in his, his drunken expression growing very serious. "I'm sorry I left you alone with him all this time."

Nic didn't know about her feelings for Magnus. Of course Nic didn't know—she'd spent her every breath denying her growing feelings for the prince for a year. "It's all right. I've . . . managed."

"Where should I put him?" Felix indicated his burden when they reached the inn.

"I'm sure we can find a deep hole," Magnus said.

Cleo glared at him, then looked at Felix. "There are empty rooms on the second floor," she said.

Felix disappeared, returning quickly without Taran.

They sat down in the meeting hall, and as Cleo looked around at the group, she couldn't tell whether she was thrilled or horrified by how this night had turned out.

Nic sat next to her at a table, and across from them were Jonas and Olivia. Felix and Magnus sat near the fireplace on the other side of the room near the bookcase, while Enzo remained standing near Cleo.

"When did you arrive?" Magnus asked.

"Today," Jonas replied. "We're still quite in the dark about what's happening here. The only information we have comes from a single Kraeshian soldier who was willing to talk."

"And?"

"He knew very little. Or, at least, very little that would help us. It appears, though, that you are on the run, your highness. And that your father is rather unhappy with how you handled things while he was away."

"That would be an understatement, yes."

Cleo watched Magnus with mild surprise. Despite how drunk he had to be by now, he seemed as sober as a Limerian priest.

"The soldier," Jonas said, nodding somberly at Cleo. "He told us that you were dead. That it happened after you escaped from Amara. That you froze to death."

"I very well could have had I not found shelter at the exact right moment." She averted her eyes, trying to keep from making eye contact with Magnus, but she could still feel his gaze burning into the side of her face.

"You were always a survivor," Jonas said. "Nic despaired, but I had hope. And here you are."

Nic shrugged. "I despair. It's what I do."

"There's so much to tell you," Jonas said. "And I'm sure there's much you have to tell us."

"Far less than you might think," Magnus said. "Amara thinks she's ruling this kingdom now. But she's wrong. And she will be defeated."

"And how do you think you will defeat her?" Jonas asked.

"I thought we might start with the earth Kindred you gave the princess," Magnus said, and Jonas's shoulders tensed. "Do you still have that shiny little chunk of obsidian squirreled away somewhere, princess?"

Oh, yes, she thought as she flinched. *This* was the Magnus she'd once despised—the one who would announce to everyone, seemingly out of spite, that she possessed the Kindred. She'd have to thank him for the reminder.

Nic grunted out a sound of disgust. "Cleo, how have you maintained your sanity being around him this long? To have sustained this unnatural alliance with him . . . there must be *some* reason behind it that you haven't told me."

"Please, Nic," Magnus said. "We're all friends here. Feel free to speak your mind."

"I just did."

Magnus rolled his eyes. "Don't worry your carrot-stained head, Nicolo. The princess continues to tolerate me—just barely—focused solely on reclaiming her throne as soon as Amara is defeated and sent on her merry way. I recently suggested your Golden Princess return to Auranos, but she refused. Don't try to tell me that this was my idea."

Cleo shot him a look as he met her gaze with something like defiance. Then she realized what he was doing.

Nic hated him. Jonas was barely allied with him. And Theon's twin had just tried to kill him.

To reveal that she and Magnus were more than begrudging allies could cause unnecessary stress, especially now that they were all together.

"Believe me, Nic," she finally said. "I look forward to the day when I return to my kingdom. But that day is not today."

"Well, now that that's settled," Magnus said, "let's discuss how to proceed, shall we?"

Felix raised his hand. "I enthusiastically volunteer to kill the empress."

Magnus eyed him with interest. "How do you plan to do that?"

"Now, I know some of you are probably going to suggest I use an arrow, aimed from afar," Felix said eagerly. "But I'd really prefer to do it up close and personal. With my bare hands, if possible. I just want to see the look on her pretty face."

Magnus blinked. "I just remembered that you're the one who sent me the flayed patch of your skin to prove your loyalty."

"I certainly did, your highness."

Cleo watched this young man warily, shocked by his words. Was he insane?

However, he *had* saved Magnus's life back at the tavern, and she was deeply indebted to him for that, so she supposed she would have to spend a bit more time around him, watching him, to see what he was truly like.

There had been a time when she'd wished for Magnus to die for what he'd done to Theon just over a year ago—she had wanted to kill him herself.

And yet, the moment Magnus's life was in danger, she focused nowhere but on the prince. Any need for revenge had fallen away from her months ago, like shedding the skin of her former self.

It wasn't forgiveness that she felt. She still hated the boy Magnus had been that day.

But she'd come to understand him over the months since, perhaps even better than she understood herself.

"There is a threat far greater than Amara in Mytica right now, I'm afraid to say," Jonas said, breaking Cleo's reverie. He was wiping the dancer's kiss marks from his face with a handkerchief handed to him by Olivia, and Cleo couldn't help but find the contrast between this silly act and his solemn tone amusing.

"Let me guess," Magnus said. "You're referring to my sister? I know you must be grieving your friend, Jonas, but there is no sense expending any of your vengeful energies on either Lucia or her companion, Kyan."

Jonas met Magnus's gaze directly. "You don't know, do you?"

"Know what?"

"You've searched for the Kindred. People have died over these crystals. You already revealed in front of everyone that Cleo has one in her possession, and we know that Amara has water and your father has air."

"Yes. This is all known to me, rebel. And we already know that Kyan has the fire Kindred."

"Wrong." Jonas's expression tensed. "Kyan *is* the fire Kindred."

Cleo stared at him, certain she'd heard him wrong. "What do you mean he *is* the fire Kindred?"

"The magic you've been seeking—that we've all be seeking—it can think. It can speak. And it can kill without remorse. And three more just like Kyan are waiting to escape their prisons. They're not magic rocks, princess, they're elemental gods."

The room went silent, and Cleo frantically searched the faces of the others, hoping to find someone rolling their eyes. Hoping this was only an amusing lie to break the tension.

This couldn't possibly be true.

But even Nic nodded his grim agreement.

And at this very moment, right in her pocket, she held one of those very prisons.

She looked at Magnus, his deep frown the only outward sign of his surprise.

"Lucia must have helped him escape the amber orb," Magnus said.

"I think that's obvious," Jonas replied tightly, earning him a dark look from the prince.

Cleo clamped her hands together to stop them from trembling. "Do we know for certain that whatever goals Kyan has are evil? The Kindred could still help us defeat Amara."

"I watched him burn Lys to nothing," Jonas snarled. "Not even a single ash was left when he was through with her." The rebel turned to Magnus. "Kyan is evil. And so is that bitch sister of yours."

Magnus rose to his feet, fists clenched at his sides. "I don't care what's happened, you will not speak that way about Lucia in my presence. I won't allow it."

"No? And do you think you can stop me?" Now Jonas also had his fists clenched, and the two of them drew closer together.

"Perhaps he won't stop you," said a new voice, cutting into the conversation and causing the rebel and the prince to freeze where they were. "But I am certainly willing to try."

With that promise, the King of Blood entered the room.

CHAPTER 14

JONAS

PAELSIA

King Gaius Damora. The King of Blood. Murderer. Sadist, torturer, enslaver, betrayer. Enemy. Target.

And currently standing in the very same room as Jonas.

There had been many surprises this evening—the first being an encounter with Laelia Basilius, to whom Jonas had briefly, and reluctantly, been betrothed—but all of them disappeared from his mind the moment the king entered the room.

Gaius swept his gaze over the group, ending on Jonas. "Jonas Agallon. It's been a long time since I last saw you. I believe it was at my son's wedding."

Jonas found he could do nothing but stare at the man who had killed so many and destroyed so much.

"Magnus . . ." Cleo said from across the room.

"Oh, yes," Magnus said, his tone now void of the outrage over any slurs against his sister. "Did I forget to mention that I'm traveling with my father?"

"You did," Jonas replied tightly.

"Yes," the king agreed. "And it's so good of my son to bring his new friends back here without prior notice."

Jonas fought to keep his composure, to not show how stunned he was. "Not as new as you might think."

King Gaius's skin was pale, his face bruised as if he'd been held down and beaten. He leaned, as if casually, against the wall by the staircase, but there was something to the angle. A weakness, a frailty, that he'd never seen in the man before.

"Go back upstairs," Magnus snapped.

"I don't take orders from you." The king smiled without humor at this. "Tell me, Magnus, do your new friends know we're all on the same side now?"

The very suggestion of an alliance with Gaius rendered Jonas utterly speechless. The others—Nic and Olivia—remained silent as well, their expressions tense.

"Oh?" It was Felix's dry growl, like the warning of a caged beast, that broke the silence. "Did you decide this before or after you allowed Amara to let me take the blame for killing her family?"

The king raised a dark brow and regarded Felix. "I never allowed Amara to do anything. She makes her own choices. By the time I knew what had happened, it was too late to intervene. I was told you were already dead. Otherwise, I would have done whatever I could to free you."

Felix kept his gaze fixed squarely on the king, his single eye bereft of anything except cold malice. "Of course you would have. Why would I ever doubt your word, your highness?"

With a sigh, the gaunt and sickly-looking king turned to Jonas. "You have every reason to hate me. But you must hear me now and realize that together we are strong. We have a common enemy now: Amara Cortas."

"Your *wife*, you mean," Jonas managed to choke out.

"Of necessity and circumstance only. I have no doubt she's already conspiring to have me killed, especially now that she has taken control of Mytica and knows her soldiers far outnumber mine. I have now dedicated myself to fixing some of my more recent mistakes, starting with casting Amara out of this kingdom."

"Sounds like a fine start," Jonas allowed.

The king moved forward slowly, wincing as if sudden movement caused him pain, and stretched his hand out. "I ask that we put our differences aside until this goal is achieved. What do you say?"

If he wasn't so stunned, Jonas would have laughed. The King of Blood had just offered him—the very same person he'd accused of murdering Queen Althea—an alliance.

Jonas looked around at the others, all of whom were staring at him and the king with silent shock. Nic's and Cleo's faces were pale, and Felix's top lip curled with disgust. Olivia kept her eyes emotionless and unreadable as always. Enzo, Cleo's guard who dressed in civilian clothing, stood with his hand resting on the hilt of his sword. In contrast, Magnus had taken a seat and leaned back in his chair, his arms crossed over his chest, his head cocked to one side.

Finally, Jonas gripped the king's hand in his right, meeting his gaze directly. "What do I say, your highness?" With his left hand, he thrust his jeweled dagger into the monster's heart. "I say go to the darklands, you lying son of a bitch."

The king grunted weakly, excruciating pain apparent in the weak sound. Jonas twisted the knife deeper then, until Gaius staggered backward.

Dimly, Jonas heard Nic howl in victory at this act, just as Enzo slammed into him, taking him to the floor. Felix was there in an instant, pulling Enzo off of him. Another one of the king's guards appeared and wrenched Jonas's arms behind him. A flash of blond hair joined the pile—Cleo was trying to pull the second king's guard back from Jonas. Magnus was on his feet, his grim focus on the king. Olivia stood in Jonas's periphery, waiting. She only ever intervened if he was in mortal danger.

The rage Jonas felt, his hatred of the king, buzzed anew within him, making him tremble. As he watched the dying king from his prone position, not a single part of him felt even the slightest fraction of regret.

Finally, he'd been given this chance. And he'd damn well taken it.

"See?" he said, looking up at Magnus. "I keep my promises."

"Yes, I can see that," Magnus said, his attention still on his father, as if curious rather than gratified at this act. "It's just a shame you couldn't have done it before now."

"And what do you mean by that?" Jonas eyed the prince, puzzled as to why he seemed disappointed by the situation at hand. Jonas had done exactly what Magnus had wanted him to do, had accomplished the task that had sent him to Kraeshia in the first place.

"Milo, let Jonas up." Cleo had the unfamiliar guard by his arm.

"He assassinated the king," Milo snapped.

"No," Magnus said. "Death has chosen to take its time when it comes to my father."

"Jonas, look at him," Felix urged.

King Gaius was no longer lying there on the bloody floor. Instead, miraculously, he was kneeling and bleeding profusely into the worn wooden slats, the hilt of the dagger sticking straight out of his chest.

The king's agonized expression was fixed upon Jonas.

"He's not dead," murmured Nic, shaking his head with disbelief. "Why is he not dead?"

In a sudden and unnaturally stilted motion, King Gaius grabbed hold of the dagger's jeweled hilt. With his narrowed gaze still focused upon Jonas, he yanked the blade from his flesh, roaring mightily as he did. The blade clattered to the floor as he pressed his hands against the wound.

"This is magic at work," Jonas managed to say through his utter shock.

"How incredibly perceptive of you," Magnus said flatly.

"Explain to me what's happening!"

Magnus nodded at Milo. "Release the rebel. I can't talk to someone pinned like a beetle to a board."

Milo released the pressure on Jonas's arm. Jonas immediately got to his feet and looked accusingly at Magnus, who shared an unsubtle and knowing look with Cleo. Cleo's jaw tightened, and Magnus rolled his eyes.

"Very well," the prince said. "I'll try to be brief in my explanation. What's happening is the result of a potion he took many years ago, a potion that has ensured that, no matter what kind of final, fatal blow destiny throws his way, my father has some time to . . . linger after being killed."

"I'm not sure that's exactly how it works," Cleo said patiently.

Magnus sighed and gestured at his struggling father. "Close enough?"

"I suppose so. Good goddess, Jonas, is that Aron's dagger?" Cleo asked, aghast. "Have you really kept that horrible thing all this time?"

"Answer my question," he said, far more sharply than he'd meant to address the princess. Finally, he'd done the thing he'd been yearning to do for so long, but once again the fates would not see him succeed—not even after delivering a fatal blow.

"You didn't kill the king," Cleo replied tightly, "because the king already met his death days ago."

As Jonas tried desperately to process this incredible statement, a woman descended the stairs. She was older, with lines around her eyes, and she wore a dark gray cloak that matched her hair. She entered the meeting hall, regarding all present with a steady stare, until finally her gaze fell upon Gaius.

She lingered upon the image for only the briefest of moments before shooting the darkest of glares directly at Jonas. "You did this to my son?"

A cool shiver moved up his arms, over his shoulders, and down his spine at the barely controlled rage in her words.

Her son?

"It's fine," the king said gaspingly, reaching for the woman's sleeve as she rushed to his side.

"This is not fine. Not at all." She looked again to Jonas, and with her stare came the frigid sensation of ice freezing him in place. "You would dare attempt to murder your king?"

"He's not my king," Jonas snarled, refusing to show any weakness or doubt. "He murdered my friends in his ill-gotten war, executed those who refused to bow before him, and enslaved my people to build his precious Imperial Road. Not one person in this room would argue that he doesn't deserve to die for his crimes."

She balled her hand into a fist. "I would."

"No, Mother," Gaius said, his voice hushed. "Let him be. We need him. I believe we will need all these young people to regain what Amara has taken."

Slowly, the king rose from the ground, and Jonas couldn't help but take an uncertain step back from him. The deep wound from the blade had stopped bleeding. The only sign that there had been a dagger in his heart only a handful of moments ago was his torn shirt and the blood on the floor.

"Only the darkest of magic could make something like this possible," a new voice said.

Jonas turned sharply to see that Ashur Cortas now stood behind them at the entrance to the inn.

"Ashur!" Cleo gasped. "You're alive! But—what? How?"

Ashur's dark brows raised. "More dark magic, I'm afraid."

She spun to face Nic, whose expression remained neutral. "You knew about this?"

He nodded. "I know, it's a shock."

"A shock? He was dead, Nic! Why didn't you tell me?"

"I was getting around to it. Thought I'd let you deal with the Taran issue first."

"Oh, thank you," she said, her voice pinched. "You're so helpful, really."

"Somehow, I get the feeling that you don't really mean that."

Jonas's gaze shifted to see that Magnus's expression was grim.

"I'm getting so damn sick of magic," the prince muttered. "And everything else over which I have absolutely no control."

"It's lovely to see you again too, Prince Magnus," Ashur said with a nod.

"So kind of you to find us, your grace," Nic addressed Ashur, his voice without any respect. "I'd begun to think you'd grown gills and a tail and started to swim back to Kraeshia."

"Not today, I'm afraid," Ashur replied curtly.

"Perhaps tomorrow."

"Perhaps."

"Shall we tell everyone about your phoenix resurrection now or later?" Nic asked.

Ashur's expression tensed at Nic's acidic tone. "It seems to me, Nicolo, that there are more pressing matters at hand. I'm right, aren't I, King Gaius?"

The attention of the group returned to the king, who was hunched over next to his mother. "Indeed you are, Prince Ashur."

"An alliance against my sister."

"Will that be a problem for you?"

"No. Provided you don't kill her, that's not a problem at all."

"Wait," Felix said from his position by the fireplace. "You know I was counting on killing her. Are you really going to take that away from me?"

Ashur shot Felix a stony look.

"Fine. It's a topic we'll save for another day," Felix said.

"Prince Ashur, you are the rightful heir to your father's title," the king said. "Take it from Amara, and all of this could be over."

"And you're now her husband, I've heard. Why aren't you by her side, guiding her decisions?"

"It's not that simple for me anymore."

"Nothing important is ever simple, is it?"

"The King of Blood wants us to work as a team," Jonas said, shaking his head. "It's the most ridiculous thing I've ever heard. That's not what I want."

Gaius let out a breath of frustration. "I know very well what you want, rebel. You want me to die. Well, I assure you, I will be dead soon enough."

"Gaius . . ." his mother hissed. "I won't have you speaking like this. I won't!"

He silenced her with a wave. "My first priority is to regain control over my kingdom. Mytica does not now, nor will it ever, belong to the Kraeshian Empire."

"Were it not for the magic rumored to be lying dormant here," Ashur said, "I can assure you, neither Amara nor my father would have bothered with this tiny island."

"I assume you're aware that Amara poisoned your father and

brothers," the king countered. "She's without remorse when it comes to getting what she wants."

Nic's dark laugh cut through the tension in the room. "That's funny. *Without remorse*, he says, as if he deems it a fault. The very man who broke my sister's neck for being in the wrong place at the wrong time." His laughter ceased all at once. "You look like death, your majesty. And I can only hope you're suffering right now."

"You won't talk to the king that way, Cassian." It was Milo, the guard, who said this.

Nic glared across the room at him. "Or what? Are you going to get your friend to help beat me up?"

Milo smiled while cracking his knuckles. "I can do it myself just fine."

"Thought you were wasting away in the dungeon."

The guard's smile darkened. "I have you to thank for that, don't I?"

"You do." Nic's eyes narrowed. "What are you going to do about it, Milo?"

"So many things. Give me time."

"Milo, is it? Listen to me very carefully." Ashur's voice was low, like the quiet snarl of a caged beast. "If you ever attempt to harm Nicolo, I swear I will personally skin you alive."

Jonas's eyes shot to Milo. He saw that Milo's only reply to this threat was a surprised blink.

Cleo spoke then to the king, after glancing worriedly between Nic and the guard. "You gave Mytica to Amara," she said, disgust clear in her voice. "Can't you simply take it back?"

"You understand nothing," the king bit out. "None of you do. Emperor Cortas would have taken Mytica by force had I not acted when I did. Tens—no, hundreds of thousands would have died in that war had I not made my proposal to him."

"Oh, yes," Magnus drawled. "My father: the savior of us all. We should erect statues in your honor. Shame that there are already dozens of them throughout Limeros." Magnus glowered at him. "Quite vain, now that I think about it. The goddess Valoria would not approve."

"To the darklands with the goddess and with all the Watchers as well," the king snapped. "We need none of their help to get rid of Amara."

"Don't forget about Kyan," Jonas added.

The king glanced at him. "Who is Kyan?"

Jonas couldn't help but laugh. "I would truly love to stay here and strategize with you, *your highness*, but I grow weary of this charade. I will not work with you now, tomorrow, or ever."

"Tell me, your highness," Felix said slowly, "do you still have the air Kindred?"

Gaius shot him a dark look.

"The air Kindred!" his mother exclaimed. "You have it? And you didn't tell me?"

"I do have it," he said simply.

"Where?"

"Somewhere safe."

Jonas tried to catch Cleo's eye, but she seemed to be occupied in a silent conversation with the prince. As they looked at one another, all amusement disappeared from Magnus's face.

"If this is true, and when I'm strong enough to locate my granddaughter," the woman said, "then victory is ours for the taking."

Once again, Jonas laughed coldly. "So that's the key to your grand plan, is it? Princess Lucia? I think you'll be disappointed to see what a cold, vicious, bloodthirsty snake she's become. Then again, she is a Damora, so perhaps you'll be neither surprised nor disappointed."

The old woman studied him. "Jonas, is it?"

"That's my name."

"My name is Selia." She drew closer, the anger in her eyes now gone, as she took his hands in hers. "Stay with us and learn more about our plans. I agree with my son that, despite our differences, we can still work together. Try to see this logically. Together we are strong."

Could she be right? "I don't know . . ."

"Stay," Cleo urged. "Please consider it, at least. For me."

He met her earnest cerulean eyes with his. "Perhaps."

Magnus stood up. "You suggest the rebels stay here?" he said accusingly to his grandmother. "In this very inn? That's the worst idea I've ever heard."

"I disagree," the king said. "My mother is right. We can find a compromise. A temporary one. We have the same enemy now."

Without even being sure of whether he was about to agree or disagree with either Damora, Jonas opened his mouth to speak, when a roar of fury broke the relative stillness of the meeting hall.

Footsteps thundered down the stairs, and Taran stormed into the meeting hall. In an instant, his furious gaze fixed upon Magnus.

Jonas's dagger—the one the king had pulled from his chest—lay on the floor. As Jonas spotted it, so did Taran, who snatched it up in a heartbeat and closed the distance between him and the prince.

Taran arched the dagger at Magnus, but the prince caught Taran's wrist before he made contact. Cleo let out a sharp shriek.

"You're dead," Taran yelled.

Magnus fought hard to keep the blade from cutting him, but Taran had taken him by surprise and possessed the vengeance-driven rage to double his strength.

Then Felix loomed behind Taran, bringing his arm around the rebel's throat and wrenching him backward. "Don't make me whack you again. I lost my piece of wood."

Jonas moved to join him, wrestling the dagger from Taran's grip.

"I'll kill you," Taran spat out at the prince as Felix dragged him backward. "You deserve to die for what you've done!"

Magnus offered no rebuttal to this. All he did was stare at the boy, his expression stony.

"I think we all deserve to die for something we've done," Jonas said, relieving a bit of the tension brewing between the prince and the rebel. "Or for something we've failed to do."

The prince broke his steely mask to send a glare of disbelief at Jonas. "Is it only my imagination, or did you just help to save my life?"

Jonas grimaced at the thought. "Seems that way, doesn't it?" He glanced over at Cleo. Her expression was filled with relief. Surely the princess hadn't wanted to see any more blood spill tonight, he thought. Not even Magnus's. "I may be about to make a horrible mistake, one I'll regret for the rest of my life, but I have decided to accept this alliance—this *temporary* alliance—until Amara has been cast from these shores."

He waited for Ashur's response to this. The Kraeshian prince's expression remained grim, but he nodded. "I can agree to that. Amara needs to realize what she's done. Even if she feels she was in the right for her actions, it was the wrong path for her to take. I will do what I can to help you."

"Good." Jonas then pointed at Taran, whom Felix still had in his grip. "I understand your grief and outrage, but your lust for vengeance has no place here."

Taran scowled back at Jonas, clutching Felix's iron bar of an arm across his throat. "You knew what I came here for before we left Kraeshia's shores."

"I did, but that doesn't mean I agreed to it. Now I've made my decision. You will not make another attempt on Prince Magnus's life. Not while we're engaged in this alliance."

"Did you hear that through your battered skull?" Felix asked Taran, his voice as rough as gravel as he clamped his arm tighter. "Or should I repeat it to you slower?"

"I abandoned a rebellion to come here and avenge my brother."

"A rebellion doomed to fail before it even began," Ashur added.

"You don't know that."

"I do. I don't take pleasure in this knowledge, but I know it. Perhaps one day the empire my father built will be torn apart, but it won't be any time soon."

"We'll see."

"Yes, I suppose we will."

Taran shifted his angry gaze to Jonas again. "You would join them freely, by your own choice?"

"I would," Jonas confirmed. "And I urge you to consider staying as well. We could use your help." He paused. "But don't misunderstand me, Taran: If you attempt to end Prince Magnus's life again, I'll end yours."

CHAPTER 15

AMARA

PAELSIA

The god of fire had been very specific about where he wanted Amara to go to achieve infinite power. It was a place, he said, that was touched by magic. A place that even the immortals themselves recognized as a seat of true power.

She instructed Carlos of the change of plans. She would not be moving into the Limerian palace after all. No, instead her destination would be farther south into Paelsia, to the former compound of Chief Hugo Basilius.

Carlos didn't question these orders but instead made immediate plans. With five hundred soldiers, Amara, Nerissa, Kurtis, and Amara's captain of the guards made their journey into the central kingdom of Mytica, which Amara hadn't yet experienced.

From the window of her carriage, she gazed out with surprise as the ice and snow of Limeros melted and gave way to parched earth, dead forests, and very little wildlife.

"Has it always been like this here?" she asked with dismay.

"Not always, your grace," Nerissa replied. "I've been told there was a time, long past, when all of Mytica from north to south was warm and temperate, always green, with only mild changes from season to season."

"Why would anyone choose to live in a place like this?"

"Paelsians have very little choice in their fates—and they are well known for accepting this, as if this acceptance has become a religion unto itself. They are a poor people, bound by the rules their former chief and the chief before him set into place. For example, they can only sell wine legally to Auranos, and wine is their only valuable export. Much of the profit is taxed, and these taxes were claimed by the chief."

Yes, Paelsian wine, infamous for its sweet taste and its magical ability to bring about swift and pleasurable inebriation with no ill effects afterward.

It was the wine Amara had brought back with her to Kraeshia to poison her family.

No matter what was said about the drink, she swore she would never drink Paelsian wine because of this memory.

"Why don't they leave?" she asked.

"And go where? Very few would have enough coin to travel overseas, even less to make a home anywhere but here. And to journey into Limeros or Auranos is not allowed for Paelsians without express permission from the king."

"I'm sure many move around as they please. It's not as if the borders are fully monitored."

"No. But Paelsians tend to obey the laws—most Paelsians, anyway." Nerissa settled back into her seat, her hands folded in her lap. "They shouldn't give you any problems, your grace."

If nothing else, and after so many problems in the past, this was a relief to know.

Amara continued to watch the barren landscape outside the

carriage window during the four days of their journey from Lord Gareth's villa, hoping to see the dirt and death change to greenery and life, but it never did. Nerissa assured her that farther west, nearer to the coastline, it improved, and that most Paelsians made their homes in villages in that third of the land, and very few closer to the ominous-looking, black and gray spikes of the Forbidden Mountains on the eastern horizon.

This kingdom was as far from the lush richness of Kraeshia as anything Amara had ever experienced, and she hoped she wouldn't have to stay here very long.

For the last leg of their journey, their entourage used the Imperial Road, which wound its way in a curious manner throughout Mytica, beginning at the Temple of Cleiona in Auranos and ending at the Temple of Valoria in Limeros. It passed directly by the front gates of Basilius's compound.

The gates were open, and a short man with gray hair awaited them, flanked by a dozen large Paelsian men wearing leathers, their dark hair plaited in tiny braids.

When Carlos helped Amara down from her carriage, the man nodded curtly at her.

"Your grace, I am Mauro, Chief Basilius's former chancellor. I welcome you to Paelsia."

She swept her gaze over the small man, a full head shorter than herself. "So you have been in charge of this kingdom following the chief's death."

He nodded. "Yes, your grace. And I am therefore at your service. Please, come with me."

Along with the empress's main group of bodyguards, including Carlos, Amara and Nerissa followed Mauro through the brown stone gates and into the compound. A stone path wound through the walled village, leading them past small, straw-thatched cottages similar to those Amara had seen as they'd passed through several towns on their way to the compound.

"These homes are where the chief's troops were once quartered. Alas, all but a handful were killed in the battle to take the Auranian palace." Mauro gestured to other spots of interest as they followed him through the compound, which at one time had been the home of more than two thousand Paelsian citizens.

There were shops here that once provided bread, meat, and produce brought to the compound from Trader's Harbor. Mauro showed them a barren area that held the stalls of local vendors, allowed through the gates on a monthly basis.

Another area, a clearing with stone seating, had been used as an arena for entertainment—duels and fights and feats of strength the chief had enjoyed watching. Another clearing was spotted with the remnants of bonfires, where the chief would enjoy feasts.

"Feasts," Amara said with surprise. "In a kingdom like this, feasts are the last thing I'd expect a leader to enjoy."

"The chief needed such pleasures to fuel his mind and help him explore the limits of his power."

"That's right," she mused. "He believed he was a sorcerer, didn't he?"

Mauro gave her a pinched look. "He did, your grace."

Chief Basilius sounded to Amara like a narrow-minded, selfish little man. She was glad that Gaius had killed him after the Auranian battle. If he hadn't, she would have done so herself.

Despite the heat of the day, the sun already beating down upon her, Amara felt the temperature around her rise. *"I know it doesn't look like much, little empress, but I assure you that this is exactly where we need to be."*

Amara didn't reply to Kyan, but she acknowledged his presence with a small nod.

"We are close to the center of power here," he continued. *"I can feel it."*

"Over here"—Mauro indicated a large hole in the ground, about ten paces in circumference, dropping down twenty paces into the dry earth—"is the holding place the chief used for prisoners."

Amara glanced down into the pit. "How did they get down there?"

"Some were lowered by rope or ladder. Others were simply pushed." Mauro grimaced. "Apologies if such imagery is unpleasant, your grace."

She gave him a sharp look. "I assure you, Mauro, there is likely nothing you can tell me of the treatment of prisoners that I would find surprising or unbearable to hear."

"Of course, your grace. My apologies."

She grew weary of men and their half-meant apologies. "Carlos, see that my soldiers are given adequate quarters after this long journey."

"Yes, empress." Carlos bowed.

"You will be staying here, Empress Amara." Mauro indicated the three-story building nearby, made of clay and stone, the largest and sturdiest in the entire village. "I can only hope it will be acceptable to you."

"I'm sure I can make do."

"I have arranged for a small market to be presented to you later today, to show you the wares of your new Paelsian subjects. Some lovely needlework, for example, might interest you. And some beaded baubles for your beautiful hair. Another vendor travels here from the coast to share the berry stain she's created that will paint your lips . . ." Mauro faltered as her expression soured. "Is there a problem, your grace?"

"You think I'm interested in needlework, baubles, and berry lip stains?" She waited for his response, but his mouth only moved without any utterance of sound.

From behind her, she heard a snicker.

She turned sharply, her gaze fixing upon the guard—*her* guard—who had a grin fixed upon his face.

"Do you find that amusing?" she asked.

"Yes, your grace," the guard replied.

"And why is that?"

He glanced at his compatriots to either side of him, neither of whom met his gaze. "Well, because that's what women enjoy—ways to look prettier for their men."

He said it without a moment's pause, as if it were obvious and not in the least bit offensive.

"*My, my,*" Kyan breathed into her ear. "*That is rather insolent, don't you think?*"

She did indeed.

"Tell me. Do you think I should buy some lip stain to please my husband when he finally returns to me?" she asked.

"I think so," he responded.

"That is my goal as empress, of course—to please my husband and any other man who happens to glance my way."

"Yes, your grace," he replied.

It was the last thing he would ever say. Amara thrust the dagger she kept with her into the guard's gut, staring into his eyes as they went wide with surprise and pain.

"Disrespect me, any of you," she said, casting her gaze to the other guards who regarded her with surprise, "and die."

The guard who'd spoken unwisely fell to the ground. She nodded at Carlos to remove the body, and he did so without hesitation.

"Well done, little empress," Kyan whispered. *"You show me your worth more and more with each day that passes."*

Amara turned a smile toward Mauro, whose expression now held cold fear. "I look forward to the market. It sounds lovely."

Later that day, accompanied by Mauro and the royal guards, Amara and Nerissa explored the market, which consisted of twenty carefully selected stalls that, as promised, mostly carried frivolous products—specifically beauty and fashion items.

Amara ignored the embroidered scarves and dresses, the lip stain, the creams meant to remove blemishes, and the sticks of coal to ring one's eyes and tried instead to focus on the vendors themselves—Paelsians, young and old, with weary but hopeful expressions as she approached them.

No fear, no dread—just hope.

How odd to find this in a conquered kingdom, she thought. Then again, the Kraeshian occupation of Mytica had been mostly peaceful so far, especially in Paelsia. Still, Carlos had made her aware of rebel groups who conspired against her, both in Limeros and Auranos.

That caused her no troubles. Rebels were an unavoidable pest, but one that could usually be swatted away easily.

Amara watched as Nerissa moved closer to a stall to inspect a silk scarf the vendor had thrust out toward the young woman.

"I'm pleased to see that you're settling in nicely," Kyan whispered warmly in her ear. Her shoulders stiffened at the sound of his voice.

"I'm trying my best," she replied quietly.

"I fear I must leave you now for a time as I seek the magic we need to perform the ritual."

The thought alarmed her. They'd only just arrived! "Now? You're leaving now?"

"Yes. Soon I will be restored to my full glory, and you will be powerful beyond your belief. But we need the magic to seal this."

"Lucia's magic. And her blood."

"Her blood, yes. But not the sorceress herself. I will find an alternate source of magic. However, we will need sacrifices—blood to seal the magic."

"I understand," she whispered. "When will you return?"

Amara waited, but he didn't respond to her.

She then felt a rustle at her skirts and looked down. A little girl, no more than four or five years old, with jet-black hair and freckles on her tanned cheeks, approached Amara tentatively, holding out a flower to her.

Amara took the flower. "Thank you."

"It's you, isn't it?" the girl asked breathlessly.

"And who do you think I am?"

"The one who's come here to save us all."

Amara shared a droll look with Nerissa, who'd returned to her side now wearing the colorful scarf, then smiled down at the child again. "Is that what you think?"

"That's what my mama tells me, so it must be true. You will kill the evil witch who's been hurting our friends."

A woman approached, clearly embarrassed, and took the little girl's hand. "Forgive us, empress. My daughter doesn't mean to bother you."

"It's no bother," Amara said. "Your daughter is very brave."

The woman chuckled. "More like stubborn and foolish."

Amara shook her head. "No. It is never too early for girls to learn to speak their minds. It's a habit that will make them braver and stronger as they grow up. Tell me, do you believe as she believes? That I have arrived to save you all?"

The woman's expression darkened, and her brows drew together with worry and doubt. She looked Amara in the eyes. "My people have suffered for more than a century. We were under the command of a man who tried to fool us into believing he was a sorcerer, who taxed us all so heavily that, even with the great profits from the vineyards, we have been unable to feed ourselves. This land we call home is wasting away beneath our feet, even as we speak. When King Gaius vanquished Basilius and King Corvin, many of us thought that he would help us. But no help has come. Nothing has changed; it has only worsened."

"I'm so sorry to hear that."

The woman shook her head. "But then you arrived. That evil sorceress was here, destroying us village by village, but when you came, she disappeared. Your soldiers have been strict but fair. They have weeded out those who oppose them, but those people are no loss to us: Your detractors are the same men who sowed discord in our kingdom in the days after Basilius's army stopped offering the little protection they once did. So do I believe, as so many here do, that you are the one who has arrived to save us all?" She raised her chin. "Yes, I do."

After her guards moved Amara past the woman and her daughter to the next area of the market, the woman's words stayed with her.

"May I make a bold suggestion, your grace?" Mauro asked her, and she spared a glance at the little man who followed her around like a trained dog.

"Of course," she said. "Unless it's a suggestion for me to buy lip stain."

His face blanched. "Not at all."

"Then proceed."

"The Paelsian people are open to your leadership, but word must spread further. I suggest that we open the compound gates to allow your new citizens entry to hear you speak to them about your plans for the future."

A *speech*, she thought. It was something Gaius would enjoy doing much more than she would.

But Gaius wasn't here. And now that she had the fire Kindred to advise her on accessing the magic of her aquamarine orb, she had run out of reasons to allow the king to continue living for much longer.

"When?" she asked Mauro.

"I can spread word immediately. Thousands will journey here from surrounding villages to hear you. Perhaps a week?"

"Three days," she said.

"Three days is perfect," he cooed. "Yes, it will be wonderful. So many Paelsians, with open arms and open hearts, ready to obey your every command."

Yes, Amara thought. A kingdom of people ready to do her bidding without question, who accepted a female leader without argument, would be incredibly useful.

CHAPTER 16

MAGNUS

PAELSIA

Magnus pondered the twelve people taking up residence at the Hawk and Spear Inn, realizing that nearly half of them wanted him dead.

"And you're definitely one of them," he muttered as Nic trudged through the meeting hall, glaring as he passed the prince. Magnus was sitting alone at a table in front of a sketchbook he'd found in a drawer in his room. "Cassian, look," he called. "I drew a picture of you."

Magnus raised the sketchbook. His fingers smeared with charcoal, he held up a page on which he'd drawn an image of a skinny boy hanging from a noose, his tongue dangling from his mouth, two morbid Xs where the eyes should have been.

Nic, allegedly a very friendly fellow to everyone else in the world, shot Magnus a look of sheer hatred. "You think that's funny?"

"What? You don't like it? Well, they do say art is subjective."

"You think spending your time doodling away in that book is

going to make anyone see you as less of a threat? Try again. This innocent, nice-guy act you're putting on is wasted on me."

Magnus rolled his eyes. "Noted," he said, tucking the sketchbook under his arm. "But I can't say I'm not hurt. I thought we'd become good friends back in Limeros."

Nic narrowed his eyes, clearly not amused. "The only thing that helps me sleep at night is knowing that Cleo sees you for what you really are."

"I certainly hope you're right," Magnus said dismissively. He'd never let Nic get to him before, and he wasn't about to do so now, but the subject of Cleo was a thorn in his side. "It's so interesting to me, the lot of you choosing to stay here in the lion's den."

"Perhaps you're wrong about who's the lion and who's the prey."

Magnus made a mock-snoring sound. "Conversing with you, Nic, is always so stimulating. Truly. But I'm sure you have other places to be, and I'd hate to waste the precious time of a brilliant wit such as yours. I'm sure I've already kept you from your next appointment, which is . . . what? Perhaps lurking about in Ashur's shadow, waiting for a moment of his glorious attention now that he's successfully returned from the dead?" Having personally witnessed Ashur's death, Magnus was still trying to process the overwhelming information that he was still alive. "So sad, truly, that no one sees what's really going on between the resurrected prince and the former stable boy."

And that was all it took for Nic's cheeks to burn with an immediate flush. "And what is that, Magnus? What do you think is *really going on*?"

Magnus paused, meeting Nic's suddenly uncertain gaze. "The taste of romantic disappointment is rather bitter, isn't it?"

"I suppose you'd know all about that, wouldn't you?" Nic snarled. "Never forget that she hates you. You killed everyone she loves. You stole her entire world. That's a truth that will never change."

With a last glare, Nic left the room, leaving Magnus glowering and heaving with a great desire to punch something. Or someone.

He's wrong, he assured himself. *The past is no measure of the present.*

And it was the present he needed to focus on. They needed to find Lucia, now, without further delay.

Why should we wait another day for Grandmother to find this elusive magic stone? he thought. Here they were, cowering like victims, when they should be doing anything they could to cast that Kraeshian from their shores forever.

Magnus shoved the sketchbook toward the center of the table and rose to his feet. He was going to find his grandmother and demand that—with or without her magic fully restored—she try a spell to find his sister.

"All alone in this great big hall?"

He went still at the sound of Cleo's voice. She stood at the base of the stairs, peering into the expansive room at him.

"Seems that way," he said. "More reason for you not to enter."

She entered anyway. "I feel like we haven't spoken privately in ages."

"It's been two days, princess."

"*Princess*," she said, biting her bottom lip. "My, you certainly are keeping this act up quite well. In fact, I can't be sure it *is* only an act anymore."

"I'm not sure I know what you're talking about." He moved his gaze over her, taking her in the way a starving man would a feast. "Is that a new dress?"

She stroked the silky skirts, the color of a ripe summer peach. "Olivia and I went to a market by the docks today."

"You and Olivia did what?" He narrowed his eyes at her, alarmed by his ignorance of the princess's choice to thoughtlessly put herself into danger. "That was a terrible idea. Anyone could have recognized you."

"Much as I enjoy being scolded, I suppose I should assure you that no one recognized me since I wore my cloak. And we weren't alone. Enzo and Milo were with us, for protection. Ashur too. He's been exploring the city to learn what Paelsians feel about the news of his sister's arrival."

"And what do they say?"

"Ashur said that most seem . . . open to change."

"Do they, now."

"Anything after Chief Basilius would be an improvement." She hesitated. "Well, not including your father, of course."

"Of course." Magnus had very little regard for Paelsians—or most Auranians, for that matter. All he cared about was that Cleo had been gone from the inn and he hadn't realized it. "No matter whom you were with out there, it was still an exceedingly bad idea."

"So is drinking to excess every night at the Purple Vine," she said tightly. "And yet that is what you choose to do."

"That's different."

"You're right. What you do is far more idiotic and foolhardy than spending the day exploring a market."

"*Idiotic* and *foolhardy*," he repeated, frowning. "Two words that have never been used to describe me."

"They're accurate," she said, her tone sharp and her brows drawing together. "When I saw you that first night with Taran . . ."

The sound of his name cut into the space between them like the sharp edge of an ax driving into a wooden block.

"I know his presence here must be difficult for you," Magnus said, his throat tightening. "His face . . . all the horrible memories it suggests . . ."

"The only horrible memory I have of Taran is that of his blade pressed to your throat." Cleo paused, searching Magnus's face as her frown deepened. "Do you assume that when I look at him I see only Theon?"

"How could you not?"

"I admit that it was jarring to see him. But Theon's gone. I know that. I've made peace with it. Taran is not Theon. He is, however, a threat."

"I see."

"Do you?" Cleo continued to study him intently, as if he were a riddle she needed to decipher. "Yet you honestly thought that I would see him and forget everything else that's happened since that day? That the hatred I used to feel for you would return and blind me? That I . . . what? Would instantly fall in love with Taran Ranus?"

"It does sound quite ludicrous."

Her expression grew thoughtful. "Well, Taran *is* very handsome. Apart from the fact that he wants you dead—which was, admittedly, a former goal of mine—he would make a perfect suitor."

"Tormenting me must be very amusing for you."

"*Very*," she teased, allowing him a small but slightly sad smile. She reached for his hands, the sensation of her warm skin against his like a salve to a painful wound. "Nothing has changed between us, Magnus. Know that."

Her words comforted his aching soul. "I'm very glad to hear that. When might you share this sentiment with the others?"

Immediately, her expression grew tense. "This isn't the time. There's far too much at stake right now."

"Nic is your closest family, your dearest friend, and he despises me."

"He still sees you as an enemy. But one day, I know he'll change his mind."

"And if he doesn't?" He searched her gaze. "What then?"

"What do you mean?"

"Choices, princess. Life seems to be all about them."

"You're asking me to choose between you and Nic?"

"If he refuses to accept . . . *this,* whatever this is, princess, then I suppose you would *have* to choose."

"And you?" she finally said after several long moments of pensive silence. "Whom would you choose, if someone or something forced you? Would it be me? Or Lucia? I know very well she was your first love. Perhaps you still love her like that."

Magnus groaned. "I assure you, there's nothing of the sort between Lucia and me. And as far as she's concerned, there never was."

His heart had evolved so dramatically over the last few months that he had to wonder if he was still the same person who had once pined away for his adopted sister. Though it had taken on a new form, that love for her was still there within him. No matter what Lucia might do or say, Magnus loved her unconditionally and was ready to forgive her for any misdoings.

But the desire he'd once had for her . . . his heart had utterly and permanently shifted to someone else—someone far more frustrating and dangerous to him than his adopted sister had ever been.

"She did choose to run away with her tutor, after all," Cleo reminded him.

His lips thinned. "Yes, and now the fate of the world rests on whether or not we find where she's run off to." Cleo looked at him, skepticism plain in her stare. "What, princess?" he asked. "You have doubts?"

"I . . ." Cleo started, then paused to stare down at her feet as if deep in thought. "Magnus, I'm just not sure she's the singular solution you seem to be counting on."

"She has dealings with the fire Kindred. I believe she must know how to draw the magic from the Kindred without also allowing the elemental god to escape."

"Seems to me that she's the one who helped Kyan escape if they're traveling together. She has to be."

"Perhaps. But her magic is vast."

"Vast enough to kill us all."

"You're wrong," Magnus said without hesitation. "She wouldn't do that. She will help us—help everyone." Whenever he spoke glowingly of Lucia, he noticed Cleo would purse her lips and crease her brow as if she'd tasted something sour.

Could she really be jealous of how I feel about Lucia? he wondered, with a sliver of amusement.

"I see thoughts of your adopted sister bring a rare smile to your face," she said, her words clipped and her tone unpleasant. "I'm sure thinking of her provides a lovely escape for you during this trying time, while we're stuck here in Paelsia, surrounded by rebels who would jump at the chance to burn this inn—and all the royals within it—to the ground."

"Is that Agallon's nefarious plan?" he asked, now pursing *his* lips and creasing *his* brow. "What else has he whispered to you in the dark of night since arriving here?"

"Very little, actually."

Magnus took a step closer to her; she took a step backward: the same dance they engaged in from time to time. They kept it up until he backed her into a corner, and she looked up at him defiantly.

"Perhaps you'd rather share a room with the rebel than with

me," he said, twisting a lock of her hair around his finger. "Then again, he'd probably prefer a house in the trees made of sticks and mud."

Cleo scoffed. "This is what you choose to focus on right now?"

"Yes. Because if I focus on Agallon, I can stop focusing on you and how badly I want to take you to my bed."

All she could do was let out a brief, breathy gasp before his lips were on hers, his hands gripping her waist and pulling her against him. And she kissed him back without reservation.

His hands slid down her sides to her waist, around to the small of her back, and over the curve of her bottom. Frustrated with the necessity to lean over to fully kiss her, he gripped the backs of her thighs and lifted her up into his arms so that her back pressed up against the wall.

Surely, she would stop him now.

And yet she didn't. In fact, she'd begun to frantically pull at the ties of his shirt, her mouth not leaving his for an instant.

"I want you," he whispered against her lips. "I want you so much I may die from it."

"Yes . . ." Her breath was so sweet, so warm. "I want you too."

When he kissed her next, all rational thought about the curse vanished from his mind. There was nothing except the maddening, blinding need to touch her, to taste her . . .

At least, not until he heard the footsteps approaching from behind him.

It was then that Magnus sensed that they were no longer alone.

Slowly lowering the princess back to the ground, Magnus forced himself to pull away from her and, shoulders tense, look upon their intruder.

Despite his intimidating stature and impressive muscle, Felix Gaebras looked positively sheepish.

"Um . . . sorry to interrupt? I was . . . uh . . . just moving through." But he remained still where he stood, then raised his chin. "Pardon me for saying, your highness," he said, looking at Magnus, "but you might want to be more discreet with the princess from now on."

"Is that so?" Magnus hissed.

Felix nodded. "Nic has happily convinced everyone that you hate Magnus, princess. And that . . . didn't look like an act of hate to me. He's going to go out of his mind over this."

Cleo stepped away from Magnus, her fingers pressed to her lips and her cheeks bright red.

"Please, Felix," she said, almost desperately. "Promise me that you won't tell Nic about this. Not ever."

Felix bowed. "Don't worry, princess. I won't breathe a word."

"Thank you."

Magnus hid his grimace. Something about how she said it, how *relieved* she sounded that it had only been Felix who'd witnessed them together and not someone whose opinion she valued more, pained him deeply.

If Ashur could seek information about Amara, so could Magnus. That afternoon, he left the inn and strode up the road to the market Cleo had mentioned, which took him by the tempting entrance to the Purple Vine. Once at the market, he barely glanced at the wooden stalls, with brightly colored tarps meant to shield the vendors from the sun, each selling a different Paelsian commodity—from wine to jewelry, from fruits and vegetables to scarves and frocks of all colors, among a plethora of other wares. The busy maze of stalls smelled of sweet fruit and smoked meat, and closer to the docks, the odor of sweat and waste buckets assaulted Magnus's nostrils. Among the numerous attendees of the market, including crews of ships and regular citizens of the city, a scattering of Kraeshian guards captured his interest.

He watched as one of Amara's men spoke with a Paelsian wine seller, who offered him a taste of their product, but the wooden goblet wasn't presented with trembling hands or fear in the seller's eyes, but with a smile upon his face.

It annoyed Magnus to see that so many Paelsians were accepting the fate of becoming a part of the Kraeshian Empire, seemingly without a care in the world. Had it really been so bad for them before that the thought of Amara as their new leader was a gift?

He continued to watch evidence of this dynamic between Paelsians and Kraeshians until the sun was high in the sky and wearing a hooded cloak became unbearably hot. Since he'd had his fill of the sights, sounds, and smells, both pleasant and foul, of the Basilia market, he decided to return to the inn.

Magnus turned in that direction only to find that someone stood in his path.

Taran Ranus.

Magnus fought not to show that unexpectedly facing the twin of Theon—someone who had nearly successfully taken his revenge on his brother's murderer—had startled him so much. But before Magnus could figure out what to say, Taran took the liberty of speaking first.

"I'm curious," Taran said, his voice low. "How many people have you killed?"

"That's a rather personal question for such a public place."

He continued, undeterred. "We know there's my brother, that's one. Who else?"

Magnus tried not to flinch, tried not to reach for the hilt of the sword he wore. Taran also wore his sword prominently at his side.

"I'm not sure," he admitted.

"An estimate will do."

"Very well. Perhaps . . . a dozen."

Taran nodded, his expression giving away nothing of what might be going on in his mind as he glanced at the busy market around them. "How many people do you think I've killed?"

"*More* than a dozen, I'm sure," Magnus replied. He pursed his lips. "Why? Are you here to taunt me with your sword-fighting skills? To tell me stories of how you've made evil men cry for their mothers before spilling their blood? How you would kill a thousand more if it meant that sunshine and happiness would reign supreme in this world?"

Taran's narrowed gaze slowly moved back to meet Magnus's. For someone who'd nearly taken apart the inn the other night with his urgent need to slit Magnus's throat, Taran seemed eerily calm today.

"Do you regret killing my brother?" he finally asked, ignoring Magnus's questions.

Magnus considered lying, wondered if he should feign remorse. But he instinctively knew he wouldn't be able to fool Theon's twin. "No," he said with as much confidence as he could. "My life was in jeopardy. I needed to protect myself from someone vastly more skilled with a sword than I was at the time, so I acted. I can't stand here and tell you that I regret taking any means necessary to save my own life, despite my choices at the time not being the same choices I would make today."

"What choice would you make today?"

"Face-to-face combat. My fighting skills have much improved over the last year."

Taran nodded once, but his face betrayed nothing. "My brother would have bested you."

"Perhaps," Magnus allowed. "So what, then? I assume you're

here to attempt to take my life before all these people. Are you? Or are we merely having a conversation?"

"That's exactly why I followed you here: because I want to decide what to do. The other night it was so simple, so clear in my mind that you had to die."

"And now?"

Taran pulled the sword from the sheath on his belt, but only enough to show the blade that had a series of symbols and unfamiliar words etched into its surface. "This was my mother's weapon once. She told me that the words carved into it are in the language of the immortals."

"Fancy," Magnus said, his entire body tense and ready for a fight. "Was your mother a witch?" he guessed.

"Yes. She was an Oldling, a witch who worshipped the elements with blood magic and sacrifice."

"I'm sure you're telling me this for a reason."

"I am. I asked you to guess how many people I've killed." Taran sheathed the sword. "The answer is one. Only one."

A trickle of perspiration slid down the length of Magnus's spine. "Your mother."

Taran nodded grimly. "Oldlings believe twins are filled with powerful magic." He shook his head, his brow furrowing. "There's a mostly forgotten legend that says the first immortals who were created were twins—one dark, one light. My mother believed dark magic was far more powerful, so to increase hers, she chose to sacrifice the light twin."

"Theon."

"Actually, no. It was me, five years ago, when I was fifteen years old. Perhaps she thought I'd let her use this very sword to kill me, but she was wrong. I fought back, and I killed her. Theon arrived then, only to see me holding a blade, our mother dead at my feet.

He didn't know what she really was. I only recently found out the truth for myself. He swore I would pay with my life for taking hers, and I knew he'd never understand. So I ran as far away as I could, and I didn't look back. Until now." He laughed, and the sound was dry and hollow. "It seems we have this in common: We both were forced to take a life to protect ourselves, an act we can't allow ourselves to regret, because if we hadn't done it, we wouldn't be here today."

Magnus couldn't find his voice; Taran's confession had managed to render him speechless. He concentrated on the market's buzz and activity, squeezing his eyes shut for a moment.

When he opened them again, Taran was walking away from him through the crowd. He followed at a distance, considering the short conversation they'd had and feeling grateful that he hadn't had to fight for his life today.

When they returned to the inn, Jonas was in the meeting hall, as if waiting for their arrival. He stood up from his seat and put down the book he'd been reading. Magnus noted with surprise it had been the same one about wine that he'd been reading.

"Taran, we need to talk," Jonas said. "Out in the courtyard we won't be overheard by prying ears. Felix is already there waiting. You too, your highness."

Magnus cocked his head. "Me?"

"That's what I said."

"Now I'm deeply intrigued. Very well. Lead the way, rebel."

Behind the inn was an outdoor space that the innkeeper and his wife referred to as the courtyard. Really, it was a patch of brown grass bordered by a small flower-and-vegetable garden and containing two animal pens—one of chickens and one of fat warlogs that chattered angrily at anyone who came close to them.

Magnus and Taran followed Jonas to where Felix stood in the far corner of the garden.

"We have information about Amara," Jonas finally said. "She's here in Paelsia."

Magnus tried not to let any intrigue show in his expression. "Information from whom?"

"There are rebels everywhere, your highness."

Magnus's first impulse was to remind Jonas that most of his rebels were dead, but he chose to hold his tongue. "Very well. Where in Paelsia?"

"Chief Basilius's compound."

"And where precisely is that?"

"A day's journey from here to the southeast. I'm surprised you don't know, considering it is a major point on your father's Blood Road."

"Imperial Road," Magnus corrected.

"*Blood* Road," Jonas said again, gritting his teeth.

Magnus chose not to get into the subject of that road with a Paelsian, nor the subject of how it was constructed so quickly on the backs of Paelsian workers at his father's command. No wonder the citizens of this kingdom were so welcoming to Amara. "And did this informant also tell you why she's come here?"

"No."

"It doesn't matter why she's here," Felix said. "This is our chance."

"To what?" Magnus asked. "Assassinate her?"

"That was the general idea."

"No, it wasn't," Jonas said, glaring at his friend.

"Killing one empress doesn't change the fact that my father gave this kingdom to her family. That her soldiers are everywhere like green splotches of mud. What about Ashur? You bring him here as if you trust him, yet we don't know what his plan is."

"Ashur is a problem, I admit it," Jonas said. "I have Nic keeping an eye on him, reporting any unusual behavior."

"Oh, yes." Magnus crossed his arms. "That should turn out just fine. So you"—he addressed Felix—"want to kill her. And you"—to Jonas—"want to wait and see." He nodded. "Excellent decisions all around. I can't imagine Amara will stand a chance against this alliance."

Jonas blinked. "Taran, weren't you planning on killing him?"

"I was."

"I'm beginning to warm up to that possibility again."

"Clearly," Magnus began, "if we know Amara's location, the best course of action is to send scouts to gather more information about her current plans, why she's here, and where she's hidden the water Kindred."

Taran groaned. "I hate the fact that I agree with him, but I do. I can go. There's no reason I should stay here with nothing to do but stare at the walls."

"I'll go too," Felix said eagerly.

Jonas gave Felix a wary look. "You think you can handle that without doing anything reckless?"

"Absolutely not. But I still want to go." Felix sighed. "I promise, we'll scout for information. That's all."

Magnus would rather take action, like Felix, and simply wipe Amara from the face of the world, but he could see how information would be useful in the broader sense of two kingdoms at war. "Shall we tell Cleo about this? Or Cassian?"

"For now, no," Jonas replied. "The fewer who know, the better."

Magnus didn't like the thought of keeping this from Cleo, but he couldn't fault Jonas's logic.

"Fair enough. We'll keep it between the four of us."

Jonas nodded. "Then it's settled. Taran and Felix will leave tomorrow at dawn."

CHAPTER 17

CLEO

PAELSIA

"Have you seen Prince Ashur anywhere?" asked Nic.

Cleo looked up from the book about Chief Basilius's life that she'd chosen from the shelf downstairs. Her thoughts were so scattered, she must've read the same page, which covered all five of his marriages, ten times.

Nic stood at the door of her private room. Enzo stood guard outside, her constant protector, but she'd made sure to tell him that Nic was not to be barred from interrupting her.

"Not today," she admitted, still stunned that the prince had returned from the dead. "Why? Is that odd?"

"He likes to wander off and not tell anyone." His expression darkened. "Does he seem different to you than before? I can't figure it out."

"He seems much the same to me, but I didn't know him well," she admitted.

"Neither did I."

"Oh, I don't know about that. Sometimes it doesn't take years to know someone. A handful of conversations can be more than enough to know someone's heart."

"If you say so."

Cleo knew that Nic and Ashur had known each other well enough that her friend had grieved the prince's loss deeply. And she also knew there was more than a simple friendship between the two, emotions they were only beginning to explore, perhaps now forever unresolved.

"Taran and Felix also seem to be missing," she said. "Where are they?"

"An excellent question. I thought I was allied with Jonas, but now it seems he conspires with Magnus."

"What?" The very thought made an uneasy laugh rise in her throat. "If you've seen the two in discussion, the subject is very likely about the king."

Ever since Jonas had successfully— yet *un*successfully— sunk his dagger into the king's chest two nights ago, the king had remained in his room, his mother constantly by his side, fearful her son was too close to death to survive long enough for the secret magic she promised to restore him.

Cleo did worry that if he died before the witch found Lucia, she'd refuse to help them, but she didn't mind at all the thought of him suffering in a tiny room in Paelsia.

A fitting end for a monster.

What had Gaius Damora been like back when he had known her mother? What horrors had he subjected Elena Corso to? It was a question that had plagued her ever since he'd spoke her name.

"Do you trust him?" Nic's voice broke through her thoughts.

"Who? Magnus?"

He laughed. "No, of course not him. *Jonas.*"

Did she trust Jonas, the boy who had kidnapped and imprisoned her—not once, but twice—and at one point wanted her dead for being present when his brother was murdered?

But he was also the boy who rose up to become a leader. To fight for his people. The boy who had risked his own life to save hers.

"I do trust him," she admitted.

So much could change in a single year.

"So do I," Nic said.

She nodded. "If he's speaking with Magnus, then it must be important."

"I still don't like it if he's keeping secrets from us."

Neither did Cleo, especially if it was a secret Jonas and Magnus now shared. Cleo vowed to get some answers for herself. She didn't care for being left in the dark.

Later that day, she got her chance. After Magnus asked to see Enzo in the courtyard, Cleo began hunting through the inn for information of her own. She happened quickly upon something potentially interesting in the meeting hall: Magnus's sketchbook.

She'd seen him drawing in it, his fingers black from the charcoal he used. Limerians didn't appreciate art as Auranians did, seeing beauty as a gift the artist shared with the world through his or her unique vision. No, if a Limerian drew anything, it was meant to be an exact likeness of the subject to aid in reference and education.

To this end, Magnus had attended a summer of art lessons on the Isle of Lukas several years ago, a trip many young royals and nobles—including Cleo's sister and mother—experienced in their youth. She'd seen Magnus's previous sketchbook, one that contained incredibly detailed pictures of flora and fauna . . . as well as multiple portraits of his sister, each drawn with unmistakable admiration and attention to every inch of Lucia's perfect face.

This, however, was not that sketchbook. It was a new one, and it intrigued Cleo down to her very bones.

"I really shouldn't look," she told herself. "He hasn't given me permission."

However, such an argument had never stopped her before.

The first drawing was that of the garden outside, clearly a quick sketch, but the dimensions and accuracy were uncanny. Before he'd abandoned this sketch, he'd focused on the detail of one rose bush, and even with the roughness of the charcoal stick, he had captured its beauty in shades of black and gray.

The second, third, and fourth pages had been roughly torn out.

The fifth page didn't have a sketch on it. It had a message.

Snooping around for a portrait of yourself, princess? Apologies, but you won't find one today. Perhaps one day I shall draw you. Or perhaps not. We'll have to see what the future holds.

—M

Cleo slammed the book shut, equally embarrassed and annoyed.

The sound of shouting drew her next to the windows, draped in rough canvas to block the light, that looked out into the courtyard at the back of the inn.

The prince had his sword drawn and was facing both Milo and Enzo, who also held their weapons. When they attacked, Cleo let out a gasp of horror before she realized what was happening.

The trio was practicing swordplay. And judging by the force of Milo and Enzo's attack, Magnus had requested that they attempt to best him.

Had she never watched him like this before, sword in hand, sweat on his brow, blocking the guards' weapons with his own? She thought that it might bring back horrible memories of that day—the day she'd lost Theon. But that version of Magnus had been a prince who had no skill compared to a palace guard, and he'd known it.

I'm so sorry, Theon, she thought, her heart twisting. *I never planned to feel this way about Magnus. But I do. I can't hold on to your memory anymore. I can't hate him for what happened, what he did that day. He's so different now.*

Or maybe Cleo was the one who had irreversibly changed.

"If you ask me, I don't think they're fighting nearly as hard as they could."

Cleo started at the sound of Jonas's voice. She looked at him standing next to her, unseen until now, with wide eyes.

"Did I surprise you?" he asked, amused.

"That you'd sneak up on someone in a darkened room certainly isn't a surprise, rebel."

Jonas grinned, but his attention was on the trio outside. "I wonder if the prince would be willing to spar with me?"

"If so, one of you would surely end up dead."

"Yes, but which one?" His brow, raised in amusement, dropped at her pained look. "Soon you'll finally be free of this unsavory arrangement with him, I promise you that."

She bit back her reply to this, being careful not to defend the prince. She felt it was still best that no one knew the truth about her and Magnus.

"He and his father—and Selia—are the means to the answers I need to unlock the earth Kindred's magic," she said instead.

"I told you: There's an elemental god inside that crystal," he replied sharply.

His tone made her flinch. After learning about the elemental gods two days ago, she'd given the matter endless thought and had barely slept a wink because of the gravity of the situation. "If there's a chance of harnessing that magic without allowing the god to escape, then I still think it's a goal worth pursuing. There's too much to lose if we don't have this power to help us in some way—even a small way."

When she met Jonas's eyes directly, his expression was grim, but his gaze had softened. "I don't entirely disagree."

She hesitated, but only for a moment. "You should know, according to a rather annoyed Nic, you're keeping secrets from him about Taran and Felix's current whereabouts."

"I've come to believe Prince Ashur is every bit of a snake as his sister. Nic knows him but says nothing useful about what to expect. I value Nic, but I don't trust him with any secrets that he might inadvertently reveal to the prince."

Another person entering the meeting hall had caught Cleo's eye. It was Ashur, only a dozen feet behind Jonas.

"Jonas . . ." she began.

"Ashur says he's this legendary hero raised from the dead to bring peace to the world. What a load of horse crap. He's just another spoiled royal raised with a silver spoon in his mouth, with any beautiful girl he desires only a snap of his fingers away." Jonas frowned. "I will admit, that would be quite a perk."

Cleo cleared her throat as Ashur crossed his arms over his chest and cocked his head. "I think that you should—" she began.

"What? Speak kindly about someone who speaks only in riddles because he's confused about his evil, power-hungry sister, who will likely destroy the world in her lust for magic and power? He could take the power from her easily. Show up, claim the title of emperor, tell everyone that Amara murdered their family. Finished and done."

Her stomach sank with every true but cutting word Jonas spoke.

"If there's one thing I'm not when it comes to Amara," Ashur said, his voice low, "it's confused."

Jonas grimaced. "You could have told me he was right behind me, princess."

"You were far too busy enjoying the sound of your own voice." And, frankly, Jonas's ramblings about Ashur had refreshed her annoyance with the Kraeshian prince.

No, not annoyance. Anger, bordering on fury.

"I would hope you're not confused about your sister," Cleo addressed Ashur directly. "She sank a dagger into your chest for crossing her."

"Amara's choices of late have been unfortunate, but I already knew she was set on this path. To be honest, I blame my grandmother for putting her own plans of revolution into action. Ironic that my *madhosha* would cut down those who equally want change in the empire. She has far more in common with rebels than she might believe."

Cleo stared at him, disgusted. "Unfortunate. You call Amara's choices *unfortunate*? She murdered you, she murdered her family, and now she's murdering any Mytican who gets in her way."

"She's lost her way. The sister I know—that I *knew*—is not one who solves her problems with mindless violence."

"Yes, of course. Kraeshians are known to be such a peaceful people."

Ashur regarded her carefully. "You're unhappy with me."

She glanced at Jonas before she laughed lightly. "Prince Ashur, why ever would I be unhappy with you?"

"You're just like Jonas. You don't trust me."

"Should we?" Jonas said. "You've told me nothing of your plans. You disappear for days on end. You keep to yourself. What is that supposed to tell me of your trustworthiness?"

"You could take the throne from Amara," Cleo said. "If you're so keen on helping the world, you could end a great deal of suffering simply by becoming emperor. You're older than Amara. It's your throne to take. Are you that afraid of her?"

Ashur laughed coldly at that. "I'm not afraid of Amara."

"You were afraid enough that you allegedly took a potion to save your life," Jonas pointed out. "Did you know she planned to kill you?"

Any amusement fell from Ashur's handsome face. "I didn't know. Not for sure. And the potion I took . . . it was well before my journey and primarily to protect myself from King Gaius, should he attempt to use my presence in his kingdom against my father. I had no idea that the potion would even work."

"But it did," Jonas said. "We need to find this apothecary, or witch, or whomever you used. Resurrection potions for everyone. Magic like that could save a lot of people."

"Death magic is nothing to be tampered with," Ashur snapped. "Not for any reason."

"Yet you did tamper with such dark magic to save your own life." Cleo was sure that the prince flinched at her accusation, which seemed very unlike him. "Do you feel guilty about that?"

"Of course not." Still, he wouldn't meet her gaze directly.

"No, no more lies, Ashur. If you're trying to give us the impression that we're all on the same side here, then you need to be forthright with us. There's more to this potion than you want to say. It's dangerous, isn't it?"

"Many potions are. Poison is simply a potion meant to kill."

Cleo took a deep breath and let it out slowly, feeling she was on the verge of uncovering a secret. "I've found that all magic comes with a price. What price did you pay for the chance to live again?"

"I've found that magic's price is often the opposite of the magic itself. For great power, you will experience moments of great weakness. For pleasure, there will be pain. And for life . . . there will be death."

"So you killed someone," Jonas said, his arms crossed tightly over his chest. "Or many people. So much for your claims of altruism."

Ashur moved to the window to look outside, his arms crossed over his chest. "You know nothing about me, Jonas. I have killed when I've had to. I haven't always been a pacifist. The apothecary warned me of the price I'd have to pay, but I didn't believe it. Amara unwittingly paid the same price when she was resurrected."

Cleo frowned deeply. "Amara was resurrected?"

"She was," Ashur said solemnly, then proceeded to tell Cleo and Jonas about what happened when Amara was only a baby, saved from drowning by dark magic and her mother's ultimate sacrifice.

Cleo found that she needed to take a seat, unexpectedly moved by this story. In Auranos—in Mytica—while women were valued for their ability to be mothers and cooks and nursemaids, they weren't prevented from doing other things, should they choose to. And a princess was able to be the heir to her father's or mother's throne without worrying about being murdered simply for the alleged crime of being a girl. Cleo wasn't sure whether she admired Amara's mother for valuing the life of her daughter—a girl— enough to sacrifice her own life or whether she blamed the woman for the fact that her daughter grew up to become a monster.

"Who died for you?" Cleo asked softly.

Shadows slid behind Ashur's faraway gaze, and he glanced at Jonas briefly before continuing. "I didn't know for sure, but I knew someone did. That's what I've been doing the last month. Traveling, visiting friends and past lovers. It was someone I spent a single summer with. I had no idea he still cared for me . . . that he'd never stopped caring." He swallowed hard. "Of everyone I've ever known in my life, someone who knew me for only a season loved me so much that he had to die for that love. I can't . . . rationalize it. I knew this price, but I selfishly ignored it. I'm told he suffered for days. He described it as a blade slowly being pushed into his chest. They tell me that in his last moments he cried out my name." Ashur's gray-blue eyes glistened. He took a deep breath. "The guilt I feel over his suffering, his death, and the fact that I erased any chance he had to live out a full and happy life . . . it will torment me forever."

All went silent in the room as Cleo tried to process what he was telling her. This Ashur seemed more like the sincere man who'd gifted her the night of her wedding with a Kraeshian bridal dagger meant to take either the unhappy bride's life or the life of her new husband. This Ashur wasn't spilling out riddles as a way to divert attention from his grief.

But then something occurred to her.

"This is why you've been so strange with Nic," she said. "He doesn't understand, thinks you're different, that you feel differently toward him, toward everything. But he's wrong, isn't he?"

Ashur didn't reply to this, but he looked down at his feet.

"You're afraid he might fall in love with you and that you might hurt him because of that love."

Jonas stayed silent, his brow furrowed. She hoped he wouldn't choose to say anything now that might distract the prince from speaking the truth.

"I had other plans for visiting Auranos," Ashur finally said. "I didn't mean for anything like this to happen. But something about Nicolo called to me, and I couldn't ignore it. I know I should have. All I managed to do was complicate his life and cause him unnecessary pain. But now, I won't let anything bad happen to him for his mistake of caring for me."

"Nic deserves an explanation," Cleo said, her throat tight.

"It's better that he thinks any feelings I might have had have changed." Ashur cleared his throat. "If you'll excuse me, I feel I've already said far more than I planned to."

Cleo didn't say a word to stop him from leaving the room. Her thoughts spun, some connecting, but most just confusing her more.

Finally, she glanced at Jonas.

"So," he said, still frowning. "Nic and Ashur, huh?"

She nodded slowly.

"Strange . . . I thought Nic liked girls, and you in particular. I'm not usually wrong about these sorts of things."

"You're not wrong. He does like girls."

"But Ashur"—he glanced toward the door—"is definitely not a girl."

"Don't try to think too hard about it, rebel. You might injure your brain. Just know that it's complicated."

"Isn't everything?" He came to sit next to her. "Now that I know Ashur's little secret, and that it's not a personal threat to you or me, I need to focus on getting my hands on the orb the king has hidden. Do you think it's here in the inn?"

"I have no idea. I wish I did. I was going to tell you . . . to unlock the magic, we need Lucia's blood and the blood of a Watcher."

His surprised gaze met hers. "That's the secret?"

Cleo nodded.

"That won't release the god?"

"I don't know. That's why it's so important that we find Lucia, to find out more from her and what went wrong with Kyan."

Jonas's brown eyes got a faraway look in them. "The prophecy . . ."

"What?" she prompted when he fell silent.

He shook his head. "Never mind. I'll tell you more when I figure out if it's true or not."

"The trouble is, I don't know how to find a Watcher." She bit her bottom lip. "Sure, there may be a handful of exiled Watchers still alive, but I think it needs to be a full Watcher. I'm hoping Lucia will be willing to help when the time comes."

"Don't worry about finding a Watcher." He didn't speak for an extended moment. "I have that covered."

Her gaze shot to his with surprise. "How?"

"Olivia," he whispered. "She's one."

She gaped at him. "You're not serious."

"It's another secret, but I'm going to trust you to keep it." He gave her a half grin then, one she'd always found equally charming and frustrating. "There's been so much that's been sacrificed on this road we've traveled together. So much loss for both of us. But I hold tight to the thought that it will all be worth it in the end."

She nodded. "Me too."

"I think you should know that Lys liked you."

"Now you're lying."

"She might not have even realized it herself, but I know she respected you more than you might think. You share the same thing: strength," Jonas's voice finally broke. "You just show it in different ways."

Cleo's eyes began to sting at the sight of Jonas struggling not to let the tears welling in his eyes fall.

She took the rebel's hands in hers, drawing him closer to her. "I'm so sorry for your loss, Jonas. I mean that from the very bottom of my heart."

He just nodded, his eyes trained on the floor. "She loved me. I didn't even realize it until it was too late. Or maybe I did and I wasn't ready to accept it. But now I see . . . she was kind of perfect for me."

"I have to agree."

"We could have had a life together. A house, maybe even a villa." He grinned again, but it was sadder this time. "Children. A future. Who knows what could have happened? I only know one thing for sure."

"What?"

"Lys deserved far better than me."

"I have no doubt about that," Cleo agreed, pleased that the surprised look Jonas gave her managed to erase the pain in his eyes. She gave him a warm smile. "My sister believed that those who die become stars in the skies. So every night we can look up and know they're watching over us."

His expression grew skeptical. "Is that some Auranian legend?"

"And if it is?"

A lock of her hair had fallen over her forehead, and he tucked it back behind her ear before leaving his hand against her cheek. "Then I like Auranian legends."

Cleo rested her head on Jonas's shoulder, and they sat there, taking comfort from each other. There was a connection between her and Jonas—something very powerful that she'd never been able to ignore. And there was a time, not so long ago, that she could have loved this rebel with all her heart.

And she did love him, but not in the way that Lysandra had.

Come what may, Cleo's heart belonged to another.

CHAPTER 18

MAGNUS

PAELSIA

It was clear to Magnus that Enzo and Milo were holding back in their sparring session, worried about harming a prince. Magnus left them both bleeding as punishment for this and went back inside the inn, feeling the surprising need to sketch.

He paused at the doorway when he saw Jonas and Cleo in the meeting hall. They were sitting close together, their voices low. Magnus inched closer to hear, but instead he watched as the rebel stroked Cleo's hair without protest from the princess, then stroked her cheek. Their eyes lingered on each other's for a second too long.

Magnus's vision turned blood red.

Part of him wanted to storm in there, to tear them apart and kill the rebel before he cast Cleo out of the inn and away from him forever.

His more rational mind told him that not everything he saw was the truth and that he shouldn't jump to conclusions.

Still, if he went in there and confronted the pair, surely someone would die.

Instead, he stormed out of the inn and headed down the road directly to the tavern, growling at the barkeep for wine. He lost track of how many goblets he'd drunk before he began to calm down.

He already knew the princess cared for the rebel, that the two had some romantic history he had not wanted to think much about. Why *wouldn't* she want someone like Jonas? Someone brave and strong—albeit poor and pathetic and a deadly jinx upon all he'd enlisted into his command as a rebel leader in the past.

Magnus could still see how someone like Jonas, who openly gazed at the princess as if she were a shining star in the night sky, would be tempting. At least in comparison to Magnus, who was dark and moody and quick to violence.

He stared down into his empty goblet. "With a million other worries and troubles upon me, I am now obsessed about where her true feelings lie." He glared drunkenly at the barkeep. "Why is my cup empty?"

"Apologies." The barkeep quickly filled the goblet until the wine splashed over the side.

Someone came to sit on the wooden stool next to him. He was about to bark at the man that he needed his space and that if he valued his life he should go elsewhere, but then he realized who it was.

"Wine never helps one forget their worries for long," his father said, his face as pale and gaunt as a corpse beneath the heavy hood of his black cloak.

Since the king had been sequestered in a private room upstairs at the inn with his mother since the night they arrived, it was a surprise to see him here. Magnus glanced around to see if he'd brought Milo for protection, but he didn't see the guard anywhere. Perhaps he still nursed his injuries from their sparring session.

Magnus ignored the king's comment and drained his cup before speaking. "Does Selia know you're here? I can't imagine she'd approve."

"She doesn't know. Her concern about my impending death has made me a prisoner. I don't care very much for the feeling."

"The feeling of your impending death or of being a prisoner? No need to answer. I'm sure both are vastly unfamiliar experiences for you." Magnus grabbed the flask of wine from the barkeep and shooed him away with a wave of his hand. He drank directly from the bottle now.

"There was a time when I indulged in such sins," the king said.

"Wine or intense self-pity?"

"Are you having trouble with the princess?"

"I'm sure that would make you very happy, wouldn't it?"

"To know that you might wish to separate from someone who I believe will only lead you to your doom? *Happy* would not be the word I'd choose, but yes. It would be for the best."

"I will not discuss Cleo with you, not now or ever," Magnus mumbled, hating that his head was so unclear with his father nearby. He'd prefer to have complete control over his senses, but it was too late to worry about that after the amount of wine he'd already consumed.

"Wise choice," the king replied. "She's certainly not my favorite subject."

"This hatred you have for her . . ." He turned it over in his mind, this seemingly unrelenting loathing the king had for Cleo. "It must have to do with her mother, yes?"

"Yes, actually it does."

A direct answer. How unusual—and deeply intriguing.

"Queen Elena Bellos," Magnus continued, spurred by the wine loosening his lips. "I saw her portrait at the Auranian palace before you had it torn down along with the others. She was a beautiful woman."

"She certainly was." The king turned away from him and wistfully looked out the tavern windows at the dark city street outside. Magnus could see the faintest smile on his ghostly pale lips.

The realization hit him hard. "You were in love with her," Magnus said, shocked at his own words but knowing it had to be true. "You were in love with Cleo's mother." This accusation drew the king's gaze back to him, his bloodshot eyes widening slightly as if with surprise. Magnus took a moment to absorb this silent confirmation and another sip of his wine to aid his suddenly dry throat. "It must have been a very long time ago, back when you were capable of such a pure emotion."

The smile quickly disappeared from his father's pale, sickly face. "It was a lifetime ago. Such weakness nearly destroyed me, which is exactly why I wanted to watch out for you."

Magnus laughed at this, a loud bellowing sound that surprised even him. "Watch out for me? Oh, Father, don't waste your breath on such lies."

The king slammed his fist down on the bar top. "Are you blind? Utterly blind? Everything I've ever done has been for you!"

The force of his sudden anger made Magnus spill some of his drink down the front of his tunic. He glared at the man. "How odd that I forgot that when you chose to end my life—and the life of my mother."

"Death would be a relief from this world for many of us."

"I will not forget anything that you've done, starting with this." Magnus pointed to the scar on his right cheek. "Do you remember that day as clearly as I do?"

The king's jaw tensed. "I remember."

"I was seven years old. *Seven*. Have you for one moment regretted it?"

The king's eyes narrowed. "You shouldn't have tried to steal from the Auranian palace. It would have caused great embarrassment had you been successful."

"Seven years old!" Magnus's throat hurt as he practically yelled it. "I was a mere child making a mistake, tempted by something shiny and pretty when I was used to living a bland, gray life in a bland, gray palace. No one would have known that I'd taken that dagger! What difference did it make?"

"*I* would have known," the king hissed. "That dagger you wished to steal belonged to Elena. I would have known because I was the one who gave it to her, back when I was a foolish boy trying to woo a beautiful girl. I didn't know she'd kept it, that she'd cherished and displayed it all the time we'd been apart. When I saw it in your hand six years after her death . . . I didn't think. I just *reacted*."

Magnus found he had no immediate reply. To have these questions answered after so long, he couldn't process it quick enough. "That doesn't excuse what you did."

"No, of course it doesn't."

Magnus tore his attention away from the king and tried to focus on something, anything else. It helped to notice that the world went on beyond this conversation. A large man walked toward the bar with an armful of empty cups, his tunic riding up high enough to show a hairy belly. A barmaid coyly slapped the hand of a sailor away. The musicians in the far corner played a lively song, and many clapped along. Several others danced on a tabletop.

"Power is all that matters, Magnus. Legacy is all that matters." The king said it as if trying to convince himself of this. "Without it we're no better than a Paelsian peasant."

He'd heard these platitudes so many times they'd become no

more than words that held no true meaning. "Tell me, did Elena Bellos love you in return, or was it a sad and hopeless obsession that turned both your heart and soul to solid ice?"

His father didn't answer for so long that Magnus thought he might have stood up and left. He turned his gaze away from the busy tavern to be sure the king was still beside him.

"She loved me," he finally said, his voice nearly inaudible. "But that love wasn't enough to solve our problems."

Magnus clenched his goblet. "Are you going to tell me a tale of love and loss now—about a boy meeting a girl?"

"No."

The thought that his father would dangle this epic love story before him without sharing it fully was as expected as it was frustrating.

"Then why are you even here?"

"To share the lesson I learned. Love is pain. Love is death. And love strips one of their power. Had I to do it all over again, I wish I'd never met Elena Corso. I've since come to despise her."

"How romantic. Since she married Corvin Bellos, I assume she felt the same."

"I'm sure she did. And now, I'm reminded of her every day of all that I've lost by that deceptive little creature, Cleo. She has become your fatal weakness, Magnus."

The hatred had returned to Gaius's voice. Magnus met his father's cold eyes. "Your ongoing hatred for Cleo seems incredibly misplaced to me. The witch who cursed Elena is the one you should blame." Magnus let out a breath in shock as he realized something. "You do, don't you? That's why you've condemned so many witches to their deaths over the years—to pay for that witch's crime. You might say you despise Elena, but you still love her—even beyond death. Why else would you have taken Grandmother's potion?"

"Think what you want." A muscle in the king's cheek twitched. "The potion was the only way to burn away the grief, the pain, and leave only strength behind. But now that strength is gone, stripped away when I fell from that cliff. The pain and grief is back, worse than ever before. And I hate it. I hate everything about this life, what I've had to do, how I've spent all this time obsessed with nothing but power. But it's over now."

"So you keep promising."

Magnus needed out of this noisy, smoky tavern. He needed the time and the space to clear his head.

When he stood up, the king grabbed his arm. "I beg you, my son, send Cleiona away before she destroys you. She doesn't truly love you, if that's what you think. No matter what she tells you, she speaks only lies."

"The King of Blood begging. Now I've heard everything." He sighed. "I've had enough to drink for tonight. Such a pleasure to have had this chat with you, Father. Try to make it back to the inn without dying. I'm sure your mother would be very upset."

He left without another word, hating how conflicted he felt about what to think, what to feel.

In the narrow alley outside the exit he'd taken, someone blocked his way to the main road, a large man with wide shoulders and a dark look on his face.

No one else was in sight.

"Yeah, I thought I recognized you the other night," the man said. "You're Prince Magnus Damora of Limeros."

"And you're horribly mistaken. Sorry to disappoint." Magnus tried to elbow past him, but the man's large mitt of a hand shot out to clutch his throat, drawing him close enough that Magnus could smell the ale on his breath.

"Ten years ago, your father burned my wife alive, claiming she was a witch. What say I do the exact same to you as retribution?"

"I say you let go of me immediately." Magnus glowered at him. "Your need for vengeance has nothing to do with me."

"He's right." The king stepped forward and pushed back his hood. "It has to do with me."

The man gaped at him as if not believing his own eyes.

"Apologies for the loss of your wife," the king said, the single lantern above the exit door lighting his near-skeletal face. "I despise witches for reasons far too long to list here and now. But I've rarely executed one who hadn't dealt in blood and death. If your wife is now in the darklands, that's exactly where she belongs."

The man's face reddened with rage, and he stepped forward with a sharp blade in his hand. Magnus watched his father as he stood there unmoving, his skin sallow, his shoulders hunched. He wouldn't—he couldn't—fight for his life.

Did he *want* to die?

The man's attention was fully on the king now, burning hatred in his eyes as he surged forward.

Magnus moved before he even realized his own intentions, grasping the man's hands, stopping the blade before it met its mark.

"If anyone deserves the right to kill my father, it's me," he growled. "But it won't be tonight."

He wrenched the sharp blade around so that it sank into its owner's chest instead. The man cried out in pain before he slumped to the ground. A pool of blood flowed freely from the fatal wound.

There was a moment of utter stillness in the alleyway before the king spoke again. "We must leave before anyone comes by to witness this."

Magnus had to agree with him. He wiped the blood from his hands on his black cloak, and quickly they returned to the Hawk and Spear Inn.

"Don't take that act to mean that I don't hate you," Magnus said.

The king nodded grimly. "I'd think you were a fool if you didn't. Still, despite your hatred for me, I want to give you something."

"What?"

"The air Kindred."

There was no way in the world that the King of Blood would hand over a piece of the Kindred to anyone, not even his own son. And yet, the king led Magnus upstairs to the room he'd been in for two straight days.

Magnus scanned the space. "Where's Selia?"

"In the courtyard." The king nodded toward the window. "Your grandmother likes to do her Oldling rituals nightly at this hour under the moonlight, which is why I was able to slip away."

The king went to the straw bed, lifted up the blankets, and felt beneath the mattress. He frowned. "Help me lift it," he said.

"That weak, are you? So you really would have let that man kill you while you simply stood there waiting?"

"Just do as I say." The glare his father shot him was much more familiar than any talk of sharing and regrets.

"Fine." Magnus went to his side and lifted the mattress so his father could search beneath.

Shock flashed through the king's watery, bloodshot eyes. "It's gone."

Magnus regarded him skeptically. "How convenient, considering you were about to give it to me. Please, Father, spare me such acts. As if you'd hide that kind of a treasure in such an obvious place."

"It's not an act. It was here. I've been too ill to find a better place to hide it." His expression darkened. "That little princess of yours stole it."

It had to be a lie. Yet another lie. Magnus couldn't believe otherwise, not over something this important.

Before he could reply, the king stumbled past him to leave the room. Magnus followed him down to the hall, where Cleo still sat with Jonas.

Magnus couldn't believe his eyes. It took every last piece of restraint he had not to make Jonas his second kill of the night.

Cleo shot up to her feet at the swift entry of both the king and Magnus. "What is it? What's wrong?"

"Did you steal the air Kindred?" Magnus asked, not liking the drunken slur to his words.

"What? I—I wouldn't even know where it is!"

"Yes or no, princess?"

Her eyes narrowed, and she lifted her chin. "No."

"She lies," the king said.

"The king of lies wishes to accuse the princess, does he?" Jonas practically spat out, his hands fisted. "How ironic."

"Where is your earth Kindred?" Magnus demanded.

Cleo's brow furrowed into a frown as she slid her hand into her pocket, her eyes growing wide. "It's gone. It was here, I swear it! I keep it with me all the time!"

A wave of nausea came over Magnus. There was a thief among them. And whoever it was would soon deeply regret their actions.

It wasn't long before the loud voices drew everyone to the room, wondering what was going on. Both Milo and Enzo had their weapons drawn, ready for a fight.

Magnus scanned the group. Everyone was accounted for—Nic, Olivia, even Selia had joined them, her face flushed from whatever ritual tonight's moon had earned. Everyone except one.

"Where is Prince Ashur?" asked Jonas, frowning. "He was here earlier with Cleo and me."

"I haven't seen him today," Olivia replied. "Perhaps he's gone out."

"Perhaps. Anyone know where he went?"

Enzo and Milo both shook their heads.

Selia went to the pale king's side as he made his way to a chair to sit down. "Gaius, darling, what are you doing out of bed?"

Magnus ignored them, his attention fully on Nic, who had remained silent. While the others argued about the location of the prince, Nic slipped out of the room. Magnus immediately followed him down a hallway toward the front door.

When Nic noticed that Magnus was close, his shoulders tensed.

"Looking for someone?" Magnus asked, his arms crossed over his chest.

"I want to go outside to get some fresh air."

"He took both of the crystals, didn't he? And he told you his plans."

Nic shook his head but didn't make eye contact. Magnus had no more patience for lies tonight. He grabbed the front of Nic's tunic and shoved him against the wall.

"Where is Ashur?" he snarled.

"You're drunk."

"Extremely, not that it makes any damn difference right now. Answer me! Ashur stole the crystals, didn't he?"

Nic gritted his teeth. "You think the prince tells me anything?"

"I have no clue what the prince whispers in your ear, but I'm not blind. I know there's something between the two of you, that you're closer than you'd like to let on. And I know that you know more about this than you're telling me."

Jonas approached from around a corner, his expression tense. "What are you doing to him?"

Magnus didn't release his hold on the boy. "Nic knows Ashur's secrets, and I'm going to find out what they are."

"Answer the question, Nic," Jonas said, his arms crossed over his chest. "Do you know where Ashur went?"

Nic scoffed. "What? Are the two of you working together now?"

"No," Magnus and Jonas both said in unison, then glared at each other.

Nic sighed. "Fine. The prince left not long ago to go to his sister. I tried to talk him out of it, but he wouldn't listen to a word I said. He's determined to do what he can to talk sense into her and if he can't, he'll claim the title of emperor."

Magnus's stomach dropped. "And he's taken her the air and earth Kindred. What a lovely gift, considering Amara has the water Kindred."

A glimmer of worry finally moved through Nic's gaze. "He wouldn't do that."

"Wouldn't he?" Magnus tried to keep his grip on Nic's shirt so that the fool couldn't slip away, but his vision had started to swim. Too much wine, too quickly. It would take till the morning for its effects to wear off. "Perhaps Amara magically summoned the crystals out of their hiding places and they flew on the wings of summer butterflies to reach her."

"I'll say it one more time." Nic's eyes narrowed. *"Let go of me."*

"And if I don't? Will you call out for the princess to come and save you?"

"I hate you. I yearn for the day when I see you dead and buried." He sent a dark look at Jonas. "A little help?"

"Nic, you need to think," Jonas said evenly. "If Magnus is right about Ashur—"

Magnus sent a withering look at the rebel. "Did you just call me by only my given name?"

Jonas rolled his eyes. "Amara Cortas cannot be allowed more power than she already has. And if her brother's taken her the Kindred, it's the worst outcome possible. She could release three elemental gods just like Kyan."

"I know," Nic replied. "I get it."

"Do you?"

"So it's my fault? Are you going to let *his majesty* break my neck? For what? Being unable to stop Ashur from doing what he wanted to do? He has a mind of his own."

"I promise *his majesty* is not going to break your neck."

"Now, let's not be hasty," Magnus said, enjoying the momentary flash of fear that entered the boy's eyes.

He'd never kill Nic.

Cleo would never forgive him.

"Here's what you're going to do," Magnus said. "You will go after Ashur and stop him from doing something unforgivably idiotic out of some bizarre and misplaced sense of Kraeshian familial loyalty. And you will retrieve the crystals he stole by any means necessary."

Nic regarded him with incredulity. "I won't leave Cleo again."

"Oh, you certainly will. And you're leaving immediately. You will return with the Kindred, or my patience with you is at an end." Magnus wracked his blurry mind to come up with a way to get Nic to do as he commanded. "You may hate me, but you've seen for yourself that I've kept your precious princess breathing all these months when others have wished her dead. I swear to the goddess I'll stop protecting her if you don't do exactly as I say."

Nic flinched, but his glare remained. "Cleo would be fine even without your so-called help."

"Perhaps. Or perhaps not. In a time of war—and make no

mistake, that is exactly what this 'peaceful' Kraeshian occupation really is—no one is safe."

Nic had no reply to this; all he did was glower.

"Threats or no threats," Jonas said with impatience, "the prince is right. Nic, you need to go after Ashur. We both do. I should have accompanied Felix and Taran when they left. There's no reason for me to be here."

"No reason, rebel?" Magnus shot him a look. "That's strange. Here I thought you were enjoying pawing at the princess's skirts, looking for table scraps."

Jonas glared at Magnus. "I would receive far more than you ever would."

Magnus smirked at him. "Don't be so sure about that."

Jonas's expression only darkened further at that. "We're done here. Nic, grab what you need for the journey to Basilius's compound. Hopefully we can catch up to Ashur before he arrives. And Magnus?"

"Yes, rebel?"

Jonas's eyes narrowed. "Harm one hair on the princess's head, and I swear to whatever goddess you give a damn about, I will make you beg for death."

CHAPTER 19

AMARA

PAELSIA

A single golden hawk circled above the Paelsian citizens gathering to hear Amara's speech. She stood at the open window in her chambers and looked out at the crowd of eager faces. Many were bewildered to be inside their former chief's private compound; its gates had been locked to the public during his command over this dusty kingdom. Today they had their first glimpse of the labyrinthine city, which reminded Amara greatly of the City of Gold, only instead of precious metals and jewels, it was made from clay, brick, stone, and dirt.

"Your grace, I wish you would reconsider this speech," Kurtis said from behind her. "You are much safer inside, especially with the news of rebels nearby."

She glanced from the window at the ever-present kingsliege. "That's why I have guards surrounding me at all times, Lord Kurtis. Rebels are always nearby. Unfortunately, I can't make everyone see my point of view. There are those who opposed my husband's reign, my father's reign. And there are those who will oppose mine as well. No, I will speak to my citizens today, those who would embrace me without question and the handful who doubt my intentions here. I must give them hope for the future—hope they've never had before."

"Which is a lovely sentiment, your grace, but . . . Paelsians are known savages, quick to violence."

She found his choice of words offensive. "There are those who say the same of Kraeshians," she replied with growing annoyance. "Perhaps you didn't hear me before. I will speak today."

"Your grace—"

She held up her hand, choosing to drop the smile from her lips. "I will speak today," she said firmly. "And no one will tell me I can't. Especially with the news of rebels, and with dissent even among my own soldiers, I need the support of these people for the future of my reign. And I will not have anyone tell me what I can and cannot do. Do you understand me?"

He immediately bowed deeply, his cheeks flushing. "Of course, your grace. I meant no disrespect."

The door opened, and Nerissa entered, bowing her head. "It is time, empress."

"Good. I'm ready." Amara stroked the silk of her gown. It was the one she wore for only the most special of occasions in Kraeshia. She took it with her whenever she traveled just in case there was the opportunity to wear such a splendid piece. Its shimmering stitches and shining beads of emerald and amethyst sparkled under the Paelsian sun as she emerged from her large villa.

An entourage of bodyguards waited outside for Amara, and with Nerissa by her side, she approached the large podium on a wooden stage high above the crowd of four thousand, who were elbow to elbow in the chief's former fighting arena.

These were her new subjects. They would hang on her every

word and spread the news of her glory to all who would listen. And one day soon, they would be the first to revere her as a true goddess.

The crowd cheered, and the air itself was infused with the sound of approval. She glanced at Nerissa, who smiled and nodded, encouraging her to begin.

Amara raised her arms, and her large audience went silent.

"I address the beautiful people of Paelsia, a kingdom that has endured many trials and tribulations through many generations." Her voice resonated off the stone pillars, which helped to amplify the words so that even those in the stands could hear her. "I am Amara Cortas, the first empress of Kraeshia, and I bring you the official news that you are no longer citizens of Mytica, a trio of kingdoms that have oppressed you for a century, but you are now citizens of the great Kraeshian Empire—and your future is as bright as the sun that shines down upon us today!"

The crowd cheered, and Amara took a moment to scan the faces, some dirty, with threadbare clothes worn down with dust and age. Weary eyes looked up at her, eyes that had seen many leaders who had made false promises and delivered only pain and suffering. Still, she saw timid hope even in the oldest of eyes.

"We will tend to your land," she continued. "We will make it rich again and ready to plant crops that will sustain you and your families. We will import livestock that will feed you. And as you continue to make the wine that Paelsia is famous for, the profits will be entirely yours, as I promise that there will be no Kraeshian taxes on this product for twenty years. The laws that have prevented legal export of this wine to anywhere but Auranos are hereby broken. I see Paelsia as a magnificent asset to my empire, and I want to show this by making my actions match my words. You are right to believe in me, for I believe in you. Together we will march forth into the future, hand in hand!"

The noise from the crowd swelled, and for a moment, Amara closed her eyes and allowed herself to soak it all in. This was why she'd sacrificed so much. This was why she'd done what she had.

This power.

No wonder her father had made so many harsh choices during his reign. This rush of obedience, of adoration, of awe was truly intoxicating.

Whether or not she could truly do all that she promised would have yet to be seen.

There was magic in the belief she felt from the Paelsian people. A magic so rich and pure that she wanted to bathe in it.

"Your grace!" Nerissa gasped.

Amara opened her eyes in time to see the glint of an arrow, and then one of her bodyguards shoved her out of the way. The arrow hit him in his throat, and he fell sputtering to the floor of the stage.

"What's happening?" she demanded.

"The group of rebels who threatened to be here today—they're here!" Nerissa grabbed her arm. Two more arrows flew toward her, narrowly missing her and hitting two other bodyguards.

"How many?" Amara managed. "How many rebels are here?"

"I don't know—" Nerissa raised her head to look out at the crowd just as another arrow whizzed by. "Twenty, perhaps thirty or more."

Amara watched with shock as her army of soldiers invaded the growing sea of civilians to apprehend the rebels. The soldiers cut down anyone who got into their way, be they rebel or Paelsian. The crowd panicked and tried to escape. Chaos broke out, cries of fear and outrage ringing all around as blood began to spill.

Paelsian men drew their weapons, their faces changing from hope to hate in an instant, and they began to fight not only with the soldiers but with each other, blades slicing flesh, fists hitting jaws and stomachs.

Savages, quick to violence, Kurtis had warned.

Mothers grabbed their children, crying and fleeing in all directions.

"What do we do?" Nerissa asked. She had crouched down next to Amara, and they were cowering now behind the podium.

"I don't know," Amara said quickly, then wanted to bite her tongue to take the words back.

Words of fear. Words of a victim.

She would not cower before rebels today or any day.

Her moment of fear quickly turned to anger. This, whatever this was, was not part of her plan. Those who wished to destroy her chance to make allies of these fierce people, who'd been ready to embrace her as their leader, would pay with their lives.

Amara bolted up from her hiding spot, her fists clenched, just as someone approached the stage from behind her. She could hear heavy footsteps stomping across the wooden surface.

She spun on her heels to see two of her bodyguards fall, their throats slashed. Behind them, a shockingly familiar face.

"Well, princess, I would bet a great many gold coins that you didn't expect to see me again."

Felix Gaebras held the tip of his sword only a couple of inches away from her face.

His was a face from her nightmares. Or perhaps they'd been premonitions. In these dreams, he'd been trying to kill her.

"Felix . . . you did this, all of this, just to get to me," she began, taking a shaky step back from the young man she thought was long dead.

He smirked. "Honestly? I was simply observing from a safe distance. This was a happy coincidence. I guess there are many other rebels who want to watch your blood spill. But it looks like I'm the one who gets the honor."

Her gaze whipped to her left to see three bodyguards racing toward Felix, but they were cut down by another young man with dark hair and an annoyed expression.

"This wasn't the plan, Felix," the young man shouted. "You're going to get us both killed."

"Quiet, Taran," Felix replied. "I'm reconnecting with an old girlfriend."

At the touch of his blade against her cheek, Amara looked right at his black eye patch. "Your eye . . ."

"Gone. Thanks to you."

She flinched. "I know you must hate me for what I did."

"Hate you?" His dark brows raised, shifting his eye patch a little. "*Hate* is such a tiny word, isn't it?"

Amara tried to see if any guards were coming to her aid, but Felix's friend Taran held them off with both the sword and the crossbow he was armed with.

Amara raised her eyes to meet Felix's and filled her voice with as much regret as she could muster. "Whatever you've endured, my beast, I promise I can make it up to you."

"Don't call me that. You lost the right to call me that when you left me behind to die." He touched the blade to her face again, nudging her gaze to turn to the crowd. "See what you did? This is your fault. Everything you touch ends in death."

Her tense gaze moved across the crowd that had gathered from miles around to hear her speak. Many Paelsians lay dead amongst the fighting, trampled by others, killed by the blades of guards or their own countrymen.

He was right: This was her fault. A moment of vanity, the desire to feel the love of her new subjects after so much pain and disappointment, and it ended with death.

Everything ended in death.

The same hawk she'd seen earlier circling above the crowd squawked loud enough for Amara to hear it. Beneath the bird, someone trapped in the middle of the chaos caught her eye, a young man with unusually bright red hair who'd been making his way toward the stage.

She recognized him as Cleo's friend—Nic. The one Ashur had become fixated upon.

Amara watched with horror as two Paelsians grabbed Nic, ripping his coin pouch off of the loop on his trousers. Nic grabbed for it, and one of the men's knives flashed in the sunlight before he sank it into Nic's chest.

She gasped.

Nic's body dropped to the ground, her sight of it quickly lost in the crowd.

This was her fault, all her fault.

She frowned at the thought. No—this had been bad luck for Nic, unfortunate circumstances. But she had not murdered Cleo's friend with her own hands. She refused to take the blame for other people's misfortune.

While she'd hated her father and equally despised her brothers, the Cortas family was not weak in any way. That included her.

And beyond the Cortas family, women weren't weak. They were leaders. Champions. Warriors. Queens.

Amara had faced far greater foes in her life than Felix Gaebras.

She forced her voice to shake as she spoke her next words to him. "You're better than this, Felix. Killing an unarmed girl? This isn't you."

"*Not me?* I'm an assassin by trade, love. Killing's what I do best."

Out of the corner of her eye, she watched his friend single-handedly fight off two more of her men. "I now rule a full third of the world and control all that fortune. Do you want to be a very wealthy man?"

He shrugged a shoulder. "Not really."

She'd forgotten that he'd been different from other men she'd known—an asset in the beginning, but a problem now. "Women, then. Ten, twenty, fifty girls who desire only you."

He fixed her with the coldest smile she'd ever seen. "And how would I know they were not cold, deceptive bitches like you? No deal, empress."

Amara summoned tears to her eyes. She hadn't cried in so long, but it was a talent she'd developed at an early age. The easiest way for a woman to avoid trouble or punishment, she'd found, was to feign weakness among men.

The tears quickly began to stream freely down her cheeks. "I planned to free you, but they told me you were already dead, killed in an attempt to escape. My heart ached for the thought that I'd lost you forever. I should have let you in on my plan, but I was afraid . . . so afraid. Oh, Felix, I didn't want anything to happen to you, truly. I—I love you! I always will, no matter what you choose to do today!"

Felix stared at her, as if stunned by her words. "What did you just say? You love me?"

"I do. I love you."

The tip of his sword wavered. But it quickly sprang back up.

"Nice try, love. I might believe that if I were a complete and utter idiot." He smirked at her. "Time to die."

A moment later, Carlos, who'd managed to get past Taran and up onto the stage, tackled Felix to the ground. Before she even had a chance to catch her breath, both Taran and Felix were brought before her and forced down to their knees.

Nerissa returned to her side, and Amara took her hand in

hers, squeezing it for reassurance that her attendant had not been harmed.

"The other rebels are dead, your grace," Carlos told her. His face bled from a vicious cut across the bridge of his nose.

She acknowledged this with a curt nod, then gazed down at Felix.

He shrugged again. "Can't say I didn't try."

"Should have been quicker."

"I like to talk too much, I guess." He gave her a wide grin, but his single eye was ice cold. It flicked to Nerissa for a brief moment before returning to her. "Let's revisit that offer of the harem of beautiful women, shall we?"

Amara touched Felix's cheek, drawing his face up. "I am regretful about your eye. I did enjoy that eye, among other parts of you. For a few nights, anyway."

"Shall we execute them immediately, your grace?" Carlos asked, his sword at his side.

She waited for fear to flash through Felix's single eye, but he remained defiant. "If I spare you, what will you do? Try to kill me again?"

"In a heartbeat," he said.

Taran groaned. "You are a damn idiot," he muttered.

Her beast had entertained her for a time. He still did.

A part of her was still drawn to him, despite everything. But it didn't matter. He should have died long ago so he'd no longer be a problem for her.

Amara nodded at her guard. "Throw them both in the pit. I'll deal with them later."

CHAPTER 20

LUCIA

PAELSIA

"She's incredible. Absolutely beautiful and glorious. More like a goddess than a mere mortal, if you ask me. I know in my heart that she will save us all."

Lucia paused at the vendor's stall as she searched for an apple that didn't have any imperfections—seemingly an impossibility in Paelsia—and glanced at the fruit seller speaking to her friend.

"I couldn't agree more," agreed the friend.

Could they be speaking of the prophesied sorceress?

"Pardon my rudeness, but may I ask whom you're speaking about?" Lucia asked. It was the first time she'd spoken aloud in over a day, and her voice cracked.

The vendor glanced at her. "Well, the empress, of course. Who else?"

"Yes, who else indeed," Lucia said under her breath. "So you believe that Amara Cortas will save you. Save you from what, exactly?"

The Paelsian women glanced at each other before regarding Lucia with weary patience.

"You're not from around here, are you?" One pursed her wrinkled lips. "No, with that accent, I believe you're Limerian, aren't you?"

"I was born in Paelsia and adopted into a Limerian family."

"How fortunate of you to have escaped these borders at an early age, then." The vendor glanced at her friend. "If only we all had been given that opportunity."

The two laughed humorlessly at this.

Lucia's patience was nearing an end. "I'll buy this apple." She pocketed the piece of fruit and handed over a silver coin. "As well as any information you can give me about the empress's whereabouts."

"Gladly." The woman greedily took the coin, her eyes narrowing. "Where have you been these last few days, young lady, that you wouldn't know all about the empress? Sleeping under a moss patch with the warlogs?"

"Something like that." Actually, she'd been recovering her strength at the inn in eastern Paelsia until she couldn't take anymore and needed to escape. Despite the barmaid Sera's concern for her health, Lucia knew she had to leave there lest her belly grow so big that she never got out of bed again.

She slid her hand over her swollen stomach, and the woman noticed, her eyes growing wide.

"Oh, my dear! I didn't realize you were with child. And so far along!"

Lucia waved off her concern. "I'm fine," she lied.

"Where is your family? Your husband? Don't tell me you're on your own here in the market today!"

It seemed that being with child made complete strangers want to treat her with much more kindness than they otherwise would. It had served her well during her uncomfortable, slow journey west.

"My husband is . . . dead," she said carefully. "And now I'm searching for my family."

The vendor's friend rushed toward her and took Lucia's hands in hers. "My deepest condolences for your painful loss."

"Thank you." Lucia got a sudden and annoying lump in her throat. Along with the swollen belly, her emotions had become much larger and harder to control.

"If you need a place to stay . . ." the vendor said.

"Thank you again, but no. All I need is information about the empress. Is she still in Limeros?"

The two shared another look of disbelief that Lucia was so vastly uninformed about such things.

"The great Empress Cortas," the vendor began, "is currently residing at Chief Basilius's former compound. From that location, she will be making a speech tomorrow, addressing all Paelsians who are able to attend."

"A speech to Paelsians. But why?"

A little compassion lifted from the vendor's face. "Well, why not? Perhaps you've forgotten because of the many years you've been blessed to live in Limeros, but life is difficult here in Paelsia."

"To say the very least," added her friend.

The vendor nodded. "The empress sees our struggles. Recognizes them. And she wants to do something about it. She values Paelsians as an important part of her empire."

Lucia tried not to roll her eyes. She'd had no true concept of what an incredibly effective and power-hungry manipulator Amara had been during the few times she'd spoken with the former princess when the Damoras had resided at the Auranian palace.

"I do, of course, question the empress's wisdom in marrying the King of Blood," the vendor mused.

"Apologies," Lucia said, staring now. "Did you say she's married to the King of . . . to . . . to *King Gaius*?"

"I did. But I've also heard rumors that he's currently missing, along with his demon heir. We can only hope that the empress has buried both of them twenty feet deep."

"Indeed," Lucia murmured, her stomach twisting at the thought. Sera had made no mention of her father's marriage to Amara. Could it really be true? "I . . . I need to go. I need to . . ."

She turned on her heel and disappeared into the market's crowd.

Once, Alexius had guided Lucia in how to find and awaken the Kindred with the ring of the sorceress. She'd hoped such a spell might work to help her find Magnus and her father. However, while she managed to make the ring spin as it had in her chambers at the Auranian palace, all her attempts to summon the sparkling map of Mytica and pinpoint their location failed. Weakened from using her *elementia*, she had to take constant rests as she made her way on foot, along with many other Paelsians, to the compound of the former Paelsian leader.

She refused to believe her family was dead. They were far more resourceful than that. And if the king had married Amara—a thought so ludicrous that she could barely wrap her mind around it—then he had done so for strategic reasons, for reasons of power and survival.

True, Amara was young and very beautiful, but her father was far too smart and ruthless to make such a choice out of mere infatuation.

There were thousands of Paelsians gathered just outside the compound walls when she finally arrived. The closest village was a half day's journey from here, and it was another long day, perhaps two in her current condition, to get to Basilia, which was Lucia's original destination.

The tall, heavy gates creaked open to allow the crowd into the compound. Lucia focused so greatly on the people surrounding her, searching their faces for anyone familiar, that she barely registered the stone pathways and clay cottages leading toward the massive, three-story residence in the center of the compound. The Paelsians were being led toward a large clearing there, one with several fire pits and raised stone seating. This made her think of the tales she'd heard of Chief Basilius hosting contests between men who wished to impress him with their strength and skill at combat. Here, there would have been fights to the death for his entertainment.

The crowd continued to grow, but from the bits of conversation all around her, Lucia heard no mention of the former chief and his pleasures. All she heard was talk of the greatness of their new empress.

Lucia had no idea Paelsians were so easily fooled. Then again, they had believed that Chief Basilius was a sorcerer for far too many years to count.

Chief Hugo Basilius. Her birth father.

And this had been his home—the place where she would have been raised had she not been stolen from her cradle.

She gazed around at the cottages and streets and fighting arena that made up the compound, expecting to feel something, some sense of loss of the life she might have had.

But there was nothing. If there was a home she longed for, it was a black palace surrounded by ice and snow.

The sooner she could leave this dry and unpleasant kingdom, the better. She'd had more than her fill of Paelsian culture after she'd first entered it with Kyan.

She'd heard no rumors of the fire god causing more havoc and death during her travels. She held tight to the amber orb that she had hidden in her pocket. Timotheus insisted that Kyan couldn't be killed. But if that was true, then where was he? What was he planning? Had she deeply harmed him in their battle? And if she hadn't, why hadn't he gone back to the Forbidden Mountains to reclaim his orb before she found it?

She curled her fingers around the amber crystal at the thought. Would she be strong enough to fight him if he found her today?

Lucia hated to admit that she wouldn't be.

No, that's not good enough, she thought. *There's no other choice anymore. I have to be strong enough.*

"She is indeed incredible," another Paelsian droned on, an old man with a hunched back. "If there's anyone who can rid our land of its current deadly disease, it's the empress."

"I want vengeance for my family's death," a younger woman replied.

"As do I," an older woman agreed.

"What disease are you talking about?" Lucia asked.

"The disease of the dark witch," the old man snarled. "Her evil has scorched this land and killed thousands of Paelsians with every touch of her gnarled, ugly hand."

Lucia twisted her hands. "I . . . I have heard of these misdeeds . . ."

"Misdeeds?" he practically yelled in her face. Some of his spittle hit her cheek, and she wiped it away, cringing. "Some say that Lucia Damora is prophesied to kill us all with her fire magic, that she's an immortal sorceress, born from the King of Blood mating with a demoness during a blood magic ceremony. But I see her for what she is—someone who needs to be slain before she harms anyone else."

They knew her name. And they hated her enough to want her dead.

It didn't matter that the old man didn't include Kyan in the telling. What was done was done. She couldn't go back and change all that had happened.

Paelsians looked at Lucia as a half-demon witch pulled from the darklands like a hateful weed. A nightmare and a disease that plagued their land.

She didn't even try to argue with them, since they were absolutely right.

The crowd began to cheer as Amara finally took the stage. Lucia tried to see as much as she could of the beautiful girl, her black hair long and flowing, her emerald satin dress with a sparkling embroidered phoenix on it, as she raised her hands. The crowd went silent.

Amara spoke clearly and passionately about a bright future for the citizens of Palesia. Lucia couldn't believe the lies she spewed, but when she looked around at the crowd, they were eating them up like a delicious, endless feast laid out before them.

The empress sounded so sincere in her promises. Lucia had to admire how easily she spoke about changing everything that was wrong with the world. Of making the decisions on behalf of these people who hung on every word she said.

Lucia stood there, her fists clenched at her sides, hating Amara and waiting for the chance to find out what her enemy had done with her family.

Then, almost instantly, the beautiful, false words Amara spoke were silenced. Someone screamed, and Lucia couldn't figure out why until she saw a guard on the stage collapse, clutching an arrow lodged in his throat. Then another guard fell, and another.

An assassination attempt.

This can't happen, Lucia thought frantically. *I need to question her. Amara cannot die today.*

With great effort, Lucia summoned air magic. Cool, windy

wisps circled her arms and hands in translucent spirals as she strode forward through the crowd and toward the dais, using this invisible magic to nudge everyone out of her path. The sight of Kraeshian guards jumping into the frightened, confused crowd with their weapons drawn only caused more panic to rise. The guards cut down anyone who fought them or stood in their way, be they rebels or civilians, which only made a fight to escape break out.

Lucia strained to see what was happening on the stage. Amara, accompanied by a girl who looked very much like the servant who used to trail after Princess Cleo, cowered before a tall young man wearing a black eye patch, sword in hand.

Lucia's cool air magic shifted to that of fire, ready to burn anyone who kept her from getting to Amara. Someone clutched her cloak, and she sent a glare down at him, ready to set him ablaze. Nicolo Cassian stared up at her, one hand gripping her cloak, the other pressed to a gaping wound on his stomach. When he coughed, blood sputtered from his mouth.

A mortal wound.

Her attention went again to the stage, but another choking sound drew her gaze back to Nic, a victim of either the bloodthirsty guards or a frightened Paelsian.

It didn't matter who had done this. She could tell at a glance that the wound was deep and deadly. What was this boy doing here, of all places?

Lucia didn't have enough magic to fight against thousands. She pressed a hand to her belly as she scanned the crowd, knowing she needed to get to safety. Many were trampling over each other to get back to the gates.

She took a step, only to realize that Nic hadn't let go of her yet. "Prinnn . . . cessss . . ." he gasped.

She cast a tentative look down at him.

"Please . . . help me . . ."

The life was fading from his eyes. He didn't have much time left. But Nic was a close friend of Princess Cleo—a girl Lucia once thought could be a true friend, until she'd betrayed Lucia.

Yet Lucia's father had destroyed Cleo's life, destroyed her entire world.

Cleo had lost everything over the last year. This friend was really all the Auranian princess had left of her former life.

If Nic died, Lucia had no doubt that it would destroy Cleo.

Lucia hated it when her conscience troubled her, especially when Cleiona Bellos was the subject.

Carefully, she crouched down next to him and pulled his hand away from his wound before pulling up his tunic. She grimaced at the sight of all the blood, the spill of his organs.

"Tell Cleo," Nic gasped, struggling to breathe, "that I love her . . . that she's my family . . . that I—I'm sorry."

"Save your breath," Lucia said, "and tell her yourself."

She pressed her hands against his bloody wound and channeled all the earth magic she had within her into him. He arched his back and cried out in pain, the piercing sound blending into the chaos surrounding them.

"Stop! Please!" Nic tried to fight her, to stop her, but he was too weak. He'd lost so much blood that Lucia didn't know if she had enough magic to fix him. But still she tried. Her hood slipped back from her head, revealing her hair and face, but she didn't bother to fix it. She drained her own energy and strength in an attempt to save this boy.

At least, until someone yanked her away from him. She spun around, furious, to come face to face with an ugly man whose lips were curled back from his teeth in a snarl.

"Look what I've found!" he announced, dragging her away from Nic until she lost sight of him. "The sorceress herself preying upon another one of us! Her hands are covered in Paelsian blood!"

Lucia tried to summon fire or air magic to blast him away from her, but nothing happened. She flexed her hand, desperate now to get away from her assailant.

"Look at me, witch," the man said.

She cast a glare at him, only to be met with the back of his hand striking her across her face so hard that her ears rung.

"String her up!" someone called out. "Burn the witch like she burned our villages!"

Disoriented, she was dragged across the dry ground, stumbling over her own feet until her attacker flung her away from him. She fell hard to her knees in the center of a circle of angry faces. Someone hurled a rock at her, and it hit her right cheek hard enough to make her cry out in pain. She touched her face and felt her warm blood.

"I'm not who you think I am," she managed, She raised her hands up before her. "You need to let me go."

"No, witch, today you die for your evil crimes. Are we all in agreement?"

The mob that surrounded her loudly voiced their approval. There was no mercy in any of their gazes. Someone handed her original assailant a thick loop of rope.

"Get her on her feet," he barked.

Someone behind Lucia hauled her up to her feet and pinned her wrists tightly together.

"Greetings, princess," an oddly familiar voice said in her ear. "Causing more trouble in Paelsia, I see."

Jonas Agallon. She strained to turn enough to meet his hate-filled gaze.

"Jonas," she managed, "please, you have to help me!"

"Help you? What? The great and powerful sorceress can't help herself?" He made a clucking sound with his tongue. "Such a tragedy. These people seem to want you dead. Burned alive, I believe I heard, yes? Seems like a fitting end for a witch like you."

Her mind reeled. "Where's my father? My brother? Do you know?"

"That's the last thing you should be worried about, princess. Truly." He turned her around, and his hand brushed against her stomach.

His brows drew together.

"That's right," she said, grabbing onto any chance at seeking help—even from someone like him. "Will you be so quick to celebrate my execution now that you know an innocent child will die with me?"

"Innocent?" Jonas's glare hadn't softened by a fraction. "Nothing someone like you could bring into this world would be innocent."

"I didn't kill that girl. It was Kyan. He . . . I couldn't control him. I wanted him to stop. I mourn your loss, and I regret what happened that day. I wish I could change it, but I can't."

"That girl's name was Lysandra." Jonas's jaw tightened, and he didn't speak for a moment while the other men urged him to follow them to a good place for a witch burning. "Where is Kyan?"

"I . . . I don't know," she said truthfully.

He met her gaze. "The child within you drains your magic, doesn't it?"

"How do you know that?"

His frown deepened. "You would have leveled this place by now if you had access to your *elementia*. Right?"

All she could do was nod.

Jonas swore under his breath. "They need you. They're depending on you. And here you are, stupidly about to get yourself killed."

If this were anywhere else, any other time, she would have resented him calling her stupid. "Then do something about it. *Please.*"

After another hesitation, Jonas drew his sword and pointed it at the man with the rope. "Slight change of plans. I'm taking the sorceress with me."

"Not a chance," the man growled.

"This isn't up for debate. I see that none of you are armed right now." He swept his gaze around the group. "Stupid move in a crowd like this not to carry a weapon, but it makes this somewhat easier for me. Follow us and you're dead." He glared at Lucia. "Let's go, princess."

He gripped her arm and pulled her along with him.

"Where are you taking me?" she demanded.

"To your beloved father and brother. May you all rot in the darklands together."

CHAPTER 21

CLEO

PAELSIA

When Cleo realized that Nic, Jonas, and Olivia had left without saying a word to her about their plans, she wasn't hurt. She was furious.

"My goodness, dear girl, you're going to wear a groove into the floor with all of this pacing."

Cleo turned to see that Selia Damora regarded her. The woman made her nervous, but she'd thankfully had little to do with her since they'd arrived. Hard to believe it had only been three days ago. It seemed more like three years.

"My friends left without saying farewell," Cleo replied tightly, forcing herself to stop chewing her right thumbnail all the way to the quick. "I find that unforgivably rude and disrespectful behavior. Especially from Nic."

"Yes, Nic. The boy with the fiery red hair." Selia smiled. "I'm sure he meant no harm. He seemed very fond of you."

"He's like a brother to me."

"Brothers *are* known for keeping secrets from sisters."

"Not Nic." Cleo twisted her hands. "We tell each other everything. Well, *almost* everything."

"Come and sit with me for a moment." Selia took a seat on a lounge chair and patted the seat next to her. "I want to get to know my grandson's new wife better."

It was the last thing Cleo wanted, but she had to pretend to be amiable. It would be wise to make friends with a woman who'd soon be filled with magic now that Cleo's magic had been stolen away—even if that woman was a Damora.

Just the thought of what Ashur had done made her tremble with outrage. How had he stolen the obsidian orb without her noticing? That Kindred had represented power to her, and a future filled with choice and opportunity. Now, because she'd allowed herself to become lazy and unobservant, it had been taken right from beneath her own nose.

And there wasn't a damn thing she could do about it.

Forcing a smile to her lips, Cleo took a tentative seat next to the older woman.

Selia didn't speak for a very long moment, but she studied Cleo's face carefully.

"What is it?" Cleo finally asked, even more uncomfortable than she'd been to start with.

"I wasn't sure before . . . but now I am. I see your father in you. Your eyes are the same color Corvin's were."

The mention of her beloved father made her tense up. "You had doubts about my parentage?"

"When it came to my son and his"—she hesitated—"*difficulties* with your mother, yes, of course I've had many doubts over the years. I thought there might be a chance that Gaius was your father."

The horror at the very idea of such a possibility made sudden nausea swell within her.

"My . . . my *father*?" She covered her mouth. "I think I'm going to be sick."

"He's not your father. I'm certain of that now that I see you."

Cleo tried to remain calm, but the woman's unexpected insinuation had blindsided her. "My—my mother would never have . . . not ever . . ."

"I'm very sorry to have troubled you with this. But wouldn't you rather be certain that you and Magnus are related only by vows and not by blood?" She frowned. "Goodness, you've become very pale, Cleiona."

"I don't even know why you'd suggest such a thing," she managed.

"I didn't think Gaius had been granted an audience with Elena after their falling out, which I know was well before her marriage to Corvin. But a mother isn't always told everything when it comes to matters of the heart, even by the most attentive and loving son."

The way the king had used what were supposed to have been his last words, his dying breath, to say her mother's name . . . *"I'm sorry, Elena."*

"I didn't even know they knew each other until very recently," Cleo said, her voice tight.

"They met one summer twenty-five years ago on the Isle of Lukas, when Gaius was seventeen and Elena was fifteen. By the time he returned home, Gaius had become obsessed with her, proclaiming that they would be married with or without his father's blessing."

Cleo struggled for breath. It hardly seemed possible, this story. It was like one from a storybook full of fantasy and imagination. "My father never mentioned anything about . . ." She frowned hard. "Did he know?"

"I have no idea what Elena may have shared with Corvin about her previous romances. I would assume that he did learn the truth eventually, if only so that he would be better able to protect Elena."

"Protect her? What do you mean?"

Selia's expression grew grave. "Elena became disinterested in Gaius once she returned home. I don't know why. I suppose it had only been a passing fancy for her, a way to spend her summer, stringing along the affections of a smitten boy. Nothing more. When Gaius learned of her change of heart, he . . . took it poorly. I confess, I love my son dearly, but he has always had a vicious violent streak. He went to her, demanding his love to be returned, and when she refused him he beat her nearly to death."

Another wave of nausea hit Cleo. Her poor mother, subject to the evil Gaius Damora at his very worst.

She'd never hated the king more.

"I only hope that my grandson isn't overly cruel to you behind closed doors, my dear," Selia said softly. "Powerful men, full of strength and anger . . . they are prone to violent outbursts. Wives and mothers can only hope to endure it."

"Endure it? You can't be serious! If Magnus ever raised a hand to me, I'd—"

"What? You barely come to his shoulder in height, and he must nearly be twice your weight. The best thing you can do in your position, Cleiona, is to be as pleasant and agreeable as possible at all times—as all women must."

Cleo straightened her shoulders and lifted her chin. "I didn't have the great privilege of knowing my mother, but if she's anything like me, anything like my sister, then I know she wouldn't have been as pleasant and agreeable as possible in the face of abuse, not by anyone at any time. And neither would I! I'd kill anyone who attempted to beat me!"

A slow smile crept across Selia's face. "My grandson has chosen to love a girl with both courage and strength, just as his father did. I was testing you, of course."

"Testing me?"

"Look at me, dear. Do I look like a woman who would let a man raise a hand to her?"

"No," Cleo answered honestly.

"Quite right. I'm very glad we had a chance to talk today, my dear. I know everything I need to know now."

She reached out and gave Cleo's hand a squeeze, then left the room.

That had been the most bizarre conversation of Cleo's entire life.

"Perhaps I'll make a visit to the tavern today myself," she muttered. "Why should Magnus be the only one around here who gets to drink wine in a foolish attempt to escape his problems?"

As she stood, something caught her eye out the window at the back of the inn. She stepped closer. Olivia stood in the courtyard. Oddly, the girl wore nothing but a white sheet wrapped around her body, one that Cleo recognized from the innkeeper's wife's daily washing.

Whatever manner of attire, the sight of the girl came as a great relief. Cleo rose and went outside to join her, glancing around curiously.

"Olivia! Are Nic and Jonas with you? Where did the three of you go?"

Olivia's expression held deep uncertainty. "I need to leave again immediately, but I wanted to return here first to see you."

"What? Where are you going?"

"It's time for me to go back to my home. Jonas's path has successfully intersected with his destiny, and my time with him is at an end."

"Apologies." Cleo shook her head, utterly confused. "Jonas's destiny? What in the world are you talking about?"

"It's not my place to explain such things. All I know is that I can't watch over him any longer, since I might be tempted to interfere." She frowned. "This must sound ludicrous to you. I know you don't know who I really am."

"You mean that you're a Watcher?"

Olivia's gaze snapped to Cleo's. "How do you know that?"

Cleo laughed uneasily at Olivia's look of shock. "Jonas told me. He trusts me, and so should you. I promise to keep your rather incredible secret, but please . . . tell me what's wrong. Are you upset only about leaving Jonas?"

"No, that's not the only reason. I . . . I went with Nic and Jonas to the compound where the empress is residing."

Cleo's eyes went wide. "That's where you were? Whose foolish plan was this?"

"Prince Magnus threatened Nic," Olivia explained. "He threatened your life as well if Nic didn't pursue Ashur and retrieve the Kindred orbs."

Cleo frowned. "That can't be right. Magnus wouldn't do something like that."

"I assure you, he did. Nic never would have left your side otherwise." Olivia's emerald-green eyes flashed with anger. "It's the prince's fault this happened. I lost Nic in the crowd during the assassination attempt on Amara. I saw him for only a moment as he fell under the blade. I . . . I believe it was over quickly."

Cleo shook her head as her palms began to prickle with sweat. "What? I don't understand. He fell under a blade? What blade? What do you mean?"

Olivia's expression held only sorrow. "Nic is dead. He is one of many who were killed during the aftermath of a rebel assassination attempt. I must leave Mytica now, and I strongly urge you to do the same. You're not safe here with someone like Magnus, who would send a boy like Nic off to his death. It's not right, princess, none of this is. The world is spiraling out of control, and I fear that it may already be too late to save it. I'm so sorry I had to tell you this, but I thought you deserved to know."

Olivia let go of Cleo's hand and took a few steps backward, her expression pained.

"Be well, princess," she said. With that, her dark, flawless skin transformed into golden feathers, her form shifting into that of a hawk, and she took flight.

Cleo watched her, far too stunned by what she'd been told to appreciate the sight of true and undeniable magic unfolding before her very eyes.

She wasn't sure how long it was that she stood in silence in the courtyard, staring up at the bright sky, before she turned and stumbled back into the inn. Her knees gave out under her before she reached a chair.

Every inch of her trembled, but she didn't cry. It was too much to process. Too unbelievable. It couldn't be true. If it was, if Nic was dead, then she wanted to die too.

"Are you all right? What's wrong?"

Before she realized what was happening, Cleo found herself swept up off the floor and into a pair of strong arms.

"Are you hurt?" Magnus stroked the hair off her forehead, cupping her face in his hands. "Damn it, Cleo. Answer me!"

Foggily, she registered the concern in his deep brown eyes and the deep crease between his brows from his frown.

"Magnus . . ." she began, drawing in deep, shuddery breaths.

"Yes, my love. Talk to me. Please."

"Tell me the truth . . ."

"Of course. What? What do you need to know?"

"Did you threaten to kill me if Nic didn't go after Ashur?"

His pained expression, utterly fixed on her, slowly gave way to the coolness of the mask he once wore to cover his emotions with her. "Did he tell you that? Has he returned?"

"Answer me. Did you or did you not threaten me to him?"

He held her furious gaze steadily. "Cassian required the right motivation."

"That's a yes."

"I told him only what he needed to hear to fix this. To—"

Cleo slapped him so hard that her hand stung from it. He pressed his hand to his left cheek and stared at her, stunned.

His eyes narrowed. "You dare—"

"He's dead!" she screamed before he could say another word. "Because of what you said! My last friend in the entire world is dead because of you!"

Confusion now crossed his face. "That can't be."

"Can't it? Don't people die when they come anywhere near you and your monstrous family?" She raked her hands through her hair, wanting to yank it all out by its roots, wanting to feel physical pain so she could concentrate on something other than her shattered heart.

"Who told you this?" Magnus demanded.

"Olivia came back. She's gone now, so you can't try to bully her into doing what you say too."

"Olivia. Yes, well, I don't know Olivia from a lump on the ground. Neither do you. All we know about her is that she's an ally of Jonas—someone who hated me enough to want me dead until very recently. For all I know, that goal never changed."

"Why would she lie about something like this?" her voice broke.

"Because people lie to get what they want."

"I suppose you should know."

"Yes. The feeling is entirely mutual, princess," he said. "Between the two of us, I believe you've racked up far more lies than I have. Also, may I remind you that you saw Ashur die with your own eyes, yet he still lives. You have no proof that Nic is dead—only someone else's words. Words are not to be trusted, not from anyone."

"That's your answer?" Cleo stared at him, realizing she barely knew this person before her. "I tell you a boy who was like my brother has been killed because of you, and you simply tell me I've been lied to?"

"Seems that way, doesn't it?"

"You take no responsibility for all the damage you've done. None at all!" She tried with all her might to stay composed, to not lose herself in the grief and rage battling within her. "I've tried to see the good in you, but then you do something unforgiveable like this. Go on," she snarled. "Try to defend yourself. Say that Nic hated you, so why wouldn't you wish him dead? Go on, do it!"

"I won't deny it. Life would be much easier for me if that jagged pebble in my shoe was discarded once and for all. But I would never truly wish him dead, because I know that you care for him."

"Care for him? I love him!" she cried out. "And if he's really dead, I—"

"What? Will you lose that last sliver of hope you've been clinging to? Will you curl up into a ball and die? Please. You have far too much riding on staying alive, fighting, lying, and continuing to shamelessly use me for what I can get you."

She stared at him, aghast. *"Use* you?"

Magnus's expression hardened. "You want power, you want magic. Staying here with me and tolerating my father's continued existence—you knew that would lead you to what you want. When the Kindred were stolen, especially knowing what we now know about them, what was I to think? That you'd continue to stay here indefinitely? I did what I did for *you*, to help return your chance for power. Ashur seems to value Nic for reasons I don't personally understand. If anyone could get through to that crazy Kraeshian, I knew it would be your dearest friend. The same friend who urged Taran to slit my throat, might I remind you."

He spoke to her like a hateful stranger, not like someone she had come to deeply value in her life. "And now you're blaming me for this. How dare you!"

He let out a deep breath. "It's impossible to reason with you."

"Then don't even try. You can't fix this, Magnus. You can't even start."

"If Nic is still alive—"

"It won't matter." Tears spilled down her cheeks. "This has proven how vastly different we are. You are unrelentingly cruel and manipulative, and I see now that will never change."

"Quite honestly, princess? I could say the exact same about you. Perhaps you'd prefer I deal with conflict by picking daisies and singing songs, but that's not me. And you're damn right: I won't ever change. And neither will you. One moment you say you love me, but you'd prefer to cut out your own tongue rather than share that dirty little secret, even with your closest friend. Goddess forbid that Nic might have thought you'd sully yourself with the likes of me. Would he hate you for that?"

She pushed her tears off her face, angry at herself for showing such weakness. "Very likely he would."

"So this proves that you'd choose him over me."

"In a heartbeat," she said immediately. "But he's *dead*."

A muscle in his cheek twitched. "Perhaps. And what about

Jonas? I couldn't help but notice you were practically sitting on his lap yesterday, cooing words of romantic encouragement to him."

"Is that what you—?" Her face flushed. "Jonas is *twice* the man you'll ever be. I'd rather share his bed than yours—any day, any time. And no curse could stop me."

"Damn you, Cleo." Fury flashed though eyes that had turned to ice. He raised his fist, his teeth clenched in a grimace.

"Go on," she snarled. "Hit me, just like your father hit my mother. You know you want to."

"What?" He frowned then and looked at his own fist with surprise before lowering it to his side. "I . . . would never hit you."

"I've had enough," she said, her voice now only a whisper. "I'm done here. I need to think." She turned toward the stairs that led up to the bedrooms.

"Cleo . . ." Magnus rasped out. "We'll find the truth about Nic. I promise you."

"I already know the truth."

"I know I can be horrible sometimes. I know it. But . . . I love you. That hasn't changed."

Her shoulders tensed. "Love isn't enough to fix this."

Without looking back, Cleo walked as calmly and slowly as possible to her room before locking the door behind her.

CHAPTER 22

JONAS

PAELSIA

Jonas had to leave the compound before finding Nic. They'd been separated after the rebel uprising. The empress's audience had panicked and began fighting against each other as well as the swarm of Kraeshian guards

His view of the stage was blocked and he'd been faced with angry Paelsians and the sorceress they wanted dead.

"You can look at me with as much hatred as you want," Lucia said to him as they swiftly left the riots.

"I appreciate your permission."

"You hate me. And yet you saved my life."

"Likely I saved the lives of a dozen Paelsian men who underestimated your ability to kill each one of them where they stood."

"And you don't underestimate me?"

"No, I don't."

"Then I strongly suggest you tell me where my father and brother are so that you won't have to risk your own life for a moment longer in my company."

Jonas knew she could make good on this threat if she wanted to. He couldn't help but shiver at the thought of how powerful this girl was and how much damage and death she was rumored to be responsible for.

"Where is the fire god?" he whispered.

She raised her eyebrows. Jonas could tell she was shocked that he knew who—or rather *what*—Kyan really was. "I already told you that don't know."

"Is he the father of your child?"

Lucia let out a sharp, nervous laugh. "Certainly not."

"I don't find anything funny about this."

"Make no mistake, rebel, neither do I."

"Keep walking," he said when her pace began to slow. "By the looks of you, you're far too heavy for me to carry."

Lucia's rebuttal to this insult was to stop walking completely. They'd entered a thatch of forest on their way to the nearest town, where Jonas planned to find transport west.

"Answer my question: Where are my father and brother? I know they're still alive. They have to be."

"If I answer your question, what certainty do I have that you won't end my life?" he asked.

"None at all."

"Exactly. Therefore, I will take you to them myself."

She gasped. "So they are alive!"

"Perhaps," he allowed.

"And how am I to believe that you want to help me?"

He spun around and jabbed his index finger at her. "Make no mistake, Princess Lucia, I'm not doing this to help you. I'm doing this to help Mytica."

She rolled her eyes. "So noble."

"Think what you want. I don't care. You refuse to answer my

questions; I'll refuse to answer yours. Our destination is not horribly far away, but you'll have to find a way to deal with my presence and my hatred during this journey together."

"I don't think so. I'm going to tell you a little secret, rebel, about a special skill I've recently discovered. I can make you tell me the truth . . . and the more you resist, the more it will hurt."

Jonas turned to face her again, more exasperated than intimidated. "Were you always this much of a bitch, or was it only after you discovered you were a sorceress?"

"Honestly?" She gave him a cold smile. "It was after."

"I find that hard to believe. You and your whole family . . . evil to the core, every one of you."

"And yet you still seem to be helping us." Lucia frowned slightly. "At least tell me that they're all right, that they're unharmed after everything that's happened."

"Unharmed?" He smirked at her. "I don't know about that. I did finally get the chance to put a dagger through the king's heart. Unfortunately, it only slowed him down for a moment or two."

Her eyes flashed with fury. "You lie."

"Right here." He patted his chest. "Nice and deep. I even twisted it. Felt so good, I can't even tell you."

A moment later, he found himself airborne, flying backward until he hit the trunk of a tree hard enough to knock his breath from his lungs.

Lucia knelt next to him, her hand clutching his throat. "Look at me."

Disoriented, he looked into her sky-blue eyes.

"Tell me the truth," she snarled. "Is my father dead?"

"No." The single word was pulled painfully from his throat.

"You stabbed him in his heart, but he's not dead?"

"Exactly."

"How is this possible? Answer me!"

Jonas couldn't look away from her beautiful, fearsome eyes. Whatever magic she'd lost during the riot—if she'd truly lost any at all—had returned. And she was far stronger than he expected her to be.

"Some sort of magic . . . I don't know. It prolonged his life."

"Magic from whom?"

"His . . . mother." Jonas was certain he now tasted blood, thick and metallic. He choked against it as he attempted to resist her magic.

She frowned deeper. "My grandmother is dead."

"She's alive. I don't know much more about her." He grimaced against the pain of speaking all of these truths to her. "Now do me a favor, princess?"

She cocked her head but didn't budge an inch otherwise. "Doubtful."

Jonas narrowed his eyes and tried with all his might to channel his own thread of magic as he'd unconsciously done on the ship with Felix. "Let go of me."

She lost her grip on his throat and fell backward as if he'd physically shoved her.

Coughing and holding his throat, he got to his feet and looked down at her.

He felt a small smile form on his lips. Olivia must have been wrong about the extent of his magic. Jonas allowed himself the briefest moment of victory over this.

Lucia looked up at him, her eyes wide. "You can channel air magic? A witch boy? I've never heard of such a thing. Or . . . are you an exiled Watcher?"

"I prefer to avoid labels, princess," he said. "And frankly, I don't know what the hell I am, only that I have to deal with this now." He pulled his shirt down far enough that she could see the spiral mark on his chest. It had only grown brighter since the last time he looked at it, and it was now glimmering with a gold that reminded him more of a Watcher's mark.

"What?" Lucia shook her head, her eyes wide. "I don't understand."

"Neither do I. And I swear, if this is my prophecy, to make sure someone like you returns to your hateful family all safe and sound, I'm going to be furious." He looked up at the trees. "You hear me, Olivia, wherever you are? Worst prophecy ever!"

"Who's Olivia?"

"Never mind that." He looked down at Lucia, still sprawled on the ground. "Get up."

She tried to push herself up. "Um . . ."

"You can't stand up, can you?"

"Give me a minute. My belly is a bit awkward at the moment." Lucia glared at him. "No, please, don't even think about helping me."

"I wasn't." He watched as she slowly and painstakingly rolled onto her side, then rose to her feet, brushing off her cloak to free it from the pine needles and dirt it had picked up. "Aren't you used to your condition by now? I've seen pregnant Paelsian women only days from giving birth chop down a whole tree's worth of wood and carry it back to their cottages."

"I am not a Paelsian woman," she said, then blinked. "Well, not exactly. And I haven't had time to get used to my *condition*, as you call it."

Such a strange girl. "How far along are you?"

"Not that it's any of your business, but . . . a month or so."

Jonas scanned her full form with disbelief. "Is this the way it is with evil sorceresses? Their unborn spawn grow much swifter than normal babies?"

"I wouldn't know." Lucia crossed her arms over her belly, as if trying to shield it from him. "I understand your hatred for me.

I understand everyone's hatred for me. What I've done since . . . since the father of this child died is unforgiveable. I know that. But this child is innocent and deserves a chance at life. The fact that you, of all people, came to the aid back there of someone like me—someone marked like an immortal, someone who doesn't claim to be a witch or an exile—that must mean something. You speak of prophesies. I'm well aware of being the subject of prophesies. To me, it means that this child matters to the world."

"Who was the father?" Jonas asked. He didn't want to feel sorry for what she'd been through or allow the catch in her voice to move him.

"An exiled immortal."

"And you say he's dead."

She nodded once.

"How did he die?" Jonas asked. "Did you kill him?"

Lucia was silent for so long that he didn't think she'd answer. "No. He took his own life."

"Interesting. Is that the only way to escape from your dark clutches?"

Lucia's look of sheer hatred made him flinch. But the look was more than that. Her eyes were pink-rimmed, a mixture of exhaustion and sadness.

"Apologies," Jonas said before he had a chance to think about his response. "I suppose that was unnecessarily harsh."

"It was. But I'd expect no less from someone who thinks I'm sheer evil. What Kyan did to your friend . . ."

"Lysandra," he choked out. "She was incredible: the bravest and strongest girl I've ever known. She deserved the life that Kyan stole from her without a second of hesitation. He was aiming for me—I'm the one who should have died that day, not her."

She nodded sadly. "I'm so sorry. I've come to realize that Kyan isn't a person, isn't someone with feelings and needs like mortals have, and he isn't someone who can be reasoned with. Kyan sees every fault and imperfection in this world. He wishes to be the one to burn it to ashes so it can begin again. I'd say that he's insane, but he is fire. Fire burns. It destroys. That is its reason for existing."

"He wants to destroy the world," Jonas repeated.

She nodded. "It's why I left him. Why he nearly killed me when I said I wouldn't help him anymore."

Jonas took a moment to absorb this. "You say fire destroys. But fire also cooks food, it warms us on cold nights. That kind of fire isn't evil—it's an element we use to keep us alive."

"All I know for sure is that he needs to be stopped." She reached into the pocket of her cloak and drew out a small amber orb, the exact same size as the earth Kindred. "This was Kyan's prison."

Jonas found himself momentarily speechless. "And you think you can put him back in there and save the world?"

"I plan to try," she said simply.

He looked at Lucia's face, determined and serious as she gazed at the crystal orb. She sounded so sincere. Could he believe her? "Given what I now know about the fire Kindred, the empress doesn't seem like much of a threat at all, does she?"

Lucia slipped the orb back into her pocket. "Oh, Amara has definitely shown herself to be a threat. But Kyan is far worse. So think me evil, rebel. Consider me someone who needs to die for my crimes. Fine. But know also that I want to try to fix some of what I've done, now that I'm able to think clearly again. First, I need to see my family. I need to—" Lucia's words cut off as she doubled over and cried out.

Jonas rushed to her side. "What's wrong?"

"Pain!" she managed. "This had been happening far too often since I left. Oh . . . oh, goddess! I can't . . ."

She dropped to her knees, clutching her belly.

Jonas stared at her, feeling completely helpless. "Damn it. What can I do? Is the baby coming already? Please don't tell me the baby is coming."

"No, it's not . . . I don't think it's time yet. But this—" When she screamed, the sound sliced through Jonas like a cold blade. "Take me to my family! Please!"

The princess's face had gone stark white against her raven-black hair. Her eyes rolled back in her head as she dropped to her side, unconscious.

"Princess," he said, trying to shake her awake. "Come on, there's no time for this."

Lucia didn't wake up.

Jonas turned to look in the direction of the riots. It wouldn't be long before the Paelsian mob found weapons and came after him and the sorceress.

Finally, swearing under his breath, he crouched down and picked the princess up in his arms, finding her much lighter than he'd expected, even with the child she carried within her.

"No time to get to your family," he said, "so I'm taking you to mine. They're much closer."

Jonas's sister, Felicia, opened the door to her cottage and stared out at Jonas for a long moment in utter silence.

Then she looked at the unconscious, pregnant girl he carried in his arms.

"I can explain," he said quickly.

"I would certainly hope so. Come in." She opened the door wider so Jonas could enter, careful not to knock Lucia's legs against the rough door frame.

"Put her on my bed," Felicia instructed Jonas. He did as she said before returning to his sister, who didn't greet him with a hug. Instead she stood there, her expression drawn and severe, her arms crossed over her chest.

He didn't expect her to be happy to see him.

"I'm sorry I haven't visited," he began.

"I haven't seen or heard from you in nearly a year, and you show up tonight with no warning."

"I needed your help. With . . . the girl."

She snorted. "Yes, I'm sure you do. Is the child yours?"

"No."

She didn't look convinced. "And what do you expect me to do for her?"

"I don't know." He rubbed his forehead and began to pace back and forth in his sister's small cottage. "She isn't well. She had stomach pains and collapsed. I didn't know what to do with her."

"So you brought her here."

"I knew you would help me." He let out a shaky sigh. "I know you're angry with me that I've been away so long, but it's been too dangerous to return."

"Yes, I saw the wanted posters. What was it? Ten thousand centimos for your capture, dead or alive?"

"Something like that."

"You killed Queen Althea."

"I didn't. It's a long story."

"I'm sure."

He glanced around, checking for any sign of his sister's husband. "Where's Paolo?"

"Dead."

Jonas's gaze shot back to hers. "What?"

"He was taken from me, forced to work on the Imperial Road. They wanted Father too, but they decided because of his age and his limp that he was useless to them. Paolo didn't return when the workers were finally released from their duties. What am I to think except that he was killed along with scores of other Paelsians who were treated like slaves?"

Jonas stared at her with shock. Paolo had been a good friend of his back when life was hard but simple. "Felicia, I'm so sorry. I had no idea."

"No, I'm sure you didn't. Just as I'm sure you didn't think keeping that little Golden Princess locked in our shed would nearly lead to his death as well."

"Of course I didn't know that." He cast his eyes downward at the dirt floor. "You . . . you say Father wasn't taken?"

"No. But from the moment he learned of the chief's death, he became very ill—ill with grief unlike anything he felt when either Mama and Tomas died. It's like his will to live began to slip away. I lost him two months ago. I run the vineyard now. Long days, Jonas, with very little help."

His father had died, and Jonas had had no idea. He sat down heavily in a chair. "I'm so sorry I haven't been here for you. I don't know what to say."

"There's nothing you can say."

"When this is over, when this kingdom is back to how it should be, I will return here. I will help you run the vineyard."

"I don't want your help," she spat out, anger that she'd been holding back until now spilling out like an overturned cask. "I can do it fine on my own. Now, I feel that's more than enough catching up. Let's deal with your current problem so you can be on your way as soon as possible. I'm no healer, but I've helped plenty of pregnant girls before."

"Whatever you can do to help is much appreciated. I just hoped you might know how to stop the pain."

"Some pregnancies are more difficult than others. Who is she?" She looked at him sharply when he didn't answer. "Tell me, Jonas, or I'll send you back into the night."

His sister was different now, harder, angrier. Every word from her mouth made him cringe.

He felt foolish to think that he could return here and nothing would have changed after being gone for so long. He'd meant to send a message, to check in, but it hadn't happened. And time had gone by.

"She's Lucia Damora," he answered honestly, since he owed Felicia that much.

Felicia's eyes widened with shock. "What are you thinking bringing that evil witch in here? She is not welcome in my home. Are you aware of what she's responsible for? A village not ten miles from here was burned to the ground, everyone in it killed, because of *her*. She deserves to die for what she's done."

Each word felt like a blow, and he couldn't argue with any of them. "Perhaps she does, but right now her magic is needed to save Mytica. To save the world. You wouldn't let an innocent child suffer because of the choices of its mother, would you?"

She laughed then, drily. "Listen to you, defending a royal princess—from Limeros, no less. Who are you, Jonas? Who has my brother become?"

"Amara can't be allowed to control Mytica," he reasoned. "I'm willing to do whatever it takes to stop her."

"You are blind as well as dumb, brother. The empress is the only one who can save us all. Or have you forgotten the past so easily now that your head has been turned by that piece of evil dung currently sleeping on my bed?"

"My head has not been turned by anyone," he growled. "But I know what's right."

"Then you need to wake up. The empress is the best thing that's happened to Paelsia in generations."

"You're wrong."

"I'm not wrong," she said, her fiery anger finally dissipating as weariness set into her voice. "But I can't be bothered to convince you of something I know is right. You're lost to us, Jonas. I can see it in your eyes. You're not the same boy who grew up wishing to be like Tomas, who went with him to poach on the border of Auranos, who chased after all the girls in the village. I don't know who you are anymore."

His heart ached at the thought of how much he'd disappointed her. "Don't say that, Felicia."

She turned away from him. "I'll let you and that creature stay for the night. That is all. If she dies of this pain she has, then let her die. The world will be better off without her in it."

Jonas reclined on the dirt floor, next to the fire, his mind in turmoil.

When he'd come here, he'd at least had a sense of direction, of purpose. He needed to get Lucia to her family.

The Damoras. The King of Blood who had oppressed his people. Who'd murdered Chief Basilius. Who'd lied to two armies about his reasons for starting a short-lived war with Auranos.

Felicia was right. Amara Cortas had ended all of that with this occupation.

How had he found himself on this path? He was a rebel, not the simpering assistant to a sadistic king.

It took a long time before he fell asleep. In a dream, he found himself in a lush green meadow under a bright blue sky. In the distance, a city that looked to be made from crystal sparkled in the sun.

"Jonas Agallon, we finally meet. Olivia has told me so much about you. I am Timotheus."

He turned to be greeted by the sight of a man who appeared to be only a handful of years older than him. His hair was the color of dark bronze, his eyes a pale copper. He wore white robes that fell all the way to the emerald-green grass.

"You're in my dream," Jonas said slowly.

Timotheus raised a brow. "A brilliant deduction. Yes, I am."

"Why?"

"I expected you'd be full of questions for me."

Of all the sensations he felt at being face to face with the immortal Olivia had told him little about, he felt no shock, no surprise, only weariness. "Questions that you'll answer?"

"Some, perhaps. Others, perhaps not."

"No, it's all right. Just let me sleep. I'm tired, and I can't be bothered with solving riddles."

"Time is running out. The storm is nearly upon us."

"Do you talk like this to everyone, so annoyingly vague?"

Timotheus cocked his head. "Actually, yes. Yes, I do."

"I don't like it. And I don't like you. Whatever this is," Jonas patted the mark on his chest, "I want it gone. I want nothing to do with your kind. I'm Paelsian. I'm not a Watcher, or a witch, or whatever you think this makes me."

"That mark makes you very special."

"I don't want to be special."

"You don't have a choice."

"I always have a choice."

"Your destiny is set."

"Kiss my arse."

Timotheus blinked. "Olivia did mention that you're rather single-minded in your observations. However, I'm sure you've noticed that you now possess a sliver of magic. Phaedra's magic. Olivia's magic. You absorbed these like a sponge absorbs water. What you are is rare and, I'll say it again, special. The visions I've had of you are important."

"Right. The visions. The prophecy of me delivering Lucia Damora to her family."

"Is that what you think?"

"Seems like that's where this destiny of mine is taking me."

"No, not exactly. You will know when it happens. You will feel—"

"What I feel right now is the need to put a knife in your gut." Jonas glared at the immortal. "You dare enter my dream now, after all this time? Olivia's helped to keep me alive, just like you told her to. I guess she's done with me now. Or maybe she's spying on me from above as a hawk, just like you all do. All I know for sure is that I'm through with this. I don't care what you have to say. You dangle half truths as if the lives of mortals are a game."

Timotheus's voice lowered. "This is not a game, young man."

"Oh, no? Then prove it. Tell me my destiny, if you think it's something I can't avoid."

Timotheus studied him. "I didn't foresee Lucia's pregnancy," he admitted. "That was a surprise to me, as I'm sure it was to her. It's been shielded from all of us by the Creators, and there must be a reason for this—an important reason. My original vision of you was that you were to assist Lucia during the storm—"

"What storm are you talking about?"

Timotheus raised his hand. "Don't interrupt me. I'm being as blunt with you as I've ever been with anyone, because I see now there is no time to be anything else."

"So spit it out," Jonas said. He felt frustrated with everything in his life, and he wanted to take it all out on this pompous immortal.

"Lucia's son will have great importance. Many will wish to kidnap this child or to kill him. You will protect the child from harm and raise him as your own son."

"Is that right? And Lucia and I will, what? Get married and live happily ever after? Unlikely."

"No. Lucia is destined to die in childbirth during the coming storm." He nodded firmly, a frown creasing his brow. "I see it now, clearly. I originally thought that her magic might transfer to you at the time of her death, making you a sorcerer, one who could walk between worlds, one whose destiny was to imprison the Kindred after they are all freed. But Lucia's magic will live on through her son."

Jonas gaped at him, stunned by his proclamation. "She's going to die?"

"Yes." Timotheus turned his back on him. "That is all I can tell you. Good luck to you, Jonas Agallon. The fate of all the worlds is in your hands now."

"No, wait! I have questions. You need to tell me what I need to do—"

But Timotheus disappeared then, as did the meadow and the city in the distance.

Jonas woke to find his sister shaking him.

"It's dawn," she said. "Your girlfriend is awake. Time for both of you to get out of my home."

CHAPTER 23

MAGNUS

PAELSIA

Magnus knew he'd never beg for anything in his life: not for mercy, not for forgiveness, and not for a second chance. Yet all he wanted to do was go after Cleo to try to make her understand.

Bloody Nic. If the stupid boy had managed to finally get himself killed, this recent rift with Cleo meant that Magnus couldn't even celebrate such an occasion.

He took a step toward the stairs.

"No," his grandmother's voice stopped him. "Let her go. Pursuing her immediately will only make matters worse. Trust me."

Magnus turned to see Selia standing in the doorway, regarding him curiously.

"I wasn't aware our discussion was being overheard," he said.

"My dear, even the deaf could have overheard that"—she cocked her head—"*discussion*, did you call it?"

"Apologies, Selia, but I don't want to talk about this with you."

"I'd much rather you call me Grandmother, like you used to when you were a little boy."

Again, he turned toward the stairs, waiting to see if a miracle might happen and Cleo might return to him. "I'll call you whatever I like."

"You are surprisingly stern and serious for such a young man, even a Limerian, aren't you? Then again, you were raised by Althea, so I'm not terribly surprised. I don't remember ever seeing that woman smile."

"Did my father happen to mention to you that he had her killed? And then he lied and told me that his mistress Sabina was my true mother?"

"No," she said simply, twisting the silver snake pendant at her throat. "This is the first I'm hearing of this."

"And you think it odd that I'm not laughing joyfully day in and day out when we're at war with an entire empire that threatens to destroy us all?"

"Of course you're right. Forgive me—my thoughts have been elsewhere."

"I envy your thoughts."

Selia pursed her lips. "You should know that your father will not survive the night. He will be claimed entirely by death by morning. Do you care?"

Magnus didn't say anything to this. No thought came to his mind, good or bad.

He'd imagined he would celebrate this moment, the impending death of a man he'd hated for as long as he could remember.

"He loves you," Selia said, as if reading his thoughts. "Whether you believe it or not, I know it's true. You and Lucia are the most important parts of his life."

He didn't have time for such nonsense. "Really? I could have sworn it was his lust for power that was most important to him."

"When on the very edge of death, matters such as fortune and legacy are meaningless in the face of knowing that someone who cares for you will hold your hand as you slip away."

"I'll have to remember that when I'm on the edge of death." Magnus glared at her. "Apologies, but is there something you require from me? Because if you're asking me to go upstairs and hold my father's hand while he dies, leaving me to fix this mess he's made, I'll have to strongly decline."

"No. What I want from you is to accompany me to the tavern this evening to meet with my friend Dariah."

Magnus's breath caught and held. "The bloodstone."

She nodded. "I want you there by my side."

"Why?"

"Because it's important to me, that's why. I know you have doubts about the choices I've made in the past, but one day soon I know you'll understand."

Magnus would go with her tonight. Not for matters of love, since those had locked themselves away in a small bedroom upstairs in a fit of anger and grief.

No, he would go because, in this uncertain time, the bloodstone sounded like a piece of magic worth killing for.

Magnus waited for Cleo to emerge from the bedroom, but she never did. When the sun set, he reluctantly left the Hawk and Spear Inn with Selia at his side. By now, he'd become quite accustomed to the Purple Vine. From its entrance, he could see the sea sparkling under the moonlight, the ships docked at port spilling their crews into the city. Basilia seemed more alive at night than during the day, when there was business to attend to. At night, all those who had toiled during the day now wished to drink and eat and pay attention to other base desires, all of which were catered to within a modest stroll from the docks.

The tavern was packed wall to wall with boisterous patrons, most of whom were already blindingly drunk by the time Magnus and Selia arrived. Still, Magnus wore his hood close around his face to shield his identity. He couldn't risk being recognized again.

Selia led the way to a table in the far corner, seated at which were a beautiful, young auburn-haired woman and a man with bronze-colored hair that reached his shoulders and eyes the shade of copper coins.

It was a man Magnus recognized immediately.

At the sight of him, the memories of the road camp in the Forbidden Mountains of Paelsia flooded his mind. This man—an exiled Watcher—had been stationed there so that he could infuse the road with the magic required to pinpoint the four points in Mytica where the Kindred would be awakened.

Magnus had not spoken directly to the man at the time, but he'd watched him steal the life from another exile during a rebel attack.

"Xanthus," Magnus finally forced the name out. "Do you remember me?"

The man rose to his feet, showing off his massive height. The thick band of the gold ring he wore on his right index finger glinted in the candlelight. "Your highness, of course I do."

"No need for such pleasantries tonight. In fact, let's forgo the use of my name or title altogether, shall we?"

Xanthus nodded. "As you wish."

"You haven't been seen or heard from in many months."

"No, I haven't," Xanthus agreed. "My work for the king was complete, and it was time for me to rest and regain my strength. Please, sit."

Magnus and Selia took a seat at the wooden block of a table.

"You look lovely tonight," Selia said to the other woman, whom Magnus didn't recognize. "Your control over air magic has improved greatly over the years."

"Do you really think so?" the woman said with a giggle, twisting a lock of her long, silky auburn hair coyly around her finger.

Xanthus placed his hand over the woman's. "Dariah always looks lovely."

Dariah? Magnus regarded the woman now with fresh eyes as he realized that she'd used her *elementia* to shift her appearance to that of a younger, more attractive woman. If he watched carefully, he could see that her features appeared obscured, as if she sat in a shadow rather than beneath a lantern set into the wall, and that she appeared slightly too perfect to be real.

"Dariah tells me that you wish to speak to me," Xanthus said. "She said it was important that I arrive as quickly as possible. For anyone else, I wouldn't bother."

"Tell me," Magnus said, curiosity building inside of him to a point where it had to be released, "are you still in contact with Melenia?"

Xanthus shifted his gaze to Magnus. "No, I'm not."

"What became of her? She stopped visiting my father's dreams."

"Melenia does what she wants when she wants. She is, I assume, focused on restoring my home to its previous greatness now that the Kindred have been awakened."

At the mention of the crystals, Magnus waited for Selia to say something, but she remained silent, her curious gaze fixed on them both.

Xanthus took a drink from the goblet before him, signaling to the barmaid to bring over another round for the table. "What do you want from me tonight?"

"One more question, if you don't mind," Magnus said, his eyes narrowing. "Are you familiar with someone by the name of Kyan?"

Xanthus returned his full attention to Magnus, his expression grim. "He is free."

"Yes. Might you have any inside advice on him?"

"Stay as far away from him as you can get, if you value your life," Xanthus said. "Melenia, believing she was doing the right thing, helped the fire god to steal the corporeal form of a dear friend of mine." He sent a dark look at Dariah as he drained his drink. "Is this why you insisted I come here tonight? To answer the prince's questions about matters I don't wish to discuss with anyone?"

"No, it's not," Selia answered on behalf of her friend. "But I find it fascinating to learn more about the fire Kindred, so thank you for that."

"The Kindred have been awakened," Dariah said, her voice filled with awe. "Is it true?"

"It is," Selia said, smiling sweetly. "Xanthus, you've been exiled how many years?"

He looked at Dariah, who nodded. "Selia is a trusted friend," she said.

"Very well. I left the Sanctuary twenty years ago."

"Incredible," Selia said, shaking her head. "All exiles I've ever heard of had their magic fade to a mere trace in a quarter of that time. Yet yours remained so powerful that you were able to bless the Imperial Road with it."

He nodded. "Melenia ensured that my magic would not drain away over the years, nor would I be at risk of death as a mortal. That promise was put to the test not so long ago, when a dagger found my heart."

The barmaid brought their drinks, and Magnus was dismayed to see that his was a mug of ale. He pushed it away from him.

"Not to your liking?" Selia asked. "Oh, that's right. You prefer Paelsian wine."

Magnus eyed her. "How do you know that?"

"Because you return to the inn smelling of it every evening." She followed this harshness with a charming smile. "Gaius had a great thirst for wine in his youth, despite all the laws against it. His father was constantly furious at him for disrespecting the goddess. Paelsian, Auranian, Terrean, Kraeshian . . . whatever he could get his hands on. I've never tried it myself. Never wanted to. I prefer to keep my mind clear and sharp."

Even with that said, Selia called a girl over and ordered two bottles of their best vintage. Magnus didn't try to stop her, and when they arrived, he uncorked both bottles himself and drank deeply from one of them labeled "Agallon Vineyards."

There truly was no escape from the rebel.

Selia raised a brow when he quickly drained the first bottle. "Wine won't ever make your problems disappear. It will only magnify them."

"Excellent advice from someone who's never tasted a drop." He sighed. "I grow weary of this horrible day. How long must we remain here tonight?"

"Not much longer."

"Good."

"Dariah," Selia leaned over the table. "The time has come."

"I understand." Dariah nodded, her cheeks flushed. "Do what you must."

Selia glanced at the exiled immortal. "I need your ring, Xanthus."

"Do you? I'm afraid it's not for sale," Xanthus said smoothly, looking down at the thick piece of jewelry on his right hand, "but I'm happy to give you the name of the artisan who created it for me."

"Dariah, you should know that I've been preparing for tonight since you left. Each day has felt like a year as I've watched my beloved son fade away before my eyes. You know I'd do anything for him. Drop your hold on your vanity for a moment and see if you can feel my restored magic tonight."

Magnus watched his grandmother, not certain what she meant. Had she not told them that she required the bloodstone to restore her magic?

Dariah's false beauty shifted and shimmered as she frowned. "Yes, I can feel the blood magic. Selia, how many have you killed to achieve this?"

"Enough. This city is full of men who'll never be missed. I like it here."

"What?" Magnus said, shocked by this admission. "When have you done this? You've been by my father's side nearly every moment since we've arrived."

"Every night after you all retire to your rooms." Selia turned her patient smile toward him. "I need very little sleep, my sweet. And neither, it appears, does this city."

"You don't think I'll try to stop you?" Dariah's voice trembled.

Stop her? Magnus shifted his attention to the other witch, his confusion only growing.

"You can try." Selia raised her chin, her lips thinning, her grip on Dariah's hand tightening. "But you'll fail."

Dariah gasped, her free hand flying to her throat. "But . . . I . . . thought—"

Without another word, the woman's beauty fell away like a mask, her older, wrinkled face revealed beneath her magic, and she slumped down to the tabletop.

Magnus regarded this with shock.

"You killed her," Xanthus said, his voice low and dangerous.

"And you didn't try to stop me."

His eyes met hers. "Your magic is stronger than any witch's I've ever witnessed."

"Witches who are willing to do what is necessary can have nearly the same magic as a sorceress. For a short time, anyway." Her gaze returned to his hand. "Now, about your ring."

His gaze hardened. "My ring is not—"

Selia brought her dagger down hard and fast, and Xanthus's index finger skittered across the table, leaving a bloody trail behind.

Xanthus roared in pain and lunged for Selia. "I'll kill you!"

Fire lit him up a moment later, covering him in an instant. He tried to bat at it, to put it out, but it was too fast and ferocious.

"Come with me," Selia told Magnus as she snatched the ring off the severed finger and slipped it into her pocket.

Magnus turned away from the screaming man on fire and rushed to follow his grandmother out of the tavern, leaving the other drunk patrons in confused chaos.

"Did I surprise you?" she asked as they made their way back to the tavern.

Magnus had remained silent, trying desperately to compose himself after what he'd witnessed. "I would have appreciated knowing your plans ahead of time."

"Would you have tried to stop me?"

"From killing a witch and an exiled Watcher? Not at all," he replied honestly. "I take it the bloodstone is hidden within the ring."

"It is. I have exactly what we need."

Magnus wanted the bloodstone for himself, but the thought of trying to take it from his grandmother after seeing what she'd done without barely blinking an eye . . .

Best for the moment, he thought, to stay entirely in the witch's good graces.

Selia didn't pause as they entered the inn, crossed the hall to the staircase, and ascended to the second floor. Magnus felt a little unsteady on his feet, thanks to the bottle of wine he'd quickly consumed, but his mind was still mostly clear. As he passed Cleo's door, he brushed his hand over it, then followed Selia down the hallway and around a corner to his father's room.

Inside, a skeletal man with flesh the same color as his bleached sheets lay on his bed.

Magnus hadn't seen his father since their chat in the tavern. He'd gotten much worse. His lips were dry and cracked. The circles under his sunken eyes were as black as the night sky. Even his dark hair had grown brittle and gray. His eyes, the same brown as Magnus's, were clouded over.

"My son," the king rasped out, weakly raising his hand. "Please, come here."

It always came as a shock to him when the king said *please*.

Magnus reluctantly sat at the edge of this father's bed.

"I know you won't forgive me. You shouldn't forgive me. My choices, especially with you . . ." The king's milky eyes were glossy. "I wish I'd been a better father to you."

"Spare me the deathbed confessions," Magnus said, his throat thick. "They're wasted on me."

"Shh, my darling." Selia sat on the edge of Gaius's bed, her hand to his forehead. "Save your strength."

How Magnus had longed to put a sword through his father's chest, to avenge his mother's death, to make the king pay for all the years of abuse and neglect. To watch the life leave his eyes once and for all.

But this wasn't how he'd wanted it to be. Magnus hadn't wanted to feel anything for this monster except hatred.

"I know you tried to save me," Gaius told his mother. "It doesn't matter anymore. You must find Lucia at any cost. You must beg her to help, if necessary. I know she won't let Mytica fall completely into the hands of Amara. Lucia will destroy all our enemies, and the throne will belong to my son."

"We will find Lucia together." Selia slipped the gold ring onto the king's bony finger, and he drew in a rattling breath. "The bloodstone is yours, my son, just as I promised. Now rest, and allow the stone to work its magic."

Magnus turned away, conflicted by everything he'd witnessed tonight. The king caught his wrist, forcing him to turn back around.

"They weren't only words," his father said, already with renewed strength in his voice and determination in his clearing eyes. "I will be a better father to you, Magnus. Whether you believe me or not, I swear this to you."

CHAPTER 24

CLEO

PAELSIA

Cleo's entire world had been reduced to the four walls of her bedroom at the Paelsian inn. The rusty lock on the door was the only thing that protected her from her enemies.

The Damoras were her enemies—not her family, not her allies, not her friends.

And yet she continued to stay with them, feeling trapped, a helpless prisoner who had no say in her own fate.

She wasn't sure when she finally fell asleep, but when she woke from the tight clutch of nightmares, her tears dried on her cheeks, she realized something very important.

She was no helpless prisoner. She was a *queen*.

She had forgotten to be brave, to be strong, as her sister and father had urged her to be. What would they think of her now, having lost her way and hoping for answers by trusting those who didn't deserve her trust?

"Enough of this," she whispered as she pushed herself out of the small bed.

She wasn't sure how, but she would fix this herself. Her goals remained the same: Vengeance. Power. Reclaiming her throne and ensuring the future well-being of the Auranian people.

Nothing else mattered.

Magnus had been right about one thing: If Nic had been aware that she was in love with Magnus, he would have hated her. Lucky, then, that she hadn't given the prince all of her heart. She'd been holding some of it back, protecting herself even with no idea that she'd been doing it.

"I'm so sorry, Nic," she muttered as she quickly ran the silver brush through her long hair, trying very hard not to think of when Magnus had done so. "You were right. You were always right."

Her stomach growled, and she realized she hadn't eaten since the previous afternoon. She needed strength to do what had to be done—to go to Auranos and find allies of her father. She had to find the rebels who would support her as they devised a plan to overthrow Amara.

If there was a way, Cleo would find it. No matter what she had to do.

Quietly, just after dawn, she descended the stairs. The inn was silent, only the Damoras now in residence in a place that, just days earlier, had been filled with a strange mix of enemies and allies.

She moved toward the kitchen. The innkeeper's wife was already up, baking bread. The scent of it made her mouth water.

"I need breakfast," she told the woman.

"Yes, your grace," the woman nodded. "Kindly take a seat, and I'll bring it to you as soon as it's ready."

"Thank you." Cleo moved into the dining room and was dismayed to find that she wasn't the only one awake at this hour. Selia Damora sat at the end of the table, reading a book in the warm glow of sunrise. She looked up as Cleo approached.

"The princess has finally emerged from her chamber," she said. "I'm glad to see you this morning."

Cleo hesitated before she took a seat next to the woman. No reason to betray her plans to leave just yet. "It's very early."

"I've always liked to get up before the sun."

Cleo had never shared that habit. There was a time when she'd slept in every morning until her sister poked her shoulder to tell Cleo that she'd already missed their first class, which made their tutor very cross. Cleo would reply by pulling her covers up over her head and grumbling for Emilia to leave her in peace.

Their tutors had always liked Emilia much more than her younger sister.

Cleo eyed the pitcher and glass goblets next to Selia. "What are you drinking?"

"Freshly pressed grape juice. It seems Paelsians do more with their famed fruit than simply make it into wine. Care for a glass?"

"Perhaps in a moment."

"You're upset this morning." Selia nodded. "I couldn't help but overhear part of your argument with my grandson last night. I must admit, you are justified in your anger toward him. He had no right to manipulate your friend and put him in harm's way."

Cleo's eyes began to sting. "I still can't believe it's true. That Nic is . . . gone."

"I know you're grieving. But let this pain make you stronger, dear."

Cleo's gaze shot to the woman. "I don't seem strong enough to you already?"

"A woman can always strive to be stronger in the face of painful emotions. If you've come to any realizations about love and how it can weaken us, then I commend you. It takes many women until they're much older than you are to learn those lessons."

"You speak as if you know my heart, but you don't. You don't know me, and I don't know you."

"Learn to take good advice when it's freely given. Life will be much easier for you if you do." Selia didn't seem the least bit fazed by Cleo's sharp tone. "I sense greatness in you, my dear. I see it in your eyes. You are determined to change the world. I saw the same expression in your mother's eyes the one time I met her."

Cleo felt her eyes go wide. "You met my mother?"

Selia nodded. "Elena was a commendable woman, strong and brave and smart. An uncommon combination, I hate to admit, especially among royals. Our kind do tend to be spoiled and coddled in our youth, no matter where we come from. It can lead to lazy adults who aren't willing to do what it takes to get what we want."

"I was spoiled and coddled," Cleo admitted.

"Such weakness has been burned out of you by challenge and loss."

"Yes. Burned out of me," Cleo repeated, nodding. "That's an accurate description of how it's felt."

"The fire that hollows us out is what allows us to be filled with strength and power where before there was none," Selia said. She poured two glasses of grape juice. Cleo took one from her. "Perhaps we should toast to that fire. Without it, we would be no threat to those who might wish to stifle our potential."

Cleo nodded. "I suppose I can drink to that."

She raised the cup to her lips. Just as she was about to take a sip, the glass flew out of her hand and shattered against the wall.

She looked up with surprise at King Gaius, who now stood next to her. His gaze wasn't on her, though, it was on his mother.

Cleo scrambled up to her feet, her chair skidding backward on the wooden floor. The king looked as healthy and strong as he ever had.

The bloodstone. He had it now, and it had worked its magic.

She'd been too busy feeling sorry for herself alone in her room to hear about this.

"Goodness, Gaius." Selia also rose to her feet. "Is that any way for you to treat your son's wife?"

"I notice you didn't take a drink yet, Mother. Go on, quench your thirst. Don't let me stop you from tasting your own dark magic."

Instead of doing what he curtly suggested, Selia placed her cup down on the table. Cleo watched her, a sickening realization dawning inside her.

The grape juice had been poisoned.

Cleo pressed up against the wall, her heart pounding hard and fast.

"You look very well, Gaius," Selia said without a glance in Cleo's direction.

"Thanks to you, it seems I've recovered."

"As I promised you would." Her expression was tight. "Now tell me what's wrong and why you look at me with hatred instead of love this morning."

He laughed hollowly. The look in his eyes was cold enough to make Cleo's blood turn to ice in her veins.

"What would have happened had the princess drunk that?" He nodded at the pitcher. "Would she have died quickly and painlessly or screaming with a hole burned through her throat as my father did from your deadliest of potions?"

"I'm not sure," Selia said calmly. "It works differently on everyone."

"You really tried to poison me?" Cleo managed, shock and outrage making her tremble.

Selia's steady gaze met hers. "You've proven yourself a problem in many ways. I see no reason why you should be allowed to disrupt this family more than you already have."

"That is not your decision to make," Gaius growled. "It's mine."

"From what I gather, you've tried numerous times to rid yourself of this thorn in your side. How difficult could it be to end the life of a troublesome child like this?"

"How did you know?" Cleo choked out to Gaius. The thought that she'd been starting to trust Selia, that she had just believed in her words of strength and bravery, made her sick. She'd been so close to drinking poison, not thinking for a single moment that her life was in danger. If the king hadn't knocked the cup from her hand . . .

"I just knew," the king said. He still hadn't looked directly at Cleo; his gaze remained fixed on his mother. "Just as I know what you did seventeen years ago, Mother."

Finally, a slight frown creased Selia's forehead. "I don't know what you mean."

"We can play this game, if you like. I'd rather we didn't. I'd rather not waste more time listening to your lies, the lies you've filled my head with all my life."

"I've never lied to you, Gaius. I love you."

"Love." He threw the word back at her as if it were a flaming arrow he'd managed to block. "Is that what you call it? No, Mother. While I've been contemplating my own death, my mind free from any protective potions, I've done a great deal of thinking about how your idea of love has only been a ruse to gather power for yourself. I did everything you asked of me and received ashes in return. You were the one to tell me that love is an illusion. Or is it only certain kinds of love that you find unsuitable?"

She stared at him, incredulous. "Romantic love is an illusion. The love of family is eternal! I waited thirteen years in exile for you to realize that everything I've done has been for you. For *you*, Gaius, not for me. And finally you appeared when you needed me the most. And what did I do without question? I saved your life!"

"I know you did. And I also I know you went to see Elena just before her death," he said, his voice quieter now. "You were troubled by thoughts that I'd return to her, despite her never replying to any of my letters. But you intercepted those letters, didn't you? She never received a single one of them."

Cleo couldn't move, could barely breathe. She knew what she witnessed was not meant for her ears. Still, she couldn't turn away.

Selia looked down her nose at Gaius as if he were a ten-year-old boy trying to argue logic with a scholar. "I have always tried to protect you from making poor decisions that would threaten your power. And yes, I knew you planned to go to her, as much of a fool at twenty-five as you were at seventeen."

He nodded slowly. "Was it grape juice you offered her too? I remember she liked cider the best. Spiced apple cider, served warm."

Selia didn't reply to this.

"You didn't have to poison her. I didn't plan to go to her, not then. My heart had already become far too black and cold to think she'd ever take me back, especially with her perfect life and perfect family. But it wasn't any vengeful witch's curse that killed her that day. It was you."

Cleo found she'd begun to tremble violently, everything she heard hitting her like physical blows. "You poisoned my mother," she whispered. "You murdered her."

"The poison should have ended both her life and the life of the child she carried." Selia shook her head. "But she was too far along in her pregnancy. Her death did seem natural to many, given how difficult her pregnancy with Emilia had been. I know Corvin believed it to be a curse, his fault for slaking his lust with a witch. And yes, it was apple cider. How strange . . . I hadn't remembered that until now. However, I assure you that she didn't suffer. She simply . . . slipped away. Peaceful."

"Lies," Gaius said through clenched teeth. "I've heard accounts of how greatly she suffered until death finally claimed her."

"Rumors only."

The cold hatred in his dark eyes chilled the room. "I want you to leave. And I never want to see you again."

Selia shook her head. "You must be able to see that I did what I thought was best. For you, Gaius. Because I love you, and I always have. You are my perfect boy, born to greatness. Together we will rule the world, just as I always told you we would."

"Leave," he said again, "or I will kill you."

"My darling, no. I can't leave you. Not now. Not like—"

"Leave!" he bellowed and slammed his fist down upon the breakfast table so hard that Cleo was certain it would shatter.

Selia raised her chin. "You will forgive me when you see there's no other way for this to end."

The king shook from head to toe as his mother left the room.

Cleo was dumbfounded, utterly unable to think clearly after such an argument.

"My mother was poisoned . . ." she began. "Because your mother thought you wanted to renew your relationship with her."

"Yes."

"And that would . . . destroy her control over you."

"Yes." It was not much more than a hiss this time.

"Selia told me that you beat my mother almost to death, that she hated you."

His eyes widened. "My mother is a liar. Elena was my world, my weakness, my suffering, my one and only love. I didn't lay a hand on her in anger and I never would have." Gaius cast a dark look at her. "I want you to leave here as well."

"What?"

"My mother was right about one thing: You are a danger to my son, just as Elena was a danger to me. I won't have it. I will protect him from harm whether he wants my protection or not."

"But I . . . I thought . . ."

"What? That I'd begun to redeem myself in some small way by stopping you from drinking that poison? That wasn't about you, princess. That was about me and my mother. Magnus would be better off if you were dead and no longer a problem for either of us."

The ache in her heart she'd shockingly begun to feel for this man and his horrific past quickly turned to stone. "I think Magnus should have a say in this decision."

"He is young and stupid when it comes to such things, just as I was. I don't forgive my mother for what she did, but I do understand why she did it. I will do you the favor of not ending your life here today, but only if you leave this very moment. Go back to your precious Auranos. Better yet, leave Mytica entirely. Elena's family hailed from western Vaneas. Perhaps you could build a new life there."

"I want to speak to Magnus," Cleo insisted. "I need to—"

"You need to leave before what little patience I have left disappears. And know, princess, I do this not for you but in the memory of your mother, who should have lived instead of her worthless child, who's brought nothing but misery to my world. Now go, and don't return."

Cleo finally turned away from him, blinking back tears.

The first person she came across was Enzo, standing just outside the room.

"You heard?" she asked.

"Not all of it," he admitted.

She hesitated. "I know you're Limerian, and despite any promises you've made, you're loyal to the king, not to me. But I must ask you anyway . . . will you come with me? I'm not fool enough to think I can go out there in this world, as it is right now, unprotected."

It didn't take long before Enzo nodded firmly. "Yes, of course I will. We'll find a ship that will take us to Auranos or wherever else you want to go."

She nodded, grateful to have his allegiance, if nothing else. "Thank you, Enzo. But I'm not taking a ship anywhere."

"Where do you want to go?"

It seemed she'd been left with very few options. It was time for her to be strong again. "I want to seek an audience with the empress."

CHAPTER 25

MAGNUS

PAELSIA

He'd drained two bottles of wine the innkeeper kept on hand. Oddly enough, the wine hadn't been a Paelsian vintage. It was bitter and dry and left a foul aftertaste in Magnus's mouth, but it was just as effective as Paelsian wine in dulling his mind and helping him fall asleep.

But not in keeping him asleep. The sound of his door creaking open woke him. He'd been certain he'd locked it. His body felt heavy and far too weary to move, and his mind was too foggy to care who entered his room.

"It's me," Cleo whispered.

Magnus's eyes shot wide open at the sound of her voice, his back to the door.

"What do you want?" he asked tentatively, without turning around to look at her.

"I needed to see you."

"Can't it wait until morning?"

"You're drunk."

"You're observant."

"You want me to leave?"

"No."

The bed creaked as she slipped into it beside him.

Magnus froze at the sensation of her hand sliding over his side to his chest. "Cleo . . ."

"I don't want to fight with you," she murmured into his ear. "I don't want to leave you. I love you, Magnus. So much."

His heart twisted. "You said love wasn't enough to fix this."

"I was angry. Everyone says horrible things when they're angry."

"But Nic . . ."

"I must have hope that he's alive. He has to be. He knows I'd be furious with him if he let himself be killed. Now look at me, Magnus."

He finally turned around and was greeted by the sight of her at his side, her beautiful face lit by the sliver of moonlight streaming through the window, her hair like spun gold, her eyes dark and bottomless.

"I need you to do something very important for me," she said.

"What?"

"Kiss me."

He almost laughed. "If I kiss you right now, I assure you, I won't be able to stop."

"I don't want you to stop. I don't want you to ever stop. Whatever happens, Magnus, we're in this together. I chose you. And I need you. Unless"—she raised a brow—"you're too drunk and you'd rather I leave."

His gaze darkened. "Hardly. But the curse . . ."

"The curse is a fantasy, nothing more. Put it out of your mind."

"Not sure I can."

"It seems that I must be the one to make the first move tonight . . ." She brushed her lips along the length of his scar, from his cheek to his lips. "Like this."

"Cleo . . ." he managed as he pulled her into his arms, but suddenly it wasn't Cleo that Magnus held. He found that he clutched only air and blankets.

He realized with dismay that she'd never been there at all. It had only been a dream.

But it didn't have to be.

He needed to talk to her, to get her to see reason. She would, he knew she would. And together they would find out the truth about Nic.

Magnus sat up, determined that today would be better than yesterday, but his head felt as if it was ready to explode. He groaned and gripped his temples, doubling over from the pain.

The wine. Paelsian wine had no ill aftereffects on those who drank it. All other inebriants, though . . .

Did others willingly choose to endure pain like this to forget about their problems for a night?

Magnus was furious with himself for giving in to something that had weakened him to this degree, but he had to overcome it. He had to focus on his goals.

He would go after Ashur himself. The Kindred needed to be reclaimed—for himself, for Cleo, for Mytica. And the way he currently felt, anyone who got in his way would die a very painful death.

The inn seemed strangely empty this morning. The princess's bedroom was vacant, the door open. Magnus's grandmother was nowhere to be seen, neither in the courtyard nor in the meeting room.

The king, however, was waiting for him at the dining room

table, a full breakfast in front of him. The innkeeper's wife—Magnus hadn't bothered to learn her name—eyed him nervously as he entered and took a seat.

"Eat something," the king told him.

Magnus eyed the spread of dried fruit, goat cheese, and freshly baked bread with disgust. The scent of it made him want to vomit.

The thought of any food at all made him nauseous.

"I'll pass," Magnus replied. "You look . . . well."

"I feel well." The king wore Xanthus's golden ring on his left index finger. He raised his hand and inspected it. "Hard to believe there's so much magic in this small piece, enough to restore me to my former self so quickly."

"How long will it last?"

"Ah, that's the question, isn't it?"

"Selia didn't tell you?"

"I didn't ask."

"Where is she?"

"Gone."

Magnus frowned, and a fresh wave of pain coursed through his head. "Gone where?"

The king tore a piece of bread off a loaf, dipped it into a bowl of melted butter, and chewed it thoughtfully. "Food even tastes better to me now. It's like a veil of apathy has been lifted from each of my senses."

"How delightful for you. I ask again, where is my grandmother?"

"I sent her away."

Magnus blinked. "You sent her away."

"That is what I said."

"Why?"

The king put down his fork and held Magnus's gaze. "Because she doesn't deserve to breathe the same air as we do."

Magnus shook his head, trying to make sense of this. "She saved your life."

The king scoffed. "Yes, I suppose she did."

"You speak, but you make no sense. Did the bloodstone steal your sanity while it restored your health?"

"I've never felt more sane than I do at this very moment." He glanced at the door where Milo now stood. "Milo, my good man, come and eat some breakfast. Magnus won't be having any, so why let perfectly good food go to waste?"

"Thank you, your highness," Milo said. "Is it true what I've heard? That Nicolo Cassian is dead?"

The king raised his brows.

"It's possible," Magnus allowed.

Milo smirked. "That is mildly disappointing. Pardon me for saying so, but I always hoped to kill him myself."

Magnus found himself nodding in agreement. "He did have that effect on people."

"Where's Enzo?" the king asked. "There's plenty of food here for him as well."

"Enzo has left, your majesty," Milo replied a bit reluctantly.

The king put down the bread and looked at the guard. "Where has he gone?"

"With the princess."

The tentative way he said it made Magnus's stomach churn. "Please be so kind as to tell me that the princess has gone shopping in the city and will return later."

"Apologies, but I don't know where they've gone, only that they left at dawn."

Magnus's heart began to race, and he shot an accusatory glare at his father. "What have you done now?"

The king shrugged, his expression unreadable. "I won't mince words with you this morning, my son. Your grandmother is gone. And so is the princess. Neither will return here."

Magnus stood up so quickly that his chair fell over backward. "I need to find her."

"Sit down," the king hissed.

"You threatened her, didn't you? Both her and Selia. You chased them away."

"Yes, I suppose I did. All while you slept away your drunken stupor until midday. You need to start thinking as clearly as I do, Magnus. Now that I've been restored, it's time for us to take action."

"Is that right?" Magnus could feel his voice getting louder and louder. "Action is what we need? Let's see . . . there's you, there's me, and there's Milo currently representing the once-great Limeros. That makes three of us against Amara's army. And we don't have Lucia with us, since you sent away the one person who could have found her!" He swore under his breath. "I need to find Cleo."

"You need to do no such thing. That girl has been a plague upon us since the first moment she entered our lives."

"Us? There is no *us*, Father. You think that anything is different now? A few encouraging words and pained looks do not make everything all right. You can try to stop me from leaving, but I promise you'll fail."

Magnus went straight for the door of the inn, his head in a daze. Cleo must have gone to Auranos, he thought. He'd start there. Someone would know where to find her.

Thank the goddess she'd been wise enough to take Enzo with her. But one single guard to protect her in the face of Amara's massive occupation wasn't nearly enough.

"Magnus, don't leave," the king said. "We need to discuss strategy."

"Discuss strategy with Milo," he growled. "Anything you have to say is utterly irrelevant to me."

Magnus flung open the door, ready to storm out of the room, but three men were already standing there, blocking his way.

"Prince Magnus Damora," one said, nodding. He looked at his companions. "See? I told you it was him. The prince of Limeros in the middle of Basilia. Who would have believed it? I remember you from your wedding tour. I brought my wife and children to see a pair of royals in their shiny, perfect clothing, to show them what we could never have as the lowly Paelsians you've always seen us as. And here you are, dressed like one of us."

"So pleased to meet you, whoever you are." Magnus's eyes narrowed. "And now I suggest you get out of my way."

"There's a price on your head—yours and your father's."

"Is there?" Magnus gave them a thin smile. "And what price is on your heads if I detach them from your bodies?"

The stranger and his friends laughed at this as if it was the most hilarious thing they'd ever heard. "All of us? Even the Prince of Blood couldn't take us all on."

"Don't be so sure."

"Kill them," the king suggested. "We don't have time for nonsense today."

"That's the first good idea you've had," Magnus replied under his breath.

But before he could make a move to grab for a weapon, or say another word, three spears sailed through the air, impaling each man from behind.

The three dropped to the ground at Magnus's feet.

Magnus looked up. Behind the men, there was a veritable army of soldiers in green uniforms.

Amara's army.

Magnus slammed the door shut and staggered back into the inn. "We have a problem."

"Yes, I see that," the king replied.

"I take it Amara doesn't believe whatever story you told her anymore if she's sent her army for you."

"I assumed it would only be a matter of time."

Magnus glared at him. "How can you sound so damn calm about this?"

There was a banging on the door. "Open up in the name of Amara Cortas, empress of Kraeshia!"

Milo was there in front of them, sword in hand, as the front door splintered inward and Amara's guards came spilling into the inn. Magnus now had his sword at the ready, but all he could do was watch as Milo—the guard he still felt deep gratitude toward for intervening when his and Cleo's lives had been threatened at the cliffside—fell after slaying only two guards.

With a roar of anger, Magnus moved forward, raising his weapon.

The king put his hand on Magnus's shoulder to stop him.

"Don't," he said.

A tall, muscular uniformed soldier strode forward, the others making way for him. "Drop your weapon. Surrender, or die here and now."

Magnus, his jaw clenched, looked down at Milo, blood pooling next to his body. Milo had wanted to fight, had wanted to kill as many of these Kraeshians as he could for the king and for Limeros.

But he couldn't kill them all. And neither could Magnus.

This fight was over before it had barely begun. Amara had won.

CHAPTER 26

LUCIA

PAELSIA

"I swear to the goddess," Lucia said, clutching her belly, "this child wishes to be the death of me."

She'd never assumed that carrying a child would be simple. In the past, she'd seen pregnant women who'd complained about their backs hurting, their ankles swelling, and constant nausea. But she knew this was different.

The road Jonas promised would lead to her family was winding and rocky. Every time the horse-drawn cart took a turn too fast or hit a boulder, she wanted to cry out from the pain.

"Do you want me to have the driver stop again?" asked Jonas.

"No. We've wasted too much time already."

The rebel had been very quiet during the journey, which, due to multiple stops, had taken them nearly an entire day since leaving his sister's cottage.

She had to ask.

"Does your sister hate you because of who I am? That you brought me to her home?"

"That would be more than enough, I think. I was wrong to bring you there thinking she'd be willing to help you. But my sister hates me for other reasons. Valid reasons. I can't argue that I didn't abandon my family. Even though I thought I was keeping them safe by staying away, I see now that it was the wrong decision. I should have been there when my father died."

"I'm sorry," she said.

He eyed her. "You are?"

"Despite what you believe of me, I'm not utterly heartless."

"If you say so."

She groaned. "Please keep talking, even if it's only to insult me. When you're talking, the pain seems to lessen a little." She scanned what she could see of the landscape, which had turned from rural to much more populated, with buildings closer together and roads that seemed smoother and well traveled. "Is it much farther?"

"Not much. I'll talk to ease your pain the rest of the way. The last time I saw my father I decided that I never wanted to be like him. But I still should have been there when he died. Like so many Paelsians, he accepted life as it unfolded before him, never working to change it. He believed blindly in Chief Basilius. I suppose I did too, for a while. At least, until I saw for myself that the chief had none of the magic he claimed and that he allowed Paelsians to starve while he lived like a true king in his compound, thanks to his high tax on Paelsian wine. He made me so many promises of a brighter future—he even wanted me to marry his daughter."

It was odd—the sound of the rebel's voice did seem to soothe her. At least until he mentioned that particular name. "Chief Basilius wanted you to marry his daughter? Which one?"

"Laelia." He studied her. "Why do you look so surprised by

this? Because the daughter of someone like Basilius would have nothing to do with a wine seller's son?"

"That's not why."

"Trust me, she wasn't complaining."

"My goodness, rebel, is your previous betrothal a touchy subject for you?"

"No. I barely think about it—or her—anymore. I have no interest in marriage." His jaw set, and he continued to mutter, as if to himself. "That leads to children, and children . . . I just don't see myself raising one, no matter how important it might be."

She frowned at him. "Of course not. You're still young."

"So are you."

"I didn't choose this."

His expression remained grim. "I keep wondering just how many of us actually get a choice in our futures, or whether they're already set and we're doomed to simply think we have control over our lives."

"So philosophical. For your information, I looked surprised about your betrothal to Laelia only because I recently discovered that Gaius Damora isn't my father by blood. He had me kidnapped because of my prophecy. My real father was Chief Basilius. Laelia is my sister."

Jonas blinked. "I'm surprised you'd share this with me."

"Why? We're making conversation, and such a secret doesn't matter to me anymore."

His brows drew together. "So you're Paelsian."

She laughed weakly. "That is all you take from that revelation?"

Jonas swore under his breath as he studied her face. "You actually look like her, now that I'm paying attention. Like Laelia. Same blue eyes, same hair color. Fewer snakes, though. And you're so pale right now. You really aren't feeling well, are you?"

"Not at all."

"So is it a sorceress thing, this quick pregnancy? All that *elementia* inside you?"

"I think it has more to do with my visit to the Sanctuary. The quickness happened only after I returned to Paelsia."

He regarded her with shock. "You've been to the Sanctuary? The actual Sanctuary where the immortals live?"

She nodded. "Briefly. A Watcher named Timotheus has been tolerating my existence because of my prophecy. Sometimes he visits my dreams. I knew I needed to see him, to ask for his help. To be honest, he wasn't all that helpful." Jonas's shoulders had stiffened at the name. "What's wrong?"

"Nothing. Timotheus, you said?"

"He has visions . . . about me, about this world, and about his world. But he's secretive about the visions that have to do with me."

"I'm sure he is." Jonas's expression was unreadable. She wasn't sure if he was fascinated by what she was saying or bored out of his mind.

"Anyway . . ." Lucia gazed around at the large village that the cart had entered, hopeful that this journey would soon end. "He hasn't visited my dreams even once since I returned here. Either he can't do that anymore or he's leaving me to discover my fate by myself. As you said, it might already be decided without any input from me."

Jonas didn't reply to this, and it was some time before he said another word. "The father of your child . . . was he good or evil?"

She was about to say that that was a strange question, but given that she already knew Jonas perceived her as nothing but evil, she decided his question was valid enough.

"I believe Alexius was good, but he was manipulated to do evil by another. He was commanded to take my life, and when the time came, he refused and took his own."

"He sacrificed himself for you."

Bringing up memories of Alexius made the pain in her belly shift to her heart. She tried to think of him as little as possible to avoid any pangs of remorse or grief about the immortal.

"He fought against the magic that forced him to move me from place to place like a piece upon a game board. He taught me more about my own magic. He even taught me how to steal the magic from others to weaken them. I didn't know why he did this at the time, but in the end . . . I understood. He was teaching me how to kill an immortal."

"You killed an immortal by stealing all of his magic?"

"No, I killed an immortal by stealing all of *her* magic."

Jonas absently rubbed his chest. "Do you think I might learn how to do that? Steal magic?"

"That doesn't sound like something I should teach someone who despises me. Besides, for all I know, that mark you showed me is the result of ink."

"It's not." He looked down at his hands. "I don't know . . . on the ship I was able to use the magic in me a little. Not much, but even now I feel it inside of me pressing outward. It's like it's trying to get out, but I don't know how to release it—or if I even want to."

"My own magic was difficult to grasp after it awakened within me. Perhaps you simply need to be patient."

"Yes, of course, because there's plenty of time to be patient with an empress and a god of fire to contend with. Brilliant suggestion, princess." He stood up as the cart came to a halt. "We've arrived."

Lucia tore her glare from the rebel to realize that she recognized the city they'd entered: Basilia. She scanned the busy streets and could smell the foul stench of Trader's Harbor from here. "My brother and father are here?"

"They were the last time I saw them." Jonas jumped down from the cart and offered Lucia his hand. She glanced at it with uncertainty. "Come now, princess, I haven't brought you this far to let you fall on your face, especially not in your delicate condition."

"I'm not delicate."

"If you say so." He shrugged but didn't lower his hand.

Grudgingly, she put her hand in his and allowed him to help her down off the cart.

"Do you need a meal?" he asked. "There's a tavern nearby where you can meet your blood sister, and I don't think you've eaten today."

The memory of Laelia only brought back unpleasant memories. "I've seen her before, and there's no time for meals. I want to see my family."

"Fine." He frowned. "You didn't tell me you already met Laelia."

"How do you think I learned who I am?"

"I don't know . . . magically?"

"*Elementia* can't solve every problem, unfortunately. No, I went in search of the truth, and that search led me to Laelia. When she learned who I was, she asked for money—a great deal of coin to help her now that her father is dead and she's afraid someone might recognize her as the daughter of the defeated chief. I'll be fine if I never see her again."

"Basilius was your father too."

"I will never claim the chief as my father."

"Yet you're happy to claim the King of Blood as family."

"Despite what you might think, Gaius Damora has been good to me in my life. He kept me safe and protected until I was stupid enough to run off on my own, thinking I was in love with a boy

I'd known no more than a handful of days. Gaius had me taken from my cradle because of my prophecy. He could have kept me locked away. Instead, he raised me as a princess, as his daughter. I was given an education and a wonderful life in a home I adored."

Jonas shook his head. "Huh, well, I guess I've been wrong about him all this time. King Gaius is a truly kind and wonderful person."

"Very well, I'll save my breath for a more useful conversation—like speaking with my father."

"Fine. Let me deliver you to your perfect, loving family, and I can be done with this. I need to go back to the empress's compound and search for my idiotic friends, who attract trouble to their lives like dirt to their shoes."

Lucia followed Jonas down the street. She felt a pang in her gut for her sharp words. Jonas had helped her a great deal.

"I want you to know that I appreciate this. What you've done, bringing me here. I will ensure that no harm comes to you, despite all your horrible crimes."

"Oh, goody. Thank you, princess. You're a peach."

Her back stiffened. "Or perhaps I won't." Just when she was beginning to soften toward the rebel, he had to make her angry again. She was about to dismiss him completely, when a wave of pain buckled her knees.

Jonas caught her arm. "Princess?"

"I'm fine," she said, her teeth clenched. "Unhand me."

"No." When he lifted her up into his arms, she was too weak to try to stop him. "You are definitely a lot of trouble, aren't you?"

"Just point me toward my family."

"No *thank you* for not letting you drop like a sack of potatoes in the middle of the street? Fine then, they're at the inn on the corner. I'll take you the rest of the way. Now, how about you save both your energy and my ears by not talking?"

Lucia couldn't speak anyway. The pain was too intense. She squeezed her eyes shut, taking deep, shaking breaths. She could bear it—she had to. As long as her child was safe, she could bear anything.

Jonas moved very quickly for someone carrying a pregnant woman. Lucia had to clutch his shoulders for safety when he entered the inn.

Ten paces from the front door, a woman was on her hands and knees scrubbing the floor. She must have only just started, since there was blood everywhere.

"Let me down," Lucia told Jonas, alarmed by the unexpected sight.

He did as she asked.

"What happened here?" she demanded.

The woman looked up, her eyes red and weary. "We're not taking any guests today. Apologies, but you can go down the street. There are plenty of inns around here."

"Whose blood is that?"

The woman just shook her head and concentrated on her task.

"Maria," Jonas said, crouching down beside her. She looked up at him, recognition dawning in her eyes.

"Jonas, you've returned." She smiled weakly. "I think you were the only one who bothered to learn my name."

"How could I not learn the name of the woman who makes the best fig fritters I've ever had in my entire life?"

Tears spilled onto Maria's cheeks. "It was horrible."

"What happened?" Lucia demanded, her fists clenched. "Tell us, or I'll—"

Jonas glared up at her. "You'll do nothing to this woman. Do not come a single step closer."

"Is this your wife, Jonas?" Maria asked warily.

"My . . . ?" Jonas let out a low chuckle. "No, she is most certainly not my wife."

How dare this peasant woman think that she would become romantically entangled with someone like this cruel, rough rebel? "I am Lucia Eva Damora, and I swear on the goddess that if you do not tell me what happened here and where my family is, you will deeply regret it." As soon as she said the words, she regretted them, and Jonas turned a look of pure fury on her.

"Lucia Damora," Maria whispered, dropping her bloody cloth. "The sorceress. You're here. Spare my husband, please, I beg of you."

"Ignore Lucia," Jonas growled. "Tell me what happened, Maria. I won't let the princess harm you or your family in any way, I swear it."

"Kraeshian soldiers . . . they came here, more than I've seen since they arrived in Basilia. There was a fight—a brief one. The king, the prince . . ." She shook her head. "It's all too much."

Jonas nodded at the floor. "Was anyone killed?"

"A young man with dark hair. He didn't have much to do with me while you all stayed here. He tried to defend the Limerians but was slayed quickly. I believe his name was Milo."

"And my father . . . my brother?" Lucia's rage had been replaced by fear. She placed a trembling hand on her belly.

"Gone," Maria whispered. "The soldiers took them. I don't know where. The city is in upheaval. So many men have been murdered in the streets in recent nights, their throats cut and their bodies left there to rot. Some wonder if it's on the empress's orders, if we've somehow displeased her."

"What about Princess Cleiona?" Jonas asked. His voice held bottomless concern. "Where is she?"

"She left early this morning. I overheard her and the king

having a vicious argument. He sent her away. The prince was displeased about that."

"I'm sure he was," Jonas muttered.

"Cleo was here?" Lucia asked, stunned.

"Where else would she be?"

"Dead by now, I'd hoped."

Jonas gave her a dark look. "Just when I start to think you aren't quite as vicious and disgusting as I thought you were, you say something like that."

She rolled her eyes. "Oh, please don't tell me you're another male Cleo's managed to seduce with her pretty hair and her helpless act. That would lower you in my regard even more."

"I don't give a damn what you think of me." He took her tightly by her elbow. "We're leaving. We've learned all the information we can here. Much gratitude, Maria. Stay safely inside until all this is over."

"And when will that be?" the woman asked.

He shook his head. "I wish I knew for sure."

Outside, Jonas walked quickly, practically dragging Lucia behind him. "We're going to the tavern," he gritted out. "We'll be able to get more information there."

"And what if someone recognizes me and I get the same reaction as I did from that woman?"

"I suggest not stupidly introducing yourself loudly by name, and we might be able to avoid that."

"She hated me."

"I'd think you'd be used to that by now."

"I am, but . . ." It was suddenly difficult to breathe, the air so warm that Lucia had begun to perspire. "I need to stop a moment. I think I'm going to faint."

Jonas groaned with exasperation. "We don't have time for more dramatics."

"I'm not being dramatic. It's just so hot out here."

"It's not hot in the slightest today."

"Do you find it hot, little sorceress?" a familiar voice said in her ear. *"How strange. Paelsia is usually quite temperate on the western coast at this time of year."*

Lucia froze in place.

"Kyan," she whispered.

Jonas whipped around to look at her. "Where?"

"I don't know—I can't see him. Can you hear him too?"

"Hear him? No. But you can?"

"Yes." The voice was the same, but it seemed to come from inside her head. He had no form that she could see or sense, other than the sensation of heat enveloping her. Was he able to turn invisible?

"Is this your new traveling companion? He seems . . . lacking. So young, so inexperienced. What a pity that you and I had a falling out."

Her heart pounded. "You wanted to kill me."

"You promised me your help, and when the time came, you refused."

"I won't be a part of your dark plan."

"Where is he?" Jonas turned around in a circle, his sword in hand.

"The boy is rather foolish, isn't he? Does he think that little mortal weapon will have any effect on me?"

Lucia could barely catch her breath. All this time, she hadn't known what had become of Kyan, despite having nightmares about him every night.

She had to calm herself. She couldn't let him know that she was now terrified of him.

"What do you want?" she asked.

"Where is he?" Jonas said again.

She glared at him. "He's no more than a voice, currently. Lower your weapon; you look ridiculous waving that around at nothing."

Jonas sheathed his sword. "Is it possible you're imagining things? You could be delirious from the pain. Or are you trying to fool me?"

"No to both questions." She tried to ignore the rebel, but he wasn't making it easy for her.

Jonas fisted his hands as if ready to fight the air itself. "Kyan, if you can hear me, if you're really here, I swear I will end you for what you did to Lysandra."

Lucia felt a waft of hot air as Kyan laughed. *"I almost forgot about that. Tell him that was her fault, not mine. She was far too eager for a taste of my magic that day."*

"You killed his friend," she snapped. "I agree that he deserves to have vengeance for that."

"Mortals and their silly need for vengeance. Death is a part of mortal life; nothing will change that for them. Yet I offered you immortality, little sorceress, as your reward for helping me."

"Helping you to destroy the world, you mean."

"This world deserves to be destroyed."

"I disagree."

"It doesn't matter what you think. I'm so close now, little sorceress, you have no idea. I don't need your help after all; I've made other arrangements. Everything is aligning perfectly. It's as if this was meant to be."

The thought that Kyan had found another way to carry out his mission to destroy the world sickened her. But perhaps he was only bluffing. "So this is just a quick visit between old friends?" she asked.

"Perhaps." The voice moved around her, and she staggered in a circle to keep the sound of it in front of her. She didn't like the idea of having an invisible god of fire behind her. *"You're with child. Alexius's, is it?"*

Lucia said nothing to this. She'd hoped her condition had been concealed by her cloak.

"Mothers are known to be fighters when it comes to protecting their children. I will give you one more chance, little sorceress. I offer immortality to both you and your child. You will survive and help to build the next world at my side."

"I thought you said you could do your evil without me."

"It's not evil. It's destiny."

"Destiny," she murmured. "Yes, I believe in destiny, Kyan. I believe it was my destiny to possess this."

Lucia pulled the amber orb out of her pocket and held it on the palm of her hand. She focused her thoughts and inhaled slowly. Her *elementia* had been easiest to access in the beginning when her emotions were elevated—hate and fear were the most useful to trigger her magic.

But now, even weakened, with Eva's ring firmly on her finger, she could coax the beast out of its cage. The fine hairs on her arms raised, and she felt the combination of air, earth, water, and fire within her rise to the surface of her skin—a crackling sensation in her veins that ached to be free. Today, she didn't wish to unleash it upon the world around her—she wished to feed it.

It hungered for stolen magic.

Just as she'd done with Melenia, she focused on the magic that existed in the very air before her, seeing it with a vision that went far beyond common sight. It was a red glow swirling around her, incorporeal, eternal. And, she sensed without any doubt, currently vulnerable.

Kyan's very essence. *Fire.*

The orb began to glow, and Kyan made a choked, pained sound.

"What are you doing?"

"Seems Timotheus isn't the only one you need to fear, is he?" she said.

Fire flared up in a circle around Lucia and Jonas. It was so hot and blazing that Lucia lost her concentration, and the sleeve of her cloak caught fire.

Was that Kyan's magic, or had she done that?

Jonas smothered the flames with his cloak, putting them out as quickly as he could. They extinguished as quickly as they'd appeared, leaving a scorched black circle around them.

"Did it work?" he demanded. "You tried to trap him, right?"

Lucia nodded and inspected the amber orb. "I don't know."

Jonas peered at the crystal. "I don't see the black swirly thing."

"*Your companion has such a way with words, little sorceress,*" Kyan hissed. "*Your magic is still formidable, but you failed.*"

"Then I'll try again." Lucia gripped the orb and tried to summon her magic, but it had weakened too much already. "Damn it!"

"*My, my, little sorceress. You are certainly not the innocent, grieving girl I met in her darkest hour, are you?*"

"No, I'm the witch who's going to be the end of you."

"*We'll see. I believe you seek your father and brother? I suggest you travel as quickly as you can to get to them before the empress tears out both of their hearts.*"

CHAPTER 27

AMARA

PAELSIA

"Fifty-three were killed in the rebel attack, empress, many of them trampled by the crowd."

"Unfortunate." Amara took a steady sip of her wine as Kurtis presented the day's news to her. "Do they hate me now? These violent peasants?"

"No. Favor among Paelsians remains high for you."

"Good."

"Do you want the prisoners executed?" Kurtis asked as scratched at his bandages. "I would suggest a swift public beheading, as well as mounting the heads of the other dead rebels on spikes, to show everyone that such crimes won't be tolerated."

Amara raised a brow as she considered this. "Is that how you do public executions here?"

He nodded. "In Limeros it is, empress."

"In Kraeshia, my father liked to have his prisoners tied to posts, publicly skinned alive, and left there until they stopped screaming. It usually didn't take long. I've witnessed many of these executions in my life."

Kurtis blanched. "That could be arranged if that is what pleases the empress."

She glared at him. "No, that would *not* please the empress."

The only thing that would please the empress would be for Kyan to finally return from his travels and give her further instructions on how to unleash the powerful being within her water Kindred.

While it was quite unfortunate, the lives of a handful of Paelsians ultimately didn't matter. And a failed assassination attempt by a former lover didn't matter either.

Only magic mattered.

Nerissa silently topped up Amara's glass of wine.

"No execution," Amara told Kurtis, sliding her fingertip around the edge of the goblet. "They can stay in the pit until I decide what I wish to do with them."

Chief Basilius had been kind enough to leave behind an ingenious prison. In the center of his walled compound was a large hole thirty feet deep, its sides crafted from smooth sandstone. There was no escaping from it, but Amara had asked for ten guards to keep watch on Felix and Taran just in case they might be able to sprout wings and fly away.

"Pardon me for saying this, empress," Kurtis went on, "but I must raise my concerns once again about staying in Paelsia much longer. As you witnessed for yourself, despite winning the people over with the promises you've made to them, they are very dangerous and quick to violence, like cornered, injured wild animals. And if there are more rebel factions here in Mytica—let alone any who might arrive from overseas . . ." He shivered. "This is far too dangerous a place for you to remain."

She squeezed her eyes shut as her head began to throb from

the sound of his reedy voice. "And what would you suggest, Lord Kurtis?"

"I would suggest that we continue on to Auranos, to the City of Gold and the royal palace there. I assure you that it would be much more suited to your greatness."

"I know how beautiful the palace is, Lord Kurtis. I've been there before."

"I've already written to my father about this possibility, and he enthusiastically approves. There will be a great feast planned in your honor, and the greatest dressmaker in Hawk's Brow, Lorenzo Tavera, will be commissioned to create a magnificent gown for you to wear to greet your Auranian subjects."

Amara stared at Kurtis so intensely that he took a shaky step backward.

"I don't know," she said quietly, still running her finger slowly around the rim of her glass. "What do you think, Nerissa?"

Nerissa took a moment to consider this. "I think Lord Kurtis is correct that Lorenzo Tavera would create a magnificent gown. He is the one who created Princess Cleiona's wedding gown."

"But what of the move there?"

"I think that is entirely up to you, your grace."

"Lord Kurtis." Amara leaned forward to regard the kingsliege, holding on to the last sliver of patience she had within her. "I think it's a wonderful idea. However, I'm not ready to leave Paelsia quite yet. You shall go in my place to personally oversee the creation of this gown and the preparation of this feast. And you will leave immediately."

"What?" Kurtis frowned deeply. "I . . . I meant that we should all go. I am your royal advisor and—"

"And that's exactly why it's so important that you are the one who'll represent me there."

"But I had hoped to be present when Prince Magnus was finally captured."

"Of course you had. But as you so graciously pointed out, other matters hold much more importance for me, such as gowns and feasts in Auranos." Amara waved him away. "You will leave the compound by sundown. That is an order, Lord Kurtis."

His jaw tightened, and for a moment she thought he might actually argue with her. She waited, considering removing his other hand as a penalty for insubordination.

Instead, he gave a firm nod. "Yes, empress. As you wish."

Kurtis left the room.

Amara gestured to a guard near the door. "Ensure that he does exactly as I commanded."

The guard bowed and followed Kurtis.

"Well, little empress, it certainly looks as if you have everything under control here."

Amara's grip tightened on her golden goblet at the sound of Kyan's voice, unexpected after three long days of silence.

"You may leave as well, Nerissa," Amara said.

"Yes, empress." Nerissa bowed and did as she was told.

If everyone were as obedient, as agreeable as Nerissa Florens, life would be much sweeter and simpler, Amara thought as she watched her lovely attendant leave the room and close the door behind her.

"When will we perform the ritual?" she asked.

"These are the words you greet me with after my travels? I have to say I'm underwhelmed, little empress."

"I'm not a *little* empress," she said, her voice rising. "I am *the* empress."

"You're upset. With me or with the world as a whole?"

"I nearly died while you were away. Rebels attempted to

assassinate me—here, where you told me to come. The very place where you promised I would become more powerful than anyone else."

"Yet you're alive and look very well. Obviously they failed."

"No thanks to you." It seemed she couldn't quite control her impatience today, not even in the presence of a god.

"And what would you have liked me to do had I been by your side? Did you have a torch I might have made burn brighter to scare the rebels away? I already explained to you that the full power of what I am is stifled in this incorporeal form."

"Yes, you did explain that." She stood up so that she could gaze out her window at the open arena where fifty-three people, including Cleo's friend Nic, had been killed. Patches of blood stained the ground. "Actually, apart from a swelling in my fireplace in Limeros and a few lit candles, I've seen no signs of your magic at all. I've heard so much about the magic of the Kindred, so I must admit my disappointment."

"I understand your impatience, little empress, as a mortal's life is short, but I will caution you not to speak with such disrespect to me."

Amara tried very hard to keep a hold on her rising anger. "I should return to Kraeshia to my grandmother's side to help her deal with the last traces of the revolution there. She's old—she shouldn't have to take on so much responsibility at her age."

"The ritual draws nearer than you might think. I have successfully gathered the pieces that we will need. We will need sacrifices, though. Blood will be necessary to strengthen this magic, since it does not come from the sorceress herself."

"I have potential sacrifices waiting." She hated to hope, but his words made her heart clench. "When do we begin?"

"When the storm comes, all will be revealed."

She was about to say something else, perhaps throw her goblet across the room with frustration and demand a plainer explanation, but a knock on the door interrupted her thoughts.

"What is it?" she snapped.

A guard opened the door and bowed low before her. "Empress, Princess Cleiona of Auranos has arrived at the compound gates and has asked to see you. Do you wish to see her, or shall we throw her in the pit with the others?"

Amara stared at him, not certain if she'd heard him correctly.

"Is she alone?" she asked.

"She has one Limerian guard with her."

"And no one else?"

"No one else, empress."

"I want to see her. Bring her to me immediately."

"Yes, empress."

"So it seems she did survive," Amara said under her breath. "And after everything, she's come to me?"

What did it mean? Cleo had to know that Amara would want her dead for what had happened between them last.

"Princess Cleiona," Kyan said. *"I know this name. I've seen her before. The sorceress despises her."*

"I'm sure many people despise Cleo."

"Do you believe her arrival here is a trick of some kind?"

"What do you think?"

"I want to know what you think."

Amara sent a dark glare in the direction of the disembodied voice. "I'm beginning to think that Cleo may prove to be of more use to me than you have. When this mysterious storm you speak of comes, please let me know."

Amara waited for his response but didn't receive one. She cursed herself for giving in to her bluntness with such an unpredictable creature.

It didn't matter. Even if she'd somehow displeased him, he would soon remember that if he wished to complete his blood ritual here, he needed her help as much as she needed his.

It wasn't very long before Cleo entered the room, flanked by two of Amara's guards. Her cheeks were red, her gaze furious. Her gown was tattered, and there were smears of dirt on her face and bare arms.

"You fought against my guards?" Amara asked, raising a brow.

"When treated with such disrespect, I'd fight anyone," Cleo replied tightly.

Amara shifted her gaze to the guard. "Where is her subordinate?"

"He's being detained in an interrogation room," the guard replied.

"No need for that. Put him with the other prisoners, but don't harm him. Not yet, anyway."

"Yes, empress."

"Leave us. Close the door."

The guards eyed each other, and Amara noticed that they both had fresh scratches on their faces. "Are you certain you don't want protection?" one asked.

"Do as I say," Amara said through clenched teeth.

"Yes, empress."

They left and closed the door.

Amara sat down and poured herself another glass of wine. "I'd offer you some, Cleo, but I'd be afraid you'd try to break this bottle over my head again." She paused to take a sip from her full goblet of sweet wine. "Have you come to apologize for that and to beg for my mercy?"

"No," Cleo replied simply.

"I'd come to think you were dead, buried under a snowdrift near Lord Gareth's villa."

"As you can see, I'm very much alive."

"You certainly are." Amara watched her over the edge of her cup. "Several of my soldiers were murdered the night you escaped. Was that your doing?"

"Will answering that question truthfully earn your respect or have me thrown in your dungeon?"

"It's a pit, actually. Quite effective. And that depends entirely on your answer."

"Fine." Cleo nodded. "I needed to defend myself. So, yes, I killed them."

"With a bow and arrow."

"Just the arrow. I confess I have yet to master the skill of archery."

"How were you able to kill men twice your size with just an arrow?"

"My appearance leads men to believe I'm harmless."

"But you're far from harmless, aren't you?" Amara couldn't help but smile as she leaned back in her chair, took another sip from her glass, and regarded the girl before her, who had surprised her with her thirst for survival at any cost. "You don't look like a royal anymore. Your dress is torn, your hair is tangled. You look much more like a peasant."

"Looking like a royal takes both time and attendants to achieve. Lately, I've simply been trying to survive to see the next sunrise and, of course, fight against your guards when they try to drag me around like a rag doll."

Something about this meeting, about Cleo's bravery in coming to visit an enemy without a trace of fear in her eyes, had quickly gained Amara's respect. "I made you an offer of an alliance when we last spoke. I believe you already gave me your answer to that." She gingerly rubbed the back of her head, which had healed, save for the memory of the wound. "I was very angry with you for your response, since I thought we could make a good team."

"We still could," Cleo replied readily.

How unsurprising that the girl's mind had changed since losing everything she once valued.

"Apologies," Cleo said a moment later, "but I've been traveling so long my feet feel as if they may drop off of my legs if I don't sit down immediately."

Amara waved a hand at a nearby chair. "Please."

Cleo sat down heavily. "I'm not here to waste any more time. Your words the last time we spoke may have been encouraging, but your actions have never given me much hope for an alliance between us. Do you really blame me for how I reacted, no matter what I was promised?"

"I appreciate your bluntness. No, I suppose the longer I've had to think about it, the less I blame you for nearly shattering my skull." She smiled tightly. "I believe I would have done the very same thing had our positions been reversed."

"I'm sure you would have."

Amara absently swirled the wine, looking down into its depths. "I was never your enemy, Cleo."

"You wanted to possess the Kindred and were willing to do whatever it took to claim it."

"True." Amara considered her for a moment. "You proclaimed Magnus king during your speech to the Paelsians, despite his family stealing your throne. Why?"

Cleo's expression shadowed. "Because I hated his father for giving Mytica to you so easily. The Limerian people weren't ready to accept me as their queen yet, so I presented them with a slightly less distasteful king than Magnus's father."

"So it's not because you'd fallen in love with him."

"Amara, you want me to be blunt? I'll be blunt. Politics and love should have nothing to do with each other. Do you disagree?"

"I don't disagree." She regarded the blond girl for a moment in silence. "Why are you here, Cleo?"

"Because I've heard that you don't trust men—any men. Yet it seems to me that you're surrounded by them. Very few women hold important positions in this world, other than being the wives or mothers of important men. I believe that should change. You control a third of the entire world now, a fraction that is sure to grow over the years and decades to come. I believe you will need help with that."

"And you're offering me that help."

Cleo raised her chin. "That's right."

"Or . . . perhaps this is just a ruse to distract me."

"Distract you from what?" Cleo said evenly.

"From demanding your head. You march in here like you have any right to be within ten paces of me. Are you that desperate now, that you would risk so much by coming here and expecting me to be kind?"

"Kindness is not something I expect from you, Amara. If you spoke to me with kindness today, I'd assume you were lying. Very well—what can I do to prove my worth to you?"

Amara considered this carefully. "Information. Tell me something I don't already know that may adversely affect my reign as empress."

Cleo chewed her bottom lip while Amara waited as patiently as she was able to. Then the girl's aquamarine eyes rose to meet hers.

"Your brother Ashur is alive." Cleo took a moment to observe Amara's shocked expression. "I take it he hasn't arrived yet."

Amara chest tightened at the possibility, but her eyes narrowed on the princess. "Impossible. Of all the lies you could tell, that was not one that will serve you well. My patience with you is finished. Guards!"

The door opened, and Amara was surprised to see Carlos, not a regular guard. "Empress, I'm here to announce that there has been another arrival at the gates," he said.

She frowned. "Send them off. I don't want to see another unexpected visitor. And take this deceitful creature away. Put her with the others while I decide how I want her to die."

"As you wish, your grace." Carlos hesitated, but only for a moment. "But I think you should see this visitor."

"Whoever it is can wait."

"He won't wait, your grace." Carlos's gaze turned to his left before he immediately fell to his knees, bowing his head.

And then Amara watched with utter disbelief as her dead brother walked into the room.

CHAPTER 28

CLEO

PAELSIA

Amara stared, still and silent, at Ashur for so long that Cleo thought she'd turned to stone.

"Sister, I'm sure you're surprised to see me," he said before turning a raised black eyebrow to Cleo. "And here you are as well."

"Yes, here I am," Cleo confirmed, her heart pounding hard. "I seem to have beat you here."

"You did. Then again, I didn't rush. I needed time to think."

"How odd. Thieves are usually in much more of a hurry."

He frowned at this. "I'm sure they are."

"Emperor Cortas, what would you like me to do with the prisoner?" the guard asked.

Prisoner. Cleo's gut wrenched at the thought that her journey would be cut short before she had a chance to make any difference. She had to think, to figure out a way to deal with this outcome. Manipulation was her best weapon. She needed to gain Amara's confidence, to get close to the most powerful woman in the world so she could help to destroy her.

"I want you to—" Amara began, then frowned. "Did you say *emperor?*"

The guard ignored her, his attention fully on Ashur. "Emperor?"

"Leave us to speak in private," Ashur told him.

The guard left, bowing all the way out of the room.

Ashur's gaze returned to his sister. "It seems now that our father and brothers are dead, I'm next in line to rule. You know very well I never wanted a responsibility like that, but I will do what I must." When she didn't reply, he continued, "Nothing to say to me after all this time apart, Sister?"

Amara now shook her head slowly from side to side. "This isn't possible."

Cleo wanted to bite her tongue, to keep from saying anything that might draw attention to her and remind Amara that she wanted her dead.

But she couldn't help it.

"It's very possible," Cleo said with a nod. "Ashur is alive and well. It was a surprise to me too, but I'm sure it's a bit more of shock to you. After all, you did murder him in cold blood, didn't you?"

"Clearly, I didn't," Amara said, her words crisper and harder-edged than Cleo would have expected, considering how stunned the empress appeared to be.

"You did," Ashur confirmed, absently stroking his chest. "There was no mistaking the pain of the blade as it slid into my skin and bone. The cold look in your eyes that I'd seen cast upon others in our lives, but never before upon me. The horrible sensation of betrayal that broke my heart just as you sliced into it without any hesitation."

"How? Tell me how this can be!"

"Let me assure you that I am not here for vengeance of any kind. Despite your harsh and questionable decisions, I do understand it all more than you might think. You are not the only one in our family who was cast aside by our father for having differences that made us unacceptable."

"Elan was different," she whispered.

"Elan looked at our father like a shining god standing before him. I suppose that pardoned many of his imperfections."

"This is actually happening, isn't it?" Amara's eyes filled with tears. "You won't believe me, but I've only regretted one of my decisions: what I did to you. I was angry, I felt betrayed . . . so I reacted."

"Indeed you did."

"I wouldn't blame you if you wanted me dead."

"I don't want you dead, Amara. I want you alive and well and willing to see everything in this world more clearly than you've ever seen it in your life. The world is not an enemy to be conquered at any cost, whatever our *madhosha* might have you believe."

"Our *madhosha* is the only one who has ever believed in me. She's guided me and been my most valuable advisor."

"So it was she who advised you to end my life."

Amara twisted her hands. "But it was I who acted on such advice. For a while, I thought you would be on my side through everything, but you chose that boy . . . that boy with the red hair . . . after becoming enamored with him after what? A month?"

"Nic," Cleo said, her throat constricting. "His name was *Nic*."

Ashur sent a deep frown toward her. "What do you mean his name *was* Nic?"

Cleo commanded herself not to cry. She refused to show any weakness here, unless it might serve her in some way. She wanted to hate Amara the most, to have that hatred fuel her, strengthen her, but all she wanted to do right now was hurt Ashur.

"When you left, he followed," she said evenly. "He was here at the compound when a riot broke out."

"And what?" Ashur asked softly.

"And . . . he's dead." It sounded far too horrible to put into words, but she had to. She wanted to twist the words into Ashur to see if this prince was truly made of steel, someone who didn't give a damn whom he hurt or used or left behind.

"No." Ashur shook his head, his brows drawing together. "No, that can't be."

"It's true." Amara nodded. "I saw it happen."

"You said it yourself," Cleo said, her throat tight. The confirmation stole away any hope she had left that this had been a lie. "Anyone who truly cares for you ends up dead. I can't imagine you're all that surprised."

"*No*," Ashur said again as he pressed the back of his hand to his mouth and squeezed his eyes shut.

"Oh, please, Ashur." Amara flicked her hand dismissively. "You barely knew that boy! You're trying to tell me you're upset by this news?"

"Shut your mouth!" Cleo roared at her, surprising herself with her own sudden ferocity. Amara stared at her, shocked. "He was my friend, my *best* friend. I loved him, and he loved me. He was my family, and because of you and your brother he's dead!"

"Because of us, is it?" Amara repeated, her voice low. "Did you even try to stop him from chasing after my brother like a pathetic, discarded lover from his past?"

"I didn't know until he was already gone!"

"Perhaps you should have been keeping a better watch over someone you proclaim to have loved."

Cleo lurched toward her, wanting to tear every piece of hair from her head, but Ashur was behind her, holding her arms and keeping her in place.

She struggled, as she'd done earlier with the guards, wanting to claw at the prince's face too. "Let go of me!"

"Violence is not the answer to violence," he said, finally releasing her to point at a chair. "Sit and be silent, unless you wish to be removed from this room."

Cleo did the best she could to compose herself, cursing the day these horrible siblings had never set foot on Mytican soil.

"You want to know why I'm alive, Sister?" Ashur said, his teeth clenched. "Because I learned what happened to you as a child. I know our father tried to kill you. And I'm not deaf or blind; I have heard you and Grandmother speaking to each other, planning what was to come and deciding who was in the way. When I felt that my life might be at risk, even though I didn't entirely believe you would do such a thing—not to *me*—I went to visit Grandmother's apothecary . . ."

A warm breeze moved over Cleo's bare arms.

"My, my, this is quite dramatic, isn't it, little queen?" a voice whispered in her ear.

She gasped.

"It would be best not to react to me. Wouldn't want to interrupt the prince and princess—or is that emperor and empress?—during their long-awaited reunion."

Cleo kept her gaze on Amara and Ashur as Ashur explained why he'd been resurrected and how he believed himself to be the legendary, peace-bringing phoenix.

"Who are you?" she whispered.

"Shh. Don't speak. Amara will be very jealous if she knows I'm talking to other pretty girls behind her back. But perhaps I don't care what she thinks of me anymore. She has been a disappointment to me, now that the storm draws closer." He paused. *"I am the god of fire, little queen, released from my prison at long last."*

Cleo began to tremble.

"You don't have to be afraid of me. I see now that I overlooked so much at our last brief meeting. My attention was more on Lucia and her brother and my search for a special, magical wheel. But you . . . your eyes . . ."

Warmth touched her face, and her muscles tensed.

"They're the color of aquamarine. The very color of my sister's crystal orb. Please nod if you understand me."

She gave a shallow nod, barely breathing now.

"There is power hidden deep within you, little queen. And a desire for more. Do you know that you're descended from a goddess? Would you like me to give you all the magic you've ever dreamed of possessing?"

Cleo knew very well what Kyan had done to Lysandra and what he and Lucia had done to many villages in Paelsia. Despite her fear and her hate for this creature she couldn't see, there seemed to be no other answer at the moment that would satisfy him and ensure she'd remain unharmed.

So she nodded.

"Amara is unworthy, I see that now. She is only after power for herself, yet she fools herself that she aspires for more than her father did. However, you would sacrifice yourself to save those you love, wouldn't you?"

Cleo forced herself to nod again, even as a shiver went up her spine. What dark promise was she making?

Did the fire Kindred truly see something in her, something special and powerful and worthy of possessing true magic?

Perhaps her wish had finally come true.

"I will return with the storm. It's so close now, little queen. Tell no one about what I've said to you. Don't disappoint me."

The warmth that had made her start to perspire faded away, and she realized Amara was speaking to her.

"Cleo," she said. "Can you hear me?"

"Y-yes, yes. I can hear you."

"Did you also hear what Ashur has suggested?"

"No," she admitted.

"He believes that together, he and I can rule Kraeshia peacefully. What do you think? Is this a good plan?"

Cleo found herself momentarily speechless at the thought of it, but then something began to rise in her throat—a laugh. "Pardon me for saying so, Amara, but that's a preposterous plan. Two people cannot rule equally. It's impossible."

Amara's brows shot up. "I appreciate your candor."

"I deeply disagree," Ashur growled.

Cleo rose from her chair, drawing from her outrage and grief and need to survive to make her stronger. "Where is it, Ashur?"

He frowned. "What?"

"What you stole from me."

"I stole nothing from you." The prince's jaw tightened. "I know you blame me for Nicolo's death. I also blame myself. If I could go back and do things differently, I would."

"Starting when? When you took the resurrection potion or when you forced Nic to kiss you that night in Auranos? Both were regretful mistakes, in my opinion."

"Vicious, heartless words don't become you, princess." Ashur turned to his sister. "The decision is in your hands, Amara, and I know you'll make the correct one. I've come here to show you another path than the one you're on. A better path."

"You have." Amara nodded. "I could choose the path to being kind, sweet, nice, and more agreeable, like all good girls should be, right?"

"You speak with sarcasm, but a gentler outlook might achieve more than you believe it would. We can rule Kraeshia together or I shall rule alone as emperor."

"If you think I'd agree to that, Brother, then you really don't know me at all. Guards!"

Cleo's wide-eyed gaze shot to the door as several guards entered the room, looking between Ashur and Amara, uncertain where to place their attention.

Amara pointed at Ashur. "My brother has confessed to conspiring with the rebel who murdered our family. He wishes to help the rebellion tear apart the Kraeshian Empire my father built."

"I've done no such thing," Ashur said, outraged.

"Wrong," Cleo spoke up, disgusted by Ashur's lies. He had hidden the Kindred somewhere, keeping it for his own gain. "He did confess. I heard it myself."

Ashur turned a look of pure fury on her.

While she'd hoped Ashur might talk some sense into Amara, that seemed to be a wish in vain. Amara had the ruthlessness that Ashur lacked. She was the predator, and Ashur, be it today or a year from now, would succumb to being her prey again.

Even if it was only a temporary ruse, Cleo had to align herself with strength, now more than ever before.

She had to align with Amara.

"Not so peaceful now, are you, Ashur?" Cleo asked steadily. "Funny how that can change so quickly."

"Put him with the other prisoners," Amara told the guards.

"Amara!" Ashur snarled. "Do not do this!"

The empress's expression remained calm. "You came here to proudly tell me that you're the phoenix legend speaks of, but you're wrong. *I* am the phoenix." She nodded at the guards. "Take him away."

The guards forced Ashur from the room as Amara sat down heavily in her chair.

"You lied about Ashur to the guards," she said.

Cleo could barely believe it herself. "I did."

"He could have taken everything from me: my title, my power. Everything. All because he's my older brother."

"Yes, he could have." Cleo kept her gaze steady. "So now what do you plan to do with me?"

"To be honest, I haven't decided yet."

Cleo bit her bottom lip, trying to stay confident in the face of so much uncertainty. "Do you really believe that you're the phoenix?"

Amara raised an eyebrow. "Does it really matter?"

A guard lingered at the doorway. When Amara's gaze went to him, his shoulders straightened. "Empress, I have information for you."

Amara flicked him an impatient look. "What is it?"

"The rebels have been captured. They await interrogation."

Cleo felt faint. Was it Jonas and Felix? Taran? Who else?

"Cleo, I want you to come with me to question them," Amara said. "I want you to prove to me that you may—just may—be able to earn a small portion of my trust once again. Will you do that?"

The fire god had made her a tantalizing promise. But would she turn her back on Jonas, Felix, and Taran if it meant that she could get her throne back?

And if not, was there a way she might convince Amara to release them before she had a chance to steal the Kindred back from her?

There wasn't time to make such decisions now, not about something so important. All she could do was buy as much time as possible.

Cleo nodded. "Of course I'll do that, empress."

CHAPTER 29

MAGNUS

PAELSIA

Magnus and Gaius spent the entire day shackled like common prisoners in the back of a wagon that journeyed west from Basilia. Magnus knew exactly where they were headed, and when they finally reached Chief Basilius's former compound at dusk, he wasn't certain that they would ever witness another sunrise.

Amara's small but impressive army surrounded the perimeter of the compound, and Magnus and his father were ushered through the gates by the guards. Once inside, they were half shoved, half dragged down a narrow, winding corridor and placed in a room with stone walls and no furniture. Guards attached new shackles to their ankles. There was nothing to do but sit and wait on the bloodstained floor.

The door had a lock on it, and it only opened from the other side.

Yes, Magnus thought, *this definitely qualifies as a dungeon.*

"I didn't want this," the king said after they were left alone.

"No? You didn't want us chained up and left to Amara's whim?

I've heard about how Kraeshians deal with prisoners. It makes your treatment of them seem almost benevolent."

"This isn't the end for us."

"That's very amusing, Father. It feels like it is. You know what would be very helpful right now? A witch to help us out. But you chased her away too, didn't you?"

"I did. And I don't regret it. My mother is an evil woman."

"I guess you came by that same evil naturally then, no potions necessary."

Magnus had had a lot of time to think during the journey here. He thought about Cleo, mostly, and wondered if anything would be different now if he hadn't sent Nic after Ashur.

Likely not. Because then Cleo might be with him and his father, and Magnus would be unable to do anything to help her. He hoped very hard that she'd finally accomplished what she should have done from the beginning and gone to Auranos to find allies, rebels, assistance of some kind.

She was much better off as far away from him as possible.

Time passed slowly, and night turned back to day as sunlight spilled into their dark dungeon room from a tiny window. The sound of a lock in the door jerked Magnus back to attention, and he shielded his eyes from more blazing sunlight as the door opened and several guards entered the room. Behind them strode the empress herself.

She nodded at him. "Magnus, it's so lovely to see you again."

"Well, I couldn't possibly feel less delighted to see you."

Amara's cold smile held. "And Gaius, I've been so worried about you. I've heard nothing from you since you went on your quest to find your treasonous son and bring him to justice. Did it not go well?"

"My plans changed," the king said simply.

"I see that."

"Is this any way to greet your husband, Amara?" Magnus asked. "By putting him in chains in a dungeon?"

"My mother once ran away from my father. I'm told he dragged her back to him and locked her in a small, dark room—for an entire year, I believe. She also lost a finger as punishment for trying to escape—she was forced to sever it herself."

She told the story without any emotion at all.

"Is that my fate?" he asked. "To lose a finger?"

"I haven't decided just what I'd like to have sliced off your body for all your lies and deceit. But I'm certain I'll think of something. In the meantime, I have someone with me whom I'm sure you'd like to see."

She stepped aside, and Magnus, still shielding his eyes, realized with stunned disbelief that Cleo stood in the doorway.

Her expression was utterly unreadable.

"I thought you said you had rebels imprisoned here," Cleo said.

Amara turned to her. "These are rebels, working against me to steal what now belongs to me. Am I wrong?"

"No, I suppose not." Cleo cocked her head. "It's so strange to think of them as rebels, though. The word doesn't quite seem to fit."

"If we're rebels, princess," the king hissed, "then what are you?"

"A prisoner of war," Cleo replied calmly, "forced to marry against my will as my freedom was stolen along with my throne. And so it has been for a very long and painful year of my life."

Magnus hadn't said a word since Cleo had entered the dungeon, stunned by every move she made and every word she uttered. This couldn't possibly be the same girl he'd come to know, the one full of passion and fire the night their paths had intersected at the cottage in the snowy woods. The one full of anger and hate when she learned that Nic was dead.

This girl's perfect mask of indifference rivaled his own.

"I gave you many chances to leave," Magnus said. "You were no prisoner."

"I was a prisoner of the choices taken from me by your father. How many times would he have liked to see this very situation reversed, to see me chained and at his mercy? *Mercy*," she snorted. "That isn't a word I would ever use to describe his actions."

"You should have woken me," Magnus said. "My father shouldn't have sent you away all alone. I know you were angry with me."

"Angry? You think I was—"

"But to come here," he interrupted her. "To, what? Attempt an alliance with Amara?"

"Perhaps," she allowed. "Since she's the only one with any power here, would you really blame me?"

"What should I do with them, Cleo?" Amara asked. "Do you want me to consider sparing Magnus's life?"

"I'll have to give it some thought," Cleo said.

Magnus narrowed his eyes at her. "Some thought? The princess needs to give *some thought* to whether or not I die? Need I remind you that I have saved your life far too many times to count?"

"This is not a scale on which we must balance such things. This is war. And in war, we must do what is necessary to survive."

He glared at her, then shifted his gaze to Amara. "Then perhaps I should arrange an alliance with you for myself."

Amara scoffed. "Really? What kind of an alliance?"

"I remember the night we spent together very well. You are . . . an extraordinary woman, one I would very much like in my bed again."

From the corner of his eye, Magnus could clearly see Cleo fidget uncomfortably.

"Really?" Amara twisted a finger through her hair. "And you don't mind that I've been with other men since we were together? Including your own father?"

"I prefer a woman with experience. So many others are so . . . clumsy and awkward in their innocence." He shifted his gaze to Cleo to see if his words, utterly untrue to his actual feelings on the subject, had any effect on her. "Don't you think, princess?"

"Oh, absolutely," Cleo agreed, though there was poison in her tone. "You should seek out only the most experienced women. Perhaps you could learn a great deal from them."

Amara kept a thin smile steady on her face. "I think such invitations are well behind us, Magnus, but I certainly appreciate the generous offer. What I'm more interested in at this very moment is acquiring the air Kindred. I want it."

"I'm sure you do," the king said. "As you've wanted everything I've had."

"Not everything. For example, I don't want you as a husband anymore. Will you tell me where it is?"

"No," he replied.

"I have no patience for this." Amara gestured to the guards. "Take the two of them to the pit."

"Yes, empress."

The two girls turned toward the door.

"Princess . . ." Magnus said, hating the sliver of weakness in his voice. Cleo's shoulders tensed at the sound of his voice.

She glared at him over her shoulder. "I thought I told you to call me Cleiona."

Magnus stared after them as Cleo and Amara left without another word.

Cleiona . . . she wanted him to call her *Cleiona.*

The name of a goddess. Her full, proper name, not a shortened version of it. The name he'd originally chosen to call her to show that he wanted her, that he loved her.

That she loved him.

Could it be that there was still hope that she hadn't abandoned him to this fate? That she had forgiven him his many mistakes?

The guards unshackled Magnus and the king and began pulling them from the dungeon and into the light. They entered a building, then moved down an echoing corridor with a open ceiling.

A pretty girl with short, dark hair and a shapely body leaned against the wall up ahead.

"Greetings," she said to the guards. "I see that you have the prisoners firmly in hand. Well done."

"Indeed, Nerissa. You look lovely today."

"You think so?" She smiled seductively, and the guards smiled back at her.

"Fitting in well here, I see," Magnus said to her coldly.

"Very well, thank you." Nerissa began walking next to them, and she slid her hand down the sleeve of the guard's uniform. "I need to ask you for a favor, my sweet."

Magnus's guard slowed down, while his father's guards continued down the hall.

The guard looked at her hungrily. "Oh?"

She whispered something in his ear that actually made him giggle.

"That is a favor I'm most happy to oblige, my lovely. Tell me when and where."

The king and his guards disappeared around the corner up ahead.

"Soon. Perhaps just a kiss for now to make you remember me."

"As if I could forget."

Nerissa pulled the guard in and brushed her lips against his. Magnus saw her reach for something in the folds of her dress. She met Magnus's eyes just as she thrust her dagger into the guard's gut. The guard immediately let go of Magnus, clutching his stomach.

"What are you—?" he gasped.

She jabbed him, quick and deep, several more times before he fell to the floor in a bloody, twitching heap.

Magnus stared at the girl in utter shock at what he'd witnessed.

Nerissa gestured to someone behind Magnus. "Quickly. Cut the prince's bindings."

That someone sliced through the ropes that tied his wrists, and Magnus turned. A familiar, angry face topped with a shock of red hair stared back at him.

"Nic," he managed.

Nic shook his head. "It goes against my very nature to save your arse, but here we are."

Magnus couldn't believe his eyes. "You're supposed to be dead."

"And I would be if it weren't for your sister's magic. Here I was prepared to despise the both of you for the rest of my life. You, I'm still undecided about. Her . . . I now owe my life." He looked at Nerissa. "What do we do with the guard?"

"This way." She grabbed the sleeve of the dead guard's uniform, and she and Nic pulled him out of the main corridor and into a shadowed alcove. "This will have to do. We need to move quickly."

Magnus, still stunned, grappled to regain his composure. "Where are we going?"

"We're going to Amara's chambers to retrieve the water Kindred," Nerissa whispered. "She knows how to perform the ritual to release its magic. I don't know how she learned it, but she's confident that it'll work. The prisoners will be used for their blood, to strengthen the magic. I want to do what I can to help them, but right now we need that Kindred in our hands, not hers."

Magnus nodded. "Then let's stop talking and start moving."

Nerissa hurried down the hallway, and Nic and Magnus followed closely behind. Finally they came to a doorway. Nerissa looked both ways before unlocking the door. They entered a lavish bedroom with several adjoining rooms full of windows that looked out at the small walled city.

Nerissa went immediately to the wardrobe, checking the pockets of a long line of gowns and cloaks. "Check everywhere else, just in case she moved it."

Magnus and Nic did as she said, checking shelves, cabinets, and under the cushions of chairs.

"Are you sure it's here?" Magnus asked.

"All I know for sure is that she didn't have it with her earlier."

"How do you know?"

"I helped her dress, and it was definitely not in any of her pockets. Check the other room."

Magnus wasn't sure how he felt about being ordered around by a servant, but he continued to do as she instructed. This girl had far more talents than simply being a personal attendant.

But, of course, he now realized that Nerissa Florens wasn't just any attendant. She was a rebel.

His search left him empty-handed, and he returned to the bedroom, but Nic and Nerissa were nowhere to be seen. "Where did you go? Nic? Nerissa?"

He scanned the large room until his gaze fell on two bodies lying on the floor.

Nic's eyes were shut, an angry red mark on his temple. A few paces away, Nerissa groaned with pain.

Her eyes met Magnus's and immediately widened with fear.

Magnus felt a sharp pain on the back of his head, and then the world went dark.

CHAPTER 30

AMARA

PAELSIA

"Little empress."

The sound of Kyan's voice surprised her, but Amara was relieved to hear it. She'd been certain he'd left her after their disagreement yesterday.

"You're still here," she whispered. She sat in the small room adjacent to her bedchambers that she'd turned into a meditation room, one empty of everything except the mat she sat upon.

"The storm is nearly upon us. It is time for me to regain my power and for you to reap every reward you so greatly deserve."

Her heart leapt. "The prisoners are waiting," she told him.

"Excellent. Their blood will seal the ritual and make it permanent."

Amara pushed away all her remaining doubts, finding that there were very few. To second-guess herself now would be the ultimate weakness after all she'd sacrificed for this day.

"Wait for me outside with the water Kindred."

She agreed to this without hesitation.

Amara wanted Cleo with her, both for support and, if required, as an additional sacrifice. Together, they left the royal chambers and went outside to the direct center of the compound, where the pit was located. Amara instructed a dozen of her soldiers to surround it, half with crossbows aimed at the prisoners below.

Nothing could go wrong now.

"Well, look who's come to visit." Felix peered up at her, shielding his one good eye from the bright sky that had only just begun to darken with storm clouds. "The great and powerful empress. Come on down here, your grace. I'd love a chance to catch up. I'm sure your brother would too!"

Amara reluctantly glanced at Ashur sitting next to Felix and the other rebel, Taran. Her brother looked up at her, not with rage or hate but with bottomless disappointment in his gray-blue eyes.

"Sister, you can still change the path you've chosen," he said to her.

"Unfortunately, you can't change yours," she replied. "You never should have returned here."

"I had no choice."

"There's always a choice. And I have made mine."

Gaius sat with his back against the side of the pit, his arms crossed over his chest. He said nothing at all, just looked up at her with that maddeningly blank expression of his. How sad it was to see the former king so defeated. How sad and yet how deeply satisfying.

There was also another young man at the bottom of the pit—one Amara vaguely recognized from the day Nerissa became her attendant. Enzo, she believed his name was.

Cleo peered down into the pit. "Where's Magnus?"

When she realized that the prince wasn't with the others, Amara frowned and turned to a guard. "Well? Where is he?"

The guard bowed. "It seems that he managed to slip away from us. There is a search being conducted, and I assure you that he will be found."

"Magnus escaped?" Cleo asked, breathless.

Amara tensed. "Find him," she told the guard. "Bring him here alive. I will hold you personally responsible if he's not found."

"Yes, empress." The guard bowed before he rushed off.

"He doesn't matter anymore," Amara said, mostly to herself. "All is well."

"*Yes, little empress. All is well.*"

A moment after Kyan spoke, thunder rolled in the sky. The clouds continued to gather, growing darker by the second. The wind picked up, sweeping Amara's hair back from her shoulders.

"So it's a true storm," she said, her skin tingling with anticipation of what was to come.

"*Yes. Created from all the elements combined by powerful blood magic.*"

Two guards approached the pit with more prisoners that Amara hadn't expected.

Cleo gasped. "Nic! You're alive!"

The boy was bloody, bruised, and disheveled, but it did appear that Cleo's friend was still very much alive. Amara nodded at the guard, who released Nic long enough for Cleo to run straight into his embrace.

"I thought you were dead!" she cried.

"I nearly was. But . . . I recovered."

Cleo took Nic's face between her hands, staring as if unable to believe her own eyes. "I'm so unbelievably angry at you I want to scream!"

"Don't scream. I have a really bad headache." He gingerly touched the red mark on his temple.

"How are you alive? Amara said she saw you die."

"Believe it or not, it's thanks to Lucia."

Amara was certain she'd heard him wrong. "The sorceress was here?" she asked.

Nic turned a look of sheer hatred on her. "Why? Are you afraid that she's going to bring this place crumbling down on top of you? We can only hope, can't we?"

Amara was about to reply, or perhaps ask for his blood to spill early, but the other prisoner caught her eye.

"Nerissa?" She turned to her attendant with shock, then glared at the guard holding her in place. "What is the meaning of this?"

"She assisted in Prince Magnus's escape, along with the boy," the guard explained. "Together, they were trying to steal from your chambers."

Amara blinked with surprise as the news registered. "Why would you do this to me? I thought we'd become friends."

"You thought wrong," Nerissa said. "I'm sure you won't believe anything I tell you right now, so I choose to say nothing at all."

"You cannot trust anyone, little empress. This girl you'd come to value managed to fool even you."

Amara raised her chin, the betrayal cutting deeper than she ever would have expected. "Put this lying little bitch in with the others. And the other one too."

"Amara!" Cleo cried.

"Hold your tongue—unless you want to join them," Amara snapped. "And I promise, that would not be good choice for you to make today. Choose which side you wish to stand on, Cleo—mine or theirs?"

Cleo's chest heaved, but she didn't say another word as Nic and Nerissa were forced by guards to descend a rope ladder that lowered them into the pit.

Amara glanced over the edge to witness Ashur's reaction to Nic's resurrection, wishing to focus on something other than Nerissa's betrayal.

"You're alive," Ashur gasped.

"I am," Nic replied tightly.

Ashur's eyes brimmed with tears as he sank down to his knees.

How weak you've become, brother, she thought with disgust and a whisper of sadness for all that had been lost between them.

"What's wrong with you?" Nic asked Ashur, frowning.

"You . . . I know you came after me, to try to talk me out of what I believed was right. And I . . . I thought you were dead."

Nic watched him warily. "Seems to be a very common belief today. But I'm not."

Ashur nodded. "It's good."

"I'm glad that you're glad." Nic's frown deepened. "Honestly? I didn't think you'd care one way or the other. Now, uh . . ." He glanced around at the others in the pit nervously. "Please stand up now."

Ashur did as requested, drawing closer to Nic. "I know my behavior has been unforgiveable of late. I wanted to push everyone away . . . especially you. I didn't want you to get hurt. But I was wrong—wrong about everything. About myself, about my choices, about my destiny. I thought I was important."

"You *are* important."

"I'm not the phoenix. I see that now." Ashur lowered his head, and his hair, loose from the piece of leather he used to tie it back, fell over his face. "Please forgive me, Nicolo."

With a slight hesitation, Nic tucked the prince's hair behind his ear. "All of this is because you thought I was dead? I truly hate to break it to you, but today isn't looking so good for any of us."

"You're right. Life isn't guaranteed, not at any time, not for anyone. Every single day, every single moment, could be our last."

"Uh, unfortunately, yes."

Ashur raised his gaze to meet Nic's. "Which means we must take what we want most in this short mortal life while we have the chance."

"I completely agree."

"Good." He put his hand behind Nic's head and kissed him hard and deep. When he drew back, Nic's cheeks were flushed nearly as red as his hair.

"Ha!" Felix said, jabbing his index finger at them. "I knew it! I *totally* knew it!"

Amara watched all of this, her heart heavy at seeing her brother finally admit his true feelings. She wasn't sure if it pleased her or if it made her sad. "How lovely for you all. My brother does put on an excellent show, doesn't he?"

"I'm not pretending to be something I'm not," Ashur growled at her. "Not anymore. Not like you."

"Trust me, brother. Today, I'm exactly who I was meant to be." She glanced at a guard. "If you successfully captured Nicolo and Nerissa, where is Magnus?"

The guard bowed his head. "Detained elsewhere, your grace."

"Where?"

"I fear I lost track of the guards who dragged him from your chambers. But I assure you, he is not a threat to you."

Perhaps not, but Amara would rather have all of her prisoners together in one place.

"Well done, little empress. You show admirable strength today."

Amara wanted this over once and for all, wanted to finally move on from these sacrifices she'd been forced to make all her life.

"I'm so glad you approve," Amara said, impatience rising

within her as the first drop of rain fell from the dark gray clouds. "Is it time to begin?"

"Yes, it's time. She is finally here."

With another roll of thunder and a violent crack of lightning forking through the dark sky, a woman approached them, her black cloak flowing in the wind. Her guards parted to make way for her, collectively taking a step backward.

"Is it Lucia?" Amara asked tightly.

"No, it's not Lucia."

The woman who approached had a mature face and long gray hair with a white streak at the front. Her dark gray eyes, nearly black, scanned the guards and the edge of the pit, then fell upon Amara herself.

Lightning forked through the sky behind her.

"Selia!" Cleo managed. "What are you doing here?"

"You know this woman? Who is she?" Amara demanded.

"This is Gaius Damora's mother," Cleo said, then gasped. "Olivia!"

Another woman trailed after Selia, a lovely one with dark skin and green eyes that darted around nervously.

"Cleo," she said tightly. "I . . . I'm so sorry for this."

"Sorry? Sorry for what?"

"The marks." Olivia extended her arms to show that her skin bore painted black symbols.

"Yes," Selia said, nodding. "Magical markings as old as time itself that will make even an immortal obey my command."

"You are Gaius's mother." Amara's thoughts spun. "And you are also the witch that Kyan summoned here."

"I am. It is an honor of a lifetime for me to use my magic to assist the god of fire in the place of my granddaughter, who foolishly turned against him. For this ritual to release the magic of the Kindred, we require the blood of the sorceress and the blood of an immortal."

"Selia," Cleo began, frowning. "Why would you do this?"

"I am an Oldling, that's why. We have worshipped the Kindred for countless generations, and today I will be the one who will help free them."

"Them?" Amara cocked her head. "I have only the water Kindred."

Selia smiled. "And I have earth and air."

From her cloak, she pulled two small crystal orbs—one obsidian, the other moonstone.

Cleo gasped. "You—it was you!"

"Incredible." Amara's frustration and doubt dissipated like mist on the wind. "I admit that I had misgivings, but now I see that all is how it must be. After all my sacrifices, I will finally receive everything I've ever wanted."

"You will?" Selia asked, her thin, dark brows rising. "Actually, this has nothing to do with you, little girl."

Amara gestured toward her guards. "Take the orbs from her and bring them to me. Make sure she does only what she's required to do. Restrain her, if you must."

Before anyone could move, all twelve guards surrounding the pit clutched their throats. Amara watched with horror as the guards gasped for air and crumpled to the ground. Each one was dead.

"Kyan! Stop her!"

"What has begun cannot be stopped." Warmth moved past her, brushing against her left ear. *"You want to possess the magic of the Kindred to use for your own gain, the same as many before you have. But we belong to no one."*

Selia flicked her finger at Cleo, and the princess stumbled

backward, falling into the pit. Amara raced to the side to look down to see that Taran had managed to catch her before she hit the bottom.

Amara turned toward the witch with shock. "You dare—?"

Selia flicked her finger again, and it felt as if a large and invisible hand had shoved her. Amara lost her footing and fell into the pit. As she slammed to the ground, her leg made a sickening crunching sound.

Felix looked down at her, his arms crossed over his broad chest. "Oops," he said. "I forgot to catch you. Did that hurt?"

Blinded by pain and unable to move, through tear-filled eyes Amara saw Selia at the edge of the pit, smiling down at all of them.

"*Excellent,*" Kyan said. "*Now, let's begin.*"

CHAPTER 31

JONAS

PAELSIA

Lucia insisted that she and Jonas journey to the empress's compound as quickly as possible. This meant on horseback, which Jonas knew, even before they started, was a bad idea for someone in the princess's condition. To Lucia's credit, she didn't complain once as they rode southeast as fast as they could.

But then she came to a halt in the middle of a forest—or what had once been a forest. Jonas saw that all around him, the bushes and trees that had once grown tall and lush were now brown and withering. He glanced over at Lucia. Her skin was so pale, she looked no healthier than a five-day-old corpse.

"I can keep going," she muttered.

"I don't think so."

"Don't argue with me, rebel. My family—"

"Your family can bloody well wait." He hopped off his horse and was at her side to catch her when she lost her grip on the reins and slid off.

The skies darkened in moments.

"Damn Paelsian storms," Jonas grumbled, looking upward. "You never know when they're coming."

A loud roar of thunder was enough to frighten the horses. Before Jonas could do anything to stop them, they ran away.

"Figures," he growled. "One bad thing leads to another."

Lucia clutched his hand as he tried to put her on her feet. "Jonas . . ."

"What?"

"Oh, goddess, I think . . ." She cried out in pain. "I think it's time."

"Time?" He shook his head, regarding her with denial. "No, it's not time for anything but finding ourselves other transportation."

"The baby . . ."

"No, I repeat, you are not doing this now."

"I don't think I have a choice."

He took her by her shoulders. "Look at me, princess. Look at me!"

Lucia raised her pained gaze to his.

"You're not going to give birth now, because Timotheus visited my dream—just one, just long enough to tell me that he had a vision about me. I am with you when you die in childbirth. And I'm supposed to raise your son."

She stared at him, her eyes widening. "He said that?"

"Yes."

"You are going to raise my son?"

"Yes, apparently."

"A Paelsian wine seller's son is going to raise *my* child?"

Jonas was far too weary to care about the insult. "Didn't you hear what I said about you dying?"

"I deserve to die for all I've done. While I certainly wouldn't pick here and now, I knew it was coming. I accept that I have no choice." Then she cried out again. "And you must accept your destiny, because I don't think you're going to have any choice either."

He hissed out a breath. "I should leave you here, just turn my back on all of this. But I won't."

"Good."

"Are you sure this is really happening now?"

She nodded. "I'm sure."

Jonas picked her up and tried to find shelter in the barren forest before the skies opened. He pulled off his cloak and put it around her shoulders for more warmth.

"I don't know what to do," Lucia said.

"I learned one thing from my mother when I was a kid," Jonas told her. "She helped other women when they gave birth in our village. She said that nature has a way of making it happen whether you know what you're doing or not. Maybe you can do something to relieve the pain, though, with your earth magic?"

Lucia shook her head. "I'm drained. I'm weak. My magic is gone. Timotheus is right. I see now why he didn't want to tell me about this. He had me believing that I could stop Kyan, but I see now that it must be you." She pressed something into his hand, and he looked down to see that it was an orb of amber. "Kyan must be imprisoned again. You have magic within you, Jonas. It all makes sense to me now." As she spoke, her voice grew weaker and weaker, until it was barely audible above the roaring of the storm. He struggled to find footing in the muddy ground as he crouched next to the princess.

"You think I can imprison something like him? *You're* the prophesied sorceress."

"Not for much longer, it seems. Jonas . . ." He had to draw closer to hear her whisper. "Tell my brother, my father . . . tell them that

I'm sorry I hurt them. Tell them that I love them, that I know they loved me. And tell . . . tell my son when he's old enough to understand that there was good in me." She smiled weakly. "Way down deep, anyway."

Jonas had started to believe this too, so he didn't try to argue with her.

"You will make a good father for my son," she said. "You might not believe it now, but I see it. You're strong and earnest and hardworking. You do what you think is right, even at great cost."

"Don't forget that I'm incredibly handsome."

Her smile held. "That too."

He shook his head, now wanting to argue. He wasn't strong, he didn't do what was right. He'd gotten so many friends killed because of his choices and plans.

Lucia took his hand in hers. Her skin was so cold, it shocked him. "You are destined for greatness, Jonas Agallon. I can see your destiny as clearly as Timotheus can."

"You know," Jonas said, pushing Lucia's long, wet hair off her forehead. "I never believed in magic or destiny before a year ago."

"And now?"

"I believe in magic. In evil sorceresses who deep down are really beautiful princesses. I believe in immortals who live in a different world than this one, accessible by magical stone wheels. But you know what I don't believe in?"

"What?"

"I refuse to believe that we have absolutely no control over our own futures, because right now? I'm damn well going to control my own. I don't want to be a father. Not yet, anyway."

"But you must! My son is—"

"Your son will be fine. And so will you." He squeezed her hand. "You said that Alexius taught you how to steal magic. So steal mine. Steal enough to heal yourself, to get through this birth without dying. Do it, and you can tell Timotheus to kiss your arse when it comes to proclaiming your future from his shiny little Sanctuary."

Lucia stared at him, confusion naked in her gaze before it faded. "That isn't how it's supposed to be."

"Exactly," he said, grinning. "Don't you like the thought of having a choice when it comes to your own fate?"

"I . . . I'm not sure I can do this."

"Try," he said. "Just try, and stop bloody well arguing with everything I have to say."

Lucia's expression of fear was replaced by fury. "You are so rude to me!"

"Good. Be mad at me—so mad you can steal the magic right out of me. You can slap me for being rude later. Do it, princess. Take my magic."

Her forehead furrowed as she concentrated. *This will work,* Jonas thought. *It has to work.*

Then he felt it—a draining sensation that made him gasp aloud. It wasn't pain, exactly. It felt like a magnetic force pulling at his insides.

His heartbeat began to slow, and spots appeared before his eyes.

"Do me a favor," he managed.

"What?" she asked, and he noticed that her voice already sounded stronger, just as he began to feel weaker and colder.

"Try . . . not to . . . kill me . . ."

Only when he woke up, rain still drenching him, did Jonas realize that he'd passed out. His wet cloak had been thrown over him like a blanket, and he slowly, very slowly, pushed himself up to sit.

"Do storms usually last this long here?" asked Lucia.

Jonas looked over at her. She was holding a small bundle in her arms. "Baby," he said. "That—that's a baby right there."

"It is." She tipped the bundle enough that he could see a small pink face looking out at him.

"Definitely a baby," he said, nodding. "You're alive."

"Thanks to you. I can't tell you how grateful I am, Jonas. Your sacrifice saved my life."

"Sacrifice?" he repeated. "Not a sacrifice at all. I never wanted magic to start with."

"Well, I didn't take all your magic. As you requested, I didn't want to kill you just yet. After all, you promised that I could slap you when I felt better." She smiled. "I look forward to that."

He tried not to laugh. "As do I."

"It seems Timotheus was wrong about many things," Lucia said. "And that destiny isn't set after all, just as you said."

"Many things? What else was he wrong about?"

"My son," she kissed the baby's forehead, "is actually my daughter."

"A girl?" Jonas couldn't help but grin at that. "Nicely done, princess."

"Please, call me Lucia. I think you've earned that right."

"All right. Now what do we do, Lucia?" he asked.

"She has a name. Do you want to hear it?"

He nodded.

"I've named her Lyssa," she said, looking up at him. "After a brave girl named Lysandra I wish I'd had the chance to know."

Jonas's eyes began to sting. "An excellent name. I approve," he said, swallowing the lump in his throat. "All right, then. Before you lay waste to the rest of Paelsia, let's find you and Lyssa a nice, dry inn so you can regain the rest of your strength, shall we?"

CHAPTER 32

CLEO

PAELSIA

Cleo took in the faces that surrounded her in the rocky pit, her heart beating out of her chest. This wasn't how it was supposed to go. She wasn't sure how she meant to stop Amara, to take the Kindred and save everyone, but this wasn't it.

"Fear not, little queen, I am with you."

Her breath caught. Somehow Kyan still thought that they were together in this. But why would he need her now? She'd never felt as helpless in her entire life as she did at this moment, even surrounded by strong young men who were normally more than capable of protecting her from harm.

Except Magnus. Her gut twisted. Where was he? Imprisoned somewhere else? But where?

Cleo watched as Selia slowly levitated herself into the pit as if standing on an invisible platform of air magic. She prayed that Felix, Taran, and Enzo weren't foolish enough to try to attack the witch. Cleo had no doubt they would fail quickly.

Thankfully, they didn't budge from where they stood.

"How long have you been planning this, Mother?" King Gaius asked from his seated position. He hadn't moved an inch since Cleo and Amara had been cast into the pit.

"A very long time, my son," Selia replied, her fingers brushing against her snake pendant. "My entire life, it seems."

"You were the one to teach me about the Kindred, to drive my passion to find the crystals."

"Yes. And you took to this promise of power just as I knew you would."

"But you didn't tell me everything."

She met his gaze. "No. It had to remain my secret until now."

He nodded. "When I was younger I thought you simply wanted the magic of the Kindred, like anyone else who'd heard their legend. But it's always been more than that, hasn't it? You wanted to help free them."

She crouched down at his side and put her hand to his cheek. "I wasn't lying to you. You *will* rule the world, only differently than I had originally planned. The fire god is in need of a new corporeal vessel. I believe that only you are great enough, worthy enough, to have that omnipotent power within you."

Before the king could respond, Cleo felt a draft of warm air slide past her.

"*No, little witch,*" Kyan said. "*This fallen king won't do at all. He's too old. Too sick.*"

"Who just said that?" Nic asked, staring around the pit.

Cleo's wide eyes glanced over to him. "You can hear him too?"

Nic nodded.

"I hear him too," Taran said, scanning the pit. Felix and Enzo stood on either side of him, their expressions tense, but they also nodded in agreement.

"*That is only because I allow it,*" Kyan said. "*Like the little empress's brother said earlier, there's no reason to hide any longer."*

"Gaius is improving, Kyan," Selia assured him. "He was horribly injured, near death. It will take more time to fully heal, but he's well on his way."

"No. I wish for a different vessel."

"Of course." Selia's brows furrowed, the only sign of her disappointment as she glanced around at the others. "What about the Kraeshian here, Prince Ashur? Young, handsome, strong."

"Again, no. I need someone already possessed by a soul of fire." There was silence for a moment as the sensation of heat moved around the circumference of the pit. *"This one. Yes, this one is perfect. I sense greatness within, greatness shielded from the world."*

Who? Cleo thought frantically. There was no way to tell to whom the fire god referred.

"Then let's begin," Selia said.

The witch held her hand out, and the three crystal orbs Amara had hidden in the pockets of her robes flew across the pit and into Selia's hands.

Cleo watched tensely as she placed the aquamarine, obsidian, and moonstone orbs gently in the center of the pit. "Where is the amber crystal?" Selia asked.

"It's not here," Kyan said.

"Where is it?"

"I am already free from my prison; there is no need for it now. The ritual must work without it. Proceed."

Selia yanked the silver chain from around her neck, and Cleo realized with shock that the large snake pendant she wore wasn't simply jewelry—it was a vial with a small stopper.

The witch tipped the silver vial over the three crystals to drip dark red liquid onto them. With each drop, the orbs brightened, glowing from within.

"You have Lucia's blood," the king said, his voice hoarse. "How?"

She raised a brow. "I bled her when she was a child, before my exile. It only took the barest trace of earth magic to keep it fresh all this time." Selia looked at Olivia. "Come here and hold out your arm."

Olivia moved toward Selia and did exactly as commanded. The witch produced a dagger and cut Olivia's arm. When the immortal's blood joined Lucia's upon the orbs, they each flared brighter than before.

Cleo wanted to rush forward, to knock the dagger from the witch's grip, but she knew it would be the last thing she ever did. She felt utterly helpless as she watched this dark ritual unfold in front of her.

But despite her anger with Magnus about so many things, she knew that he wouldn't leave the compound if he managed to escape from Amara's guards again. He wouldn't focus on saving only himself.

No. He would intervene when it seemed like all hope was lost.

Had he understood the signal she'd tried to give him—having him call her Cleiona? She needed him to know that she'd tried to align with Amara only out of necessity and opportunity. That she had meant to use that alliance to regain her power.

To regain Magnus's power as well.

The storm above grew more violent. Rain began to fall in sheets, soaking Cleo.

Selia raised her hands, her eyes glowing. The crystals flared with light, like tiny suns. Cleo gasped aloud as the wisps of magic that had been inside the orbs streamed outward.

Three crystals. But there were now four wisps streaking through the air all around them: red, blue, white, and green.

Why did Selia say the ritual required the amber orb if Kyan was already here? Cleo wondered. Did it matter? Could it make a difference in stopping this?

"Fire god," Selia said. "You have chosen. And now it is time for you to claim your new flesh-and-blood vessel."

The flame-red wisp of magic swirled violently around the pit before it finally plunged deep into Nic's chest.

"Nic, no!" Cleo yelled.

Nic's eyes widened as he cried out. Choking, he collapsed to the ground in a heap.

Then her dearest friend slowly turned to face her.

"Nic," she gasped. "Are you all right?"

He frowned. "I took the name of my last host, Kyan. I like it much better than *Nic.* I shall keep it."

She stared at him with disbelief. "What? What have you done? Nic, can you hear me? You have to fight this!"

"Nic is gone," the boy who looked like Nic told her. "But I assure you that he's been sacrificed for the greater good of the world."

Hot tears rolled down her cheeks. She'd just gotten him back, and now he was lost to her all over again.

"Earth goddess," Selia said, stealing Cleo's attention from Nic, "you are free. Claim your flesh-and-blood vessel."

The green wisp of magic swirled around the pit, and this time everyone stepped back from it, watching it with fear.

Olivia gasped as the magic plunged into her.

Nic . . . or Kyan . . . or—Cleo didn't know what to think—went directly to Olivia and took her hands in his. "Sister?"

"Yes." She looked up into his eyes. "You did what you promised. I am finally free!"

"Yes. And you've chosen an excellent vessel."

"What was her name?" she asked.

"Olivia," he told her.

"Olivia," she repeated, nodding. "Yes, Olivia will be my name now."

"Mother." Gaius had moved to Selia's side, his black hair slicked to his face from the rain.

"I'm sorry, my son," she said to him, shaking her head. "You have the bloodstone; it will have to be enough."

He nodded. "You've always put me first, no matter what you had to do."

She searched his face. "I shouldn't have done what I did to Elena. I see now that it hurt you more than I thought it would. But I just wanted you to be free."

"I know. And you were right. My love for her clouded my mind. It threatened to destroy my thirst for power." He took her face gently between his hands and leaned forward to kiss her forehead. "Thank you for helping to make me the man I am today."

She touched his hand, then frowned. "Wait. Where is the—"

With a sharp twist, he snapped his mother's neck and let her body fall to the ground.

Kyan stared down at the witch, then his furious glare turned to the king. "What have you done?"

"I've interrupted your self-serving ritual," Gaius said, glancing down at the body of his mother. "I knew there was a good reason I hadn't killed her yet."

Kyan eyed the remaining two wisps of magic with anger in his stolen brown eyes. "Little queen, I need you now. I need blood descended from a sorceress—your blood. The magic from it will be enough for now. Later, I'll find another obedient Oldling to seal all that's been done here."

He was right next to Cleo, holding Selia's dagger. "I will give you your throne. All of Mytica. All of this world and beyond. Anything you desire."

Tears mixed with the streaming rain on Cleo's face. "Give the dagger to me."

He did as she asked, and she looked at the dagger in her hand, knowing she had to do this. Knowing there was no choice.

Kyan could not leave here today, no matter whose body he had stolen. But just as she raised the dagger to thrust the blade into Nic's heart, Ashur caught her wrist.

She stared up at him as the rain came down in torrents upon them.

"No," he said. The single word held no room for argument. He squeezed her wrist until she gasped with pain and dropped the weapon.

When she turned back to face Kyan, he slapped Cleo so hard she spun backward, hitting the wall of the pit.

"You disappoint me, little queen," he snarled.

Magnus, she thought with panic. *Now would be a perfect time for you to save the day.*

The walls of the pit began to crumble inward. The blue and white swirls of magic—the water and air gods—continued to spiral around the pit.

"Brother, we have a problem," Olivia, now possessed by the earth Kindred, growled. "The others are ready, and time is running out. How do we finish the ritual without a witch to help us?"

As if in reply, the white wisp of magic shot toward its chosen host and disappeared into Taran's chest. He gasped and fell to his knees.

Before Cleo could say a word, cry out, or stagger away from the rebel, the blue wisp was right in front of her.

It felt as if she had been hit by a thirty-foot wave, knocking her backward and choking her on its salt water.

The water Kindred had chosen her as its vessel.

Cleo stared upward at the stormy sky, the rain falling upon her as she fought to retain control over her body. She knew she couldn't weaken now, but how was she supposed to fight against a god?

"We will return to fix this," Kyan roared with anger before he turned into a column of flame and shot out of the pit. Olivia, casting a hateful glare at Cleo, crumbled as if made from dirt and disappeared into the ground.

Taran was at Cleo's side, helping her to sit up.

She stared at him, confused. "Taran . . ."

"Are you still you?" he asked. When she didn't answer, he shook her roughly. "Answer me. *Are you still you?*"

She managed to nod. "I—I'm still me."

"So am I." Taran frowned and held out his right hand. A simple spiral—the mark of air magic—was on his palm, as if branded there.

Cleo looked down at her left palm to see the two parallel wavy lines that created the water symbol.

"The witch was killed before she could make it permanent with us," she said. "We have the elemental magic inside of us, but we haven't lost our minds or our souls."

He searched her face, his brows knitting together. "Do you really think so?"

She shook her head, her mind a jumble of confusion. "I don't know. I don't know anything for sure right now."

Cleo searched for Magnus again, peering up at the edge of the pit and hoping he would suddenly appear. When he didn't, she held her hand out to Taran. "Help me up."

Taran did as she asked. "What happens now?"

The rain still poured down on them. New guards arrived and stared down at the group at the bottom of the pit.

"Empress?" one asked tentatively.

Amara tore her shocked gaze from Cleo, a deep frown creasing her forehead, and looked up at the men. "Get us out of here."

The guards brought a ladder that sank into the mud at the bottom of the pit. One by one, the group silently exited. With her broken leg, Amara required two guards to physically assist her.

"Kyan wanted everyone's blood to spill," Amara said at the top, her tone void of any discernable emotion. "That, with the witch's magic, would have made the ritual permanent."

"And you agreed to that—to killing us all," Felix said, his hands fisted. "Why am I not surprised?"

Amara flinched. "It didn't happen, did it?"

"No thanks to you," he said, scowling. "Don't worry, I'll make sure you pay for what you did here today."

"So, what does it mean?" Nerissa asked. Enzo stood protectively beside her, his hand at her waist. "None of what the witch did is permanent? Not even with Nic and Olivia?"

Amara shook her head. "I don't know."

"You stopped me," Cleo said to Ashur, who hadn't said a word since they'd exited the pit.

"You were going to stab Nicolo. I couldn't allow that."

"He's lost," her voice broke. "He's gone."

"Do you know that for sure?" His expression hardened. "I don't. And if there's a way, I will bring him back to us. Do you hear me?"

All she could do was nod, hoping desperately that he might be right.

The king was the last to climb out of the pit.

"Where is my son, Amara?" he asked.

"I don't know that either," Amara said.

Magnus's continued absence wasn't right. He should have been found by now.

"You have to find him," Cleo managed, fresh panic swirling inside of her.

"I will," Amara said.

"Yet you don't sound like you give a damn. Listen to me carefully: You *need* to find him."

"He's likely dead," Amara said bluntly. Then she choked and started spitting up mouthfuls of water. "What—what are you doing?"

Cleo realized that her hands were clenched at her sides so tightly that her nails dug into her palms. She felt like she was spinning. She forced her left hand open to see that the water symbol had begun to glow.

Water magic. The water Kindred was inside of her, but not in control of her actions.

She felt something warm under her nose and touched it to realize that it was blood.

"The power of a god within the form of a mortal," Gaius said with awe. "Without the full ritual to finalize it . . . it is a dangerous position for you to be in, princess. And you as well, Taran. But you're right: We must find my son."

Nerissa stepped forward, tentatively taking Cleo's hand in hers and squeezing it. Cleo met her anguished gaze.

"I saw a guard hit him, princess," she whispered, shaking her head. "He hit the prince hard and then dragged him away. I . . . I fear that Amara might be right. I'm so sorry."

Cleo stared at her friend, her eyes burning. "No," she managed. "No, please no. That can't be true. It can't be."

Taran and Felix shared a worried look. The rebel uneasily glanced down at his own palm that bore the air magic symbol.

"What do you care of Magnus's fate, Cleo?" Amara asked, her voice holding a tremor that Cleo had never heard before. "I thought you hated him."

"You're wrong, I don't hate him," Cleo managed softly. Then

stronger: "I love him. I *love* Magnus with all my heart. And I swear, if he's . . . dead . . . if I've lost both Nic *and* Magnus today . . ." Her voice broke as she raised her gaze, seeing that the others now watched her with fear in their eyes. The bottomless sensation of cool, powerful water magic flowed just beneath the surface of her skin, as if waiting to be unleashed. "I don't think this world will survive my grief."

CHAPTER 33

MAGNUS

PAELSIA

Magnus blinked his eyes open, frowning with confusion at the aching pain in his arms. It took him a moment before he realized that he was vertical. His arms were raised above his head, shackled and chained to the ceiling.

He was in a dark room lit only by a few torches.

"He wakes. Finally. I was about to send for some smelling salts."

He frowned, not understanding. Still dizzy.

"Greetings, my old friend." The voice was familiar. Painfully familiar.

And then he understood all too well.

"Kurtis," Magnus said, tasting coppery blood in his mouth. "How delightful to see you again."

"Ah, you say the words, yet deep in my heart I know you're lying." The former grand kingsliege walked a slow circle around Magnus, a smug smile on his thin lips.

"What did you do with Nerissa and Nic?"

"Don't worry about them, old friend. Worry about yourself."

Magnus tried to summon a sense of where he was, casting a look around the room. It was difficult, since one of his eyes was swollen shut.

"I saw your lovely wife earlier," Kurtis said. "She didn't see me, of course. Given how we last left things between us, I feel like Cleo might still be cross with me."

"Don't you dare speak her name," Magnus growled.

Kurtis stopped in front of Magnus and cocked his head, still smiling that damned smile of his. "Cleo. Cleo, Cleo, Cleo. Do you know what I'm going to do to her? I would love it, truly love it, if you could be there to watch."

He leaned closer and whispered in Magnus's ear a list of horrors that would cause anyone—man or woman—to beg for death long before such a relief finally came.

"I swear to the goddess," Magnus said, "I will kill you long before you lay a single finger upon her."

"I thought I might be getting close enough to do just that, with our archery lessons. I know you watched us. Was that jealousy in your eyes? It seems the rumors of hatred between the two of you are far from true, aren't they? Yet what do you care about her fate anymore? She betrayed you for a chance to align with the empress."

"I wouldn't give a damn if she betrayed me to align with every demon in the darklands, I will still kill you if you even look at her again."

"Yet, in your current predicament," Kurtis glanced up at the chains, "I'd really, really like to see you try."

"You wish to torture me? Some sort of retribution for what I did to you?"

"Oh, yes, I wish to torture you. And then I wish to kill you very slowly." He raised the stump where his hand used to be. "And

I would advise you to save your breath rather than beg for your life. You'll need it for all the screaming you'll do."

Part of Magnus, deep inside, knew the truth of what he saw in Kurtis's eyes. There would no mercy here. But Magnus Damora would not beg for his own life.

"I would make a better living ally than a dead enemy," he said instead. "Remember, you are currently a Limerian in the center of thousands of Kraeshians and tens of thousands of Paelsians."

Kurtis's lips peeled back from his teeth as his sinister smile widened. "One problem at a time, my old friend. Tell me, when you returned to the palace and displaced me from the throne, I could have sworn you had a broken arm. Was it your little sorceress sister who healed it for you?"

"Perhaps I have a few tricks of my own that you don't know about," Magnus bluffed.

"I hope so. I sincerely do." Kurtis glanced at two Kraeshian guards who had been behind him in the shadows. "Break both of his arms, if you would. And, I think, his right leg."

The guards moved forward without hesitation.

"Kurtis," Magnus said, his eyes glancing between the kingsliege and the approaching guards. "You think you'll kill me here today and no one will know about it?"

"Today? You think I'll kill you today? No. Your death should take quite enough time for you to suffer very nicely." He nodded. "See you soon."

Magnus swore to himself that he wouldn't beg. He wouldn't plead.

But Kurtis had been right about the screaming.

When Magnus opened his eyes, he could see a sliver of the moon above him in the dark sky. Consciousness meant he was alive, but it also brought with it ceaseless pain from the injuries inflicted upon him by Kurtis's sadistic orders.

Where was he? Outside, yes. He was outside if he could see the moon. And he was still in Paelsia, since the chill in the air matched neither the bracing cold of Limeros nor the warmth of Auranos.

He realized that he lay in a box made of wood. "What is this?" he managed.

"You're awake," Kurtis said, and his loathsome face appeared above Magnus. "You do sleep very soundly. Like the dead, I might say."

"I . . . I can't move."

"I would imagine not. You're in terrible shape, my friend. Strong, though. I've watched that kind of torture as it killed men and women alike. Well done."

"You are a lord and a kingsliege, Kurtis. A born Limerian. You're also a pathetic, weasely little shit, but you have to see that what you're doing is wrong. There's still time to stop this."

"All these compliments, Magnus, they're going to my head. I never liked you, but I tolerated you because of your father's power. Now that is gone, along with my hand. All for following orders." Kurtis's eyes bugged as his face reddened. "Tell me, is the rumor true that you have a fear of small, enclosed spaces?"

"No, that's not true."

"I imagine it will be true soon enough." Kurtis smirked. "I'll cherish this moment for the rest of my life, my old friend. Farewell to you."

Magnus tried to sit up, but pain flashed through him, blinding him like lightening.

And then the moon, the night, and Kurtis Cirillo all disappeared as a wooden lid came down on top of him.

A coffin. He had been put into a coffin.

Nails were hammered into it. Magnus felt airborne for a split second, and then he landed hard, his back slamming against the wooden bottom.

Then came the scrape of shovels and the soft thud of dirt filling the grave as Kurtis and his loyal guards buried him alive, deep in the Paelsian earth.

ACKNOWLEDGMENTS

Just like in Mytica, there is a trio of kingdoms on the Morgan Rhodes author map, and I seriously couldn't survive without all of them existing in harmony.

Kingdom #1 is called *Razorbillia*

My publishing family at Razorbill and Penguin Teen make the Falling Kingdoms series (and a shout-out to its sister trilogy A Book of Spirits and Thieves) a possibility. Thank you to Liz Tingue, Jess Harriton, Ben Schrank, Casey McIntyre, and the rest of the fantabulous team who have my eternal gratitude for allowing me entrance to this golden palace. And thank you always to Jim McCarthy, my wonderful agent and part-time dragon slayer.

Kingdom #2 is called *Realworldia*

Thank you to my magnificent friends and family who help keep it real when I'm in my huge mansion eating bonbons, drinking expensive champagne, and having Ian Somerhalder, my manservant and future husband, give me my daily massage by the pool. . . . Wait, that's not actually happening? Okay, FINE. But they're still awesome at supplying pep talks, shopping trips, entertainment, food, and margaritas when I get time off for good behavior.

Kingdom #3 is called *Readerlandia*

Thank you to my amazing readers, who make all the work worthwhile. And, yeah, writing books is sometimes work . . . even writing about Prince Magnus. I know—it's hard to believe. Never stop believing in magic. And books. Magic + books . . . who needs anything else? (P.S. Sorry about that cliffhanger! *evil laugh*)